THE TENTO SAGA

MANKIND'S PERILOUS JOURNEY

BY

JASON WILLIAM EGROFF

ISBN 13: 978-0-6152-0664-6

"Origins of Annihilation" Prologue by Samuel Orlando
Editing by Arlene Prunkl
Cover Illustration by David Whitecraft
Interior and Cover Layout by Jason William Egroff
Executive Producer: Eileen J. Egroff

First Printing – April 2008

First Edition

Published by Jason W. Egroff
Printed by Lulu Press, Inc.

Contents

The Tento Saga: Mankind's Perilous Journey

PART I

THE EXILE

Prologue: Prelude to Agony

The president of the United States sat in the oval office. He studied the national security estimate laid out by his security advisor. The title of the report read, "Austria Determined to Dominate the World." The president's national security advisor paced, contemplating the nation's response to the rising threat.

"Sir, I don't see any alternative to regime change in Austria. The dictator has proven through his actions that he isn't willing to negotiate peace with his neighbors. I fully believe that he will continue on his current course of action and eventually dominate the entire region," the advisor concluded gravely.

"I agree. I'm disappointed in the lackluster intelligence estimates leading up to this current report. This man is the worst tyrant since Adolph Hitler. It's as if we've gone back in time a couple of thousand years. If unchecked, this man's plot for world domination will succeed and his disgusting ideology will rule," the president stated.

Suddenly, the president's phone rang. He picked it up with dread.

"This is the president."

"Sir, NORAD reported thousands of incoming Austrian military craft by air, land, and sea. It appears as if a large-scale invasion of the United States is in action. Early intelligence reports state that it's General Zonfer's brigade," the military official said calmly.

"Deploy forces throughout the country immediately," the president asserted decisively. "That psychopath needs to be stopped immediately."

"Yes, sir. I'll keep you updated on operations."

The president hung up with a somber expression on his face.

"Sir?" the president's security advisor inquired.

"We're at war on American soil. Within the hour, Zonfer's forces will be at our doorstep. I'd better phone the vice president and prepare an address. Meanwhile, we need to move to the underground security bunker. General Zonfer and his brigade are advancing."

The president's associate swallowed hard. "I've heard of this man's tactics. God help us…"

***

General Zonfer stood on American soil surveying the battlefield, assault rifle in hand. The Austrian forces had taken most of the country with little opposition. The United States' preparedness was flawed at best. The ruthless military leader oversaw Austrian-dominated New York City. His transport chopper thudded in the background atop the United Nations building. He thought about his next militaristic action when a captain chimed in on his communication channel.

"General, our forces are advancing on the American capital. Deployments of American forces are currently unfolding. Combat operations are going as planned."

"Excellent. I've landed in New York City and will be overseeing the holding of the territory. I will expect hourly updates on progress. When the capital falls, I want to know," commanded Zonfer.

The general ran down to the ground level of the city streets, with the sound of tanks and jet fighters booming through the world's economic capital. An officer approached Zonfer and said, "Sir, we have to pass the bridge that connects the city but civilian vehicles clutter the bridge—"

"Take them out," Zonfer declared without hesitation.

"Yes, s—sir," the soldier stuttered, startled by Zonfer's heartlessness.

***

When the breeze on Tento blew, the planet shivered. It was a cold and desolate planet, the kind of place that not even the commoners liked. For this reason, no one ever visited the planet. Its overcast, dreary clouds wrapped it in a charcoal-gray prison. Tento seemed to cry to be freed from its cold desolation.

Science labs in various states of disrepair stood in the middle and far-reaching parts of the planet. The buildings looked as if some new-age weaponry had decimated them. This was only somewhat accurate. There had been an uprising between the scientists on the planet. This and the naming of the planet signaled the only defining moments in Tento's history.

From Earth, an astronomer named Evan Tento had discovered the new planet. Upon discovery, Tento reported that the planet didn't appear to hold any promising qualities. At this time in Earth's history, nothing interested the inhabitants of Earth more than the possibility of life on another planet. Whenever an astronomer spoke, his words pertained to this subject. But the discovery of this planet received the label of a useless discovery. Little did those who dismissed it know that the planet's discovery would change the course of mankind.

The discovery of Tento came at a very inopportune time. It proved to be the worst time for something significant to happen in the realm of intergalactic biology. If this discovery had come at any other time, Earth's inhabitants' excitement would have skyrocketed. Earthlings worried about the direction of their leader. After the great leader Zonfer had devised a plan to eliminate all threatening inhabitants of Earth and to begin his campaign for world domination, all of Earth's nations united to defend their home. Earth chose to resist. Zonfer had assembled a massive army. When all of the battles had concluded, Zonfer emerged victorious. This signaled the arrival of the great slaughters. Zonfer entered nations and wiped out complete dynasties. Generations of great leaders perished at the hands of the tyrant.

This turned out to be a transitional period for the planet Earth. Zonfer had successfully extinguished all of his possible enemies through a masterful plan of deceit and conspiracy. It took many years for the residents of Earth to accept his unconscionable actions. However, it signaled a very prosperous time in Earth's history, when the economy was strong and the crime rate was almost nonexistent. It was unclear if this was because of Zonfer's "final solution" or just because there were fewer people to commit crimes. Unemployment disappeared—a problem of the past. The only people who experienced poverty were those who deliberately decided to not work. Along with addicts and the mentally ill, they became vagrants. The super corporations in the world flourished. Manufacturing boomed and people purchased things just as fast as production took place. For the first time in Earth's history, 98 percent of the population enjoyed the benefits of an unlimited job market. Little did anyone know that a terrible evil, an evil far worse than Zonfer, stood poised and ready to strike down the inhabitants of Earth.

***

The architectural wonder that was Zonfer's headquarters dominated the landscape where it resided. No leader had ever possessed a more imposing or awe-inspiring structure. Custody of such a structure surely proved an individual's supremacy over all others.

Sitting in his majestic main office, Zonfer contemplated what the new day would bring. As he sifted through the various thoughts that crowded his mind, he stood and strolled through his domain, with arms folded, at a leisurely pace. Zonfer personified the very essence of intimidation. He stood strong at six feet two inches tall, and his posture was flawless. He appeared somewhat younger than his years, with a flowing, shoulder-length, gray and auburn-tinted mane and facial hair. Exceptionally malevolent facial features completed the striking visage—arching eyebrows and deep scowl marks. Little escaped Zonfer's intellectual ability; he was a man of infinite intelligence and foresight. This combination of mental acumen and physical prowess made Zonfer a *tour de force* of coercion. Make no mistake, Zonfer ruled planet Earth and its tenants with an iron fist. Nonetheless, the subsequent weeks and months would prove to humble the brutal leader.

As he sifted through the Intelligence reports, he slowly caressed his beard. The last few sentences troubled him. The United States continued to be a thorn in his side. He now regretted not eliminating the government completely. It was a precarious and unusual political situation. Zonfer had ultimate rule over the country but the leadership fought him in every way they could. The pundits described it as the "Zonfer occupation of the United States." This was as accurate a description as could be formulated.

Zonfer read the transcription of the latest Senate and House activities. "The amendment hereby states that the United States remain steadfast in our resolve against our occupier. The CIA in unison with the U.N. shall monitor Zonfer's actions and hold the tyrant accountable."

Zonfer sighed and closed the cover on the tan folder. It was little more than rhetoric. Both he and the rebellious U.S. leadership knew nothing could touch Zonfer. A unifying evil stood poised to strike.

Chapter 1: Genesis of Destruction

Taber sat in his lab chair examining the new samples from the region of concern. Reports of outbreaks of mysterious infections caused by long extinct diseases had been piling up on Taber's desk. Whenever something of this nature occurred, research would immediately commence. Taber worked for the biochemistry department of Zonfer's administration. What he was looking at baffled him.

Staring back at him laid the biological makeup of a destructive force that could very well bring about the demise of Earth and its vulnerable life. Taber performed various tests on this biological anomaly. He determined that it was a single-celled organism that could reproduce asexually. This hypothesis represented the only logical and viable conclusion that the current research information provided. But without more reliable information on the actual organism, the biological calculations didn't make much sense. He determined that in a period of about twenty-four hours, this organism could cover the entire face of the Earth. The resulting report, with little more than a barely feasible educated guess, came off more than a little ridiculous. Taber, a scientist, wanted to back up his information with solid, well-informed facts. This, given the current state of the facts as he knew them, would be impossible. He knew that, if he was left without further research and data gathering, this threat could assemble in a frightening maelstrom of unimaginable proportions. He gathered the research reports and projections that made the most sense and filed them for submission to Zonfer's main office. He prepared for—and dreaded—an inevitably awkward presentation.

Zonfer stared at the various information packets Taber had assembled for his boss's consumption. He examined every report, all the while in subconscious conversation and contemplation. After he finished the final page of the research summary, he sighed and threw it upon his enormous desk, where it landed in a heap. To say the least, he didn't take it seriously, but he requested the presence of his science officer to discuss the controversial report. Minutes later one of Zonfer's aides announced Taber's arrival.

Taber entered Zonfer's office, hoping fervently that the meeting had nothing to do with his research pertaining to the biological anomaly. However, he wasn't so fortunate.

"Sir, you requested my presence?"

"Yes," said Zonfer, "please come in—come in."

"Did you digest all of my report?" Taber asked with dread.

"Yes, Taber, I did. Please sit and have a drink with me." He poured some fresh coffee from his sideboard into a second mug and placed it before Taber. Zonfer's expression frightened the timid science officer.

Taber took his seat and slowly sipped the hot coffee.

"Taber, you take me as an intelligent man, don't you?"

"Yes sir, of course," replied Taber humbly.

"Then please explain to me how, Taber, you expect me to buy this horse manure?"

Zonfer's eyes blazed with fury. He wasn't the type of man who hid his emotions. His personality didn't allow it.

"Sir, all I have done in this report is presented the facts to you as I know them. With the information provided, you must understand that little is certain about this organism," Taber confidently concluded.

"These 'facts' you refer to—they include the ridiculous theory about the possibility of this being a biblical Plague? You do realize that nothing like that has been mentioned in thousands of years? The Bible was rejected as fiction long ago, Taber. You being a scientist, I would assume this is something you are aware of."

There was more than a hint of sarcasm in Zonfer's voice. Taber didn't appreciate this in the slightest little bit. He momentarily forgot whom he was addressing and made a fatal error.

"Sir, I really don't appreciate being made to look like a fool. I merely mentioned the biblical-type Plague as a comparison. I did not mean it as, literally, a biblical Plague. To be perfectly honest with you, the research data couldn't definitively confirm anything about this thing. I need more time and samples to come to any kind of viable conclusion in this matter."

Zonfer shifted in his seat and clenched the ends of the armrests of his large chair.

"And *I* don't appreciate my biochemist talking back to me. You speak to me like that again and you'll find yourself at the barrel end of a pulse cannon."

"My apologies, sir. I don't know what got into me." Taber shriveled back into himself like a snail into a shell. He knew Zonfer wouldn't directly eliminate him because the watchdog agencies studied his every move. Zonfer, however, had his methods of discreet action. Taber had witnessed them on several occasions. Now he appeared to be the latest in a long line of science officers who had lost favor with Zonfer.

"So, are you going to recommend that I tell the public about this inconclusive report or should I let it slide?" asked Zonfer sarcastically.

"Well, sir, I think that's up to you. Upon further research, I can submit a more conclusive report. Until then, I think the decision would be best made by you."

"Taber, you know that I'm required to carry out whatever actions you recommend. This entire conversation is being monitored by that organization that had me by the balls when I wanted to eliminate all of the senators on Capitol Hill in Washington. No more beating around the bush. What is your recommendation?"

Taber searched for an acceptable response. He stumbled over his words, his mind in mental disarray.

"Well, sir, I th—think this certainly—"

Zonfer clenched his fist hard. He gritted his teeth and glared at the terrified scientist with absolute contempt.

"I ah—my recommendation would be to—ah—"

Zonfer stroked the pulse cannon that rested on his desk while staring at Taber with a murderous rage in his eyes. Taber silently interpreted Zonfer's body language and responded accordingly.

"I—I recommend that you not mention it. It would cause an unnecessary panic among the inhabitants of the planet. This is appearing only in a remote region of what used to be the Holy Land. At worst, the casualties would be limited given the general location of interest. The consequences of panic would be far more—dire."

"All right, Taber. I appreciate your visit and I will think about every option. Now, there are many things that demand my attention. I would appreciate some privacy now."

Taber froze, staring blankly in Zonfer's general direction, unblinking.

"Taber!" Zonfer exploded in anger, striking his desk furiously. The science officer jerked back in fear, his body trembling uncontrollably.

"Yes, sir, I'll be—begin my follow-up report immediately."

"Don't bother, Taber."

Taber exited with a heavy chest and a heavy conscience. He realized the possible outcome of what he had just done.

Chapter 2: First Emergence – November 22, 3033

The Council for Scientific Research sat in session. The topic of discussion was the violent heat waves that gripped the Middle East. The lead member of the panel, Dr. Gilian Waters, stood prominently in the center of the conference room.

"Ladies and gentlemen of the council," he began, "Dr. Taber, the lead scientist in the science department of the Zonfer administration, has submitted a frightening report to the council for discussion. It concerns the recent climate change in the Middle East. Apparently, in this same remote region, a biological threat of an unknown origin has surfaced. Our goal today is to examine the findings thoroughly and discuss the possible origins of this organism."

Displays embedded in the desks in front of the scientists flickered in activity as the report loaded onto the council's research equipment.

"Please examine the findings thoroughly," said Waters. "When you're finished with your research, please activate your indicators. At that time, I shall return. Thank you for your cooperation."

Dr. Waters exited the conference room. He walked to an adjacent room, took a seat at a desk, and turned on a display with the research data loaded. Deep in thought, he examined the preliminary biological test results, scanning images and text. He frowned and rubbed his forehead, baffled by the data.

Meanwhile, in the conference room, the council wasn't doing much better. Clicks of keyboards sounded intermittently. The council members tirelessly attempted to piece together the puzzle. Gradually, completion indicators were activated. Finally, the last scientist activated his indicator. Soon after, Dr. Waters entered.

"I am excited to hear your findings. To be honest with you, I can't begin to understand this organism. Ms. Barber, you are the designate for presentation."

"Thank you, sir. I think I can speak for the rest of the council when I say that I've never seen anything like this. We couldn't even confirm that this organism is, in fact, living. One theory says it could be a chemical weapon of some sort made to look like a single-celled organism, but we can't confirm that. In terms of the climate change, this is another mystery. I wish I could tell you more, but..." Her voice trailed off.

"Don't apologize," Waters responded in a tired voice. "I suspected this would be the case. I've been studying the—whatever it is, since Dr. Taber first filed his report. I haven't been able to come to any definitive conclusion myself. All I know is that the projections are terrifying."

"Indeed, sir, we concur. Unfortunately, we cannot aid this investigation any further without more information," Barber responded.

"I understand. Dr. Taber is performing a follow-up on his inconclusive first report. This report will be made available to the council upon completion.

"Well, that concludes this session. Thank you all for your efforts."

The scientists rose from their seats, still in a state of disbelief at what they had observed. Several discussions ensued as they left the conference room.

Dr. Waters stood outside his office. His cell phone rang and he answered.

"Waters here. Hello, Dr. Taber. How is the follow-up report going?" The doctor's eyes widened. "You have got to be kidding me! He's ignoring it?"

***

A resident of Center City in the Middle East sat in his residence viewing the evening news on television. The commentator began the telecast.

"The heat wave in the Middle East continues, and reports of mass hallucinations are increasing. Citizens are reporting alien beings roaming in their presence, sands catching fire, and various other supernatural phenomena. The death toll continues to rise as new victims are discovered. Over a thousand citizens were found dead today—victims of various fatal circumstances. Suffocation and dehydration were among the culprits."

The viewer took a deep breath, turned off the set, and threw the remote to the side of his couch. Feeling thirsty, he went to the kitchen to get a glass of water. He took a glass from the cupboard and turned the faucet to the on position. The sink produced a clunking noise, but the faucet gave not a drop.

"Shit—not again."

The man left his home and headed for the local market to pick up some bottled water. The heat was as oppressive as ever. The sweat on his brow accumulated quickly. He breathed heavily, with each breath harder than the last.

After what seemed like hours, he finally reached his destination. The market was eerily inactive, the only noise being the annoying elevator music playing in the background. He found his water and searched for a clerk to pay for it.

"Is anybody here? I want to buy this!" the man yelled while pulling out a handkerchief to wipe his brow.

After the futile attempt to find a sales clerk, he left the store with his unpaid item. Something was strange about tonight. It made sense that few people were about because of the heat but this was extraordinary.

As he began his journey back to his house, he saw a group of people gathered together and gawking at something in the distance. He approached the onlookers.

"What's going on? Is something the matter?" he inquired.

"Look, do you see that hazy cloud in the distance?" a woman responded. "It's moving toward the city. We've been watching it for about an hour now and it seems to be picking up speed."

"Yeah, I see it." His voice trembled. "What the hell could it be?"

"Notice the way it moves. It's almost as though it's alive," Another onlooker observed.

"Look! It's passing over that herd of sheep!" shouted the woman.

The ominous cloud rolled toward the helpless animals. As the force passed, the crowd watched in horror as the flesh of the creatures began disintegrating from their bones.

"My god, what is happening?" another woman screamed.

Another pedestrian gazed at the sight in sheer terror.

"Mister, what should we do?" she said, shaking with fear.

"Come on, we can take shelter in my house!" The man began to run, urging the others to follow him. One man collapsed in a heap, dead from exhaustion. Then, as they approached the man's house, the other male member of the group succumbed to the Plague. The cloud engulfed the man's being, ripping his flesh from his body in a disgusting display.

The female onlooker and the owner of the house were the only members of the group that remained. The woman collapsed to the floor, crying desperately.

"What the hell is going on? This heat—and now this—" she sobbed.

"Maybe the news has something on about this—"

He picked up the remote from his couch and turned on the set. The familiar tag line of "Breaking News" was scrolled across the bottom of the screen. They sat and watched the images in horror.

"...and the cloud just swooped into the city and started eating everything in sight! I saw a guy get caught in the cloud and after it passed, there was nothing left of the guy! I'm tellin' you! This is the end of the world! This thing is—"

"All right, thank you for that eye-witness account, sir." The newscaster interrupted.

"To update our new viewers, an unknown disease has engulfed Center City and most of the Middle East. Projections on the casualty rate are not yet available. An address from Zonfer has not yet been scheduled. This is Trina Kall live from Center City for Global News Now."

Suddenly, the now familiar organic movement of the Plague appeared in the distance behind the telecaster. It advanced with tremendous speed. The camera captured the image of the reporter being mutilated by the cloud and collapsing dead on the street, a pile of bones. The cloud engulfed the camera's lens and obliterated everything.

The man quickly turned the television set off.

"I think that's enough TV for tonight..."

The woman continued to cry and moan, the images burned into her mind.

"Listen, I think we're all right. If it hasn't gotten us yet, maybe it won't come near here," the man said in an attempt to comfort the distraught woman.

"I need a glass of water," the woman choked.

"Yeah, so do I.".

The two entered the kitchen. He retrieved two glasses from the cupboard and poured the bottled water. She stood behind him, awaiting her glass. Without looking, he handed the glass to her and she took it. Suddenly, her glass crashed to the floor

"Shit! Did I drop it?" he asked.

He looked in her direction. Her eyes were wider than two full moons and her hands covered her mouth. She was staring out the window, and the man also turned to look. The cascading cloud of the Plague confronted the man. The woman grabbed him in a deep embrace as the menace broke through the window and devoured them.

Chapter 3: The Reaction – November 23, 3033

Stroking his Fu Manchu, Zonfer studied the sizeable pile of documents on his desk. The title page of the collection of papers read, "Incident #4004: Plague." Immediately, he recalled his discussion with his main science officer. With a steady hand, Zonfer began to thumb through the incident report. As he scanned each document, his concern grew with each progressive paragraph. Gradually, and with careful contemplation, Zonfer began to accept reality. Initially, he had resisted, even denied the facts. However, by the conclusion of the report, heavy-hearted, he was forced to accept what he held responsibility for.

In the depths of the evil tyrant's psyche, a switch had been flipped. Long ago, before the formative events in his life had taken place, Zonfer had fought for peace and understanding between cultures. Long gone were those days, a mere heartbeat in time to him. Forced to accept the gravity of the situation, he contemplated the consequences of inaction and immediately began pondering a solution to the problem. He organized his top advisors and began a dialogue in pursuit of a viable way forward.

Zonfer and his associates decided that an address to the populace concerning the catastrophe would be the logical next step. In classic Zonfer style, the address would be quick and to the point. In the past, leaders had orated for hours. The planet's inhabitants had grown weary of the long, tiresome speeches of their leaders and Zonfer had recognized this fact. His new flair embodied a much-needed and well-received change to political culture, and the result of this change in the public relations arena was an attentive audience. This approach also gave the people of Earth peace of mind; they thought their safety would remain unthreatened as long as Zonfer remained in power. While perhaps a deviant method of reassurance, it sufficed.

Zonfer sat in his main office, alone, his only company the whirling thoughts of how to present a palatable address. He slowly compiled his thoughts and recorded them as they came. As he worked, he realized how much of this entire situation depended on a power greater than himself. He contemplated, of all things, God. The "seeing is believing" leader noticed a strange brainwave pushing him in a direction of a faith-oriented speech. Apparently, the images that had accompanied the Middle East council report had left an indelible mark on Zonfer's subconscious. Perhaps some soul-searching would be in his immediate future.

Zonfer scribbled down notes on a small pad. He had never warmed up to computers. Individuals around him thought it strange but they respected it. He liked a pen in hand. Soon, he entered full-on speech-writing mode. He carefully injected a pinch of "faith talk." Zonfer had never witnessed anything like the devastation the Plague had caused, and the images were burned in his memory for a lifetime. The rise of this new, seemingly undefeatable foe forced him to think outside of the proverbial box. The seeds of change had taken root in Zonfer's mind and there would be no turning back. Luckily for Earth, a new man would be birthed from the dark and eccentric leader who currently dominated the human race.

At nine o'clock international time on November 23, 3033, Zonfer appeared on all of the major networks. He began:

"People of Earth, thank you for tuning in. A time of great concern has arrived. About one month ago, my science officer and I sat in my office and discussed a terrible situation that had arisen. He explained to me that a single-celled organism of unknown origin had surfaced in the Holy Land. He advised me not to concern the entire world with this because the organism inhabited a region of a very remote location and the probability of this organism actually spreading and causing problems elsewhere was slim to none. I now regret this immensely. Yesterday, this organism attacked a part of the Holy Land. It was tragedy on a grand scale; over ten thousand perished. Now, we must focus on what we do from here. The report stated that the problem showed no sign of returning. However, from studying the report that my biochemist gave me, I believe this will be a catastrophe that will resurface. Unfortunately, we have absolutely no way of fighting something that disappears within seconds of doing its damage. We are faced with a great problem, a dilemma that we can only pray we will never have to deal with again. I have come to you tonight to let you know that we are going to have to be strong. We are going to have to play this by ear. I can guarantee you that I am doing all that I can to ensure your safety as inhabitants of Earth. We must unite and we must be strong. Thank you and good night."

* * *

The citizens Zonfer called his own had faith in him. The enigmatic enemy wasn't a tangible reality to them. Most wrote the emergency off as a fluke, a freak occurrence. As far as most were concerned, it didn't require a second thought. But those ideas were soon to change.

Chapter 4: Disaster – December 1, 3033

The sun rose on New York City in the United States. This city had long been the capital of the world's economy. The base of operations for an inconceivable number of super corporations lined the city's streets. The roar of every possible method of transportation was deafening. People scuttled as they engaged in their morning routines. "Shorts in December!" many of them thought. Indeed, it was stranger weather than had ever been seen.

The sun hit the site of the Statue of Liberty first. It had been victimized by a terrorist attack in the year 2010 and had been neglected ever since. The now defunct terrorist group Al Qaeda claimed credit for the attack. The once graceful structure appeared to moan in pain; Liberty's crown was broken and her paint badly faded. The scene was desolate, more than depressing, even in the beautiful morning sun. No one visited her anymore. She seemed lonely.

The site of the WTC disaster of 2001 remained dormant as well. Procrastination was an awful thing, but the former presidents of the country exercised it thoroughly. The promised memorial never materialized. There always seemed to be a bigger objective for the country. "Those were times past. We must focus on the future." Zonfer assured them of a proper erection in 3040. He may have had a greater sense of urgency if it wasn't for the U.S.'s hardheadedness. The Zonfer administration longed for the day when the U.S. fully caved to their—rather Zonfer's—will. It remained a precarious situation, a new age cold war of sorts.

During this time of year, it rarely got past 40 degrees Fahrenheit on the thermometer. However, on this day, the temperature went far past the 90-degree mark. It was record breaking. It was the highest temperature in the winter, in the region, since record taking had begun. Early-morning weather reports played on televisions throughout the city. "Well, I thought I'd seen everything. Ninety degrees in December…Armageddon anyone?" a weather reporter joked on a television in a coffee house.

To the north, near sad Lady Liberty, a large cloud emerged. At first, most thought a cloud of smog had formed. But something was different about this cloud. Its movement was poetic, organic. It appeared to follow a path, billowing and churning forward. For a time, it covered the sun, and the sky was illuminated in crimson red and midnight black—a physical manifestation of death itself.

Suddenly, the cloud came upon a prominent skyscraper. The paint melted and dripped down the side of the building like ice cream in summer heat. Deafening metallic groans resounded as the dying structure collapsed. Bloodcurdling screams ensued upon the New York streets. It was flashback to days past; until now, the current generation had only had nightmares of such horror.

The enigma continued on its murderous path, with its next target a congested stretch of highway. The cloud passed over the left bridge first. A thunderous clang echoed throughout the entire city. The sound of sheer terror and brutal slaughter rang through New York. Citizens threw themselves over the bridge guardrails in desperation—anything to escape the horror. Upon contact with the menace, a human body didn't stand a chance. Flesh, muscle, and bone alike were eviscerated. The only thing that emerged from the other side of the cloud was mangled and twisted pieces of metal mixed with pulpy human remains.

An immediate response began. The first to arrive were the fire departments. A fire department chief approached the bridge and immediately gagged and vomited. It was an inhuman sight, incomparable to anything that had ever occurred before. The stench was unbearable, an indistinguishable combination of metal, fuel, and flesh. The impregnated steel oozed with spongy human remnants.

In the years following the 9/11 attacks, the NYFD had lived up to their new identity as "keepers of the city." Every major incident since then had been handled almost entirely by the city's fire departments. They responded in such a way that the police weren't required to get involved in any way.. In fact, the NYPD had become an almost obsolete tool in fighting most tragedies. The past three attempted attack plans were foiled by the fire department without any help from the various security departments. Islamic fundamentalism was not only a thing of the past, but it was far from handholding World Peace. Threats to the city were still very real.

This time, the fire department officials were baffled. The cloud had disappeared as fast as it had done the atrocious damage. The cleanup would be painful for the crew. The smell of rotting flesh grew stronger by the second. "First the heat and now this…" the captain thought.

***

Zonfer's headquarters was awash in activity. A constant stream of advisors and underlings traipsed in and out of his office. The report of the NYC incident had just arrived on his desk. He was overcome by a sense of urgency. This time there would have to be more decisive action taken against this new phantom enemy. Zonfer decided to declare marshal law on the entire planet, and a protective quarantine was also in order. This was another first for the Zonfer administration. The action would not cause a problem within Zonfer's force structure. Zonfer's defense forces made up the largest military organization the world had ever seen. Each nation had a mandatory minimum number of active force members. The United States, always rebellious, remained the biggest minority in the organization. With incentives and coercion, Zonfer attempted to change this situation. Perhaps this show of concern would help unite the Zonfer Administration and the United States.

What this new action would do still remained a mystery. Zonfer's method of thinking never changed. If you have an enemy, meet him face to face. This new enemy, however, was unapproachable. The best course of action would be to hunker down and defend as best as possible. Erectorbots would immediately begin building massive defense barracks. Older facilities would also be utilized. The human race would need to unite and fortify their homeland.

The time had come to seriously discuss a viable plan of action. Zonfer organized a meeting with the top members of his defense force. Zonfer's communication panel began to beep.

"Sir, General Hayden is here to see you."

"Yes, I've been awaiting his arrival. Send him in," Zonfer responded.

General Tyrone Hayden was the commanding officer of Zonfer's defense force. He was massive, standing seven feet tall and weighing around three-fifty. His coffee-colored skin was marred with scars from years of combat. His black uniform fitted him perfectly. The "Z" crest was displayed prominently upon his right pectoral. He was a veteran of the United States Marine Corp. Former U.S. combatants were few but coveted; statistically, they rose in rank faster than all other demographics.

"Good afternoon, General. I've highly anticipated our meeting. I'm hoping you will have a viable plan of action," Zonfer began.

"Sir?" queried Hayden, confused.

"Naturally, I turn to you, my defense force general, in search of a plan of attack," Zonfer responded matter-of-factly.

"I understand, sir, but I really don't see how you fight an enemy of this sort. Maybe the best offense is a good defense, sir?" Hayden responded confidently.

"Preparations are already in order for defense, General. I want to fight this thing."

Hayden looked puzzled. He searched for a response.

"Given the circumstances, sir, may I make a bold suggestion?"

"That's what I pay you for, General." Zonfer said blankly.

"Planetary evacuation." Hayden said.

Zonfer glared into the massive man's eyes with vitriol. It wasn't deliberate. Hayden had affirmed his worst fears. Deep within himself, Zonfer knew.

"Unacceptable—absolutely unacceptable! That is not a plan, General! That is a cop out!" Zonfer exploded.

Hayden was unaffected. "I don't know what you want me to say, sir. You know what I know about this enemy. How can we possibly fight something that we can't begin to understand, let alone face? Our forces will simply be fodder for this thing! I refuse to knowingly send my men into their certain death."

Zonfer's raged boiled underneath the surface.

"Your forces? Have I ceased to be, General?"

Zonfer felt his anger approaching the point of no return.

Hayden recoiled. He knew he had gone too far.

"No, sir, I'm sorry…" He paused to contemplate his next words.

"I'm not telling you anything you don't already realize, sir. We're at the mercy of this thing. If it wants us dead, we're gonna be dead."

Hayden's tone changed. Suddenly he had an idea.

"Sir?"

"Yes, General?"

"You are a religious man?"

Zonfer smiled wryly. "I never was, General. Why?"

"I heard your last speech. I was touched. I've always had faith…I thought I was the only one nowadays. To hear your words…I think we need to think about that more. Prayer, sir. That might be all we've got now."

Zonfer shook his head in bewilderment. "That will be all, General."

Hayden clicked his heals and quickly turned to exit.

"General." Zonfer quickly said.

"Sir?" Hayden responded without turning.

"Do that."

"What, sir?"

"Pray."

Chapter 5: A Tyrant's Final Murder – January 3034

The Plague was as relentless as ever. The slaughters continued. Scientific studies were constantly being performed on the available data in an attempt to uncover vulnerability in the foe. Zonfer's science department, headed by Dr. Helmut Taber, worked twenty-four seven on the matter. This was the subject of the current meeting.

Taber stood in the middle of Zonfer's office. "Sir, I tried to tell you months ago, this was a serious problem. You decided to ignore me. In fact, you threatened me into not giving a recommendation that I thought was the right one. Now, we are at a point where the only option is planetary evacuation."

"If I hear that one more time from anyone, I swear that person will end up in a grave." Zonfer's patience wore frightfully thin.

Usually timid, Taber finally grew impatient. "Sir, I don't know what you want from me. I am giving you my honest and best opinion in this matter. We have lost three fourths of our military power in less than a month. That is unmatched by anything that has ever happened in history. Especially since the reserves had over 30 billion men and women ready for deployment. This seems like the only plausible solution."

"I will never consider this as an option. There must be something that can be done about this." Zonfer paused and thought for a while.

Taber began, "Sir... may I suggest we take the defensive to another level?"

Intrigue bubbled in Zonfer's mind. "Please, do tell, Taber."

"Well, sir, I was thinking—could the oxygen supply to the planet be temporarily rerouted to a central location?"

"I guess this may be possible. I would have to discuss this with my construction consultant. What is your idea?"

"It is a very simple idea. We make a super craft, essentially a manmade planet. Like the idea that Tokyo had to make more living space for their residents. We outfit it with the latest in aeronautical technology and be ready to leave the planet when necessary. I think that this would be possible now that we have the type machinery that would make this a doable plan."

Zonfer contemplated. "Yes, you are correct that we have the machinery necessary to make such a craft. The Erectorbots have been working tirelessly since the beginning of this catastrophe. However, do we have the materials necessary to make such a massive structure? You must remember. We would be housing the entire planet."

"Yes, this could pose a problem. This is a question that I could not answer. Let me brainstorm with my colleagues on this matter and I will return."

Taber exited the office. Frustrated at the leader for not heeding his warning, he muttered to himself in disgust. He fiddled with his close-cut black hair in frustration. As he walked to his destination, he adjusted his glasses. In the fury of his frustration, he broke the left stem. "Son of a..." he muttered to himself.

Zonfer's headquarters bustled with activity. The entryways to the various offices emitted a neon glow from monitors and various research and communication terminals. Zonfer's headquarters was a combination of a "majestic palace" and "logistical base of operations." Zonfer had experts and consultants based all over the world. The headquarters represented Zonfer's hub. Where all problems found solutions.

Taber couldn't believe that Zonfer had the nerve to call on him and complain when he wanted Zonfer to warn the inhabitants. He was sure to be the scapegoat if things went south and he knew it. His reputation as a scientist depended on the successful outcome of his brainchild.

Taber entered the office of Donald Conlind. He was a dapper man with a five o'clock shadow upon his face and longish brown hair. His suit was impeccable. Donald was the materials expert on the Zonfer council. He was known to have had words with Zonfer from time to time.

"Good evening Don. I was just in Zonfer's office."

"What's he bitching at you for now? Don't you take anything from him! He's no better than you or me!"

"Yeah, easy for you to say. I'd like to keep my job and—and my life! Anyway, the reason I am here is to ask you about a materials matter."

Conlind smiled and snickered. "Shoot."

"Can you come up with enough hard materials to develop a craft that could support the entire population of the Earth?" Taber's tone was blank. A craft that could carry the whole human race—piece of cake!

Conlind was speechless. "Well, I would have to look at the numbers—"

"Do that," Taber said, exiting quickly.

Taber entered Zonfer's office once again. "My colleagues need time to perform various calculations on logistics of this idea."

"Excellent," said Zonfer. "This may be a solution. I must commend you on your troubleshooting. A promotion may be in your future, if any of us have a future. This idea may just give all of Earth a future that is worth living. Not running and leaving this beautiful planet to be eaten by that evil. I sincerely hope we don't need to leave this planet."

"Sir, your courage is amazing. Most leaders before you would cower and run. The fact that you are steadfast in the face of such turmoil is admirable. I commend you."

"I am a different kind of leader, Taber. I thought you knew this by now. The first man to actually rule Earth, Napoleon tried it, but I did it."

"It is truly impressive, sir." Taber responded in a less than sincere tone.

"Thank you, Taber. I've been thinking, doctor, what difference would it have made if I did tell the citizens about this? The only thing that I could foresee happening was a mass panic. Enlighten me, Taber—please."

Taber scratched his upper lip. "Umm…" He then wrapped his bottom lip over his top. He was nervous. Zonfer had an odd air about him. He seemed distant and cold, more so than normal. He stared unblinkingly at the mousey science officer.

"Well, sir, my thoughts are—" With these words, blood poured from Taber's mouth. He squirmed in his seat and retched. He then realized what had just transpired. Zonfer had used a toxic substance on the door handle.

Taber fell in a heap to the ground. "Sir, I don't understand," he choked. "I thought we understood each other. I thought we had worked out everything."

Zonfer folded his hands, emotionless. "I told you, Taber. No one makes a fool of me and lives to tell about it."

Taber gasped his last breath. Zonfer had always been known to grossly overreact to people correcting him or questioning his authority. Perhaps it was his ego. Soon after this took place, the person found himself or herself in a morgue. Zonfer didn't get to where he was by being forgiving.

The main reason that he controlled himself was because of the sanctions that the United States government had placed on him since the assassination attempts on the senators. The United States remained the main focus of Zonfer's aggression. He respected the authority of the government, but he grew tired of the constant sanctions that they put on him. However, the United States Armed Forces had always been one of history's most formidable combat organizations. Of Zonfer's international force, the largest minority remained North American males. Time, however, did not side with the Americans. It was only a matter of time before the international force took over the U.S. military as well. This task proved to be a daunting one. However, this battle had not been won on the battlefield. Recently, the forces had negotiated with D.C. In fact, this occurrence was so recent that Taber had no idea of the news.

This was unfortunate for Taber. Since Zonfer's influence finally made the U.S. cave, the sanctions that had been put in place by the United States were no longer of any importance. One of the clauses in the sanctions was that Zonfer could not indiscriminately murder people. If this sanction were to be violated, he would be subject to military action. This, needless to say, was no longer an issue.

The tyrant remained tyrannical. Dr. Taber would be Zonfer's last thrill kill.

Chapter 6: Zonfer's Admission - (late) January-April 3034 (end of Earth timeline)

After Taber's "untimely demise," Zonfer decided to go through with his drastic solution to the problem. The idea of planetary evacuation was quickly becoming the operative plan. The report from Conlind was optimistic. This would be no easy task, even with the advanced machinery that would be performing the work. Materials turned out to be the least of Zonfer's worries. The main problem would be time involved to create the craft. The estimated amount of time would be one to three years. Something would have to be done in the meantime.

Although he opposed it at first, the Renaissance, as it became known, was fitted with engines. Its transition to a massive spacecraft took shape. This was more than the first intergalactic bus. It was a dream, a vision. It would be mankind's second chance.

Zonfer once again went to his military advisors for a solution. He met with Hayden and found nothing but contemptuous criticism of how the problem had been handled so far. This, to say the least, did not make Zonfer happy. He stormed out of the meeting with his entourage following close behind. He vowed to himself that he would make the critics pay for their remarks someday.

Reports of Zonfer's murdering ways circulated throughout the press. His approval rating was plummeting. Zonfer was concerned about resistance groups. Recently, various attacks had been attempted on his headquarters. Individuals dressed in street clothes had a red fist insignia plastered across their chests. It appeared that a tangible resistance force was forming. Zonfer hoped it wasn't true.

It was a cold day in Zonfer Square in Vienna, Austria. The dampness on the steel building walls froze immediately. The smell of the early winter loomed. The winters were longer now because of the environmental situation. This was a moot point with the citizens. At some point, they just stopped caring. Ninety-five percent of Earth's air had been polluted beyond repair. Smog and filth floated in the atmosphere. On certain occasions, one could taste it.

The motorcade left Zonfer's headquarters deep in the Austrian mountains. The glossy dark paint on the large utility vehicles glistened in the Earthling sun. Zonfer sat silent as he contemplated his meeting with the CGC. The low hum of the vehicle's engine rumbled in his chest. It was comforting. This was a welcome rest before he had to deal with the council members. The meetings were increasingly tense. Zonfer sensed the council's distain for him. However, he knew he needed them. They were bright individuals and their wisdom was priceless.

The motorcade quickly approached its destination. The cylindrical shape of the erection was awe-inspiring. The war-torn old leader still loved architecture. He gazed at the structure in delight. A slight smile crept upon his face. The transports came to a slow stop. Two large-framed men dressed in Zonfer's defense force garb flanked both sides of Zonfer's vehicle. They tapped the window signaling an "all clear." Zonfer's black and golden garments glistened in the morning sun. His cloak rippled gracefully through the light breeze. Any sign of joy or delight was long dead upon Zonfer's countenance. He was all business now.

The door cycled open and shut on the Central Governing Complex in Vienna. The inside wasn't nearly as appealing as the outside. Plain stainless steel walls, bland black floors—it was the typical government facility. He stood outside the main chamber. He dreaded the meeting. He knew he had mishandled the situation from the onset. This wouldn't be pretty.

The CGC had been the place where Zonfer had met with his advisors for years. He had a meeting on this day with most of the members of the Alliance for Peace. This was an organization of the leaders of each nation around the world. Zonfer appointed each of these leaders himself. They had been waiting for Zonfer for a good amount of time. This was often the case. Many of his advisors had grown tired of Zonfer's disrespect. He often acted as if they were peons.

The meeting was about to begin. The council speaker announced, "Zonfer in chamber!"

The members of the council rose—a panel of a couple of thousand men. They were dressed in boring attire, basic suits, and ties. A muted hiss was heard from a few unknown locations. Zonfer's eyes bounced from man to man. This was the first time in a long while that Zonfer had felt nervous. Nonetheless, his expression remained angry and stoic.

"Be seated, everyone." The rattle of seats commenced. "I meet you today with a heavy burden on my conscience. We all know of my lack of foresight in this matter. I ask you to forgive me." Muted chatter erupted. Could it be? The unquestionable Zonfer admitting fault?

"Order!" the council speaker yelled.

Zonfer continued. "I hope to not be interrupted again. I have received no useable advice from my military advisors and have decided that you are the final hope for a solution. The Plague has played hell on the population in the affected areas. My science advisor had told me that this Plague showed signs of spreading randomly throughout the nations of the planet. Neither the origin nor the physical composition of the Plague is known. The only thing that is definite is that it first showed up in Center City, near the Holy Land and then in NYC. The random nature of the Plague makes it next to impossible to defend against. I am hoping that some of you have some productive ideas for defending against it. We know that it can destroy literally anything. What I am looking for from you are suggestions as to what we can do, collectively, as a whole. This is a time of great peril. We need to put behind us any differences we have had in the past. The fate of our race is at stake. We have had challenges in the past, but nothing as defining in our history as this. The entire fate of the world lies in our hands. What we do will forever decide the world's fate. Will Earth remain the domain of the human race?

We will seriously have to consider this question. I have discussed this matter with all of my personal advisors and have had no luck in finding a solution. This is why I stand before you today. I have put my trust in you to govern the various nations around the world. Prove to me that I did not make a mistake. Show me that the trust I have instilled in you was not misspent."

"Zonfer has addressed the council. Council members may now yield and make comments or ask questions," the council speaker announced.

"May I yield?"

"Councilman Feldman of the Holy Land yields." The speaker confirmed.

"Sir, as you are well aware, I have dealt with this situation personally. We have discussed this together on several different occasions. You made it quite clear that the human race would not tire. We would wait this out. Find an alternate means of survival until this menace left our domain. I find it quite hard to swallow that with all of the advisors' advice, you cannot come up with an alternative to leaving the planet."

Zonfer steamed, "May I yield?" The moderator confirmed and Zonfer spoke.

"I don't appreciate the tone in your voice, Feldman. I have discussed this with every advisor and they don't have the first clue as to how to handle this situation. This isn't exactly a textbook problem. The human race has never faced an enemy like this before. There is no weakness to this phenomenon."

"May I yield?" Feldman retorted. It was confirmed.

"I was under the impression that we could speak freely, Zonfer. I guess even in this time of peril you cannot be questioned—"

Loud chatter cascaded across the expansive boardroom. Zonfer began to realize that most, if not all, of the council had lost respect for him. He needed them, however. He knew that they were the last hope of the human race.

Zonfer adjusted his tone. "Feldman, do you think I want to do this? Do you actually think I would leave the planet for the fun of it? We're losing citizens, councilmen and women! This needs to end!"

Feldman continued. "My concern is how we will get all of the inhabitants of Earth on a vessel. I discussed this with you some time ago and suggested that we evacuate but you would have no part of it. In fact, you were quite offended that I would even suggest it.. Now, here we stand with countless attacks behind us, millions dead, cities in ruin, and still no concrete plan as to how to get out of this situation. I see only one thing to do and that thing has not changed since we spoke on that day. We must evacuate. I am calling for a vote."

Zonfer hung his head low. Feldman was correct. Nothing could change that reality. This was why Zonfer needed the council. They were about to do what needed to be done.

The moderator confirmed. The electronic voting panels exploded in light in front of each councilperson. The panels read, "Councilman Feldman has called for a vote on an Earth evacuation—yea or nay?" Zonfer waited in suspense.

The moderator tallied the votes. "The results of the vote—a unanimous yea."

Conversation resounded in the corridors of the CGC. Word would certainly spread quickly. This obviously was a huge turning point in Earth's history, an Exodus of mass proportion.

Zonfer left the CGC quickly, with no conversation. The atmosphere was intolerable to him. He felt the council's hatred. It was palpable. Thankfully for Zonfer, all eyes would be trained on the progress of the Renaissance. Zonfer could take a back seat for now.

Chapter 7: Construction Revealed

Another day began. Zonfer awoke to the same unfortunate progress reports from the Plague-afflicted regions. It appeared to be spreading at an alarming rate. The latest science report taunted Zonfer. He opened it and skimmed its contents—more of the same. No progress. He scowled and pressed on his temples in frustration.

Zonfer's disappointment was not only in the council but also in himself, in fact, mostly himself. He always strove to pursue the best possible solution to a problem. Over the years, he had become arrogant. Toward the end of the Earth timeline he'd begun to think of himself as almost godlike. Taking life where and when he chose became a grotesque habit. It took this disaster to snap Zonfer out of the haze of power he had been living in for years. Zonfer never had the foresight to recognize the problem of having to face an enemy that even he was weak and powerless against. Zonfer was in the solutions business. But this was different. It defied logic. When faced with this catastrophe, he experienced fear for the first time. When Zonfer witnessed the effects that the Plague had on its victims, he was affected in a way that he never experienced before. The mutilation was a shocking sight even to him.

In the hours leading up to the evacuation planning, Zonfer had time to reflect on his empire and what his impact on history would be. Had this Plague come about because of him? Had he needed this wake up call? Was this a take down executed by a higher power? Historians would decide Zonfer's role in the world, not he. Now he knew without a doubt that he needed to focus on saving mankind.

Talk had been surfacing about an evacuation to the planet of Tento. Initially, the citizenry thought of this as a joke. Surely, no one would choose to live in such a place. The idea of moving to such a barren wasteland did not appeal to the masses. But the truth was that this was the only possible planet that could support life much like life on Earth had thrived for billions of years. It had the biological requirements to sustain the amount of life that Earth supported. However, the planet was severely underdeveloped. There were only a few dilapidated buildings remaining on the landscape of Tento. The Erectorbots would have had a field day with the development of Tento City. For the time being, the Earth's inhabitants would reside in the super-craft, the Renaissance. While the construction of cities and towns took place, the citizens would adapt to the new surroundings of Tento.

Just when Zonfer thought his day would be dominated by negativity, General Hayden entered with a massive stack of documents.

Hayden began, "Sir, I come to you with good news. The bots are close to completion of the craft. Mr. Riddick has requested your presence. I have visited the craft and have come to tell you that I am very optimistic about our future. The craft is of sound architecture and is aesthetically appealing. The people of Earth will be pleased."

"I am extremely pleased to hear this, General," exclaimed Zonfer. "What documents have you brought to me?"

"This is the report of progress from Mr. Riddick. He has informed me that the craft will be done in a matter of months, not years."

"This is excellent news. The Plague attacks have been increasing in rate steadily. I've never seen anything like this, General. Have you seen the footage?"

Hayden swallowed hard. "Yes, sir. The science department requested I study it and show it to the force. I don't really understand why. I guess so that we'll know what to expect during recovery missions. First time I saw it I nearly lost my lunch."

Zonfer narrowed his attention. "Understandable, General, no one should be used to that kind of devastation."

"Yes, sir, I guess so. The sooner we can call that spaceship our home, the better." Hayden said shifting his weight to his right leg.

"Absolutely, General," Zonfer said. He gazed up at his office clock. "Let's get going. I don't want to keep Mr. Riddick waiting."

***

Zonfer's transport approached the construction hangar. The latest incarnation of the Griffin Wing dropship neared the destination. The designated construction area was the Sierra Desert. The Erectorbots had their hands full with this project. The craft was inconceivably massive. Nothing like it had even been attempted in the past. Zonfer was making history again.

Riddick was standing near the front of the hangar. He waved the Griffin Wing down. It landed and Zonfer and Hayden emerged.

"Hello, sir!" Riddick said.

"Greetings, Mr. Riddick. I'm anticipating seeing your progress," Zonfer said in his less than commanding voice.

"Follow me, sir."

Zonfer, Hayden, and Riddick entered the hangar. They were confronted with the wonderment of the flagship Renaissance. Small pod like machines with long steel arms welded and checked their work. Seeing the Erectorbots at work was an amazing sight.

"Well, here she is, sir," Riddick declared confidently.

"Fantastic. I don't quite know what to say, Mr. Riddick," Zonfer said. It was true. He was speechless. He looked at General Hayden. He smiled and nodded in agreement.

"Shall we enter?" Riddick asked.

"Absolutely!" Zonfer responded enthusiastically.

They approached the entry ramp. Riddick entered a code on the keypad and stepped back.

"You'd better stand back, gentlemen," Riddick said.

The three men paced backward slowly. They peered toward the ceiling of the hangar. The massive entry ramp to the Renaissance gracefully lowered to the hangar floor. It was almost silent. A barely audible hum pervaded the hangar.

"Wow," Hayden whispered.

Zonfer stood, arms crossed, in a wide, silent stance. As the ramp touched down, the three men entered the Commons Area. There was activity in every corner of the craft—workers welding panels and checking if they were secure; scientists conducting experiments on the air in enclosed spaces and various other detailed activities.

Riddick was a fit man, standing six-feet-four inches tall. He was formerly a hit man for an organized crime family in Italy. Riddick had come to the attention of Zonfer when he had been assigned to assassinate Zonfer. Needless to say, Riddick was not successful. Zonfer decided to keep Riddick alive and use him as an asset. Riddick had come closer than anyone before him to actually getting the job done. It turned out that this was a good judgment call on Zonfer's part. It turned out that Riddick was a contractor for a large corporation before he had taken up the business of being a hit man.

There had been several attempts on Zonfer's life over the years. No one ever even came close to the man himself. Zonfer had developed the best and most effective security force ever known by any man. The fact was that Zonfer was—or had been—untouchable. If someone wanted to get to Zonfer, they would have to get to him through the security force.

"Well, sir, what do you think?" Riddick inquired.

"I don't quite know how to respond to that question, Mr. Riddick. I'm astounded. Your work is to be commended. I knew your worth when I recruited you but never foresaw anything close to something like this. It's amazing." Zonfer kindly responded, (certainly out of character.) "Thank you, sir. I have to admit. I've impressed myself. When Don Conlind approached me with the idea, I really wasn't sure this was possible. I can't take all the credit, though. The Erectorbots are life savers" Riddick motioned to one of the hovering bots working.

Zonfer nodded in agreement. "They are amazing. How long until the artificial atmosphere is up? I want to witness that firsthand when it happens."

"The scientists are about a week away from perfecting it. Mind you that this will last forever. So, this craft will be able to be used even after the cities on Tento are built. If the unfortunate situation that we have here on Earth were to happen on Tento, we could use this as a life boat." Riddick informed.

Zonfer flinched at the mere notion that something like this would ever happen again. Not on his watch, anyway. This was one thing that Zonfer had not worked out. There was no heir apparent to the throne of the human race. What Zonfer intended on doing was to give the governing powers back to the people of Earth. He believed that after years of rule under himself, that the people of Earth would be ready for a change. But the people of Earth had learned to live fairly simple lives, aside form the CEOs of large companies. Most of those people lived lavish lives of luxury and pampering. In this simple mind set, crime had been virtually eradicated. Zonfer was to thank for this. He had done the unthinkable of politically cleansing half of the population of Earth. This did, however, result in the prosperous times under Zonfer's control. The citizenry feared Zonfer. His ultimate intentions of the Great Slaughter had been realized. No one dared to challenge him. This Plague made Zonfer think about consequences to actions. What did the Plague ultimately mean?

Zonfer turned to General Hayden. "Sorry for ignoring you, General. I guess I'm rather engrossed with this."

"Don't think twice, sir. This is your moment," Zonfer nodded to Hayden and cracked a half-smile.

Now, with the Exodus at hand, Zonfer was writing a new chapter in the book of human history. For the first time ever, Earth would no longer be the domain of the human race. He was proud of his accomplishments. Most of the population had now rallied behind their leader. There were a select few sects of the population that were protesting the evacuation and were refusing to leave. They were however, a very small minority. Most of the population had recognized the danger in the Plague and were excited about leaving for Tento.

Zonfer was pleased at Riddick's progress. He saw a sound craft that appealed to the eye while being extremely effective and efficient in its design.

Zonfer began. "Well, Mr. Riddick, I am very impressed. You have made quite a lot of progress. I am very pleased of the status of the schedule. I can't wait to see the artificial atmosphere up and running. I look forward to meeting with you again."

"Thank you, sir."

Zonfer shook Riddick's hand with a firm grip. Hayden did the same. He was truly pleased at the progress that the project had made.

Zonfer and Riddick appeared on all the major news networks. In a news conference at the hangar, they gave the inhabitants of

Earth a preview of the craft they would call home for a time. It
was a welcome break from the constant coverage of Plague attacks.

The Exodus was at hand and the population was jubilant
about the situation. There were large celebrations. The mood had
changed completely.

***

The streets were cold in New York but the atmosphere was
not. People gathered and celebrated their chance at a new start. It felt
like a New Years' Eve bash. A bar on the corner of 5th Avenue was
packed with many citizens. The televisions inside lit up with
optimistic images of Zonfer greeting people. The headlines on the
newspapers read, "A NEW BEGINNING!"

Then, as the celebrations continued, a Griffin Wing appeared
in the distance.

"Look! Do you see that?!" One of the onlookers on 5th
Avenue exclaimed. People, as they heard the commotion, paused
from their activities to observe the grandiose entrance.

The dropship neared 5th Avenue. It found the designated
building and landed. Zonfer emerged from the craft and waved to the
now frantic crowd. A podium was conveniently present. All the
major news outlets were there.

After a greeting, Zonfer approached the podium and began.

"People of Earth, a new era is upon us. The death and
destruction of the past decades is behind us. I make a new pledge to
you on this day. Tento is the next step for the human race. We must
all pull together. Unfortunately, those who died in the attack on New
York were not the last to die in the name of this Plague. It has
claimed far too many lives. Many may say that we are bending in the
face of this evil. I beg to differ. You, the people of the human race
and inhabitants of Earth, are showing great courage. You are leaving
the only place that mankind has known as home for the past several
million years. This, my friends, takes enormous courage and I bow to
you. I bow to you because of the enormous task you are undertaking.
Some of you maybe saying goodbye to loved ones that have decided
to stay. To you, I also bow. So, I call on you, citizens of Earth, to
come to Zonfer Square in Vienna. This is where the launch will take
place. There is no fee to board. This is a flight for life, a flight for the
future, a flight to remember. We are all Gods' children and we must
unite to overcome this burden of the Plague. I was not a man of faith

before this menace. The Plague showed me that God is real. God is watching over us and God allowed us this great opportunity of life. I, as your leader, have taken this chance for life and I believe that God himself helped the people who built the craft, The Renaissance. This is a renewal of faith and life! This is the new beginning! Thank you!"

The onlookers exploded in cheers of joy and some confusion. Where had all of that come from?

Chapter 8: The New Beginning and the Resistance

The crowd was truly amazing. The line could be seen for miles. No one could begin to estimate the amount of people that came to Zonfer Square that day. This was not the day that they would leave, however. That was still months away. The people were excited to see the amazing craft for the first time. They were mesmerized by its sheer size. No one had ever seen such a grand craft before. There were millions of rooms throughout the Renaissance. Every corridor could hold countless inhabitants. This was also a humbling experience for the affluent people of Earth. They knew that they would be living like everyone else for some time to come. But, strangely enough, none of them cared. Most people truly believed that this was a new day in the lives of every person on the face of the Earth. People were giving up everything to take part in this new culture. Zonfer had done it again. Never had the people of Earth been this united. The new beginning had begun. Zonfer was meeting with people in the Renaissance. Most people were casual and very thankful to Zonfer. Zonfer spoke to them about his newfound faith and the future of the human race. Optimism was the new attitude. Negativity was no longer a word that anyone understood.

Zonfer stood at the entry ramp of his crowning achievement. General Hayden stood next to him in a strong posture. His assault rifle rested across his chest ready for combat. The line of citizens of all ethnicities and creeds approached the seemingly humble leader and greeted him.

"Hello, sir, it's so exciting to meet you in person! Thank you for this opportunity!" a middleclass woman exclaimed, shaking Zonfer's hand vigorously.

"The pleasure is all mine, miss. Please, enter and enjoy," he said humbly.

Hayden couldn't help but smile. He had never seen this side of Zonfer. Not many had. The stream of humanity continued and Zonfer enjoyed every second.

A large framed man dressed in old, tattered Austrian Armed Forces fatigues stood motionless in the background. His longish dark brown hair fell into his pitch black eyes. His stare was terrifying. His massive arms were folded in front of him. An ancient standard issue sidearm was strapped to his thigh. He showed no sign of interest. In fact, one surmised the man felt contempt for the people that surrounded him. "Pathetic," he muttered to himself.

Then, a few individuals behind the man unfurled a massive banner. Painted on it was a large red fist in a circle. Behind our seething onlooker stood members of the Resistance. The man that stood in the forefront was known as Blaine Danken. He had been organizing an opposition group to Zonfer's power for years.

Through no effort of their own, Zonfer and Danken had an intertwined past. They had served in the AAF together during the War for Humanity. Both of them had also been inductees of the controversial Warrior Program, a scientific experiment in pursuit of a super soldier. Danken also had held a combat position in Zonfer's defense corporation for a period. All of that seemed like ancient history to both the men. Danken thrived on war and death. The years of peace under Zonfer's rule had sickened the unstable man. In hopes of sparking a huge conflict, he and his Resistance had been attempting provocative attacks on Zonfer's outposts for years now.

Danken stood away from the crowd with a maniacal grin on his grim, scarred face. "I love the smell of rocket fuel. Do you smell it?" He sighed.

A voice from behind him responded, "Yes, sir."

Even though he never spoke the language anymore, he still had a heavy Austrian accent. There were many times when he gave orders to his men and they failed to obey him only because they didn't understand him. Many men had died for this fatal mistake. Most of the globe spoke English exclusively. The U.N. had declared it the language of free nations. Hence, the generations afterward inherited it. Danken was old enough to remember the days when each nation had their own way of doing things. Now, it was the Zonfer way or death. Not while he was still breathing. Danken vowed to be the monkey wrench in Zonfer's New Beginning. He was sickened by Zonfer's display of affection for the inhabitants. Danken was colored by his experiences of war. He had no more faith in the human race. He thought every person was a corrupt entity.

The crowd began to respond to the Resistance jeers. Zonfer heard the commotion and peered in the direction of the large group. He observed the massive banner looming over the group. He immediately recognized the red flag. Zonfer tapped Hayden on the shoulder.

"You see that, General?"

"Yes, sir—I saw them earlier. I was hoping they wouldn't start a scene," Hayden said as he gripped his assault rifle.

"Well, I guess it was inevitable. We know they've been trying to start a war for years now. This would be the perfect opportunity…Danken…damn you."

Zonfer's gaze was concentrated on the leader of the Resistance. An amalgamation of memories suddenly attacked his psyche, things he thought he had buried long ago. He decided to not prolong the inevitable.

"I'm going to try and take care of this, General. Keep an eye on the situation. Have the force ready," Zonfer said.

"Yes, sir. You sure you don't want me to back you up?" Hayden responded.

"No, General—I'll handle Danken."

Zonfer walked toward the group of rabid Resistance members. His stride was deliberate and unwavering. His Redfield assault rifle slung upon his shoulder. He approached the gathering.

"What the hell are you doing here?" Zonfer exploded.

"Zonfer—Nice to see you too, old friend. Is this not a public affair, Wolf?" Danken grinned at Zonfer with a sarcastic grimace.

Zonfer's eyes blazed with anger. Nobody called him that, especially not the likes of Danken.

"Get your filthy crew out of here," Zonfer spat. A Resistance member began to lunge forward. Danken immediately interceded with his monstrous arm.

"Hold it—There can't be a war without opposition, Jayson," the Resistance member stood down.

Zonfer's patience grew thin. "I know what you are planning and I won't stand idle and let it happen."

"You said it yourself, Zonfer. This is a gathering for all of us, the pathetic inhabitants of Earth," Danken sarcastically laughed and shook his head.

Zonfer briefly peered at General Hayden. He was watching every second of the confrontation as he oversaw the elated citizens' entry to the Renaissance.

"You all right, sir?" Hayden enquired on the comm. channel. Zonfer nodded.

"Earth—What a shit hole this place is. I wouldn't send my worst enemy to live here. Except you, Zonfer, you deserve these idiots, these mindless vermin. Why do you bother with them, Zonfer? I guess that it is appropriate. You were one in the same at one time, before you became drunk with power. I hope that that goddamn albatross goes down with all of you in it!" Danken spewed.

Zonfer grabbed Danken by his collar. A physical confrontation seemed inevitable. The collection of Resistance members yelled in rebellion.

"Calm down, boys! It's all right," Danken said calmly.

"Leave—now," Zonfer whispered.

Danken laughed. "Sure, I'll be going now. You can have all of these peasants. Send the best to Taber for me—Oh, that's right."

Zonfer watched the ragtag group file out of sight. A few obscene gestures were thrown his way. Zonfer accessed the comm. channel.

"General, we're going to have to keep an eye on this. I've got a bad feeling."

Hayden pushed the comm. deeper into his ear. "Affirmative, sir."

Zonfer did not appreciate the interaction. He was glad to see Danken leave with his followers even if it was only temporarily. The New Beginning faced its first obstacle.

The question remained in Zonfer's mind. Why was Danken going to Tento if he was so against the idea? The answer was obvious to Zonfer. Danken's Resistance would attempt to ignite a Civil War. Danken's force structure was far more formidable than Zonfer could imagine. Danken had formed a force of around one million followers who were opposed to the evacuation. The majority was ordered to lie low. Danken wanted to retain the element of surprise. The Resistance vowed to end the New Beginning and take as many lives as possible.

After Danken left, the mood returned to being jubilant. However, if the people of Earth had known what was to come, there would have been no celebrating. This was the beginning of the bloodiest conflict in human history. Unfortunately, there was nothing that Zonfer could do to prevent these events from happening.

Zonfer turned to view his people. He knew Danken well and what he sensed scared him. Danken had plunged off the deep end; his psychotic nature now defined him. Zonfer's heart sunk at the sight of the massive celebration. He hoped this would be the last roadblock to the New Beginning. But deep down, he knew otherwise.

***

The celebration went on for many hours. Zonfer retired to his palace long before the celebrations had concluded. He had grown tired of mingling. Sleep didn't come easy to Zonfer. The many years of war and violence had affected his mind in the worst possible manner. Nightmares plagued his nights, images of dismembered bodies and of baby corpses. He was a troubled soul. The many ghosts of his past indiscretions and atrocities haunted him. His sins did not go unpunished.

The next months flew by quickly. The future continued to look up. The inhabitants of Earth had found something to look forward to. The time of the Exodus was fast approaching. The anticipation was quickly rising. Plague attacks were declining and the human race breathed a collective sigh of relief.

Danken had also been eagerly anticipating the launch. He decided this would be the best time to begin the war. He finally had a meaningful task that he would be involved in. The wars were significant but he played limited roles in those conflicts. This uprising would be of his making, an accomplishment all of his own. The Resistance was like a nomadic tribe. They gathered wherever it was most convenient and planned their eventual attacks.

***

The Exodus now was a mere month away. Zonfer's daily routine remained unchanged. His advisors entered his office and provided hourly updates on the progress of the various matters at hand. During his brief moments of inactivity, he observed the vast expanse of his view of the Alps. Something was happening. The sky was changing. The science officials had been playing catch up with the changing biology of the planet for months. Any ironclad explanation remained elusive. The sooner Earth could treat the Renaissance as home the better.

Zonfer's communication panel sounded. He lightly touched the answer button.

"Sir, General Hayden to see you."

"Send him in, please."

The general walked into Zonfer's office. He had a perplexed look upon his face. Zonfer shifted his attention to his commanding officer.

"General, how are—" Zonfer sensed the general's bewilderment. "What's the matter?"

The general's posture straightened. "Sir, the Resistance appears to be amassing weapons and transports."

Zonfer gazed down at his desk. "Yes, recon has been reporting the same activities. Just keep an eye on them. I don't want to be the one to start a war."

"Yes, sir."

"Was that all, General?"

"Yes, sir."

Zonfer nodded. "Dismissed." Suddenly, Zonfer's console toned again. He answered.

"Sir, a man is here to see you. He refuses to—"

"Let me in!" the voice interrupted. "I just want to talk!"

Zonfer immediately recognized the voice. Danken. "It's him," Zonfer said to Hayden.

"What!" He exclaimed. "You mean him—him?"

Zonfer nodded. "I think it would be wise for you to stay during our meeting."

"Absolutely, sir."

Zonfer appeared unaffected, but his strategy was hard to discern. "Send him in."

"I'm on my way," Danken responded on the console. Zonfer's eyes widened. Danken kicked in the steel door. It swung in with a massive crash.

"Man, there's a big mess out there! You should have somebody clean it up!" Danken said jovially.

A pool of blood was visible from Zonfer's vantage point. His attendant had been murdered. The culprit was obvious.

Danken had made his grand entrance. The grandiose décor and busts of Zonfer he viewed upon strolling the headquarters' entrance sickened him. He viewed this as a weak man's ego getting the best of him. He thought to himself that he would enjoy killing Zonfer more than he had enjoyed killing anyone before him. Danken's hatred for Zonfer was seething at this point. He wanted to kill him right then but he managed to control his anger. The general was a formidable deterrent as well.

Hayden raised his Redfield assault rifle. "Please, sir, let me take this maggot out!"

Zonfer held his arm out and shook his head. "We'll have real problems if we kill him now."

Danken was manic. The adrenaline from his kill was just entering his system. "Goddamn, this place is hideous! I've never seen more gaudy things in my life. You sure do have bad taste, Wolf."

"Don't call me that!" Zonfer exploded, pounding the desk with furious rage.

"Haaaa! Touched a nerve, did I?! I know your past well, you old bastard! Your mindless sheep like that big mongrel might not remember—but I do!" Danken proclaimed.

Zonfer clenched his fist. He was between a proverbial rock and hard place. He couldn't imprison nor eliminate Danken. If he did so, it would appear that he was the one agitating the situation. Also, Danken's followers would surely lead a rescue mission for their leader.

Zonfer considered his words. "Danken, despite your wanting to thwart the Exodus—"

"Nonsense!" Danken interrupted. "You are quite mistaken, my old friend. I can't wait for the Exodus. This is a new beginning for me as well. The Resistance will rise on the day of the Exodus! This is my defining moment, Zonfer, not yours!"

Zonfer bit his bottom lip. He grew tired of this idiocy.

Danken paused and fiddled with his hands. "Zonfer, do you remember what it is like to kill a man? Do you remember the rush of adrenaline that comes from getting another man's blood on your hands? We're alike, you and I! We're Warrior Program grads! You remember—Sullivan—the conditioning—It's all right there, buried deep within your mind. All you have to do is call on it. Just like yesteryear." Danken's voice had trailed to a disturbingly evil hiss.

Zonfer found his demons gaining on him fast. His old AAF partner was dredging up very dangerous memories. Memories long forgotten. Memories long buried. He glared at Danken blankly.

Danken snickered. "Do you remember our fishing trips at the barracks?" Zonfer's eyes narrowed on Danken. He remembered that?

Danken continued, "I thought we'd have a great partnership. I trusted you. We trained hard, harder than all the others. We got that Leopold—together! Somehow, you— alone—became Mr. Leopold in 2993! Then, after all the bullshit, just before our first deployment, you dropped me like a bad habit! And I'm not supposed to be mad!"

Zonfer shook his head. "Ancient history—ancient history."

"Not to me!" Danken was emotional, vulnerable.

Zonfer sensed an opening. "Danken, time heals all. Why don't you take a breather? See a psychologist. Get some help. The New Beginning will be for all of Earth. You included."

Danken nodded. "Maybe you're right, Wolf. Maybe you're right." Danken left Zonfer's headquarters. Medics were attempting to resuscitate Danken's victim, but he casually walked by barely noticing the scene. It was as if he were sleepwalking through the mess.

Zonfer ascended from his seat and ran to the scene.

"She going to make it?" He inquired.

"She's gone, sir. Sorry." The medic responded.

General Hayden approached soon after. "Sir, I don't understand why you didn't take that nut into custody. He can do a lot less damage on the inside than out!"

Zonfer stared at Hayden wide-eyed. The look was plenty. Hayden stood down. He was probably correct but the possible damage to Zonfer's image was too high of a risk. They would fight Danken and the Resistance. At this point, a scarred reputation would be far more devastating.

Chapter 9: A Rebirth of Hope / A Resurrection of Fear

It was the day of the Exodus. It was cold. Everyday since the Plague disappeared seemed colder. The Earthling sky continued its odd transformation. The color was familiar, crimson and black, the colors of the Plague.

Zonfer, Hayden and three silhouetted figures stood surveying the crowd. No sign of Danken and the Resistance. Zonfer hoped he had decided to end his opposition to the Exodus.

The collective population of Earth was joined in a giant celebration. Zonfer Square in Austria was packed with citizens eager to get the launch under way. Zonfer approached a podium near the Renaissance's ramp and began his address.

"Citizens of Earth, welcome to the day of Exodus!"

The crowd came alive, screaming and cheering for their leader. With his head held high, Hayden looked on in pride.

"In a matter of hours, we will all be on our way to Tento. This is the day that we have all been waiting for. I hope that you are as excited as I. In a few short hours, we will write a new chapter in the book of our history. This is the single most important day in human history and you are all a part of it!"

The crowd approved. They cheered once again with even more vigor. Zonfer's approval was at one hundred percent. The people saw him as almost a savior, the new age equivalent to Moses.

Zonfer had completed his speech. As he descended from the podium, Hayden's targeting system went crazy.

"Sir, we've got hostiles!" Hayden urgently proclaimed.

"I see them, General," Zonfer responded.

In the near expanse, Danken's Resistance could be seen approaching the site of the Renaissance. It was a terrifying sight. Their formation was scattered. There was no clear organization. It was a million-man posse, all of them armed and very dangerous.

The Resistance circled the crowd around the flagship. The three silhouetted figures stepped forward, slowly revealing their identities. They were Zonfer's three best soldiers. Their black combat armor held the noble Zonfer crest upon their chests. With their rifles at the ready, the three prepared for combat. Upon their right breasts were inscribed their names, Vankman, Galant and Williams.

Danken was in front, his eyes wild. He paced uncontrollably. "Listen up!" he yelled.

The crowd immediately turned silent. They stared at the madman in absolute terror. What could they do?

"I am declaring war on every man, woman, and child here today! This is the start of a civil war like no other! I am taking this conflict right to Tento! We will battle on that hunk of junk there and we will battle on Tento! I will not rest until all of you peons are lying at my feet!" Danken grinned. His teeth chattered. He was manic.

The crowd roared in anger. They were having no part of the man's attitude. They were ready for a fight.

"Who the hell are you anyway?" a brave voice said from the crowd.

"Shut up! My name is not important! We are the Resistance! Before long, you vermin will be calling us leader and not Zonfer!" Danken roared.

Zonfer approached the podium. "Danken! Stand down! My DF is ready for deployment! You don't stand a chance! You'll be slaughtered like pigs!" Zonfer could take action now. Danken had publicly declared war. This was it—D-Day.

Danken laughed manically. "Try it! How about this? Will this get a reaction?" Danken raised his old assault rife and fired on the crowd. Screams erupted, citizens scattered, destroying the perfect line.

"That's it, General. Deploy the DF. He wanted a war. He's got one," Zonfer said.

"All units—This is Hayden—" He turned to begin the offensive posture.

The three top DF members were already engaging targets.

All over, men, women, and young adults were seeking out firearms and weapons of all sorts to fight the Resistance. Citizens were beating resistance members in the streets with primitive blunt weapons, pipes, and large rocks, whatever. Gunfire lit up the sky like the forth of July.

Danken struggled with a Defense Force member. The two exchanged punches. Danken blocked and retaliated. He parried another hit and pinned the young soldier down.

"Do you honestly serve this pathetic idiot willingly?" Danken hissed.

"I serve him and only him," the soldier replied.

Danken laughed. "Then face my blade."

Danken drew forward and made one long stroke of his bayonet. The blade sliced through the flesh of the guard's neck like a hot knife cutting through butter.

Zonfer leaped the protective barrier. He sprinted to a DF armored personnel carrier. He approached Captain Vernon Sillus.

"Sillus, get me a Redfield!" Zonfer exclaimed.

"Sir? You're going to fight?" Sillus responded, shocked.

"Why else would I ask for a rifle, soldier! Double time it!"

The captain quickly retrieved the requested weapon and returned. He handed it to Zonfer carefully. Zonfer turned to the battlefield.

"Sir!" Sillus said hastily. Zonfer paused and turned again. "Good luck."

Zonfer nodded and saluted quickly. He ran headstrong into the epicenter of the battle. Captain Sillus watched his leader fade into the fog of war. He was thoroughly astonished. Zonfer was around sixty years old. However, his physique and endurance was that of a man in his mid-thirties. No one but Danken knew of Zonfer's secret past. This past explained his vitality.

A river of blood slowly formed in the streets of Zonfer Square. The New Beginning looked doomed. Zonfer fought tooth and nail with his DF and his determined people. As long as there remained a breath in his body, he swore to preserve the New Beginning.

***

"Fall back! Everybody! fall back!" Danken cried.

The gruff crew fell into a sloppy formation and abandoned their current offensive. Zonfer lie prone in a dimly lit alley near the resting place of the Renaissance. He held his breath and inched the trigger back. Thrack! Thrack! Thrack! His A-92 Redfield threw its death. Every bullet collided with its intended target, dropping the enemy mercilessly. Zonfer sensed their retreat. He downed a few fleeing combatants and ended his offensive.

"General, we good?" Zonfer asked into his comm. link.

"Looks as if they're falling back, sir. This could be our chance to board!" Hayden's voice squawked back.

The time had arrived to board The Renaissance. With the members of the Resistance nowhere in sight, this was the perfect opportunity to begin. The civilians boarded slowly. Zonfer was at the helm waving his people to safety. General Hayden accompanied him in the endeavor.

"Come on, people, we need to get this whale in the air!" The general jokingly said in an attempt at some levity in the face of peril. Zonfer nodded and smiled. "There it is again," he thought. A smile.

The boarding continued until every man, woman, and child were safe under the care of the flagship Renaissance. In a matter of hours, they were safe and conversing with one another. Zonfer observed with his faithful general at his side on a perched catwalk high atop the Commons Area.

"Would you look at that—quite the sight," Hayden said in wonder.

"Quite the sight, indeed, General. Quite the sight."

***

"Come on! We gotta do this quick. They'll be firing up the engines any second now!" Danken exclaimed. He and the Resistance began to pile into the jets of the Renaissance. It was insane. It was more than insane.

"Hurry up! Get in there!" he yelled.

A stream of humanity continued on the suicide descent to the engines of the biggest spacecraft ever built.

Danken stood in front of his crew. "If we continue down, this will lead directly to the Maintenance Block! That's gonna be home for us—for now." His voice bounced off the thick steel walls of the Renaissance's internal workings. Danken's right-hand madman stood appropriately to his right.

"Jayson, we need to get our crew moving. If we lag, we're dead," Danken proclaimed.

Fillmore Jayson was massive. Danken had met him years prior at a Austrian gym. He stood an inch over seven feet tall. His hair was impeccably trimmed to a perfect crew cut. He had been working a dead-end job in retail when Danken discussed his idea of a resistance force against Zonfer. Misguided and somewhat simple, Danken's influence prevailed.

Jayson raised his primitive rifle and shot a short burst. "You heard the man, get sprinting!" he barked, the bass booming in his voice.

This received the desired result. The huge group of scruffy combatants traversed the awkward engine block. The clink of countless boots resounded. It was almost deafening.

They neared the Maintenance Block. Suddenly, an Earth-shattering roar emitted from every corner of the engine block.

Danken staggered. "Gahh! Run! Quick! Everybody sprint as fast as you can!" Danken exclaimed.

Seconds before the engines initiated, Danken entered the Maintenance Block. Jayson followed close behind. Danken peered into the now almost active jet block. A few members still were inside running as fast as humanly possible to escape their certain demise.

"Run!" Danken exclaimed.

Suddenly, a rush of flames flooded the jet blocks. Danken saw the three men engulfed in the unforgiving flames. He shrugged his shoulders casually and laid upon the warm Maintenance Block floor. He laughed quietly.

"What a day—What a day."

The Resistance had lived to fight another day. Danken had proved himself to be a competent leader—uncaring and insane but competent.

***

Activity in the Commons Area hadn't ceased. The atmosphere had calmed considerably after the first wave of fighting. The Commons Area was in lockdown. Zonfer thought it wise to be safe rather than sorry.

Large pillar-shaped machines lined the whole of the Commons Area. A large makeshift banner indicated their purpose, *"All citizens find their assigned rooms."* Upon them were touch-sensitive panels.

A tone that resembled the sound an airplane intercom made beeped.

"Attention: All residents approach the touch-panel pillars and follow the on-screen instructions. Thank you," a calming female mechanical voice said, repeated in an infinite loop.

The millions of people lined up to await their turn. They had seen plenty of activity for the day. It was time for sleep.

Chapter 10: A Renaissance of Conflict

Zonfer stood in Renaissance Control, the main area of logistical and security operations on the craft. Perplexed by Danken's fixation on death and war, he hoped a large-scale conflict could be avoided. The old warrior's eyelids were heavy. He felt them sagging. He'd sleep for a year when this was over.

General Hayden entered and approached him. "Sir, the citizens have settled nicely. Everybody found their respective quarters promptly."

"Glad to hear it, General," Zonfer's gaze was distant.

"You all right, sir? You look like you could use some rest," Hayden commented with concern.

"Some, General? Your powers of observation may need tweaking."

Hayden smiled. "Good news on the anti-Resistance front, it looks like Danken might be dead. Either that or left behind. His quarters haven't been accessed."

Zonfer looked at Hayden with cynicism. "Do you actually think he would be dumb enough to try and go to his quarters? Come on, General, I'm starting to lose respect for you!" Zonfer laughed. First smiles and now laughter—what would be next?

***

The soft glow of the pot lights that lined the Living Quarters walkways melted across the expanse. Danken's room was empty and dormant. The lights were out and no belongings could be found. Suddenly, the door cycled open. A small LED light softly illuminated the entry. Standing at the entrance was Danken, bloody but very much still alive. His bayonet was soaked in fresh blood. He also carried a standard issue sidearm, the latest incarnation of the Beretta, a 3020 model. He jacked it from a fallen DF soldier. The semi-automatic weapon was still a mainstay in defense organizations. It was known as "old faithful" in Zonfer's DF.

He found a seat and took it. He knew he didn't have long. He inhaled deeply and closed his eyes. He asked the servant bot to get him a can of diet cola. The servant bot returned with the requested beverage and promptly left Danken to his thoughts. Danken knew that from this moment on, he was a marked man. Not only would Zonfer be seeking him but also Zonfer's DF and Recon. A contract would surely be put upon his head. All of this and more furiously coursed through his mind. Enough. There was no time for thinking.

Danken decided to abandon his quarters for good. He knew that Zonfer would look for him here. He had in his possession a dank, old rag. He could use this and the old pair of pants he had to disguise himself and blend in with the less fortunate former inhabitants of Earth. He would no longer be able to use his battle fatigues. The citizenry knew him from his AAF garb.

Danken took his tattered battle garb, threw it in the bathtub and burned it. "Out with the old, in with the new," he muttered to himself.

The remnants of the clothing washed down the drain. The sewer system on The Renaissance was dumped every five to seven days. So, no one would ever know what he had done to cover his tracks. This was painful for Danken. That clothing had meant a lot to him in the past years. It was the last remaining symbol of the lives that he had taken. It was now time for Danken to take the walkways of the craft. He would soon meet up with his fellow Resistance members to brainstorm on a plausible way of igniting the conflict. First, he wanted to get acquainted with the interior of what would be the battlefield, The Renaissance.

As Danken exited his quarters, he heard the clunk of boots in unison. Zonfer's DF was on to him. He bowed into the shadows and disappeared. His demon like visage dissolved into the cloak of obscurity.

***

Over the preceding weeks, the citizenry spent their time adapting to their new lives on the Renaissance. Commerce Square was packed. It was the cultural and entertainment hub of the craft. Bars, nightclubs, storefronts and the like lined the walkways. The new businesses were flourishing. People were spending money like water. The constant chatter of citizens echoed throughout the area. The occasional outburst of laughter was heard. Mankind was flexible. They had an uncanny ability to adjust.

It was hard to understand the size of the Renaissance until one was actually inside it. When placed upon land, the ship covered eight hundred thousand square miles. There had never been anything like this built in the past and especially in the realm of spacecraft. Its boundless ceiling stretched farther than the eye could interpret. The atmosphere processors hummed in constant activity.

Looking quite different, Danken scuttled the walkways. His hair was now fully grown in and coiled into dreadlocks. A full, long beard obscured any of the madman's recognizable characteristics. He wore baggy, droopy clothing. He wore a camouflage pattern hooded sweatshirt with the hood up and kaki-colored pants. He was simply frightening—and armed to the teeth.

He searched the walkways for new recruits. His message didn't find much support. War was old hat. Everyone buzzed about the New Beginning. The Renaissance was on course for arrival on Tento. Timeline projections were cautiously optimistic. Zonfer left wiggle room for unforeseen delays. The citizenry was anticipating the descent into the planet's orbit. Zonfer promised a fantastic show.

Danken had learned how to keep a low profile while in public. Even with his drastically different appearance, there was still a risk of detection. Zonfer's DF would surely have his digital face framework programmed into their helmet heads-up-displays.

His first destinations were always the various bars. This was one area that Danken knew plenty about. He was an alcohol aficionado, beers, whiskeys, and wines, everything. He had requested countless different concoctions at the many different bars along the walkways of Commerce Square. The bars offered another priceless benefit. They were the best recruiting grounds. Nothing freed the inhibitions like a deep glass filled with bourbon. He was a date-rapist with an entirely different payoff, a dedication to the cause. A human life willing to risk it all for his twisted vision of the future.

It was an especially active night at *RenaiSauce*. Fluorescent diodes pulsated to the beat of the bland, repetitive techno. No one cared about the music. Danken was no exception. He had bigger fish to fry.

His posture slouched, Danken approached the bar.

"Yo, Bee, what's goin' on, dawg," the dark-skinned bartender said happily. Danken was a regular. They took care of their regulars.

"I'm good, Reggie," Danken responded shortly.

"What'll it be—Bee? Ha! Never gets old does it?" he said, slapping Danken on the shoulder.

Danken half-smiled. "I guess not—the usual, Reg."

"Dang, dawg, you ever change it up? Dat' shit's gonna pickle your liver, man!" Reggie playfully commented.

Danken looked up peering through his dreadlocks. "You're not my mother, Reggie. Don't act like her. Vodka—straight."

"Yeah, yeah, I know. Com'in' up. Settle down," Reggie said as he walked toward the opposite end of the bar.

"To answer your question—yes! I like everything! But I like the vodka here!" Danken yelled, pointing at the humble bartender.

Reggie turned, nodded, and smiled.

An average built and handsome man sat next to Danken. He snuck a glance at him and then focused his attention forward again. "You look really different." The man commented.

Danken recognized the voice immediately. It was Dr. Waters, Zonfer's lead research scientist. "You would too if you were wanted by as many people as I am."

Waters snickered and took a sip of his whiskey. "I guess so."

Danken took his own glance at his neighbor. "So, you're my contact? How the hell did that happen?"

Reggie sat Danken's drink in front of him. Danken nodded in approval.

Waters sneered. "Pffft. I never liked Zonfer. After Taber, that was it for me. I wanted to see that guy pay for the crap he'd pulled."

Danken peered into the glass. The reflections of the diodes danced throughout his drink like UFOs in the nighttime desert sky. "Lucky me," Danken proclaimed.

"You're damn right, lucky you!" Waters paused and looked at his conspirator quickly. "You got the account keycard?"

Danken slipped him the requested object. Waters removed a small card reader from his jacket pocket and inserted the keycard. The small LCD screen confirmed the details of the account. "10,000,000 International Credits Avail." "Perfect," he thought to himself.

"Hello retirement," Waters whispered under his breath. He tucked the card and reader deep within his inside jacket pocket for safekeeping.

Danken kicked back the remainder of his drink in a quick shot. "The research documents?" he extended his hand.

Waters reached into his other jacket pocket and pulled out a thumb drive. He held it between his index and middle fingers in front of Danken's face. He quickly snatched it.

"Handle with care, my friend. You're dealing with Night of the Living Dead shit there," Waters said casually.

"When can I expect my new recruits?" Danken enquired with a grin.

"My colleagues will be—'transferring—'" he motioned quotations dramatically. "—to facilities near the Maintenance Block of the Renaissance tomorrow around four a.m."

Waters glared at Danken and pointed a judgmental finger. "You'd better treat them right—I don't want any murder investigations with my name involved."

Danken glared around the bar in search of listeners. "Why don't you just announce it to the world? You'd better get out of here and sober up."

Waters looked into his empty glass. "Yeah, I've been here a bit too long. I wouldn't have been if someone hadn't kept me waiting!"

Danken had what he needed. He was gone before Waters even noticed. Waters looked at Danken's discarded cocktail napkin. He ignored the message scribbled upon it.

***

Renaissance Control was quiet. The only sounds were the occasional clicks of keyboards and mice. Zonfer's advisors monitored all activities at all times. They found themselves working over, over overtime. A full pot of coffee was always available. Their mugs needed constant refreshing. They could sleep on Tento. Until then, their eyes were needed. For now, they belonged to Zonfer and the Renaissance.

Zonfer was in his quarters. His scheduled meeting with Riddick was taking place. He sat behind his steel desk, legs crossed and stroking his facial hair. It was a habit.

"Yes, sir. The framework of the craft is acting exactly how I thought it would. It creaked for a bit but it's absolutely stable now. We're making good time too. The projection estimates show that we will arrive in Tento's orbit in a matter of about seven to ten months. A year from now, at the latest, is when we'll be laying our eyes on our new home."

Zonfer nodded in approval. "Unbelievable. Weeks ago I feared for our future— now—it's so bright."

"Yes, sir. We're fortunate. May I say that your leadership has been the reason for our good fortune. Without you, our race would certainly be extinct," Riddick sincerely stated.

"Without individuals such as yourself, Mr. Riddick, we would've been just as finished," Zonfer swiveled back and forth in his seat. "You're going to have a lot more work on your hands on Tento! Building plans will be needed to be drawn up, the layout of main city, vegetation—you'll be working for ten years straight!"

The two laughed in unison.

"That sounds fantastic, sir!" Riddick said jokingly.

"I'm sure you're up to it."

"Let me think about that one—you're going to have to give me time on that."

Zonfer nodded and smiled.

Suddenly, as Zonfer and Riddick continued to converse, the muted sound of an explosion caught their attention.

"Sir, did you hear that?" Riddick asked urgently.

"I did. Come on—Let's get to Control!"

They sprinted the short distance. Upon arrival at Control, Zonfer knew the dung had hit the proverbial fan. His advisors barked back and forth. The group was a network. If one was clueless, the rest fell like dominos. The security cameras were useless, all disabled.

General Hayden approached Zonfer and Riddick. "Sir, Recon and DF patrols have reported Resistance opposition in Commerce Square. I suggest we deploy immediately."

"I agree. Do it now," Zonfer responded.

"Yes, sir! All units, this is General Hayden. We have a go for deployment in Commerce Square—I repeat—"

Zonfer hung his head low in a lazy posture. Riddick stood idle observing the activities. Zonfer shook his head. He'd gotten his hopes up too high.

***

In a matter of seconds, troops arrived at Commerce Square. The scene was despicable. There was no reason for this. Thousands of innocents rested dead on the Renaissance walkways. Streams of blood paved a path down the cold steel. There wasn't a Resistance member in sight. Captain Sillus, the commanding officer, was appalled by the sickening display of cowardice. Sillus' HUD displayed targets everywhere but the platoon saw nothing. He attempted to address the Resistance. His tone was direct and livid.

"We can do this the hard way or the easy way! You can show your sorry asses and fight like grown ups! Or, you can keep on killing innocent civilians like the spineless worms you are! What'll it be? Huh?"

Sillus was beyond the point of return. His anger boiled. In a distant position of protection, a shot rang out. Before the good Captain had a chance, he was dead. The bullet decimated his skull, blood surging from the decapitation.

It was an ambush of epic proportions. The shadows had concealed the silent assassins. They appeared quickly and began to slaughter Sillus' platoon. Bullets shot out from every orifice that concealed a Resistance member. The bullets tore ruthlessly through their victims. The screams were heard from every corner of the craft.

Round two went to the Resistance.

***

The Commerce Square security camera reactivated at the perfect—or worst possible time. It witnessed the entire episode. Zonfer, Riddick, and Hayden looked on in horror. Hayden broke the silence.

"I can't believe what I just saw."

Zonfer was steadfast. "General, deploy the heavy machinery."

"Right," Hayden responded. These were his men and he wasn't about to see them slaughtered.

***

Armored Personnel Carriers and light tanks rolled into Commerce Square. The roar of barked orders and moving combat apparatus prevailed.

"Hustle!" Captain Vinci said to his squad. "We need to do a full sweep of Commerce Square, boys! Let's get this show on the road."

The tanks and APCs lined up front to back creating a solid wall of steel. DF soldiers were perched atop the APCs scouting for Resistance movement. Transparent heads-up-screens sat atop the gun emplacements on the combat vehicles. The screens glowed and clicked doing their job.

The APC in the front of the pack sat dormant. No one had exited it yet. Then, the rear door cycled open revealing the vehicle's contents. Inside stood three members of Zonfer's defense force, the same three silhouetted figures from the Zonfer Square conflict. John Galant, Dorian Vankman, and Trevor Williams had been in Zonfer's DF since the beginning. When Zonfer first came to global power, attempts at his life were constant. The Elite Three, as they were known, were the leader's personal security detail. They all held the official rank of "Vanguard" placed directly under General Hayden. This rank was exclusive to the Three. They abstained from further promotion. They wanted to remain field operatives. That's what they did best.

Their combat attire was unique to only them, deep gray in color with silver trim. The default "Z" crest scrolled across their chests. Countless DF honors were displayed upon their right upper-arms. Their specialty combat helmets completely covered their faces. The Three each stood at six feet with perfect physiques. Their A-92 Redfields were hoisted upon their shoulders. They were ready for anything.

The Three exited the APC in search of Captain Vinci. While they all held the same rank, Vankman was the most senior member. Williams and Galant agreed that Vankman was their superior. He had served for ten years in the United States Navy Seals and seen almost every possible combat situation. The other two were younger, top grads at Zonfer's military training facility. Vankman ran the show.

The Captain wasn't hard to find. "Vinci, does your platoon have the marching orders?" Vankman inquired.

Vinci gave a quick nod. "Yes, sir, my unit's currently doing a full sweep of Commerce Square. If any of those rats are still out there, they'll take care of them."

Vinci studied Vankman's unique combat headgear. The perfect gray dome gracefully enclosed his entire cranium in protection. The black-tinted visor hiding his features glowed a muted blue where the warrior's eyes would be positioned. The familiar "Z" crest was etched on the right side in a glossy platinum finish.

Vankman was pleased. "Affirm, Captain."

Williams and Galant stood close behind Vankman surveying the horrific scene that confronted them in the middle of Commerce Square. "My God—" Williams said.

The Three paced slowly with their A-92s readied. Vankman spied a downed DF member. He shouldered his rifle and knelt beside the fallen comrade. He observed the embroidered nametag. *Keller.* He knew him. He took a deep breath and exhaled slowly.

"You all right, Vank?" Galant asked, his voice sounding almost robotic under the headgear.

Vankman shook his head. "Yeah…I just don't understand this. Why are these nut jobs doing this? We should all be thankful to Zonfer for leading us to safety from the Plague. I don't get it."

"Murphy's Law, Vank. Something had to go wrong. This is it," Williams said chiming in on the conversation.

"I guess so," Vankman said hopelessly. He observed a Resistance corpse close to the fallen DF member. The Resistance member's eyes were closed. Vankman closed his own eyes in search of solace. When he reopened them, the fallen enemy's eyelids were raised. "What the hell?" He muttered to himself. Somewhat disturbed, he quickly got up from his kneeling posture. He stared at the corpse closely as he walked away.

They continued on their trek. Vinci's squad was spread out all over Commerce Square. Aside from the bodies, every establishment was completely abandoned. The civilians immediately fled upon the initial explosion in Commerce Square. Sporadic gunfire was heard time to time.

The Renaissance was built like a layer cake. A huge number of levels and sectors stretched for miles vertically and horizontally. Sounds behaved oddly in the craft. Sounds of activity in an area miles away could travel through ducts and confound one's senses. This made for an almost constant low-tone drone of noise, sometimes prominent, other times muted.

The Three were now doing a quick sweep on a bar. A large flat panel display above the bar flashed a graphic. *The RenaiSauce.*

"You hear the noise, Vank?" Williams asked.

Vankman listened. "Yeah, it's louder than normal. We'll probably be getting a comm. call soon."

Galant stood observing the animated sign. "Clever name…"

Williams rolled his eyes. "Yeah—right."

Galant looked down at the bar. A crinkled cocktail napkin caught his attention. He picked it up and read it. *THE RESISTANCE LIVES!* was written in red ink as well as a crudely artistic drawing of the red Resistance fist.

"Yeah—no shit," Galant whispered to himself and dropped the napkin.

Abruptly, the Elite Three's comm. links activated. "This is Hayden! We've got Resistance all over! The Central Living Quarters, the Maintenance Block, the Commons Area—everywhere! We need you back at Renaissance Control! We need to come up with a plan of action! We've gotta stop these maniacs! Hayden out!"

"Goddamn—" Galant said.

"Come on, let's get back to the APC," Vankman said hastily.

They exited the *RenaiSauce* and sprinted back to their APC transport. The war was on.

Chapter 11: Villains and Vanguards

The Maintenance Block was dark. It was the perfect place to lie low. The Resistance quietly organized discussing operations. Danken was the only member with any real military experience. He had been the main architect of the attack on Sillus' platoon in Commerce Square. He may not have made it too far up the totem poll in the AAF but he had plenty ideas for taking lives.

The Resistance higher-ups, if there were such a thing, sat around a dimly lit steel surface in the Renaissance's mainframe room. Enormous cooling fans lined the walls, whirling in constant activity. The mainframe room held a supercomputer that stored and analyzed all of the various readouts from the Renaissance's systems. It was checked about every month or so for study by Zonfer's science department, the main focus of study being the artificial atmosphere and gravity regulators. This technology was still very new and there was much to learn. The scruffy looking gathering listened closely to their leader.

"Two groups are plenty. I'll be heading one and Jayson the other. I'll break up the roster soon—that's it—oh! One last thing—don't forget to kill a lot of people," Danken said, laughing uncontrollably.

The Resistance members scattered randomly. Many of the million-member posse had already begun wreaking havoc. Danken's recruiting tactics proved effective. He had compiled a frightening group of individuals. Murderers, rapists, mental patients, he scraped the absolute bottom of the barrel of humanity. He needed every life he could get his hands on to be formidable against Zonfer's DF.

Danken exited the mainframe area of the Maintenance Block. He trekked the long corridor en route to his next meeting. The yawning of the still settling steel engulfed the massive passage. He turned the corner and found a small crawlspace leading to a lower level. He reached the exit of the crawlspace and entered the makeshift scientific research facility. A group of about seventeen scientists worked feverishly. Laptops, various analyzers and organized stacks of papers cluttered the steel counters.

"Boys! How are things going?" Danken said jovially. Several of the men jumped in shock. One of them approached Danken awkwardly.

"Ummm—things are progressing well, sir," said a mousy man with badger eyebrows and glasses.

Danken threw his fist in the air. "Fantastic! So, you've done most of the operations already?"

"Yes, sir, it's a fairly simple procedure. Little to no risk of death. We've experimented with this alteration for years. It was nearly ready for full implementation— But he was having no part of it!" The scientist's tone changed completely.

Danken scowled. "Who?"

"Our proud and—stubborn leader. He thought I was mad when I suggested the program. He said, 'I've known scientists like you—better than you could possibly realize and I won't let things like this happen under my watch.' Whatever the hell that meant— Then he threatened to fire me if I even discuss Project R with anyone," the scientist whined.

Danken nodded. He knew what Zonfer meant. The Warrior Program in the AAF—Part of Danken and Zonfer's entwined pasts. Danken's mind wandered for a bit. Then, in a sudden motion, he clapped his hands.

"Well! We're gonna show him! Aren't we, buddy?" Danken said, wide-eyed.

The scientist squinted at the Resistance leader in confusion. "I guess so—sir."

Danken fake cried, "No one's ever called me 'sir' before," Danken said, feigning a whimper.

The scientist wasn't even close to feeling comfortable around Danken. Waters had told him what to expect but it was far more serious than he had let on. He began to wonder if the huge financial payoff was worth the risk of being around Danken.

"Doc—suit me up! How do we do this?" Danken said quickly.

The scientist was confused. "What?"

"I got things to do! People to see! Come on, Doc—I don't got all day!" Danken barked. The others present tried their best to ignore him. They went about their business nonstop.

"Very well, sir—follow me."

Danken followed the little man into an adjacent space. Rows of makeshift operating tables cluttered the area. Bloody gauze was soaked in stainless steel bowls near the tables. Random operating tools were scattered throughout.

Danken looked around casually. "Nice place you got here, Doc…"

The scientist ignored the comment. "If you could please remove your shirt and lie on the table, sir—"

"I'm not that easy, Doc. You gotta buy me a drink first!" Danken yelled, laughing hysterically.

The scientist continued preparing his medical equipment. He retrieved one of the metal bowls and scrubbed the equipment thoroughly. An infection meant certain death in these conditions. He found it easier to ignore Danken's odd humor rather than respond to it. He hoped it would stop.

"All right—I get the point. You're all business right now. That's fine. That's what I paid for," Danken said, feeling dejected.

The scientist filled a syringe with a clear fluid.

"That my night-night juice?" Danken inquired in a childish tone.

"Indeed, sir," the scientist said as he plunged the needle head into Danken's muscular forearm.

"Ahhh…" Danken euphorically sighed. "Good stuff, Doc… See you on the flipside," Danken said as he trailed off.

***

Activity in Renaissance Control hadn't stopped for a second. The neck-breaking pace at which the war had begun was astonishing. The Resistance seemed to be everywhere. Zonfer and Hayden had severely underestimated their numbers. The security cameras were all functional. The images that confronted them were horrific. The subdued blue glow of the LCD monitors bathed the room. Silence prevailed. Zonfer could only watch in horror as posses flooded the walkways and roads of the Renaissance killing and terrorizing his people. In the conflicts, the DF was prevailing. The problem was confronting them. They were using hit and run tactics flawlessly. The Resistance was an immaculate insurgency.

Zonfer had seen all he could take. "What a nightmare," he thought to himself. He stepped out of Renaissance Control to regain his equanimity. He stood in the hall of the executive wing peering out of the massive viewing pod below. The infinite blackness and dots of white stared back coldly. The reality of the situation confronted

Zonfer. Questions haunted him that coursed through his mind.
The Plague—this war—Danken—was he to blame for all this? His
eyes widened.

"Exile," he thought to himself. More of his past confronted
him. The Seers—he had written them off as a bad dream. He
remembered vividly the night they had touched him.

"May this scar be a reminder of your crime."

He peered into the shiny finish of the wall in front of him.
He touched the scar upon his face. He slowly lowered his head in
angst. Perhaps his father had been wrong. Maybe he shouldn't have
ever had the amount of power that he had acquired. His pursuit of
power had always been driven by his want for peace. During the
latter years on Earth, he clung to power through questionable means,
sometimes criminal means. He found himself revisiting the Great
Slaughter. It was the only way he could capture the power he sought.
He shook his head in torment. His sins didn't go unpunished.

"It was the only way," he thought.

Suddenly, Hayden exited Renaissance Control. He turned and
saw Zonfer peering into the vast nothingness. The two stood next to
each other glaring into the never-ending expanse of the cosmos in
silence. The whirl of the Renaissance's engines was the only comfort
for Zonfer and Hayden.

"Sir?" Hayden said finally breaking the silence.

Zonfer failed to answer. He just stared.

"Sir?" Hayden repeated.

Zonfer inhaled deeply. "Yes, General?"

"We've got Danken on comm."

Zonfer flinched. "What did you just say?"

Hayden nodded. "He must've gotten his hands on a DF
helmet comm. He's—"

"Why the hell didn't you tell me right away!" Zonfer
interrupted in fury. His deep blue eyes pierced through the general's
soul.

"I'm sorry, sir. I—"

Zonfer promptly left Hayden for Renaissance Control. A fire
of vehemence boiled in his belly. If this were a year ago, Hayden
would be on the unemployment line.

***

Danken scratched at his chest with vigor. "Ouch! I'll kill that damn butcher myself if I get sick from that operation."

Jayson looked down at his own chest. "Mine's all healed up."

Danken was aggravated. "Well, isn't that fantastic, Fill! Now—shut up! I got the big guy on the line."

It was true. Zonfer waited patiently on the other end listening to the comedy routine.

"You had an operation?" Zonfer asked, interrupting the act.

"You see what you did, Fill? Idiot—" Danken cleared his throat. "No, no. I just had a bit of a pain in my chest. It's passed."

"Too bad," Zonfer said definitively.

Danken giggled. "We've got big surprises for you, Wolf. That's why I comm'ed! Thought you'd like to know what to expect."

Zonfer's brows raised. "Surprises?" he responded.

"That's right! Big ones—Well, one big one," Danken quickly retorted.

Jayson's booming laughter erupted in the background. "Hey! Dumb-ass—go do something," Danken said angrily.

His tone and demeanor had taken a scary turn.

"Out!" he screamed at the top of his lungs.

Zonfer listened in an angry confusion. This was odd, to say the least. This man that so casually joked with him was mercilessly killing the innocent. His ego was taking a hit. This was the guy he couldn't catch? Then, Danken's dark side surfaced.

"I'll say this and nothing more. Just when you think we're dead, we're not. Energizer Bunnies—we'll take a lickin' and keep on tickin'," Danken said in a deep-toned hiss.

The next sound was the comm. link being thrown to the ground and stomped on. Zonfer shook his head and searched for solutions. Hayden listened at the entrance of Renaissance Control. He didn't want to make his situation any worse than it already was. He knew that he had ticked Zonfer off. His eyes told the story.

"Sir?" a seated female advisor said.

"Yes?" Zonfer responded.

"May I make an observation?"

"Surely—name?" Zonfer inquired.

"Alexia Denison, sir. That man is clearly bipolar. I studied psychology and had a practice for years before I worked for you. I've heard hundreds of people just like him— most of which called a prison home. He's as dangerous as they come."

Zonfer stared at the gorgeous woman curtly. "Is this supposed to be news?" he said rudely.

Alexia was caught off guard by Zonfer's hostile attitude. "No—I—I just meant that if you can get him into custody and medicate him, he'd be fine."

"Well, miss, if I could get him into custody, none of this would be a problem—right? Am I missing something?"

"No, sir," Alexia said, clearly upset.

"Right," Zonfer said as he exited Renaissance Control hastily.

The war raged on. Danken was free. Times were not good.

***

The crescendo of conflict had peaked to an inconceivable level. The Civil War's main front was in the Central Living Quarters, a tragic twist of fate. No one was safe. The Resistance plundered and murdered ferociously. They had gotten their hands on plenty of firepower, grenades, mines, RPGs, even some Redfield A-92s. Danken's Resistance force had developed into a life form with many heads and tentacles. Some evil power must have guided the way for their organization was unpredictably sound. Danken split the million-man group into two major force structures. The individual members took it from there. They broke off into thousands of small posse-like hordes. Danken and Jayson, the group leaders, remained in the safety of the Maintenance Block.

Vankman, Galant, and Williams, the Elite Three, led Zonfer's DF in the area. Williams and Galant knelt near the cover of an APC firing and reloading in a nonstop cycle of efficient and necessary killing. Their Redfields were loaded with the latest in ammunition technology, the Killer Bee. Only the Vanguards possessed these picayune murdering machines.

The Three were perfect fighting machines but they were also friends. When addressing Hayden or Zonfer, they went into "respect mode," as they called it. In the field, they let loose a bit.

"Hey, Will! Does it seem to you like we have to put a whole clip into these guys to down them for good?" Galant asked on the comm.

"Now that you mention it—yeah," Williams retorted as he emptied his clip on the corpses scattered on the ground.

Williams went prone and prepared to take a steady shot at an approaching Resistance member. He engaged. The Redfield fire sailed through the air. He hit the combatant multiple times in the chest. He spied the body closely. After a wait of about twenty seconds, he observed the corpse pop back up. He dispatched it accordingly.

"What is this, the Night of the Living Dead or something?"

"What?" Galant inquired.

"You know—that ancient zombie movie," he retorted in a matter-of-fact tone.

"You're weird, man."

Vankman wasn't as lucky as his two fellow Vanguards. He was pinned down inside an abandoned apartment room. He laid with his back to an overturned steel table jockeying for a better position. His targeting system within his helmet beeped and clicked constantly. It was becoming more of a hindrance than help.

"Son of a bitch!" he yelled as a bullet grazed the floor next to his position.

A grenade landed feet in front of him. He promptly grabbed the frag and tossed it back. "Frag out!" a Resistance member screamed urgently. The villains scattered to the wind.

"Droooooom!" It exploded in a furious maelstrom of chaotic shrapnel and flames killing a few but not nearly enough to free him from his deathtrap.

Suddenly, he had a brilliant idea. It was time for the Killer Bees in his Redfield to do their job. He unlocked the helmet that coated his head like an exoskeleton. He placed it carefully under the steel table in a position of safety but aimed toward the combat so the targeting system keyed up the bogies. He glanced at his Redfield.

"All right, little buddies, do your thing," he whispered and tapped the butt of the rifle on the steel table.

Upon hearing his targeting system's lock-on-confirmation beep, he blind-fired on the attacking Resistance members, emptying his entire clip. The Killer Bees immediately sprung into action. They floated through the air gracefully guided by the Vanguard's targeting system. A lock-on meant certain death.

The Bees began their attack. Heads started to pop. Each Killer Bee equaled a kill. The realization of inevitable death quickly entered the minds Vankman's opposing force. They ran in a panicked frenzy attempting to escape the swarm—impossible. Before long,

Vankman's suppressors were vanquished. He panted in nervous relief. That was a close one.

"Vank, you all right?" Galant finally chimed in on the helmet comm. link. There was no answer.

"Vank! Goddamn it! Vankman!" Galant said in panic.

Williams railed on the continuous flow of Resistance that poured from a massive breach in the east CLQ wall. "Where the hell are they coming from?" he whispered under his breath.

"Will! I think Vankman might be down!"

"I'm fine! I'm fine! Had my helmet off," Vank's comm. at last resurrected.

Galant exhaled hard. "You scared the tar out of me, Vank!"

"So, now you're worried! When those scumbags had me pinned down, you didn't comm.!" Vankman hastily squawked as he prepared to regroup with the remainder of the Three.

"Come on, Vankman, we've got our hands full down here! We've gotta keep pushing them back!" Williams barked in frustration.

"Already en route," the battle-hardened Vanguard responded. Upon his arrival, he decided it was time to update Zonfer.

Chapter 12: Reconciliation

Feeling completely hopeless, Zonfer sat in his presidential quarters. However, he didn't have the luxury of time for sulking. The video comm. device on his desk was active. The video showed Vankman knelt behind a DF Armored Personnel Carrier with Galant and Williams directly behind him staying off the enemy. He yelled at the top of his lungs to override the deafening combat.

"Sir, this thing doesn't show any signs of letting up! We put them down and they file in twice as fast! I don't know what to say, sir! I'll keep you up to date! Out!"

Vanguard Vankman's assessment was dire and accurate. Every field report was identical. The Resistance was strong, very strong. Suddenly, his intercom toned.

"Who is it?" he enquired.

"General Hayden, sir."

Zonfer beeped him in. Hayden slowly walked through the entry. Hayden's superior glared at him, his vitriol apparent.

"What is it, General? What are you going to fail to tell me this time?" Zonfer screamed.

Hayden stood motionless and expressionless. He understood Zonfer's anger. It was nerves. No one, even the leader of the entire human race, could withstand the pressure this sixty-year-old man was under. He was around the same age as Zonfer and couldn't imagine holding the same amount of responsibility. Yes, he commanded the DF, but Zonfer aspired to protect all of mankind, even those the likes of Danken. Hayden knew he had to do some consoling. If he didn't, nobody would.

"Permission to speak freely, sir," Hayden said in an official tone of voice.

"Great—here it comes. Yes, General," he shot back.

"Back in the corp., we used to say that we were closer to each other than our family members were. Times like these require that type of brotherhood. You were in the military—you know what I'm talkin' 'bout—don'tcha?"

Zonfer squirmed uncomfortably. "My experience was much different, General. Although I was a different type of recruit. During my time in the AAF, our soldiers were dropping like flies. Those SAT bombs were tearing us a new orifice—" Zonfer smiled and laughed.

"God, the CO was happy when the satellites went down for good. He talked about it for weeks! Anyway, I digress. It felt safer to not make friends. My partner Webb and I got along all right but we didn't have a brotherhood. I knew plenty of fellow troops that felt like you describe, though."

"What are you doing?" Zonfer thought to himself. He had always promised himself to not discuss his past with anyone. There were many skeletons cluttering Zonfer's closet of the past and none of them were pretty.

Hayden was pleased with himself. He had even got a laugh out of him. "Score one for the corp.! *Hooray!*" he playfully imagined.

Hayden closed his eyes and sneered. "Sir, I just realized how odd this pact of ours is. A former U.S. Marine Corp. general and a former AAF general—we should be at each other's throats!"

Zonfer inhaled deeply and exhaled slowly. "I never fought the U.S. because I hated them. I fought for peace." Zonfer paused, shifted his weight, and pointed at the general.

"As you well know, the War for Humanity was started by your side. Not ours!" Zonfer yelled in a non-threatening tone.

Hayden's smile was gone. He stared at the floor like a scolded child as he bobbed his head slowly. "Can't argue with that one, sir. I was just doing my duty."

"As we all were, General." He said in a consolatory manner.

The general raised his head and smiled. "I came in here hoping to make you feel better and you end up making me feel better—"

"Well, Tyrone, why don't we call it even?"

Hayden's smile shone brightly upon his face. "I should be getting back to Control."

"All right, General. I'll see you soon."

Hayden saluted and turned to exit.

"General," Zonfer said as he exited.

Hayden turned back. "Yes, sir?"

"I think I understand the brotherhood now—thank you."

He nodded and almost left but there was one last detail. "Oh, one last thing, sir. Alexia wants to speak with you."

Zonfer scowled. "Really?"

"Yeah, yeah—I think she might have a thing for you. In my experience, sir, women love power—even if it is—" Hayden paused and chose his word carefully.

"Ruthless."

He left the entryway hastily to avoid another inquiry.

"Interesting," Zonfer thought to himself. It had been— forever since he had experienced the love of another. Perhaps the gaping void inside the once-heartless Wolfgang Zonfer could still be filled.

Chapter 13: Mending a Damaged Soul

He had no idea how to do this. The leader of the human race and he didn't have the first clue about how to approach this non-threatening woman. She may have been non-threatening but she was breathtaking.

She was young, about thirty. Her long, light brown hair was elegantly streaked with blonde highlights. Her mane ended near the small of her back. As she moved, it flowed poetically from side to side. Her body was toned and fit but not skinny. Her white, administration-issue uniform clung to her body like a second skin. Her facial structure was perfectly feminine, high arching eyebrows, almond-shaped eyes and a graceful nose. The perfect profile—Alexia was a living, breathing dream.

Zonfer had fought countless battles in some of the most challenging circumstances imaginable. On none of those occasions had he ever feared or faltered. At this moment, mere days before the arrival on the new planet that mankind would call home; the unwavering leader found himself trembling. With all the activity, he still focused on her. The New Beginning hung dangerously close to failure and yet he focused on her. He slowly walked to her seat. His palms were sweating. He inched closer.

"Alexia—" he said softly and hesitantly. His voice was unrecognizable.

"Not now," she retorted as she furiously pounded the keyboard in front of her.

He cleared his throat. "It's Zonfer."

Alexia flinched. "Oh! Sir—I—"

"It's okay. You were obviously busy." The transformation of his vocal pattern and tone was puzzling.

She turned and smiled, brushing her hair away from her magnificent face. His pulse was racing. Their eyes were fixated. A mildly uncomfortable silence followed.

"Listen—" Zonfer began, "I wanted to apologize for earlier in the week. This war has taken its toll on me and I—I was short with you. You offered a good observation and I attacked you..." he trailed off.

"Will you forgive my ignorance?"

She tilted her head slowly and gazed into the hardened soul's eyes. "I don't know..." she said slowly.

His stomach sank to the floor. She had to forgive him.

"Alexia—I'm really—"

Her laughter interrupted him. "Of course I forgive you!"

Zonfer smiled. Of course, she was kidding. Why didn't he think of that?

"Well, since that's all cleared up, I was wondering if you would like to visit the presidential—"

"Yes," she abruptly interrupted.

He coiled back. "Really?"

She nodded with a devilishly provocative gleam in her eye. Zonfer might not have been very good at this but he wasn't brain-dead.

"That was easy," he thought.

Chapter 14: Mad Science

With the insurgency in the Central Living Quarters mostly quelled, The Elite Three were onto their next objective. Their APC rolled down the center of the CLQ roadway. It approached the vehicle lift quickly. The entrance to the lift cycled and the APC roared onto the platform. Vankman, Galant, and Williams breathed heavily. The combat had been nonstop since deployment. They were spent.

"For God's sake, I totally underestimated how many of these freaks there are out there," Vankman sighed as he checked the clip in his A-92.

"Yeah. But something really troubles me more than anything else," Williams said in a dire tone.

"What's that?" Vankman inquired.

"Well—the whole 'getting up after we put them down' thing. I don't know what to make of it. Do you?"

"I think I have an idea," Vankman said definitively.

Williams and Galant looked at each other in shock. Silence gripped the brothers in arms for a moment.

"Well?" Galant pushed.

"This one time, Zonfer was talking to his science officer. This is going back a few years. I don't know the exact details but I heard stuff about a certain science project— Project R, I think it was called." Galant and Williams peered at Vankman, listening intently. Their combat helmets rested beside them, occasionally bumping in the movement of the vehicle lift. Vankman compiled his thoughts and continued.

"All I know is that it had something to do with the DF…and surgical procedures being performed. Zonfer exploded on the communication line when he heard the details. I guess R and D was performing tests on people without his knowledge—"

"What the hell does this have to do with the Resistance?" Williams interrupted.

"Settle down, I'm getting to that! I'm thinking if Danken could get his hands on some of Zonfer's science department research documents and then kidnap some of the personnel…" Vankman eyed his two comrades.

"He could implement it into the Resistance," Galant said, completing the thought.

"Exactly."

"You think that's what this zombie stuff is all about?" Williams inquired.

"It's the closest thing that I can come to an explanation," Vankman concluded.

The Three sat in silence. They hoped that Vankman's hypothesis was dead wrong. The vehicle lift boomed to a stop. The lift exit cycled open slowly. The APC roared to life as it quickly exited the Renaissance vehicle lift.

"Last stop, boys," the APC driver exclaimed.

"You've got to be kidding me," Vankman said, upon looking out the APC porthole. "The Maintenance Block?" he said, scratching his forehead.

"What?" Williams exclaimed.

"That's just great—don't we get backup?" Galant inquired.

"Apparently not. We are the Elite Three," Vankman said curtly.

"Yeah, but not gods!" Williams retorted.

Vankman scanned the area. "Looks quiet." He activated his comm. link with the DF. "General, this is Vankman. We're at the Maintenance Block. What are the current directives?"

The comm. link hissed and popped. Suddenly, Hayden's voice buzzed. "We've reason to believe that certain members of Zonfer's science department may have defected to the Resistance. We've already uncovered a mole in Dr. Gilian Waters. He's been feeding Danken Level One classified research documents. You are to scan the area for a makeshift science lab, dispel any Resistance members and retrieve any sensitive documents. Details as to what to watch for will be sent to your HUDs in a moment. Any questions?"

Vankman rolled his eyes and looked at his partners.

"Yes, sir, just one. Can we expect backup?"

"You are to carry out the current parameters alone. All units are currently engaged elsewhere. You shouldn't encounter much retaliation. Is that all?"

Vankman hissed in frustration. "Yes, sir, Vankman out."

Galant immediately sprung into disbelieving action. "Vank, this has gotta be a joke! There could be a million Resistance out there. We can't know for sure!"

"This is what we do. You know that. That's why we're Vanguards. That's why there are only three of us to hold that rank," Vankman said proudly.

Williams and Galant nodded at their noble leader. He was right. "Let's gear up," Williams proclaimed.

They rose their cybernetic helmets to their upper torsos. The graceful domes hissed and clicked into their iridescent shoulder guards.

"Come on, guys! I gotta be somewhere for a pickup!" the driver yelled.

The Three turned and looked at the driver in concert.

"All right, all right. Sorry," he said, almost peeing himself.

The APC hatch cycled open quickly and the Three exited. Their transport hastily returned to the lift and left the warriors to their objective. With their A-92s locked, loaded, and readied, they prepared for the inevitable.

*****

"Well, this was a pleasant surprise," Williams said.

Vankman nodded. "Agreed. I thought this area was going to be crawling with those nutjobs."

"Don't you guys get all cozy. We're not out of here yet," Galant chimed in.

"Always the optimist!" Williams said sarcastically.

"Keep it down!" Vankman said, as though reprimanding his children.

The Maintenance Block was eerily quiet. The only sound was the occasional bang from the mainframe room. The whirl of the cooling fans and atmosphere processors surrounded them. They inched toward the end of the massive walkway. Vankman spied an opening in the steel wall.

"What's this?" he said, inching his head inward.

"What you got, Vank?" Galant inquired

"Looks like we got something here, boys. Stay frosty."

The Three began their descent into the murky blackness of the Resistance's makeshift science lab. Vankman finally reached the exit to the crawlspace. His A-92- mounted flashlight illuminated the darkened expanse. He peered into the darkness.

"Lights out, guys. Enable night." Vankman ordered.

The Three deactivated their flashlights and keyed up their night vision on the sides of their helmets. The sight that confronted them was horrific.

"Holy—" Galant said.

The science lab was a slaughter house. Blood pools flooded the entire area. Corpses of men and women wearing white coats littered the ground. Vankman was unaffected.

"Just what I thought. He used them and threw them out like the morning garbage," he said.

"What's this mean, Vank?" Galant asked.

"We already know. We've been dealing with it all along. If this Resistance keeps up, we're going to have a big problem on our hands," Vankman concluded. He activated his comm. link.

"General, this is Vankman. The lab is filled with dead scientists. They're all from Zonfer's science department."

They heard Hayden exhale in frustration. "Damn! All right, collect their nametags and return to the DF. I've gotta sort this out."

"General, you should know that the procedures performed were definitely successful. We've been noticing the effects. Please tell Zonfer that Project R has been implemented."

Silence on the other end of the comm..

"Affirm, return to the DF," Hayden finally responded.

Eyes from a hidden position of safety in the science lab shifted manically. They watched every move the Three made. As they left, the visage emerged.

Danken.

Chapter 15: The Arrival

The flagship Renaissance chugged through the cosmos like an intergalactic supertanker. Immersed in the ultimate sea of infinite black, the gargantuan craft inched toward Tento, mankind's destination, their only hope. Zonfer, General Hayden, Dr. Alexia Denison and the Elite Three, minus their combat gear, sat in the observation dome. Thousands of speechless citizens lined the walkways with the gathering observing openmouthed. Danken agreed to a cessation of violence for the event. Even he wanted to see this.

Zonfer and Alexia sat next to each other closely. He embraced her tightly with one arm. They peered into each other's eyes with smiles upon their faces. Zonfer's void had been filled. He pressed his lips gently upon her head and inhaled. Her scent was the smell of his salvation.

The now-familiar female mechanical voice spoke. "Approaching destination: Planet Tento. Decent in...five minutes...weather conditions...moderate. Wind velocity..."

That's where everyone stopped paying attention. The group chatted quietly as they looked upon their new home in wonder. While boring in color, mostly pearl-white and light gray, the three hundred sixty degree view made for fantastic theater. Tento's opaque cloud cover coiled around the planet like a giant anaconda. The iridescent flash of random Tentonian storms confronted the group's senses. Earth's beauty made Tento look like the Earthling moon. But it would have to suffice.

The Renaissance punctured Tento's atmosphere. A low-toned rumble commenced. Flames showered the viewing dome. Suddenly, the intercom tone sounded. "This is Renaissance Control. The entry may be a bit rougher than we thought. Thank you for your understanding and sit tight."

Their descent continued. Their seats lightly rattled beneath them. Zonfer held Alexia tighter and her grip tensed as well. Finally, the roar ceased and the rattling settled. The flames across the viewing dome disappeared.

The craft broke through the thick cloud cover dramatically revealing the perfectly flat expanse of the Tentonian landscape. Immediately, the first thing to catch the group's attention was a Tilothan, massive wooly mammoth like creatures that roamed the landscape constantly.

The thousands in attendance exploded in cheers. All eyes were fixated on their leader as they clapped in pride. Zonfer looked at Alexia. She was crying. Then, something Zonfer barely understood happened. A tear fell. It dropped upon her face. She jumped in shock and laughed. They kissed and embraced.

Zonfer's promised New Beginning was about to be realized. But what about Danken and the Resistance? Would Danken's promised cessation to the conflict last? Had he been touched at the sight of Tento?

Unexpectedly, among the continuing cheers, alarm bells rang. The room quaked underneath the crowd. Zonfer and Alexia looked around in confused concern. "It's all right, Alexia. I'm sure it's just natural turbulence." He consoled. Alexia nodded wiping the tears from her eyes.

Vankman, Galant, and Williams were nowhere in sight. After the unveiling of the Tentonian landscape, they quickly ran back to the DF headquarters to gear up. They were always on call, even on the day that mankind met its new home.

Zonfer's advisor who oversaw the descent chimed in on the intercom.

"We've got some problems here. We've lost one of the turbo thrusters. Nothing to worry about—sit tight." The advisor said in an unaffected tone.

Zonfer's attention piqued. He sprung into action. "Listen, Alexia, get back to Control. Whatever happens, I want you safe. I have a bad feeling about this."

Alexia was distraught. "Wolf! What are you going to do?"

Zonfer's expression was cold. "I have a feeling—I think Danken might not make this day the peaceful celebration it should be," he said in a stoic tone.

Without warning, his comm. link activated.

"Zonfer! It's Hayden! We've got a Resistance posse in the Commons Area!"

Zonfer was steadfast. "Is he with them?"

"Yes, sir. It's strange. They're just standing in the middle of the Commons. I don't understand it—God—there's so many of them."

Zonfer's gut was correct. He bowed his head. He wished he would have been wrong. He prepared mentally for his final battle. This was going to end. He grabbed Alexia by her shoulders gently.

"I want you to go back to Control. I'm taking care of this for good."

***

The Renaissance continued on its rocky descent toward the Tentonian soil. It was nearly time to set down. The flight plan had decided the landing spot almost a year ago. The perfect position had been chosen for the site of Tento City. Soon after the landing, Erectorbots would begin their job of constructing the city.

After gearing up, Zonfer accompanied General Hayden and his own squad to the Commons Area. The APC waited patiently in the DF hangar ready for deployment to the area. Hayden was astonished and confused at Zonfer's insistence to engage in combat.

"Sir, I'm confused. You have an entire defense force ready to give their lives for the cause of the human race's survival. Why do you insist on fighting with us?" the general said, genuinely curious.

"I don't know what they taught you in the Marine Corps, General... but I know what I was taught as a private in the AAF. A leader should care about his troops. I do."

Hayden smiled and nodded. He was impressed. Zonfer was a man to be admired.

"You've really changed, sir. You seem—" Hayden paused.

"She found me, General," Zonfer interrupted. "I had lost myself years ago...and she found me."

Hayden's smile remained. She certainly had.

The APC driver chimed in on the comm. links. "All right, we're set."

The combat vehicle came to life, the engine roaring. Just before they left, there was a massive quake.

"The Renaissance has set down on the Tentonian soil, sir," Control chimed in on the comm. channel.

"The start of a new era—after arrival," Zonfer said softly.

The APC exited the hangar en route to the Commons Area. Zonfer fervently hoped the Resistance would end with the new era.

***

The Resistance stood at the exit to the Renaissance. None of them moved an inch, but clung to their firearms tightly. Their numbers stretched nearly the entire expanse of the exit. Terrified citizens fled in panic. Thankfully, most were in their rooms in the Central Living Quarters.

Zonfer and Hayden's transport roared into the Commons Area. It stopped abruptly and they exited quickly. The collective force structure of the DF flanked in front. The Elite Three were nearby. They approached the APC and knelt beside Zonfer and Hayden.

"What the hell is going on, Vankman?" Hayden asked.

Vankman's cybernetic helmet glistened in the lights.

"I wish I could tell you, sir. They haven't attacked. They're just standing there," Vankman's robotic voice buzzed.

Zonfer silently contemplated a plan and addressed his dedicated warriors.

"I'm going to talk to Danken," Zonfer said quickly.

His four comrades were shocked.

"Do you think that's wise, sir?" Vankman asked.

"I think I can talk him down. I've known him for years," Zonfer said shortly.

Suddenly, the sound of the Renaissance exit cycling open resounded. Danken had initiated the start. The Three, Zonfer and Hayden popped up from their knelt positions.

"What the hell are they doing?" Hayden exclaimed.

Zonfer was already approaching Danken's position. The Renaissance's ramp finally rested on the soil. The strong Tentonian breeze flooded the cabin. It had a damp sting to it. However, it felt good in the lungs. Tento's coiling clouds could be seen in the background moving slowly in the sky. Danken spoke first.

"Well, here we are! It ain't no Earth. I'll tell you that."

"Danken, I want this war to come to an end for good. Please, extend the cessation indefinitely. Please, agree to it," Zonfer pleaded.

"You know what I've got to say about that?" Danken said reaching into the humanity behind him.

Muted female cries confronted Zonfer. Zonfer cringed. His eyes widened. "No!" he thought to himself.

Danken had her. He pressed his 3020 Beretta to her head and...

Chapter 16: The New Beginning Realized – Five Years After Arrival (A.A.)

The construction of the Tento super city was taking shape. Erectorbots had been deployed and were creating the structures of tomorrow. Zonfer was a shell; emotionless, cold, and filled with nothing but rage. A picture of Alexia was face down on his desk.

She was dead.

On the day of arrival, Danken staged a massive attack in the Commons Area upon landing. Apparently, he had heard about Zonfer's newfound love. He vowed to destroy it. Her life had been taken by the crazed madman. "And for what…" Zonfer thought. Wolfgang died that day—for good. Soon after Alexia's murder, Danken and his followers fled deep into the Tentonian wilderness. They had lived like nomads for years. Now, with the construction sites taking shape, Danken and the remainder of the Resistance squatted in abandoned, incomplete facades.

Zonfer called upon his most trusted warriors to meet him in his presidential quarters. The "Z" crest upon the flat panel monitor aside the entrance to his quarters transitioned to an image of The Elite Three. "Sir, Vankman, Galant, and Williams reporting," Vankman proclaimed.

Zonfer cycled the door open and the Three entered. They stood at attention. Zonfer sat idle; hands folded in front of him. He sighed and cleared his throat.

"Gentlemen, I fear Danken is hell-bent on restarting this conflict. This needs to end immediately. I want you to search every street, building, and shack in this city. Don't stop until you have him in custody. A Griffin Wing transport spotted him in an abandoned framework near center city," Zonfer said wearily but with determination. He was tired. Retirement or death sounded very good at the moment.

"Yes, sir. You won't see us again without Danken. You can count on us." The Three turned to exit.

"Gentlemen…" Zonfer said softly.

"Sir?" Vankman responded.

"Be careful. I want you returning alive."

"Yes, sir," Vankman responded.

As usual, the Three were all business. They never flinched under any circumstance or level of pressure. Danken was as good as captured.

The last bastions of the Resistance were quickly meeting their end. Zonfer's DF was fully deployed throughout the city doing sweep missions. Danken and the Resistance's decision to venture into the unfinished and underdeveloped Tento super city was suicide.

The end was near.

***

The underdeveloped streets and structures of Tento City were dormant. The Civil War was coming to a close. The once million-member strong fighting force had been exterminated down to a few sad mobs. Rickety and battle-worn Resistance vehicles resounded through the unfinished roadways of mankind's new home. Zonfer's forces were relentless. A constant pursuit of the final remnants of the Resistance was in full swing.

Galant, Williams, and Vankman found themselves in the heart of the last known Resistance stronghold. The massive, half-completed structure was barren. Spent ammo clips littered the ground. The Resistance was gasping for its last breath. Within the Resistance base, Zonfer's forces had eliminated most of the force structure clearing the way for the Elite Three to do their duty. The Three walked in perfect unison, their stride and posture flawless. The Civil War had been a proving ground for the Three. Their charcoal-colored combat gear glistened in the Tentonian street lights. Their combat honors meant more to them than ever before. Their A-92s were pointed forward ready for any opposition. They hoped this would be the end.

"Galant, you take our six. Williams, take noon. I got level two," Vankman ordered.

"Affirm," The two said in unison.

The atmosphere was tension-filled. It was too quiet. Vankman's senses were tuned and focused. His in-helmet heads-up-display clicked and beeped, no movement. He adjusted his grip on his rifle, his knuckles cracking. As he passed a dark corner, he observed multiple Resistance corpses laid out on the cold, damp ground. Emotionless, he moved on.

Galant chimed in on the comm. link. "All clear."

"Affirmative. Await Williams and I at the noon," Vankman responded. Galant confirmed.

Vankman continued on his path. The place was dead. Danken wasn't here.

"All clear," Williams said on the comm.

"Affirm. Meet Galant at the noon," Vankman responded in a blank tone.

Suddenly, a voice emerged from Vankman's rear.

"Looking for me?"

A scruffy-looking Danken emerged from the shadows. His tattered garments clung to him like body paint. His dreadlocks appeared to be coated in unmentionable materials. His beard was grown to ridiculous proportions.

"Hands up! Let me see 'em!" Vankman yelled. He looked different but Vankman knew those eyes, the stare.

Danken tilted his head and smiled. He slowly offered his arms to the Elite Three members. Vankman, puzzled, squinted at the awful man.

"Well?" Danken said. "You gonna cuff me or what?"

"Shut up! Galant, Williams, I got him. Meet me on two," Vankman ordered.

The sound of the soldier's sprint clopped through the abandoned structure. Their boots greeted the stairway with a clang on the steel steps. Rifles pointed, they greeted their partner with the prize.

"You all right, Vankman?" Galant inquired.

"I'm good. He didn't put up any kind of fight."

"I could have!" Danken screamed. "You'd all be dead right now if I didn't want this!"

"Yeah, yeah, shut up!" Vankman smashed Danken's abdomen with the butt of his rifle. Danken coughed and laughed at the same time. Vankman activated his comm. with their transport.

"Biff? This is Vankman. We need immediate transport to the Renaissance. We got him."

The dropship landed in the vacant Resistance stronghold. Vankman pushed the battered Resistance leader down the cold, metal steps and out the exit. Finally, the Civil War was over for good.

***

Danken stood in the middle of Zonfer's presidential quarters on the Renaissance. His demeanor was completely different. He seemed resigned to his fate. Danken's battered visage glared blankly at Zonfer.

Zonfer began, "I never understood you. From the day I met you in the AAF, you bewildered me. Somehow, I knew that one day you would cause me hurt. But never did I imagine the magnitude of that hurt."

The battered man remained silent. He breathed heavily and quickly.

Zonfer slowly shook his head. "What did I ever do to you, Blaine? How did I deserve the fate you dealt me?"

Danken's eyes widened. "What did you just call me?"

"You thought I'd forgotten, hadn't you? I had discovered my former self on this journey, Blaine! Do you remember when we met in the AAF? We were a lot alike. It scared me at the time but it was a fact—I had found Wolfgang again. I thought he was long dead…but she helped me find him! The scared little kid in bed in Austria!" A tear formed in the corner of Zonfer's right eye.

Zonfer pulled out his 3020 Beretta.

"Wolf, wait! Forget the war—forget about her—"

He aimed for the center of Danken's person.

"Wolf! Please! Think about this!"

"No more, Danken. I won't risk my people's futures any longer. No more war, no more murder, as long as I'm king," Zonfer paused and aimed.

"This is for Alexia."

"Tharp!" The shot rang out.

Zonfer took his shot and he didn't miss. Danken's body fell to the ground with a thud. Blood pooled on Zonfer's majestic floor.

Suddenly, Danken's corpse shot back up, reanimated. He must have been the last to have the procedure done before the scientists had been assassinated. Zonfer fired several more shots into Danken's reanimated corpse. With Danken's death, the Civil War would fade with time. Thankfully, Zonfer had managed to contain a situation that could have raged for years.

***

Zonfer stood strong, peering out the massive, open window of his presidential quarters. The weary leader had ended the journey as he had begun it, alone. The Renaissance had served the Tentonian people well. He hoped to live to see the cities of Tento pouring with life.

A single line of smoke streamed out of his 3020 Beretta that he casually rested on his thigh. He thought about the future of mankind's new home. It had been a tumultuous journey and the future was as uncertain as ever. The old leader had found love and lost it at a traumatic speed. Zonfer bowed his head, hoping that this final act of violence would usher in a solid era of peace for his people. Suddenly, he found himself thinking about the past. He thought about his father and his days in the Austrian Armed Forces. All of that led to this moment. His heavy heart told him that his past deeds of unthinkable evil hadn't gone unpunished. The Seers…they had told him this would happen. He wondered if a final visit with the beings was in his future.

As the Tentonian breeze blew lightly, it caressed Zonfer's face. The scar stretching from his upper forehead and ending at his lower cheek greeted him in his reflection in the window, another reminder of the past. It no longer bothered him. Because it hadn't bothered her…he closed his eyes in comfort but also with deep angst…

Alexia…

He hoped there could be a day when he'd hold her again.

The End

PART II

MEMOIRS OF A
TYRANT

Prologue: A Future Political Commentary

Luckily, earlier leaders of the United States government had reconciled their differences in the regions that had troubled them for years. 2050 A.D. was a watershed moment for world peace. This marked the year of the creation of the Coalition for Middle East Reconciliation. It was a group comprising the greatest minds in foreign policy at the time. Compiled by the United States, this organization vowed to undo the seemingly irreconcilable damage former administrations had done in the past to American credibility. This group managed to negotiate the disbandment of virtually all Middle Eastern terrorist groups. All Middle Eastern countries signed the Accord of Lasting Peace in 2052. This agreement garnered support from every nation and Islamic extremism breathed its last breath. With not a drop of blood spilled, this accord finally proved that the pen was truly mightier than the sword.

Earth experienced a period of lasting peace for centuries, the United States being the main bearer of credit. With the natural ebb and flow of political climate, times were bound to change. With the world pacified, malicious organizations brainstormed, planned, and waited to implement their agenda. Power was what they craved. Power was what they sought. Power was what they got.

***

The year was 2993. Formerly the moral compass of the world, the United States now embodied the ultimate enemy to freedom. Unfortunately for the cause of world peace and understanding, North America continued on its campaign for geopolitical supremacy bombing and invading its enemies for political power and the ever-decreasing natural resources of the planet. Governments around the globe were in a constant defensive posture against the superpower. Planet Earth faced its most tumultuous era.

In an extremely bold foreign policy move, the United States declared its intention of establishing a permanent military footprint in every European nation. This new agenda passed the United States Congress and the U.S. military began the campaign for global domination invading all nations that didn't already have a base of operations. It was a clear repeat of the same policy it had attempted in the Middle East in the beginning of the millennium. The policy-makers decided that this would be far easier than the Middle East mission for ideological reasons.

The United Nations became a far more powerful organization. It had always been meant to be the great mediating force of the world. Finally, this vision was realized. In an unprecedented action, the U.N. declared the English language the "uniting dialect." This meant that all participating nations needed to declare English their primary language of operation. The other major U.N. mandate was the declaration of an international Election Day. This new international law was created for logistical reasons. The United Nations now oversaw all governmental elections in an effort to protect the citizen's voice. It appeared that the United Nations was providing the required balance during an extremely volatile era of human existence.

During this highly confrontational time in history, a formerly neutral country rose as the new moral compass. The European nation of Austria decided that it was no longer possible to ignore the attack on European sovereignty. The Austrian president, along with the full support of parliament and, most importantly, the people, organized the Austrian Coalition for Humanity (ACH). This new alliance of nations vowed to stand strong against the United States' global power grab. The alliance was composed of Africa, parts of Asia and every European nation, minus the United Kingdom that remained neutral in the current political climate.

North America's intentions were clear. This "guarantee for peace," as United States politicians put it, was a thinly veiled grab at a one-world government accountable to no one and nothing. Former Austrian leaders had stood by and watched such events take place in the past. President Gerhard Hensted vowed to permanently thwart the United States' attempt at global domination. When America began their incursion near Austrian interests, this was the final proverbial straw.

Philosophically, for better or for worse, the world had transformed into a secular, "realist" society. The concept of peace through violence exploded in the current generation of mankind. In reality, no one in places of power truly wanted peace. The truth of the matter remained that much treasure was to be gained from warfare, resources and influence being the most attractive capital. Human decency was at an all-time low. Collectively, society plunged toward oblivion, the moral minority muzzled and silenced.

A perfect storm of chaos, war and political paranoia loomed over planet Earth. The consequences of such turmoil were about to be fully realized.

Chapter 1: Live by Example

As the Austrian sun rose beginning another day, the Zonfer residence initiated its daily routine. The fresh morning warmth caressed Wolfgang Zonfer's young, chiseled jaw line. He waited for his father's morning wakeup call. Every second of peace the boy could harness was priceless to him. Suddenly, the sound of his bedroom door violently sliding open shattered his serenity.

"Wolfgang, it's time for breakfast! You need to be at the barracks at 0:800!"

Wolfgang sighed and rubbed his eyes.

"Yes, sir, I'll be down in a few minutes."

"Make it fast, son. This is an important day in your young military career."

Wolfgang hastily dressed in his fatigues. He examined the cuffs and collar for imperfections. When satisfied with his appearance, he ran out of his humble room and down a grand spiral staircase. The difference between young Wolfgang's surroundings and the rest of the estate was astounding. It was as if he was a world apart from the rest of the Zonfer clan. As he entered the impressive kitchen, he took a deep breath and composed himself.

"Good morning, son. Are you prepared for your first real military honor?" his father inquired.

"Yes, sir. I feel that I have earned this title and my commanding officer isn't going to regret this decision."

"That's my boy. Now you know why I insisted that you join the AAF right after your primary education. This is the Zonfer family way!"

Wolfgang's nineteen-year-old chest flared out in pride.

"Yes, sir, I was born to serve the Austrian Armed Forces. This will be the first day of my long career serving our citizens."

Sigmund Zonfer nodded in agreement and motioned toward the massive television mounted on the wall. They listened to the commentator.

"Another day of hostile confrontation between AAF reinforcements and enemy combatants ended yesterday with the signing of the first peace accord between Austria and the United States. Many experts believe that this outburst of violence will be short-lived and that all-out war is inevitable. Later today—"

Sigmund Zonfer muted the television and began to consume his morning sustenance. Wolfgang felt the tension in the air. His father was a man of war but he didn't want to see conflict for erroneous reasons. The current Austrian president was less than experienced in foreign affairs and international tension was running high.

"Father, do you think this may spark another conflict?"

"To be perfectly honest with you, son, I have no idea. With the way our current chancellor handles himself, I would say that anything is possible. That's why you need to be prepared. For all we know, you could be deployed in a few months."

Wolfgang's eyes widened and he clenched his fist. The elder Zonfer sensed his son's bewilderment.

"Remember, son, you need to be strong. After all, Hensted doesn't have much more time in office. It's 2993 now, in 3000, we'll be having new elections."

Wolfgang's brow rose.

"If you think I am frightened of going to war, you're dead wrong."

Sigmund quickly changed his tone.

"The tone you just addressed me with needs never to be used again!" he commanded sternly. "Do you understand!"

"Yes, sir. It will never happen again," answered Wolfgang submissively.

Shouting at Wolfgang was commonplace. His father, while a caring man, didn't tolerate disrespect. Sigmund Zonfer was a former AAF general, after which he was elected to public office. He currently presided over the armed services committee in the Austrian Parliament. He had great hopes for his son, hopes that he would never give up on. Occasionally, when Wolfgang was especially rebellious, Sigmund would resort to cowardly tactics. He saw physical discipline as a mainstay in parenting. The consequences of these tactics would prove to be tragic.

As the young soldier devoured the last morsels of his morning meal, he became distant. The two were no longer in discussion of the current state of affairs. Wolfgang quickly wiped his mouth clean and washed up. Without a further word, he gathered the soiled dishes and placed them in the farmer's sink for cleaning, then quickly exited the Zonfer estate through the front door.

Outright hostile confrontation wasn't a mainstay in the Zonfer household. But Sigmund Zonfer's booming orders were.

When the two did cross swords, the fireworks were palpable for miles.

***

Wolfgang peered out the AAF main barracks window. He awaited the acknowledgement of his achievement from the supreme commander of the Austrian Armed Forces. He was proud but not overly confident. The praise from his father was more than adequate payoff for his accomplishment. He watched as AAF members went through their daily routines. Finally, the woman typing on a computer keyboard addressed the young soldier.

"General Puck will see you now," she said, barely looking away from the monitor.

Wolfgang quickly glanced at her with a mildly contemptuous look and started for General Puck's office. He entered and stood at attention.

"Ah yes, Private Zonfer, I'm so glad to see you. I would like to officially congratulate you on your amazing feat of being the first private to receive the Leopold Medal of Achievement. I saw your performance at the training outing and I must say that I have never seen a more effective use of modern military strategy," the general said enthusiastically.

"Yes, sir, thank you. I appreciate your encouraging words. I hope to someday lead the AAF to victory in battle, sir."

General Puck grinned.

"With your amazing understanding of military tactics, I may have to worry about you taking my job today!"

The general laughed. Wolfgang was suddenly very uncomfortable. He could feel the urge to lash out at the general. However, he understood the ramifications of such an action and knew he would never be so bold. That wasn't his style.

"Yes, sir, I would be lying if I said that I didn't want your position someday."

"I'd be worried if you didn't, private. Now, to get to the official business, this is just a meeting between the two of us. You will be getting full honors for your achievement at a later time. Currently, there are more—how shall I say it—trying matters that face the AAF."

Wolfgang's interest was piqued.

"Are you referring to the conflict with the United States, sir?"

General Puck began to squirm in his chair. He could scarcely believe he was discussing very confidential information with a private.

"Not at all, son. These are matters that are far above your current rank. When you are Corporal Zonfer, perhaps I will discuss such matters with you."

"I understand, sir. Well, if that will be all—"

"Yes, Private Zonfer, and once again, congratulations on your remarkable performance. I know the AAF will have a stellar warrior in you."

Wolfgang's eyes pored directly into General Puck's soul. The general felt the burning fury inside of young Wolfgang Zonfer and somehow it deeply disturbed him.

"Yes, sir, thank you, sir," Wolfgang said in a deadpan voice.

He saluted and left the office. General Puck stared at the position that the young soldier once occupied. He thought to himself, "that young man has issues."

***

Wolfgang sat in his designated seat at the dinner table. Every night he was expected to be in that same position at the table. Sigmund had taken discipline to a new level of strictness.

Soon after taking his seat, his father entered the room for dinner and sat at the table. He picked up his eating utensils and began to partake in the feast. After a few minutes of awkward silence, Sigmund addressed his son.

"Wolfgang, how did the meeting with General Puck go?"

"As well as it could have, father. He explained to me right away that this was nothing official. The real ceremony will happen at a later date. Apparently, other things are more important than my Leopold," Wolfgang said glumly.

"Listen, son, you've been walking around here with a chip on your shoulder for long enough!"

Wolfgang Zonfer's rage had peaked and he was at the breaking point.

"Isn't that how you raised me to be? You are the one that's always telling me, 'I expect nothing but perfection out of you, son! You are inheriting the great Zonfer family legacy'—all of that garbage! Why didn't Edward join the AAF? Why was it me who you expected to be perfect?"

Sigmund Zonfer gripped the tablecloth in front of his seat, seething with anger.

"There are many things that I could say to you right now, Wolfgang. I am going to choose my words carefully. When you were younger, I noticed a quality in you that your brother did not possess. One day, while you were playing a game of rugby, I saw this quality shine. It wasn't like a child playing a game. I saw a spark in you that I had when I was that age. That spark was ruthlessness. I knew from that day forward that you would be the son to carry the Zonfer family torch. I always tell you that you need to be tough for a reason. That's what has worked for our family for decades."

Wolfgang, for the first time in a long time, felt encouraged by his father's words. He relaxed. He felt as though he had a real place in his family. The Leopold was nothing compared to the honor of carrying on the Zonfer name in the AAF. At that moment, he realized the importance of the years to come.

Chapter 2: First Combat – 2995 A.D.

The war between the Austrian Coalition for Humanity and the United States had been waging for over a year. The first battalion of the ACH forces sat in anticipation as their commanding officer, General Stein, stood in front, ready to give marching orders.

"First battalion, listen up! This is it! The overzealous capitalists have overstepped their boundaries for the last time! Their president will regret the moment he contemplated conquering the motherland. Today, we stand united by our cause, a peaceful society that doesn't covet the possessions of free societies that are not their own. We are the fist of the teacher! We are the bullet in the gun! We are the pen writing history! And we shall never falter!"

The general's pep talk achieved the desired effect. Thousands of soldiers from all walks of life and ethnicity, from various nations and organizations, exploded in unison. The screaming could be heard through the entire military outpost. A twenty-one-year-old Private Wolfgang Zonfer sat silent, arms crossed, as the jovial celebration unfolded. He stared into the eyes of General Stein as he slowly caressed the sleeve of his military issue jacket. Thoughts of being in possession of such power and influence traversed through his mind.

Wolfgang's time in the AAF had begun to manifest ambitious goals in the young ground troop's mind. He often imagined himself as chancellor of the Austrian parliament, making the difficult decisions he knew needed to be made. At the same time, these moments of military brotherhood felt surreal to him. This time, they were nothing more than a pit stop before he reached his true calling. As the cheers continued, Wolfgang felt a brush on his back. He ignored it. Then a more vigorous slap jolted his attention. His brow furrowed and he turned.

"Hey, Wolf—where's your sense of spirit?"

"Blaine, I was thinking. I don't like it when people bother me when I'm thinking."

"You'd better get with the program, brother. We're going to be killing today. I can't wait!" enthused twenty-one-year-old Private Blaine Danken.

Wolfgang sighed in quiet anguish. Blaine's attitude was the very reason why he felt so out of place. He didn't enjoy killing. He understood the unfortunate necessity of just wars but didn't thrive on violence. During the short time he had spent with his foxhole partner, Blaine Danken, he recognized his mental instability. Wolfgang hypothesized that he was bipolar. One second, Blaine would be smiling and upbeat. The next, he could be found in a corner sulking over nothing.

After Blaine's attempt to motivate his partner, Wolfgang decided that he'd had plenty excitement for the time being. The general had completed the mission briefing and the warriors now had some time to themselves. The mental preparation for waging war became Wolfgang's main focal point. He left the outpost and pulled out a massive cigar. He thumbed his lighter and puffed the contraband to a steady burn. Smoking was encouraged but a cigar was an indulgence. As he puffed away, his mental preparation inched toward completion. Just when he thought he was free from all distractions, the inevitable happened.

"Hey buddy, how'd you get that thing through the Gestapo?" Wolfgang's tenacious partner inquired.

"Blaine, listen. I'm sure it isn't the easiest thing for you to understand, but I need time to think. Can you give me that luxury?"

"Wolf, you do realize that we're going to be sharing the battlefield together, right? If you have a problem with me, I think it would be best to get that out in the open right now," Blaine said authoritatively.

"Of course I do, Blaine. Listen—this has nothing to do with you. It's a personal matter."

"Is it the killing? I bet it's the killing," smirked Blaine.

Wolfgang blankly stared at his partner. He couldn't possibly relate to such talk. After a somewhat awkward silence, Blaine continued.

"I know this is your first time in combat. I was stationed in Switzerland last year during the Yank invasion. That was my first taste of taking a human life. Wolf, I have to tell you—there's nothing like it. It's the greatest rush you will ever feel. To understand that the life you just ended wanted to end yours—there's nothing like it."

At this point, Wolfgang wanted nothing more than to leave his partner. It was clear as day to him that Blaine was not a stable human being. Politically, accepting Blaine as a partner could turn out very bad for Wolfgang. Merely associating with such an individual could hinder his rise to power. As he realized this, Wolfgang made his final decision.

"Blaine, I have to go."

"Wait! Are we still partners?"

Wolfgang turned toward Blaine coldly.

"No."

As Private Zonfer walked toward his commanding officers' quarters to request a new partner, the flame of a new hatred was kindled inside Private Danken. As Wolfgang entered the outpost, Blaine's mouth slowly formed a maniacal grin.

Soon after he had entered, Wolfgang once again emerged from the barracks. As he walked by his former partner, Wolfgang addressed Blaine for what he hoped was the last time. "It's nothing personal," He said again.

***

The Hungarian conflict raged. Wolfgang and his new partner, Private Tyler Webb, lay prone at the first battalion rallying point. The commanding officer shouted orders over the constant bombardment of explosions, gunfire, and jets.

"Listen, we've got to take the position ahead of us immediately if we want any chance of victory! Privates Zonfer and Webb, I need you front and center!"

The two young warriors sprinted to the requested position.

"I've been watching you two. You're the best qualified for this objective."

Zonfer and Webb looked at each other in satisfaction.

"Yeah, yeah, get the love fest over with, said Captain Stahl impatiently. "Now, this Yank outpost has been giving us hell for this whole conflict. I need you two to covertly take control of it. The rest of the battalion will be providing covering fire. I don't need to tell you to stay in constant contact with me. I want real time updates."

"I know we can depend on the support for constant cover fire, sir. We're ready to go," Zonfer said with conviction.

"Just watch those rail gun emplacements. They've been railing from this position constantly. We've been taking massive casualties because of this. Your main objective once inside is to disable the rail gun targeting systems. Secondarily, take control of the outpost and set up shop. Reinforcements will arrive soon after."

"Yes, sir, you can count on us," Wolfgang reassured him.

Privates Zonfer and Webb sprinted to an advancing cover position. The rest of the fighting force readied their M2-A2 automatic rifles and prepared to provide covering fire. Upon Captain Stahl's command, the collective presence of the ACH rose in unison and delivered a hail of gunfire toward the enemy. Chunks of concrete and earth flew into the air in dramatic fashion. The captain chimed in on the communication channel.

"Zonfer and Webb, prepare to make the rush! On the second volley, you're up!"

Wolfgang felt his nerves tingle with anticipation. He had imagined this moment since his first day at AAF training. With a tilt of his wrist, he checked his vital statistics on his bioreader. His heart rate was relatively calm. In the final seconds he had remaining, he checked his M2-A2 Ravager. The green LED shone, reflecting the status of the mission.

"All units rise, covering fire!" the commanding officer shouted.

Privates Zonfer and Webb powered out of their prone position. The deafening drone of an amalgamation of combat clatter bounced in Wolfgang's brain. The unfolding pace of combat was nothing more than a fleeting thought in the back of his mind. He systematically eliminated every combatant who crossed his path. Webb was comparable to his partner but not as comfortable as Wolfgang. Still, they approached their objective with little effort.

"You sure this is your first time, Wolf?" Webb said with a smile.

Wolfgang eyed the security keypad. He knew it had to be hacked.

"Webb, get the hacker out. We need to get this door open. I'll give you cover."

Webb noticed Wolfgang's state of mind and saw that he was unshakable.

"Ten-four, brother. I'll have this cracked in no time."

As Webb worked feverishly to crack the security lock, the young warriors noticed the sound of chaos beginning to subside. Soon thereafter, the only sound the privates heard was static inside their combat helmets.

"Did they give up?" Webb jokingly said while he continued his task.

Suddenly, the commanding officer's voice filled their helmets.

"All units prepare to take cover!"

Wolfgang and Tyler looked at each other with concern.

"I bet it's a SAT bomb," Wolfgang said calmly.

Webb's eyes widened in fear at the mere thought of experiencing a satellite bombing. He felt himself thinking about the reality of the situation and refocused on the task at hand. "I'm almost there," he said.

The beeps and blips of Webb's hacking tool bounced throughout the entry corridor of the U.S. outpost. The crack of gunfire or boom of a passing jet occasionally broke the relative silence. Suddenly, a chorus of military voices shouted from various positions.

"SAT bomb!" they screamed as they gazed into the skies above.

Portions of the sky began to glow and ominous rumbles soon followed. The few warriors present who had experienced a SAT bomb and lived to speak of it knew what horror they were about to face.

"You're going to be cutting it close, Webb. We need to get inside before this starts," said Wolfgang.

"I know, I know," said Tyler frantically, "I'm going as fast as I can. They have a solid encryption on this pad."

"You've got time. Just take a deep breath and focus."

"Clearly an easy task for Mister Leopold 2993," Private Webb said sarcastically.

Wolfgang ignored the remark and continued his support role. As the seconds ticked by, the roar of the approaching bombardment from the cosmos grew.

"Christ, do you hear that?" said Webb nervously.

"You'd better double time it, Tyler," said Wolfgang.

Then, with the boom of a thousand conventional bombs, the first SAT bomb struck with hair-raising precision. Wolfgang and Tyler flinched and ducked at the catastrophic explosion.

"Come on, come on, Webb, get us in there!" Wolfgang said, now in overdrive.

Webb's fingers trembled with tension. Wolfgang, with his back to the wall and Ravager readied, peered out a nearby porthole. He observed luminous hues dotting the surrounding area.

"My god, they must be carpeting the entire battlefield! Tyler, we need to get low now if we want to survive!" a now frenzied Private Zonfer said hoarsely.

"We're in!" Webb yelled.

Then, with a hiss and a clang, the once secured door inched upward. The two warriors crouched and ran into the enemy stronghold. Crimson hues and alarm bells assaulted their senses. A mechanical voice boomed throughout the hallways.

"Attention! All personnel report to the lockdown area. This is not a drill. Attention!"

Apparently, all hostile entities had already obeyed the monotonous mechanical voice. The privates found themselves in a safe haven. They stared out a nearby viewing window in terror as the SAT bombs devoured the battlefield. Their comrades did the same. The ruinous devastation rolled across the landscape. Wolfgang and Tyler listened to the insanity as it unfolded on their helmet communication links. As young Private Wolfgang Zonfer listened to the screams of his dying compatriots, he searched his soul for feelings of compassion but to no avail. As far as he was concerned, they all deserved their fate. As do I, he thought without emotion.

"We need to help these guys! I'll cycle the door and flag them down!" Webb said, feeling helpless.

A loud pound and hum signaled the door's opening. Wolfgang checked his weapon and gazed onto the battlefield. Stray limbs lay upon the damp soil, and a light rain began. A combination of blood and fresh water collected in selective areas of the terrain. As soldiers filed into the enemy outpost, Wolfgang spied a large-framed man sprinting toward the safe haven. It was Blaine. As he passed his nemesis, their eyes met. Blaine's mouth contorted into an almost inhuman shape. The young men said nothing to each other.

The number of casualties taken was staggering. Most of the first battalion of the Austrian Coalition for Humanity was extinguished in this apocalyptic scene. As the last surviving members filed through the door, Wolfgang took a moment for contemplation.

"Look at this—the human race is so fragile. Why do we do this? Killing each other over land, resources, influence, power—it doesn't make sense to me. Our leaders take us to war, claiming it's the only way to peace. So, here we are, in the name of peace—killing," he said, the statesmen in him shining through.

"Sounds to me like you are working for the wrong organization," Tyler said.

"Perhaps…my father likes to remind me that he has big plans for my future.

'You're the Zonfer family political heir.' he says. 'I see it in you. The AAF is merely a stepping stone.' He bombards me with that crap all the time."

"I don't know. He might be on to something. You sound like a member of Parliament to me," Webb said with a smirk.

Wolfgang guffawed. "Is that a compliment or an insult?"

The two young soldiers laughed in unison.

"To be serious for a second, I must say I think this war is just," said Webb. "We didn't attack the Yanks. This time the preemption doctrine is going to bite them in the ass."

"Bah!" argued Zonfer. "Sometimes I wish the just nations in the world could systematically terminate the unjust. If I had my way—well, why discuss it? It's futile!"

"You're preaching to the choir, buddy," Tyler responded.

As the heavens ceased to fall, Wolfgang dreamed of an era free of useless violence. That day, he made a commitment to himself. Peace through violence would become an ideology of the past.

Chapter 3: The Prophet

General Puck walked down the pristine sidewalk in New Vienna. The drone of passing cars and clop of footsteps surrounded him. As he approached a dilapidated church, one loud voice stood out. Standing on the front steps was a grungy, unkempt fellow. His tattered clothing clung to him like a second skin. He was psychotically reciting a speech to a nonexistent audience.

"The end is near! Read the good book and see all! The signs are everywhere!" he preached.

General Puck increased his pace in an attempt to avoid any confrontation. It was a futile effort. The vagabond grabbed at the stately-looking, uniformed military man.

"I know you! You can help the cause! You know the eighty-four man! He is the key to salvation! He is our only hope!" the tramp said in a feverish state.

"Sir, please take your hands off me!" Puck said in shock and anger.

"I apologize, sir! I've seen you! In my visions, you were the man I approached! This is it! Praise God, this is it!"

Puck felt the urge to run. He had a meeting in minutes with the United Nations Security Council, followed by another meeting with the Austrian Parliament to report on progress of the war. However, at his core, Puck was a compassionate man. He gave the lost soul a chance.

"What exactly are you speaking of, sir?"

"You know the man of eighty-four! I saw this number in my vision. It is the number of the man who will save the human race from extinction! We have strayed, sir, strayed from the path of righteousness but God is with us still! He is ever present!"

Puck looked into the eyes of the scruffy man. What he saw was insanity. He turned and began to walk away.

"Sir, wait!" the man said.

Despite his misgivings, Puck stopped and turned.

"I realize this sounds crazy. I have visions. But I saw you. I need you to find the man of eighty-four," the man said, experiencing a moment of clarity.

Then, once again, his sanity fell apart.

"You know him! He is the only hope! I see the way you are looking at me! You judge what you do not understand, sir! You are not a perfect man! Just last night you cheated on your wife!"

Puck's brow furrowed, his eyes widened. He stood open-mouthed, staring at the man. How could he have known this?

"Have you been stalking me, sir? If I ever see you again, I'll be contacting the authorities!"

Puck turned and left the man on the church steps. The vagabond just smiled and entered the once beautiful church. As Puck made his way to his destination, all he heard was the man's singing echoing from the inside of the church.

"A...ma...zing grace, how sweet...the sound..."

***

Puck closed his portfolio containing the appropriate information for reporting progress in the war. He sat before the Austrian Parliament feeling confident in his position.

"General, before you go, I have one more issue to discuss with you," one of the members of Parliament said.

"Of course, sir, my schedule is clear for the rest of the day," said Puck compliantly.

"I appreciate your patience. We in Parliament have been hearing great things about a Corporal Wolfgang Zonfer. His name has been mentioned countless times during briefings from various sectors of the defense force. I wonder what your take is on this man."

"Thank you for the question. I was thoroughly impressed with Corporal Zonfer. I only met with him once, soon after his winning the Leopold award for his outstanding performance in the AAF training program. Since then, he has been deployed in various fronts in the War for Humanity and has proven his worth to the defense force. The Austrian Coalition for Humanity is demonstrably stronger and more efficient for his service."

"I thank you for your answer, General. We heard one story in particular about Corporal Zonfer from past testimony that certainly raised my brow. During his time in the Hungarian conflict, he allegedly dodged enemy fire while taunting the United States forces. Apparently, he shouted things like, 'Why are you trying to kill me?' and 'You're nothing more than a slave obeying his master.' Have you heard this tale?"

"Yes, that sounds familiar, sir. When I heard about this, it concerned me. Honestly, I didn't know whether to be impressed or disturbed by this story. My initial impression of Corporal Zonfer was one of confusion. I thought about recommending a psychological evaluation but after his exemplary performance in the force, decided against it."

"Well, General Puck, after careful consideration, the Parliament has decided that Corporal Zonfer holds special potential. While an extremely proficient warrior, his place is not on the battlefield. The Chancellor of Parliament is recommending his name for an appointment to the United Nations. With its growing influence, the United Nations will very likely become the main front in the War for Humanity. Immediately after President Hensted leaves office, a better opportunity for real peace talks will arise."

Puck looked at the chairman in confusion.

"I don't think I understand, sir. Are you saying that you want to appoint a twenty-two-year-old corporal to a position at the United Nations? Where does this confidence in Wolfgang Zonfer come from? It certainly can't be from this ridiculous tale."

There was a short, awkward silence before the chairman responded.

"Absolutely not. The truth is that this has more to do with Mr. Zonfer's father than anything. As a highly distinguished former commander of the AAF, he has an incredible amount of influence on the chancellor. He recently requested that his son be relinquished from his duty. Corporal Zonfer can do much more for Austria off the battlefield rather than on it."

Puck was shocked and appalled that Parliament would even consider giving any single member of the AAF special treatment.

"Sir, I would like to respectfully disagree with this action. The other members of the defense force will not take this too kindly. If you start something like this, I doubt you'll be able to stop it. This will cause a mass exodus of soldiers. Trust me."

The chairman gazed at Puck in deep contemplation. "You make a valid and compelling point, General," he said. "Perhaps this is not the time for the corporal to be relieved."

"I appreciate your consideration, sir. After all, Corporal Zonfer is an excellent soldier and the force would be weaker without him," Puck humbly replied.

The chairman nodded.

"Yes, the Parliament was presented footage of Corporal Zonfer's Leopold award-winning performance at AAF training. Quite impressive."

"Indeed, sir, he's an extraordinary tactician. He has better knowledge of engagement tactics than some captains."

"Well, the last thing I would recommend before we close would be a promotion for the corporal—perhaps a large promotion. Do you understand what I am saying, General?"

The chairman tapped a pen rapidly on the surface in front of him with an intimidating look upon his face. General Puck didn't take kindly to this scare tactic.

"I understand what you're saying, sir. I'll consider it."

"All right, General Puck, we all appreciate your service to the nation and the world. We stand adjourned."

The chairman of the defense force committee slammed the gavel authoritatively. Puck collected his materials and exited the Parliament building.

Puck made his way to the nearest bus stop. He took a seat and examined his materials. As he glared at Wolfgang's last name, his thoughts drifted back to the vagrant's rant.

"Find the man of eighty-four! You know him!" echoed through his mind.

According to the English language, he quickly added the respective numbers to the letters in Zonfer's last name. As he realized the fact that the name Zonfer added up to eighty-four, he quickly closed the file and his eyes as he awaited his transport.

Chapter 4: Battle Weary

"Another day, more death. This cycle needs to end," an exhausted Wolfgang Zonfer sighed as he awoke from a deep slumber. "Eighty-four—what the hell does that mean? Weird dream—" he thought to himself.

Wolfgang and Tyler rested as a new day dawned in the War for Humanity. Unfortunately for corporal Zonfer, the Austrian war for the preservation of freedom showed no signs of ending. Battle fatigue became a serious concern. The war had been raging for almost three years. Deployments were nothing short of brutal.

"Let's get the morning grub, brother," Sergeant Webb said enthusiastically.

Wolfgang said nothing and left the sleeping quarters. During his time in combat, he had earned a formidable reputation. As he walked down the barracks hallways, every warrior greeted him. He only nodded his head in acknowledgement. The young man was drained, emotionally and otherwise.

He entered the vast line to receive his fare. The trays were stacked neatly, ready for use, in front of him. As he walked, he felt his feet drag. What made things worse was the fact that Wolfgang knew he lacked the wherewithal to continue. He found himself longing for his leave. Perhaps he had leaped into this war too enthusiastically and was now paying the price for his zeal.

Wolfgang filled his tray and found a secluded seat in the mess hall. Corporal Webb found his partner hiding among the crowd and approached him.

"Hey, buddy, why aren't—"

"I need some alone time, Ty," Wolfgang said abruptly.

His partner, not recognizing this new personality trait of the soldier he had bled with, was taken back. He squinted at Zonfer in confusion.

"All right, I understand," said Tyler, even though he didn't. "If you need to talk, I'll be around."

Wolfgang's eyes slid down to his trough. The simple act of feeding himself felt like brain surgery. Halfway through his meal, he realized the war had taken a massive toll. He emptied his tray and left the mess hall. Tyler saw his partner leave but ignored his exit.

As Wolfgang approached the commanding officer's main office, he stopped. He clenched his fist, his knuckles cracking loudly. He slowly walked up to the door and raised his arm. Then he froze, again contemplating what he was about to do. "Just do it," he thought to himself. Suddenly the door opened.

"Ah, Corporal Zonfer, I was just about to get some grub and meet with you."

"Meet with me, sir? Why?"

"Yes. Why don't you come into my office and have a seat." It wasn't a question but an order. Wolfgang's fatigue was clearly visible.

"How are you feeling, son?" the CO said.

"Honestly, sir, I'm feeling drained. I was about to—"

"Say no more. This comes at a perfect time. I was just on the phone with General Puck. Apparently, the chancellor thinks you have a higher calling. They are recommending your name for some kind of new program."

     Wolfgang was confused but happy. "New program? What exactly do you mean, sir?"

     "I don't have the particulars. You'll be briefed upon your return to Austria."

     Wolfgang cracked a smile for the first time in months. "Pardon my ignorance, sir, but is this effective immediately?"

     "Oh, yes. In fact, you should get packing. Your transport to the safe zone should be here very soon."

     Suddenly, Wolfgang began to feel his energy surge. "I'll do that, sir. It's been an honor."

     "The honor is mine, son. You're a fine warrior, one of the best. I know I'll be hearing about you," Captain Briggs said in a fatherly tone.

     Wolfgang nodded and smiled. He saluted and departed the captain's office with a new bounce in his step. As he quickly walked to his quarters, he thought to himself, "New program—"

     A lamb whistling his way to slaughter…

Chapter 5: The Homecoming

     Wolfgang yawned and squeezed his eyes shut. The first actual restful sleep in many months repaired his brain and body quite well. The chopper rested lightly on the roof's landing pad in Vienna. A small crew of media vultures crowded near the chopper to film the war hero.

     His debriefing had immediately followed touchdown. He found himself lost inside his thoughts as he struggled to contemplate the words that the Coalition commander had spoken.

     "Your promotion is effective immediately, Colonel Zonfer. So, twenty-three years old, Leopold award winner, and youngest colonel in Austrian history. That's quite a resume," General Puck had warmly said.

     "I can only bow and thank you, sir. As far as I know, you're the one who did this."

"Not exactly, son. Don't get me wrong. You are one of the most effective and talented tacticians I have ever seen. But this decision is far above my pay grade."

Wolfgang found himself intrigued and curious. He crossed his arms and stared at the general, wondering how this had happened.

"You didn't make this decision? I don't understand."

"It's a combination of factors, Wolf. Can I call you Wolf?"

"Sure—if not you, then who, sir?"

"As I said, Colonel, various people and factors were involved. You don't need to understand."

Wolfgang didn't like this. Something didn't feel right about the situation. Why would the ACH grant him a leave and promotion for no apparent reason? Wolfgang gathered his thoughts and responded. "There's got to be a catch."

The general's expression changed immediately.

"I knew you were going to catch on. You're a bright one."

A somewhat awkward silence followed before the general continued.

"The Coalition Experimental Medicine and Science Pavilion of Vienna is starting a new program for exemplary members of the military. Your name has been recommended for induction into the program."

Wolfgang's tension level doubled at that statement. "Wait a minute! Is this that Frankenstein program that the politicians—"

"Absolutely not!" the general interrupted. He calmed himself and continued.

"This is a legitimate scientific venture. I'll let Doctor Sullivan explain the particulars."

General Puck checked his digital wristwatch.

"In fact, he's expecting us soon. We should get to the hummer now."

The two exited the office and made their way to the front entrance, where a large military transport awaited. The grandeur of the vehicles awed Wolfgang; he had seen them every day for the past three years, yet somehow was still impressed in their presence. The glossy, metallic paint glistened in the early afternoon sunlight, the smell of fuel fumes thick in the air.

"Here we are. After you, son," the general said politely.

Wolfgang humbly nodded, smiled, and entered the transport. The institution of conversation was uncomfortably absent within the vehicle. The promoted youngster could only wonder what future lay in front of him. While Wolfgang was in mid-thought, the general nervously spoke.

"How is your home life? I would think living with the legendary Sigmund Zonfer would be quite an experience."

Wolfgang felt his back and neck relax. Of all things to calm him, a question about his father seemed the least likely. He almost chuckled to himself at the thought.

"Not all it's cracked up to be, sir. I respect him but—"

"He expects a lot out of you, big things. I know, it's really all he can talk about," Puck replied matter-of-factly.

Wolfgang broke into half a smile in surprise.

"I had no idea you had spoken with my father."

"Not on a regular basis, but we have video chats every now and then to catch up."

Wolfgang paused for a moment and thought about how to phrase his next question.

"Sir, to be honest with you, I don't understand why or how my name was magically picked for this mysterious new program. Could you shed some light on this for me?"

Puck rubbed his hands on his wool slacks, appearing somewhat nervous.

"You're an effective warrior, Wolf. I don't think you fully understand how impressive your training test numbers were. We haven't seen ratings like that in—well—forever."

"Sir, may I be frank with you?"

The general squirmed a bit.

"Of course, Wolf."

"I think my father had something to do with all of this. Am I correct?"

Puck looked down at the interior carpeting of the vehicle, then up at Wolfgang. He looked down once again and sighed.

"You have a third eye or something, don't you?"

"Sir?" Wolfgang asked sternly.

Puck immediately became more defensive.

"Listen, son, I'm still your superior. Don't address me like that."

"My apologies, sir, I'm just a bit frustrated," Wolfgang said quickly.

In this moment, Puck saw the personality quality that had shocked him when he'd first met Wolfgang Zonfer—an indescribably cold stare. One needed to experience it first-hand to understand its power. All of a sudden, Wolfgang was vacant, distant.

Instantly, Puck's expression went from cordial to fearful. The military man of strong stature recoiled back, defeated by the young man's powerful aura.

Wolfgang gazed out the window, deep in thought. Once again, the general broke the silence.

"Man of eighty-four—" Puck whispered under his breath.

Wolfgang's eyes widened to the size of large almonds.

"Sir, what did you just say?"

***

The front of the Coalition Experimental Medicine and Science Pavilion inspired awe in all who approached it. Stretching stories high, many taxpayer funds had been invested in this sparkling new facility. Some said it was a whole lot of money spent on nothing. Its development was shrouded in secrecy. Only high-ranking members of Parliament and the biochemists who worked there knew of its existence. The LCD sign glowed with intensity. It read, "CEMS Pavilion: Creating a Better Warrior." The monitor displayed the Coalition crest. The screen phased between the two images and occasionally would display an informational video.

Wolfgang exited the transport first; General Puck followed close behind. The warrior stopped and observed the advertisement of sorts. A soothing female voice greeted him.

"For the past four years, the CEMS Pavilion has been conducting vital research on human genetics. Technological advancement as well as dedicated biochemists, led by Doctor Hannibal Schiller, have made the past years' landmark momentous in scientific history. Recent achievements include the discovery of the cancer code, a certain sequence that appears in the genetic structure that can be restructured so the afflicted can be cured."

"Yeah, I heard about that. They never credited the biochemist that uncovered it," Wolfgang mused.

"Anything having to do with this place is confidential. That's a reminder to you, son. Speak of nothing you see here."

Wolfgang began to wonder what he had gotten himself into. He uneasily cocked his head back in the direction of the screen as the video continued.

"In more controversial subjects, unproven but compelling evidence of the existence of the human soul and newly discovered imaging methods and devices provide the means to a new era of human understanding of science and medicine as a whole. Finally and perhaps most impressive, there is lead biochemist at CEMS Pavilion, Dr. Hannibal Schiller's invention of the bioscanner. While in an early developmental stage, its possibilities are endless. Using genetic and biological calculations, the bioscanner can map an entity's biocode and produce a firm calculation of said entity's genetic and biological components."

A stately-looking man with graying hair appeared on the display, with "Dr. Hannibal Schiller" tagged at the bottom of the screen.

"The uninhibited atmosphere of CEMS's studies makes this the perfect venue for truly remarkable discoveries. Every day we are making enormous strides in medical and scientific understanding. I believe that the CEMS Pavilion reports will go down in history as one of the most influential and provocative groups of studies in the history of the human race."

Wolfgang listened intently. His eyes were glued to the crisp images of real scientific progress.

"You'll get this video in the welcome package, Wolf. We need to get going. Dr. Sullivan is waiting."

They walked down the concrete pathway. The lawn was perfectly manicured, almost as though someone trimmed it with scissors.

"They sure do take care of this place," Wolfgang said quietly.

The majestic entrance to the CEMS Pavilion was iridescent. The glare caused Wolfgang to squint. The massive titanium doors slid back with lightning speed. The action seemed almost alien in its smooth execution.

As Wolfgang entered the facility, he made a surprising and disturbing observation. He scanned the territory in search of familiar faces. Eventually, he spied the last person on Earth he expected to see. It was Blaine Danken. Bewildered and somewhat disgusted by the discovery, Wolfgang inquired quietly, "Sir, all due respect, what the hell is Blaine Danken doing here?"

The general's face went white with nausea.

"Dear God—" he said flatly.

Wolfgang's desire to flee overwhelmed him. Nothing had seemed right about this to him from the beginning. Another lesson his father had always preached was "Trust your instincts." He decided to push for an answer.

"Sir, I'm trying to keep it together here but I need some answers. What is going on here?"

"I told you!" the general said, almost creating a scene. He adjusted his tone accordingly. "I told you. I don't have the details. Dr. Sullivan is going to explain everything."

Puck was a good man. Wolfgang knew this. If something wasn't right, he wouldn't green light it. Wolfgang accepted his answer and just nodded with a neutral look upon his face. He stared at the floor, observing the beautiful and spotless tile. Wolfgang had a passion for architectural design. He dreamed of the day when he would own his own property and could execute his vision of the perfect dwelling. Then, lost in the repeating triangle pattern on the tiles, Wolfgang was roused from his daydreaming.

"Hey, buddy, we should go fishing like we used to at training. We'll be seeing a lot of each other now that we're both in the program. Sounds so scary—'the program'—" Blaine Danken said in his inimitable wicked fashion. He laughed almost hysterically.

Wolfgang continued to ponder the tiles, scarcely responding.

"Yeah, sure, Blaine, maybe later, let me settle in first. Find out what this is all about."

"That's my man. We're going to be juiced up murdering machines in no time, Wolfy! Yeah!" Blaine said in a clearly manic state.

He left Wolfgang with the general, noticing Puck's presence as he left.

"Why the hell do you have the big welcoming committee? I come home and get a damn staff sergeant to escort me! Goddamn!"

To everyone's delight, Blaine Danken finally made his grand exit.

"That boy certainly has a way, doesn't he?"

"I guess you could say that, sir," said Wolfgang. He decided to continue on his quest for answers.

"Sir, what exactly did Blaine mean about 'making us murdering machines'? I'm starting to wonder what this 'new program' is all about and if I even want to be a part of it."

Puck's personality morphed again.

"You don't have a choice, son. You were given your leave for a reason, soldier. This is where your future lies."

Wolfgang's temperament wasn't fragile but this came close to breaking the young man.

"But, sir, what if I don't want them to do these—whatever—"

"Listen, Wolf, I'm sorry. This is above me. You're in other hands now. I'm here now because I truly care about you. I can also inform your father as to what CEMS's plans are for your role in this program," Puck stated honestly. He felt the need to further comfort the obviously distraught soldier.

"Everything is going to be—"

Suddenly, a tone interrupted the general and a voice soon followed.

"Dr. Sullivan, 1200 hours. General Arnold Puck and Colonel Wolfgang Sigmund Zonfer, the doctor will now see you."

Wolfgang's brow rose at the booming voice. Everything was grandiose about the Pavilion. The large door, surrounded by security cameras and monitoring paraphernalia, cycled open for the men. They entered and were greeted by a tall, scrawny man. Standing about six foot three inches tall, he was gawky and clumsy in appearance. The classic balding pattern atop his head completed the picture.

"Hello, sirs. I'm Doctor Sullivan, head of the Warrior Program. It's an honor to see you. What is it, Colonel Zonfer?"

"As of today, yes it is," Wolfgang proudly stated. The two shook hands firmly.

"Ah, I've been eagerly anticipating your arrival."

"Why is that, doctor?" Wolfgang inquired.

"Well, naturally, because you are the first official test subject. You should be—"

"Wait, wait, wait! I'm the first and only inductee to this program?"

"Well, yes, the first to be cleared for Tier One placement. The man who just left not long ago has been cleared for Tier Five, just basic alterations. Why don't we take a stroll to my office and discuss the details of the Warrior Program?"

Wolfgang and the general looked at each other in confusion.

"Don't look at me, Wolf. I've never seen this guy before in my life. Apparently, these guys live like hermits," said Puck frankly.

"That's not fair, General. We have lives. People fear what they don't understand." said Dr. Sullivan. But suddenly they could only hear his voice, and it came from his office down a long hallway, far from Wolfgang and the general.

"What the—it's like he teleported—and how did he hear us?" Puck whispered lightly.

"Through human engineering, General," Sullivan said, now right in front of the two shocked military men.

"All right Houdini, what's this program all about?" Puck barked, clearly annoyed.

"Simply put, it is technology helping us evolve, man pushing the ball of achievement up the slope of progression that God decided to abandon. Operations and procedures that geneticists and biochemists previously thought were impossible."

Colonel Zonfer and General Puck looked at each other, mystified. What was this crazy man muttering about?

"It's improving the modern warrior by addressing the core issue, that being that humans have physical limitations. Colonel Zonfer, what if I told you that I could give you nerves of steel, a Super Mario Brothers jump, hypersensitive senses, and superhuman strength?"

"I would say you're completely insane. That's graphic novel and video game nonsense," said Wolfgang with a hint of doubt in his voice.

"That's what you think, boy. How do you think I heard you perfectly clearly from so far away? What about my disappearing and reappearing act? What do you think, General Puck?"

"I thought you said Wolfgang would be the first to be inducted into this Tier One. How could you have procedures done on yourself?" Puck asked.

"You should check your ears for wax, General. I said that Mr. Zonfer would be the first Tier One inductee. We have, of course, tested these methods on subjects before, some less successfully than others. I happened to retain some of the effects. Nevertheless, Mr. Zonfer is the perfect candidate. We ran his genetic code through Dr. Schiller's bioscanner. You gentlemen should see that thing—quite amazing to see it at work. But I digress; Wolfgang's genetic biocode is of hardy roots. These alterations should take easily," said the doctor confidently.

Wolfgang thought about the prospect of being the perfect warrior. Though he was almost ashamed to admit it, Wolfgang knew he wanted to do this. He decided to be straightforward. "All right, doctor, suppose I decide to embrace this idea. What exactly are the risks of these procedures and the odds of them failing?" he asked.

"You have nothing to worry about. There are no negative physical effects to an unsuccessful procedure. At worst, you'll come out the same old Wolfgang."

The eccentric doctor was one hell of a salesman.

"Sign me up!" smiled Wolfgang.

At that moment, the young man made a decision only a fully developed adult should tackle. He determined that Wolfgang would be no more. All that would remain would be simply, *Zonfer*.

Chapter 6: Engineering Cruelty – 2999 A.D.

The blurred ceiling was the first image that greeted Wolfgang Zonfer. It had been almost a year since Colonel Zonfer had been inducted into Tier One of the Warrior Program. No one heard from or seen him in months. The CEMS Pavilion officials explained his extended stay away as, "unforeseen reactions" and "uncontrollable variables." The truth was that the Pavilion had systematically dissected and restructured a human being. Wolfgang's mind and body were no longer his own.

Zonfer was hardly an active participant in this transformation. Unfortunately for him, during an early stage of his "psychological conditioning," he experienced a severe psychotic break. Allegedly, he almost killed an attendant. Due to the questionable lack of security cameras inside the CEMS Pavilion labs, nothing was known for sure. The young warrior's only hope lie in an internal investigation of the CEMS Pavilion's research methods and, more importantly, its inductee and patient treatment.

The genetic engineers visited once a week. They recorded his progress or lack thereof and made recommendations for "the next step of progress."

As he glared at the ceiling in a stupor of tranquilizers, scattered thoughts traversed his subconscious. Sudden, violent flashes of unimaginable murder and chaos, pooling blood, killing fields, dismembered body parts, decapitated heads—all caused a scream to build in his throat. The shrill noise echoed throughout the CEMS facility. But biochemists, geneticists, and attendants alike ignored his cries. As each second passed, the young warrior, Colonel

Wolfgang Zonfer, slowly died, a black transfiguration. The genetic alterations and psychological conditioning bled the man of all sane and coherent thoughts. The Warrior Program reduced Wolfgang to nothing more than his darkest qualities—the cold stare and militaristic talents were untouched. Essentially, he was a machine, unfeeling and uncaring. The fond memories of brotherhood in the AAF and tender moments with friends and family were merely a murky afterthought.

Dr. Sullivan stood outside Zonfer's room as he argued with Dr. Schiller, the lead biochemist at the Pavilion.

"Don't you understand, Sullivan? You're destroying human minds! If you look at Wolfgang's current biocode and his initial read, you can clearly see the consequences of this program!"

Sullivan laughed.

"What do you think the point of this program is—to make the inductees gentle puppies? No, we're building killing machines, bloodthirsty demons! You want to win the war, right? This war will be won with soldiers from the Warrior Program!" Sullivan boasted.

"Not with that one," Schiller said as he nodded his head toward Zonfer's torture chamber.

"That man's biological makeup is ravaged to the point of no return. He'll be good for nothing but sleep thanks to you. If you don't change your methods, I'm pulling the funding," Schiller asserted.

Sullivan was insulted by Schiller's lack of confidence in the program.

"Do you actually think I would've started this venture with Colonel Zonfer if I thought there was the slightest possibility his body couldn't take it? Do you take me for a complete fool, Hannibal! Trust me, it may take longer than expected, but this man will lead our forces to victory! He's the one and only Tier One inductee and his limitless potential is worth that cell. It's worth ten cells!"

Schiller had turned off the crazy doctor's ranting long before his last proclamation.

"Listen, just fix him up—God bless him—and get him out of here. His father has called once a day for the past year wanting to talk to him. I've covered your ass long enough!"

Schiller promptly stalked away, the clop of his shoes the only sound throughout the ward.

Sullivan peered into Zonfer's cell. He watched as the transformed warrior writhed in agony. Zonfer gritted his teeth and randomly twitched. Sullivan smiled crookedly and spoke.

"Baptism through fire, Zonfer."

Like clockwork, as Doctor Sullivan entered his office, General Puck approached the Pavilion labs entrance. The continued stonewalling from the CEMS officials kindled his interest. While he shook off any responsibility, he cared for the young soldier.

He accosted the night attendant for access.

"General Puck, AAF, I'm here to see Wolfgang Zonfer."

"It's a bit late, wouldn't you say, General?" said the night attendant sarcastically.

"I apologize for that, miss. I've got a lot on my plate right now and I wanted to check on the boy before I went home."

The attendant's attitude remained toxic. Expressionlessly, she pushed a glowing button in front of her and began a conversation. Puck's patience ran thin.

"Miss, if this is going to be a problem, I could—"

"One moment, General. I need to clear this with Dr. Sullivan."

"Miss, could you please hang that up? All I ask is for one second!" Puck insisted.

The attendant lifted her finger away from the call button and looked at Puck with disdain.

"I only want to look in on him. His father has been calling me for weeks and I don't know what to tell him. Please—"

The attendant rolled her eyes but acquiesced and opened the door.

"Thank you," said Puck quickly as he gave up attempting to be affable.

The general slowly walked the hallways as he searched for Wolfgang. Most of the quarters were empty. Puck wondered where all the other candidates were. As General Puck passed Room #84, he noticed a soft glow coming from the room. He looked inside the door window. In hopes of attaining a better view, he cupped his hands around his eyes. Lying in the bed was the broken warrior. Puck immediately recognized him; he noted Wolfgang's blank stare. At this time, the person who had been Wolfgang Zonfer was dead. What lay in the bed was a psychological Frankenstein.

Puck had known that Wolfgang was a youth on the fringe with his rage simmering just beneath the surface. He recognized the stare on Wolfgang's face all too well. It was that same look that had shaken him when he'd first met Wolfgang.

"My God, they're turning him into a monster. I have to get him out of here," Puck muttered to himself.

He approached Sullivan's office and violently rapped on the door.

"Sullivan, open the door! I need to speak with you!"

The door slowly folded inward.

"Ah, General Puck, what a pleasant and unexpected surprise. To what do I owe this—"

"Enough! What the hell are you doing to that boy?" Puck interjected.

"He is the first Tier One member of the program. He's a bit of an experiment. But things are looking positive for the future. Colonel Zonfer will be a killing machine, tactless but tactically faultless. It's going to take time, though. The AAF and Parliament need to be patient! Rome wasn't built—"

"Shut up! I'm not here for the goddamn AAF! And certainly not for Parliament! I'm concerned for the boy and now I see my suspicions were correct! That boy is leaving this hellhole! If I have to carry him out myself, I will!" the general bellowed and abruptly left the doctor.

Sullivan stared out his office doorway as General Puck stormed away.

"I think it may be time for Mr. Zonfer to awaken," mused Sullivan to himself.

***

"This was not agreed to, Mr. Chairman! I was not informed about any kind of new program! As far as I was concerned, I was promoting Wolfgang Zonfer and he would be taking his post at Coalition Command!"

General Puck sat in front of the Parliament in a furious rage. The members were barely able to get a word in edgewise.

"The committee understands your concern, General. I would like to ask you to calm yourself," the chairman requested.

"I care about my soldiers, sir. That boy is being tortured in that place! How could you endorse such barbarity?"

"This war will not be won with conventional thinking, General. If we are going to prevail against the United States, we need to make our forces more formidable. As you well know, the United States has been developing programs such as this for decades. We need to keep ahead of the curve!"

The General saw that his effort was futile. A threat was the only option.

"Gentlemen, if you will not help Colonel Zonfer, you leave me no choice other than to help him myself. If you don't release him from the CEMS Pavilion, I will relinquish my post as commanding officer of the ACH."

Frantic chatter erupted in the grand room.

"Order!" the chairman barked.

Slowly, the bickering faded.

"Talk of such nonsense is unnecessary, General Puck. Dr. Sullivan informed me before this session began that Colonel Zonfer would be at Coalition Command sometime today."

Puck was shocked. Sullivan told him that it was going to take time.

"I don't understand. He told me just last night that this process was going to take time. Gentlemen, it was clear to me that this madman was destroying this young boy! I saw the look in his eyes!"

The chairman looked at Puck without emotion.

"Once again, General, we understand your concerns. I stress—there is nothing to worry about. Dr. Sullivan is a professional and thorough scientist. Colonel Zonfer is in good hands."

Puck felt defeated. He hung his head low and breathed slowly. He only hoped that the chairman spoke the truth and Wolfgang would be in his new office at Coalition Command.

"Well, General, if there is nothing else."

"No sir," Puck said solemnly.

"This meeting is adjourned."

The slam of the gavel ricocheted off the interior walls of the Parliament building. Puck felt a tear stream down his cheek, not a familiar feeling to the general. He wished this meeting had happened a year earlier when the boy would still have had a chance. He tried to calm himself. Perhaps Wolfgang Zonfer was fine.

Chapter 7: An Unlikely Post – 3003 A.D.

Wolfgang Zonfer, now appointed to the United Nations' Peacekeepers' Office in Vienna, sat in his office as he contemplated diplomatic means of ending the War for Humanity. In search of answers to the present predicament, Zonfer decided to peer into the past. A historical fiction book entitled *Elusive Peace* lay spread out before him. It was a modern-day *War and Peace*. In an entertaining and informative fashion, it outlined mankind's tribulations throughout the centuries. He carefully digested each verse as he pondered a solution.

Finally, after hours of reading and contemplation, Diplomat Zonfer deduced the same solution as prior thinkers. In some cases, brutal conflict had been entirely necessary. Perhaps, in the grand scheme of time, wars were an earmark in history, a vital snapshot of an era, their ultimate purpose being a lesson not to repeat them. Mankind had clearly been missing his lessons.

Weary from hours of taxing his brain, Zonfer closed the massive tome. Sighing and pinching the bridge of his nose, he found himself reminiscing over his military days. "Peace through war," he thought repeatedly as if it were some sacred mantra. Suddenly, he found himself having terrible flashbacks—bloodletting, dismembered bodies, pooling blood—all the same visions from his Pavilion torture. As the agonizing memories emerged, Zonfer realized his time was being wasted.

His psychological conditioning finally took hold. In the heat of his psychosis, the once peace-oriented warrior completed his dark transformation. All the remnants of his former ideology were now eradicated. If anyone else had been present, they would have shuddered at the sight of Zonfer's groans and inhuman facial contortions. He grabbed his cranium tightly in hopes of white-knuckling the experience. Finally, the pain subsided. His emotions cascaded in an almost pleasant manner. Zonfer made a decision.

He rose from his seat and left his office. His destination was his superior's office. What felt like an eternity passed as Zonfer finally approached the door. He pounded on it so vigorously that the office window rattled.

"God, are you trying to break the door down? Come in!" the head of the UN Peacekeepers' Office said.

Zonfer opened the door and stood in the doorway. William Bauer immediately noticed Zonfer's metamorphosis. Something had changed.

"Wolf, I didn't know you were still working. What's the problem?" he said nervously.

Zonfer said nothing. He simply stood in the doorway staring coldly at Bauer. Finally he spoke. "Sir, could you just call me Zonfer—please?"

"I didn't realize you didn't want to be called *Wolf*."

Zonfer just stared. His eyes were completely vacant. His expression was like a black hole that sucked the courage and bravery from anyone with the audacity to stare back. Nothing could break its influence.

"Wolf—I mean—Zonfer—I don't understand this visit. Why are you here, exactly?"

"I'm relieving my post to return to active AAF duty. This war needs me. It's never going to end if I don't do what I have to do," Zonfer said with a totalitarian air.

"But all your work—you've spent countless hours attempting to broker these peace accords! You can't just—"

"Yes, I can. This has been my paramount responsibility here, and I'm telling you they don't want peace. They want to dominate our people and our way of life. I'm going to stop them."

Bauer admired the man's candor as well as his determination. If Zonfer were to give up, no one had a chance at success.

"Thank you, Zonfer. I wish you all the luck on the planet. You're going to need it," Bauer said, genuinely appreciative.

Zonfer's blank expression hadn't changed. He slowly bowed his head and turned to leave. As he walked away, he was more determined than ever to be victorious. For some reason unknown to him, he thought of the phrase "baptism by fire."

***

Initiating a now familiar brutal action, Sergeant Tyler Webb reloaded his Ravager. He and his new partner had been on the frontlines in Hungary for what seemed like forever.

"Goddamn, are they ever going to stop pushing?" Webb yelled over the noise of warfare.

"Shit, I hope they keep it up! This is what I live for!" Webb's partner shouted in excitement.

The overzealous warrior that dueled alongside Webb was none other than Blaine Danken. After his successful Tier Five alterations, Danken was immediately deployed to the most active front—Hungary. If Danken was any indication, the Warrior Program was a stunning success.

Fortunately for all the members of the Austrian Armed Forces, Tier One of the Warrior Program was terminated soon after the Wolfgang Zonfer fiasco. However, all lower tiers of the program remained intact. Danken was the only member who successfully completed the post-program training. The CEMS Pavilion hoped that, in time, 100 percent of inductees would go back to active duty. A certain amount of preparation was required for the "Über Troopers," as they became known, to complete before they could return to the theater.

Danken's aim was flawless. Every shot met its target with deadly accuracy. With each kill, his bloodlust only intensified. Suddenly, whatever had held Danken back from jumping head first into oblivion evaporated.

"Ha! Enough of this crap. I'm moving up!"

"Blaine, wait!" Webb shouted.

"The name's Danken, Ty!" said Danken as his murderous melee began.

Webb watched in awe. Danken ran from point to point with incredible speed. At one juncture, surging forces actually stopped pushing. Some even took cover as they attempted to reassess the battlefield. Danken was wolf like; he relentlessly hunted his prey. The stunning display continued until silence and inactivity swept the expanse. Webb scarcely believed what had just transpired.

"Man, where'd you learn that?" asked Webb from across the almost tranquil war zone.

In response, Danken said, "Long live the program, brother!"

"Where do I sign up?" Webb whispered to himself.

***

Before returning to Coalition Command, Zonfer decided the time had arrived to pay a visit to a face from his past. His stride was long and fast. He wanted to finish this as quickly as possible.

He entered the CEMS Pavilion. Memories of atrocious events assaulted his mind. The negative effects, however, were no longer apparent to Zonfer. As each second passed and more memories bombarded him, it only fueled his psyche. He hadn't experienced this before and he loved it.

He finally reached his destination, the CEMS Pavilion psych ward. Dr. Sullivan was admitted to the ward soon after his maniacal experiments were exposed. When Dr. Schiller realized the full extent of Sullivan's madness, he immediately committed him to a lifetime sentence in the psych ward. Zonfer approached the attendant and spoke.

"I'm Colonel Zonfer. I'd like to see Sullivan."

Zonfer's demeanor and tone negated any chance of the attendant not granting him access.

"Yes, sir, just a moment," said the attendant. "You'll find him in cell #10."

The security system buzzed and the door slid open. As Zonfer walked the ward hall, random screams and clatter resounded ominously. Zonfer remained unflinching and focused on his task. He no longer understood the meaning of fear.

He reached cell #10 and gazed up at the security camera. The attendant pushed the door-opening mechanism for Sullivan's cell. The darkened cell was suddenly illuminated by a white neon light overhead. Sullivan was in a fetal position at the corner of his cot. Being such a tall man, he appeared especially awkward in this posture.

Arms crossed, Zonfer stood and stared at Sullivan. He wanted the prisoner to be truly shocked. Finally, Sullivan rose his head. Astounded, he said, "Ah, my beautiful masterpiece, I've awaited your arrival! I knew you'd show up eventually!"

Zonfer continued his infamous cold stare. It had quickly become his default expression in his new mind.

"I see the conditioning has finally activated. How do you feel?"

Zonfer said nothing.

"Well, damn it, you've turned into a dumb Mongoloid," Sullivan moaned. "That's unfortunate. All that work—down the drain,"

Sullivan buried his head in his arms once again, occasionally whimpering.

"I feel nothing. And I thank you for that," Zonfer said softly.

Before he could respond, Zonfer was gone. Sullivan broke into a small smile and cuddled his pillow.

"Consider yourself baptized."

***

General Puck was inundated with work. The occasional worker bee entered and barked new developments at the good general. He felt his head spinning at the pace of activity. The war on the Hungarian front had stepped up. The United States made the decision to flood the region with hardly a second to contemplate his next move. Puck found himself in the middle of the chaos without a second's worth of solace.

"Yes, Captain, I understand the circumstances. If you calm down, I think you'll be able to understand the consequences of failure. You need to keep pushing. Failure cannot even enter into your mind. It's not an option," Puck said softly into the secure communication channel.

The response was favorable. Puck ended the conversation and continued his work. Suddenly, one of the worker bees entered.

"Sir, there's someone here to see you."

"Who the hell would be visiting me at this hour? Send them in, Sergeant."

The sound of footsteps greeted Puck before the individual. He stood in anticipation at his office doorway. The visage that greeted him brought a smile that could comfort a thousand tormented souls.

"Wolfgang, what a pleasant surprise. How are you?"

There was that name again. Zonfer twitched, a sliver of recollection shooting through him.

Puck noticed his state. During the silence, the general bowed his head in distress. He knew Wolfgang was, for all intents and purposes, an entirely different person now. Still, he hoped their past might revive something inside the man's mind. It quickly became apparent to him that Wolfgang was gone.

"I'm here to resume my duties as an active member of the AAF, sir. What are my current directives?" Zonfer said without emotion.

Puck squirmed in psychological torment. The cold stare, the emotionless expression, and all the traits that concerned him the most were all that remained of the man that stood before him. He had already accepted it.

"You return at an opportune time, Zonfer. The Hungarian front is as active as ever. In fact, the Yanks have flooded the region in huge numbers. Consider yourself promoted, soldier. You'll be commanding officer of the Hungarian front battalion. Congratulations, General Zonfer. God, I remember the day you stood in that exact same spot and we talked about this moment—amazing."

Zonfer stood strong, his posture perfect, as always.

"Thank you, sir. You won't regret this decision. I intend on ending this war," he said in a determined tone.

He turned to walk away when Puck called him back.

"General, one more thing, I've been hearing chatter about plans for a large-scale invasion of the United States. If you're comfortable with the idea, I would like to recommend your battalion for the main surge."

For the first time since his induction into the Warrior Program, Zonfer felt a modicum of joy. His mouth contorted into a crooked smile. "Pen me in, sir," he said in a disturbingly playful manner.

Chapter 8: General Zonfer

A Coalition APC roared down a Hungarian roadway. Inside sat the newly appointed leader of the Hungarian battalion. Zonfer wasn't cognizant of his newborn personality. However, it was apparent to all who encountered him. An uncomfortable atmosphere pervaded the vehicle interior. None of the inferior officers dared even to address Zonfer. During his time in the United Nations, Zonfer had been allowed to develop his own image. No longer bogged down by the ties of the AAF constraints, he had allowed his hair to grow, nearly to shoulder length. Also, he now sported a Fu Manchu. The resulting combination struck fear into the bravest of individuals.

He stared out one of the APC portholes, scanning the terrain. Smoldering craters and charred earth dominated the landscape. Zonfer was indifferent to the visuals. On his face was a blank expression.

The APC had finally reached its destination. It pulled up to the Coalition Command outpost with a monstrous boom. The inconvenience of warfare was absent from the area. With the secure status, General Zonfer made his grand entrance.

The vehicle's rear door slowly lowered. Several underlings exited the rover first, assembling in a perfect line at both ends of the door. They held their Ravagers close to their chests, clinging to them as if they were life itself. Finally, with a thick theatric air, Zonfer made his first appearance. As he stepped onto the Hungarian soil, the wind blew through his flowing auburn locks. He took a deep breath and closed his eyes, listening for the sounds of war. Instead, a vaguely familiar voice greeted him.

"General Zonfer, it's an honor. I remember you when you were only a private. You're the most talented soldier I've ever had the pleasure of commanding."

Zonfer found his senses quite in tune to his surroundings being back in the field.

"Thank you, General Stein. I've waited for this day for my entire career. Trust me, you needn't worry about leaving your soldiers under my command. I fully intend on ending this war as quickly as possible."

General Stein patted Zonfer on the side of his arm. "It's not as easy as you think, General. You'll find that out soon enough."

Zonfer didn't respond. Stein noticed Zonfer's dissatisfaction with his last statement and revised it.

"However, anything is possible. Maybe you're the man to do it. I hope so."

Zonfer's expression stayed cold. Stein's *mea culpa* fell flat.

"Sir, Coalition Command in Vienna is eagerly anticipating your return," Zonfer said, wanting to end the increasingly gruff exchange. "You'll be receiving full honors upon your arrival. I'm sure you want to be getting back."

Stein nodded and entered the vehicle. "Good luck, General," he said as the door slid closed. "The world is counting on you."

Zonfer looked toward the outpost as the transport roared into action. The weight of his new responsibilities suddenly hit him with tremendous force. His reaction to this realization was one of exhilaration. He found himself invigorated by uncertain situations, which was a complete one-eighty from his prior outlook. As he walked toward his new workplace, Zonfer shrugged off the last of his self-doubt. The determined leader had completed his transformation.

***

Coalition Command on the Hungarian front was frantic. General Zonfer paced the situation room as he observed and digested incoming reports from the theater.

"General, we're taking massive casualties in combat sector one. What are your orders, sir?" an officer inquired.

"I want all active forces to stand down. They're to return to Coalition Command immediately and await my new strategy," Zonfer said without hesitation.

"Yes, sir, I'll inform all units."

Zonfer retreated from the chaos of the situation room to his main office. It was in a state of flux. Massive maps of the Hungarian theater and status reports cluttered his workspace. Stein hadn't been briefed on Zonfer's promotion. Thus he left the office in its state of disarray.

General Zonfer skimmed the materials quickly. He hoped to assemble a fresh plan of attack. He knew the Yanks would try to claim victory upon the ACH force retreat. Zonfer realized how rapidly his mind was functioning. He marked certain positions on the map well suited for flanking action, his favorite war tactic.

The United States had embedded itself very effectively within Hungary. All ACH attempts to invade the stronghold were held off by SAT bombings or reinforcement arrivals. Thankfully, the combat technology branch of the CEMS Pavilion had successfully developed a tool for disrupting the SAT bomb satellites. The U.S. had recently attempted an electromagnetic pulse bombing of the Pavilion but failsafe redundancies thwarted the effort.

In a matter of hours, Zonfer had completed the new tactical maneuvers. The ACH troops awaited their new marching orders. General Zonfer exited his office and headed for the troops' barracks. On the way, he met his commanding captain.

"Captain Sutherland, are all squads back?"

"Yes, sir, the last of them arrived just a few minutes ago. They're awaiting your orders."

"Excellent, I just finished the framework of the new offensive and will be addressing the forces in a moment."

They parted. Realizing where the general was headed, Sutherland adjusted his current agenda. He ran toward the situation room, entered, and found the dispatch operator.

"Listen, all troops need to report to the barracks," he panted. "General Zonfer will be expecting them."

"Yes, sir," said the dispatcher.

The enormous situation room screen was impossible to ignore. Sutherland studied the combat theater observation screen, a relative calm presence. Steaming craters and billowing black smoke dominated the display. The brutal SAT bombings were over but the ACH forces were still taking massive losses. Bodies littered the battlefield—ACH and American forces alike. The United States began a redeployment of troops within their Hungarian command post. Some soldiers remained on the battlefield as they collected the fallen.

Sutherland admired this quality in the U.S. military. Though fraught with flaws, the American tradition of honoring the dead stayed intact. He stared at the display and spoke in earnest. "You have to respect that."

He left without another word.

***

"How the hell did that bastard make general? I've killed twice the Yanks he has," Sergeant Blaine Danken muttered as he sat in the barracks briefing room. An audience for his words absent.

Danken's advancement in the ACH was indefinitely stalled. His superiors recognized the warrior's instability and recommended he remain a mere ground troop. He was unaware of his plight. He constantly dreamed of the day when he would lead a battalion into combat. Unfortunately for Danken, this day would never come. Just as Danken was contemplating this possibility, General Zonfer entered. With his head tilted down, Danken raised his eyes in Zonfer's direction, hatred boiling within his mind. Captain Sutherland stepped up to the briefing room podium and began.

"All right, men, listen up! Our new CO has arrived and drawn up the new plan of attack. As you are all aware, General Zonfer has been a member of our battalion in the past. Some of you may have served with him."

Corporal Tyler Webb's eyes widened. He'd thought he would never see Wolfgang again. Suddenly, he found himself enamored with Sutherland's words.

"Without further delay, let me introduce General Zonfer," Sutherland said as he stepped aside and bowed to the general.

General Zonfer approached the podium from behind the briefing room display, the ACH crest glowing in animation. Zonfer had morphed into an almost mythological creature. His black military garb was impeccable. His shoulder-length, auburn hair was styled elegantly and his chest armor, combat boots, and gloves shone in the fluorescent lighting of the room. His military rank metals were perfectly positioned on his shoulder. The thud of his boots pounded within the soldiers' hearts. To complete the impressive and intimidating persona, the general wore a flowing, midnight black cloak.

The room grew silent as the troops stared in awe of this perfect specimen of a man. Even Danken was impressed.

"He sure does clean up good," Danken thought. Webb had a small, wry smile on his face. He knew Wolfgang was going places but this was amazing. Just a few years ago, they had fought side by side. Webb abruptly realized his expression and changed it.

As he prepared to address the soldiers, Zonfer relaxed his stance a little. But he remained standing strong, his posture perfect, with his arms folded behind his back. With his gray-blue eyes he slowly browsed the gathering of warriors.

"The art of war—"

The general shifted his weight and rethought his choice of words.

"The fog of war—I'm sure many of you are experiencing this phenomenon. I certainly did. Moments of clarity in this environment are few and far between. I'm here to create clarity out of chaos."

The soldiers continued to gaze at Zonfer in awe. His presence was stunning. Zonfer slowly paced the stage near the podium.

"You're all going to learn quickly that I am a different kind of leader. I won't send you out to battle alone. Consider this meeting a bonding moment. We are all a part of each other now. General Stein was an effective leader and he deserves our profound respect. With that being said, I have come to this front to end the American occupation. Stein wasn't willing to take the necessary steps to bring this quagmire to a positive conclusion."

Zonfer noticed his slightly negative tone and adjusted.

"The ACH isn't lacking in heroes. We all realize this. Stein, Puck, Captain Sutherland, they're all honorable and valorous warriors. However, I come to you a new man, reborn. I was a part of Tier One of the Warrior Program—"

With this declaration, murmurs arose among the soldiers. Danken's face contorted into one of his infamous grins. He discovered that he liked Wolfgang again. The psychopathic sergeant could relate to the "new and reborn" Zonfer.

While the mild disturbance ensued, Zonfer revisited his podium and raised his arm. With that action, silence once again hastily cascaded on the hall. Zonfer continued.

"I anticipated that reaction. Let me demystify this operation. I am sure many of you have heard strange things related to the Warrior Program. Take most of those notions and throw them out of the proverbial window. The truth is that the Warrior Program is vital to the future of the ACH. The Yanks have had their own genetic engineering facility for decades. We are merely keeping up."

Zonfer had the crew mesmerized.

"I stand before you today the first and only Tier One candidate. If you have noticed someone fighting with you who seems stronger or more agile, chances are they spent time at the CEMS Pavilion. My time there was different—and not without trials."

Zonfer paused, obviously reflective.

"I've had more than just physical alterations. My ability to develop military strategy has greatly improved. I'm not going to bore you with the details, but I've enjoyed this advancement in my makeup."

Danken stared blankly at the stage. He wondered why Zonfer had been picked for Tier One and not himself. Regardless, Danken realized their link. He hoped Wolfgang felt the same.

"I've disclosed all I can about the program," Zonfer carried on. "I decided it would be wise to inform all of you about my induction. I don't want any secrets between us. I'm going to ask you to give me one thousand percent from here on out. If you've already been giving it one thousand, I need ten thousand."

Zonfer bowed his head and closed his eyes.

"We are one. I will stand with you until the last millisecond of combat. I will brief Captain Sutherland and he will lay out the new strategy for victory. The war on this front will end."

General Zonfer walked off the stage and exited the briefing hall. Loud discussions erupted between the soldiers. Statements like, "I'll follow that man into hell" and "I'll be proud to serve under this general" were among the phrases heard. Morale was higher than ever before.

Chapter 9: The Defining Moment

With their new war strategy in place, the ACH forces converged on the American stronghold. The roar of APC engines rolled across the expanse. Zonfer occupied the passenger's seat of the first combat APC. He rested his hand on the pulse pistol that resided at his hip. An aftermath of chaos and death surrounded the ACH motorcade. Zonfer activated his communication device.

"Are all units in position?"

"That's an affirmative, sir," the voice on the other end responded.

"Copy that, all units. APC stealth mode engage."

With this order, all the transports cloaked in a chameleon technology, and their engines were silenced. The ACH forces positioned themselves around the parameter of the Yank fortress. Like a pack of wolves, they waited with bated breaths. Zonfer chose his orders carefully.

"All units await my order, disengagement in a moment."

Captain Sutherland sat directly behind Zonfer. His trepidation peaked.

"Sir, it's far too quiet."

"I agree, captain. That's why we're waiting," Zonfer said, his eyes locked on the enemy fortress.

Sutherland nodded in agreement.

Silence had been never so disturbing. Not a crack of gunfire or a voice, only the occasional boom of an ACH jet jarred the men. As Zonfer observed the stronghold, he noticed pulsating red lights dotted around the structure.

"I'm getting a bad feeling about this," he said under his breath.

Suddenly, a monotone alarm screeched, breaking the uncomfortable silence. However, this was the last sound Zonfer wanted to hear. The ACH forces watched as the four corners of the stronghold rooftop opened. Large rail guns reared their ugly heads. Zonfer knew exactly what was happening.

"All units disengage stealth and push into the base!" he commanded.

The ACH transports roared into action. They blazed new trails to the front of the American base. The first battalion it its entirety now resided closer to the enemy stronghold than ever before. Safe from the utter devastation of the U.S. rail guns, Zonfer immediately knew his next move. He activated his communication link and spoke.

"This is it, men! All units disengage from your transports and engage the base! Do not stop pushing until you see the American general dead on the floor!"

Every APC entry hatch opened at the same time. The soldiers piled out in unison. Zonfer stepped onto the active war zone for the first time in a long time. He gripped his Ravager Elite tightly and ran for cover. Sutherland followed close behind. He was puzzled by the general's active role.

"Sir, you don't have to fight! You're our general!"

"Captain, did you not listen to my address at the barracks? You're dealing with a different kind of general."

Sutherland managed to crack a small smile. Then, without any warning, the U.S. stronghold's walls began to scroll upward. The plan of the American forces was slowly revealed. The entire fighting force of the U.S. stood behind massive barriers, prepared for combat. Finally, the war resumed.

"Fire at will!" screamed the opposition captain.

Assault rifle and gun emplacement fire exploded. The ACH soldiers lobbed pulse grenades inside the enemy barricades. Using the devastated landscape as cover, they slowly moved toward the stronghold.

General Zonfer and Captain Sutherland remained safe in their cover position. Zonfer barked a few final marching orders and prepared to engage the enemy himself. Sutherland spied certain positions and took occasional pot shots with perfect accuracy. Zonfer noticed his effectiveness.

"You're quite good, captain."

"I'm Tier Four. This is as good a time as any to tell you." Sutherland responded, not missing a beat.

Zonfer grinned with pleasure. He was beginning to view his time in the CEMS Pavilion as a gift. Wolfgang's father had been correct. He had a greater purpose. The fulfillment of that prophecy was unfolding with every second.

With the speed of a cheetah, Zonfer leaped from his cover. Sutherland observed the following happenings while providing cover fire. Gripping his Ravager Elite tighter than ever, Zonfer sprinted to an overturned American transport. As he studied every angle of advancement, in an almost superhuman action, he launched himself over the spent vehicle. While in midair, he eliminated three enemy combatants with unprecedented precision.

Upon landing, Zonfer rolled into another area of safe cover. Knee deep in an impact crater, he periodically peeked toward the base. His push was astonishingly swift. He found himself within a few hundred feet of the stronghold vehicle storage facility. Because all of the enemy forces were engaged in combat, this area was clear, save for a few personnel. Zonfer made this area his objective. Once inside, he would secure the region and flood the ACH soldiers into the base. Zonfer activated his communication link.

"Sutherland, how's my position looking from your end?"

"You're clear, sir."

In a beautifully fluid motion, General Zonfer popped out of his safe haven and began a mad dash toward his objective. In a crouching position while he held his Ravager Elite in firing mode, Zonfer felt his senses tingle. He eyed targets yards from his position and eliminated them swiftly. As he entered the garage, he modified his pace, going from full-on sprint to stealth in a split second. He held his breath and listened intently. The insanity of war raged in the background as Zonfer paced the corridors of the vehicle storage facility. Blue fluorescent lights lit small areas in a mostly midnight black building. He found a dark corner and pressed his back against a near wall, then slung his weapon to his side. As his heightened senses kicked in, whispers greeted the general. Two U.S. personnel grunts discussed the matter at hand.

"We need to prep these transports! The general will have our asses if they aren't ready for the next offensive. He plans on wiping the floor with those krauts this time," one of the men said.

"Yeah, yeah, like we haven't heard that before. Those ACH guys really know how to fight. It's not going to be so easy to wipe any floor with them," the other man replied.

"You're not prepping anything," Zonfer said, suddenly in their presence, weapon drawn.

Flabbergasted, the two men turned in unison. They both immediately pulled out their tasers.

"You don't want to do this, guys. Leave now or I'll put two in both your skulls," Zonfer said.

"What do we have here? What are you, Captain Kraut?"

Without another thought, Zonfer squeezed the trigger of his Ravager Elite. The bullets decimated the two men's craniums. An explosion of red soaked the wall. The general paused. He looked down upon the two African American males. Zonfer could not understand his newfound love of killing. Suddenly, he grabbed his head in pain. He collapsed to the floor in a heap. The same set of images bombarded his subconscious: bodies, dismembered heads, killing fields, and blood pools. Slowly, the pain subsided and gave way to euphoric pleasure. As he let go of his head, Zonfer grinned and chuckled. The psychological scarring of what Zonfer had endured had come to a head. Then, as he recognized his manic state, he took a deep breath and focused. While in a pile on the floor, he activated his communication link.

"Sutherland, gather the brigade. File them in from the path I took. We're ready to take this from the inside."

"Yes, sir, how'd it go?"

"Easier than I thought, Captain."

He closed the communication link and said to himself, "in more ways than one."

***

The invasion of the enemy stronghold was a success. General Zonfer and the ACH forces now controlled the Hungarian front. He paced the U.S. general's office, the general now a prisoner of war. Zonfer observed the strategic plans that lay on the general's desk. He studied them closely when he was suddenly distracted.

"Well, well, well General Zonfer, nice job on the invasion. I would have expected the great United States to have a much more impressive layout," a familiar voice muttered.

Zonfer glanced up at the source of the statement. It was Danken.

"Hello, Sergeant. It may not look like much but this general knew his strategy. If we hadn't taken action when we did, they could have taken us."

"I was on today, Wolfy. You should have seen me! I took out five Yanks in five seconds! You'd have been proud!" Danken said, barely taking note of Zonfer's point.

"Is that right? Tier Five was good to you, huh?" Zonfer said matter-of-factly.

"The Warrior Program was the best thing to ever happen to me, Wolf. I feel superhuman, like those comic book freaks, crazy stuff," Danken said with the familiar crazy eye.

Zonfer nodded. "It's a great tool for guys like us. It makes our jobs a lot easier."

Just then the office phone rang. "I need to take this, Blaine. I'll talk to you later."

"Congrats, Wolfy, you're doing well," Danken said as he saluted the general and left. Zonfer picked up the phone and answered.

"This is General Zonfer."

"Hello, Zonfer, this is General Puck. I was just briefed on your successful taking of the Hungarian front. I really don't know what to say. I'm astonished. A week after your promotion, you take the one front left that we needed. The chancellor will be more than pleased with this development."

"Thank you, sir."

"This is the one-up we needed. The plans are almost complete for a full-scale invasion of the United States. I'm sure the chancellor will want you to help in the final preparations."

"Excellent, sir, I'm fully prepared to take on any and all new objectives. I assume this means I will be returning to the home front?"

"Absolutely. The final plan for invasion is in its final stages of development. Your touch will be vital. The transport chopper will be arriving soon. Really, Wolfgang, I can't express my respect in words. You will go down in history as a hero to Austria and the world. I'll see you soon."

Puck's use of his first name turned him off. Zonfer hung up the phone without another word. With the Hungarian front secure, the beginning of the end had begun.

Chapter 10: Dominating the Superpower

The U.S.S. Humanity chugged across the North Atlantic waters near the eastern coast of the United States. A savage storm raged. The waters were treacherous. General Zonfer stood on the main deck as he yelled orders to his underlings. The Zonfer Brigade was assigned the invasion of the eastern front. Jet fighters were currently assaulting infrastructure resources within the enemy territory.

Most of the eastern front was without power, water, or telecommunications resources. With this lack of communication between governmental agencies—the military and the executive branch—a perfect storm of anarchy percolated into reality. This complete lack of infrastructure also gave General Zonfer and the ACH unfettered safety in the American coastal waters.

Zonfer was the main architect of the psychological operation. As a result of this attack on basic services, widespread panic descended upon the country. Paranoid citizens began to take up arms and revolt against their own governmental facilities. Instances of United States National Guard troops slaughtering their own citizens were reported. Fortunately, the American government had contracted many private security firms to deal with this new threat to national security. With American forces well versed in non-lethal tactics, casualty levels began to drop quickly. American prisons swelled with "enemy combatants." The brilliant tactician's grand plan for internal chaos was succeeding.

Not a single ACH troop had stepped onto United States soil. The only military action was from the long arm of jets, cruise missiles, and psychological operations. The effect of this tactic was phenomenal. Confusion among the citizenry, as well as the leadership, was contagious. Americans distrusted their government and this affliction now took its toll. Many believed that the government was attacking its own people. Conflict zones began popping up across the nation, with a second American civil conflict becoming a tangible possibility.

General Zonfer was pleased at the progress of the offensive. He knew that cultural and political weaknesses within the country made it vulnerable to this type of operation, but he never anticipated the swiftness of the fall. The idiocy of red, blue, left, and right politics had become poisonous during recent years in America. Apparently, the most recent endeavor in geopolitical domination had been the breaking point. The vitriolic tension between political enemies had reached the boiling point. Democrats and Republicans wished death on one another. The general exploited this problem to the fullest extent.

The deck on the destroyer was rife with activity. Colonel Sutherland approached Zonfer.

"Sir, you requested my presence?"

"Yes. The surrogate nature of this operation will be transitioning soon, Colonel. Begin preparing the drop ships for the main influx of soldiers. We've bled their will plenty."

"Right away, sir," Sutherland said and quickly left the general.

Zonfer stared at the massive ACH drop ships. Another technological marvel, the ACH Griffin Wing was the workhorse craft of the infantry. The jet propulsion system lay directly beneath the enormous titanium wings that cascaded over the heads of its occupants. Soldiers felt safe under the protection of the Griffin Wing. Its stark black finish glistened in the deck lighting. The rainfall continued to intensify the sparkle. As he gazed at the fleet of crafts, Zonfer delightfully recalled its embrace. During his time on the Hungarian front as a private, the presence of the Griffin Wing had meant solace to him. The low-toned hum of the propulsion system soothed all who heard it. This resonance blanketed the deck as preparations began.

As the rain continued to drive down, Zonfer gazed at the eastern coast. His proverbial crosshairs were dead set on the target. Nothing would stop him.

***

The Griffin Wing fleet enveloped the overcast night sky of the American East coast. The ACH forces began their approach and descent upon their rivals. With the utterly terrifying image of thousands of incoming halogen spotlights invading the coastline, the United States government quickly realized its new reality. It immediately mobilized all entities of defensive positioning. As the Griffin Wings began their descent, American forces confronted them. Tanks and combat rovers filled with American forces converged on the area. The rail cannons upon the tanks quickly opened fire on their targets. The crafts bobbed and weaved as they evaded most projectiles. Some ACH forces parasailed out of the crafts as they met their enemies. The invasion was massive. The War for Humanity had finally arrived on United States soil.

Blaine Danken sat in anticipation. The man was ravenous when it came to combat. His eyes, wide as saucers, glared at the combat. He rocked in position while he mumbled to himself, "Yeah, blood, just a little longer."

Webb squirmed uncomfortably in his seat. Danken's instability had taken its toll on the warrior. However, he realized Danken's benefits outweighed his psychotic nature.

"Blaine, you wanna calm down a bit?" Webb said calmly.

"You know me, brother! This is how I work!" Danken laughed hysterically.

Webb rolled his eyes in fatigue of Danken's exhausting personality. He scooted left as he attempted to ignore his crazy partner.

Danken and Webb's Griffin Wing quickly approached its designated front. As it neared the Chesapeake Bay, the Griffin Wing dove sharply and landed gracefully. Danken leaped out of his seat.

"Time to die, baby—time to die!" Danken yelled almost incomprehensibly.

The warrior was ravenous for blood. With vigor he leaped onto the enemy soil. He carefully aimed at his targets with pinpoint accuracy, his Ravager steady as a stone. Each hostile entity swiftly met his demise. Danken, a consummate master of cover tactics, found his quarter. He chucked combustion grenades into the immense gathering of fortified U.S. forces. This wiped out a considerable amount of the fighting forces. A continuous stream of reinforcements, however, made the likelihood of a long battle almost certain.

The sheer perfection of the Warrior Program's genetic engineering shone. During the battle, a Warrior Program graduate stood out. As time progressed, more individuals were persuaded into the CEMS Pavilion's murderer-making factory; the true War for Humanity veterans were the only remaining unaltered human specimens. With Sullivan in an institution, the saner minds prevailed. The Warrior Program now strove to improve only a soldier's agility, speed, and aim. Dr. Hannibal Schiller and his colleagues discarded the controversial mental conditioning, which were the same tactics used on General Zonfer.

Before long, the ACH forces had secured the coast. Coalition reinforcements flooded the ACH-held territory; Zonfer's strategy was now fully implemented. Griffin Wings dominated the dark, stormy skies. The idea of American resistance became increasingly remote.

***

General Zonfer stood on the U.S.S. Humanity's main deck. His eyes were glued to his target, and the picture was now very different. He finally took a moment between giving new orders to appreciate his tactical genius. Zonfer now believed that the Pavilion's torture had been worth the benefits. Nevertheless, Sullivan's influence lived on in the ACH general. Like a ticking time bomb, Zonfer's fragile psyche ebbed and flowed. Yet he found it easier to bury the visions than before. With the frenzied atmosphere of warfare, the general was delivered from his cross. His convictions were stronger than ever. Deep in thought, Colonel Sutherland approached the general.

"General, I apologize for the interruption. I've just been informed that the eastern coast has fallen. ACH reinforcements are solidifying our upper hand in the region. Several brigades from ACH Central Command are on their way to complete the occupation force. Congratulations, General. The world owes you a great debt of gratitude."

Zonfer shifted his head to the colonel.

"I fully intend on cashing in on that debt, Colonel," said General Zonfer somewhat wildly.

Sutherland was taken aback by Zonfer's attitude. His current state seemed unstable at best.

"Have we been taking prisoners?" Zonfer inquired.

"Yes, sir. The enemy's will to fight is fading fast," said Sutherland.

"That's encouraging. The new directive is to take no prisoners," Zonfer said decisively.

"What exactly do you mean, sir?"

Zonfer's brow furrowed.

"Did I stutter, Colonel? Take no prisoners," the general slowly growled.

"Yes, sir," Sutherland replied, leaving the general to his thoughts.

Dreams of global domination coursed through Zonfer's mind. "I can own the world," he thought. And even as he observed the final stand of the American forces, the Zonfer era was beginning.

He approached a Griffin Wing pilot who had just returned from a run.

"Are you free, Sergeant?" General Zonfer inquired.

"For you, General, of course."

"I think it's time to visit my old U.N. post."

Chapter 11: Genesis of the Zonfer Era – 3020 A.D.

With the ACH dissolved, the United States defeated, and United Nations sanctions imposed, the world ushered in a period of peace. Austria and the collective membership of the ACH represented the just nations of the world. The ACH now folded into the European Union and had full representation in the U.N. as peacekeeping enforcers. Soon after the capture of North America, the ACH and the collective United States leadership—Congress and the president—signed a peace treaty entitled "The International Peace Accord." It outlined the consequences of the United States engaging in unilateral, unprovoked militaristic operations. The War for Humanity marked the last American attempt at geopolitical domination. Ironically, from the side that defended the freedom of the world, the notion of global domination by a single power still loomed, ready to become a reality.

Zonfer proved himself as the needed entity to bring a definite end to the War for Humanity. His tenure as a general made him a globally known figure, a legend. However, as might be expected, in some cultures, Zonfer was a villain, in others, a hero.

Having recently retired from the Austrian Armed Forces, Zonfer took his shot at the private sector. In 3015, he founded Z-Defense Industries. During the first five years of its existence, Z-Defense recruited a fighting force bigger than that of most countries. The young Wolfgang Zonfer's dreams were now a reality. He built an architectural phenomenon that became known as Zonfer's Headquarters in his home country.

Upon their first sighting of the building, onlookers would gasp in wonder. It was an absolutely impenetrable structure. Built upon the highest point on the Grossglockner, composed mostly of solid titanium and steel, the giant "Z" hung strong atop the incredibly enormous structure. At certain times during the day, the sunlight glinted off the metal. This caused the building to shimmer and made it visible from almost anywhere in the country. Zonfer's office, of course, resided on the side with the best view. A wall-sized window gave Zonfer one of the most awe-inspiring views in the world.

This remarkable structure was where Zonfer spent most of his days. He oversaw all operations Z-Defense took on from this central command of sorts. The daily briefing was taking place. Zonfer's employees were more like political advisors. No one had any illusions. It was obvious what the former general wanted: power and a lot of it. Zonfer paced in front of the table that was surrounded by his advisors.

"Stinton, how are operations on the African front progressing?" he inquired.

"As well as can be expected, sir. Fortunately, our casualty levels are nil. Apparently, the governments in the region want nothing to do with our force structure. Intimidation can be a weapon in itself. On the political front, government–citizenry reconciliation is on track. Hopefully, by the end of 3020, there will be a lasting peace."

Zonfer gripped his chin with his thumb and index finger.

"Amazing. I was assigned that region for a time while in the United Nations. It took a steady hand and fear, serious fear, to get anything done. Great work, Stinton. Mr. Deshlocke, give me the rundown," Zonfer said as he continued his brief.

"The North American front is secure, sir. Our presence is not welcome but they realize they have no choice. Their new leadership has adopted a non-confrontational agenda. I think the War for Humanity has pacified them for good," Deshlocke concluded.

Zonfer nodded in approval.

"If they know what's good for them, they'll stay pacified. How are talks within their Congress?"

"As I said, sir, they have adopted a pacifist government. This is across the board. There have been rumblings about possible unilateral sanctions on Z-Defense but nothing worth paying attention to. They can't touch you," said Deshlocke.

"I would expect those types of actions. Let them try to impose anything on anyone. They've damaged their standing in the world so gravely that their long-time ally the United Kingdom wouldn't even support it. Well, the two main fronts are secure. It appears that an era of peace may be near—or it would have been."

"What do you mean, sir?" one of the advisors said.

"Well, there are certain times in your life when you know you have to do something you never wanted to do. This is one of those times for me. The golden ring is right in front of me and it's time to grab it."

Zonfer's enthusiasm was obvious. He stopped speaking and just paced for a time. The panel stared at him with bewildered looks upon their faces. Then Zonfer's booming voice broke the silence.

"Think about it. We have command posts and bases all over the world. In every major city, province, county, state, or commonwealth, we have a footprint. What if the 'Z' in Z-Defense decided that he wanted to have governing powers within those areas with our footprint? What if they didn't? Would we immediately withdraw from our contracts and end our agreements? I don't think the governments of the areas we patrol would like the idea of us leaving," Zonfer said, his powerful voice echoing in the grand room.

Deshlocke furrowed his brow and nodded his head.

"I see what you are saying, sir. I assumed this would be your agenda eventually. However, I didn't foresee it so soon." The tall and dark advisor cleared his throat and accessed a manila folder.

"A large-scale PR campaign would be the most effective course of action. If you feed the people your version of the truth enough, they'll buy it. In democracies, Z-Defense could be written into the ballot. In dictatorships, the dictator could be exiled from the country by Z-Defense, the company taking over the leadership role. Before long, you'd control the entire planet."

Zonfer was visibly elated. He pointed at Deshlocke.

"That's what I want to hear. Absolutely brilliant! Deshlocke, consider yourself promoted. You're going to head up this edict. Do what needs to be done."

"Yes, sir," he said and swiftly exited Zonfer's office.

"Gentlemen, this is merely the beginning. Napoleon tried it; I'm going to do it."

Chapter 12: A Doomed Fate Decided – 3021 A.D.

The public relations campaign was in place for a year. Television advertisements gave Z-Defense's motto: "Z-Defense Industries: Securing a Peaceful Tomorrow." Deshlocke's idea went precisely as planned. Public support for Z-Defense, while never low, increased daily. The propaganda took hold. Public polls indicated that the people of the world trusted Zonfer's corporation more than their own governments.

At this point, Zonfer had influence practically everywhere on Earth, the last bastion of opposition coming from the stubborn United States.

Zonfer sat in his office awaiting Deshlocke. The former general was becoming increasingly isolated. After all, Zonfer was challenging every major government in the world. Paranoia came with the territory. Also, he feared his psychological state might be deteriorating. The visions had made a horrifying return. In the worst episodes, he woke from a deep sleep swiping at the shadows. Suddenly, two of Zonfer's personal security detail entered his office.

"Sir, Mr. Deshlocke has just arrived."

"Thank you. Send him in, please."

Carrying a laptop and various reports in his briefcase, Deshlocke entered with a somber look upon his face. He stood before Zonfer, almost paralyzed.

"Mr. Deshlocke, what's the problem? It's obvious there is one," Zonfer said, cutting to the chase.

"In terms of the PR campaign, things are going far better than I could have anticipated. However, I'm not sure I'm entirely comfortable with where the next step in this process will take us."

"Well, if this is the time to confront it, let's confront it. Tell me what you think," Zonfer said as he shifted his weight to his left leg.

"As you are well aware, sir, no entity seeking ultimate power finds no opposition. This case is no different. In certain regions, I don't think Z-Defense will ever be able to capture the collective support of all the people. In these areas, cleansing of the population may be the only viable option. We could blame it on the governments and repopulate."

Zonfer was suddenly distant. It was as if he were asleep with his eyes open, an expression of silent torture distorting his face. He vigorously rubbed his temples, searching for clarity. Suddenly, he felt his neck begin to pulsate with pain. He shifted his attention to this new aggravation, gripping the back of his neck. Finally, the episode ended with flashes of the familiar, horrifying images. His pathological condition was bubbling to the surface at a very dangerous time.

"Sir—sir—are you all right?" Deshlocke said, trying to determine his superior's state.

"Do it," Zonfer said without hesitation.

"Excuse me, sir?"

"You heard me!" Zonfer shouted, slamming his fist on his desk and leaving a small indentation in the steel.

Deshlocke, on the verge of defecating himself, decided that wrapping up the meeting as soon as possible was the best course of action.

"My colleagues and I have drawn up a plan of action that I think you would approve of. Shall I implement it?"

"Yes, do what needs to be done. I don't want to hear about this again. I could use some privacy, Mr. Deshlocke," Zonfer said, obviously in distress.

"Yes, sir, and thank you for your time," Deshlocke said, quickly leaving Zonfer's office.

And thus the fate of the human race was determined.

***

Blaine Danken and Tyler Webb, now full-time employees of Z-Defense, were performing their daily patrol in Nigeria. The lack of combat made Danken restless. He was used to constant warfare and bloodshed. The War for Humanity days had spoiled the psychopath. There was the occasional uprising that required quelling but nothing more. Tyler Webb had joined Danken in his decision to follow Zonfer after the war. Together, the two managed most operations on the African front.

Their glossy, black combat gear shimmered in the hot, midday Nigerian sun, the giant "Z" on their backs indicating their allegiance. They carried the latest incarnation of the highly efficient Ravager. Their body armor was the latest version of Dragon Skin. Their combat helmets, equipped with highly advanced targeting and global positioning systems, beeped and clicked when prompted.

Z-Defense Industries specialized in weapons, combat vehicles, and armor development. The company devised new technologies and sold them to the highest bidder. In the rare instances that said bidder had enough, the company would leave out most details on the actual production of the product. Z-Defense Industries quickly became the largest private sector defense company in the world. Z-Defense not only sold weapons, combat vehicles, and armor but also private security forces. No other company in the world had seen profits like Z-D Industries. It was as close to a corporate government agency as there ever had been in the past.

Danken felt especially restless.

"Hey Webb, how do you feel about leaving the AAF?"

"Well, I almost certainly wouldn't still be serving. I guess I could say I have no regrets. Besides, you know Zonfer's going to rule the world. You want to be on the right side, don't you?" he asked, slinging his weapon securely on his shoulder.

"Yeah, yeah, he might. But I tell you, it's going to take him a lot more than just patrolling to stop these governments. He's going to have to beat some sense into them. They're not going to just give up their sovereignty."

Webb looked at Danken in surprise. "You haven't heard?" he asked incredulously.

"What?" Danken responded, confused.

"Well, I've heard rumors about a new directive, a pretty crazy one."

"Tell me more!" Danken nearly choked.

"Yeah, I knew you'd love that. It has to do with a very large-scale slaughtering of people. I don't know if this is across the board or just here. I don't even know if this has any truth to it. Nonetheless, that's what I've been hearing."

The first bit of exciting news made Danken giddy.

"Yes, I knew the old man would come around eventually! Ha, this is a great day!" Danken said gleefully.

"You should really seek help, buddy."

The two continued on their way as the blazing heat continued to beat down on them. After a time, Danken stopped and slumped down. "Goddamn, it's hot," he said wearily.

Suddenly, their helmet communication links activated.

"Orders from above, buddy," Danken joked.

"All Z-D forces, listen closely. This is Council Dietrich Deshlocke. A new directive has been ordered and is in effect immediately, the details of which will be communicated to your in helmet HUD units in a moment."

Webb closely watched his heads-up display. A corner image flashed and then maximized in front of his eyes. The message read as follows:

Directive 84: Stranglehold
08/21/21 00:12:00 Intl.

Eliminate citizenry as according to your targeting systems. New threats to Z-Defense Industries have been determined and this new directive is in immediate and permanent effect. All employees are required to carry out said directive until all targets are neutralized.

> *— Z-Defense Industries Board of Progress*
> *Dietrich Deshlocke – Chair and Council*

Webb and Danken looked at each other in disbelief.

"This couldn't possibly mean what I think it means," said Webb as he attempted to remain calm.

"Man, I hope it does!" said Danken, considerably more excited.

Then, as they passed a Nigerian citizen, their targeting systems began to activate. Red reticules highlighted the passing innocent. "My god, what is happening?" Webb thought. Without another second for Webb to think, Danken fired a short burst of Ravager ammunition into the civilian.

"It's hunting season!" Danken yelled as he ran toward the next target on his helmet HUD.

Webb stopped dead, the realization of the directive's purpose hitting him hard. He began to cough and gag uncontrollably. "You can't go along with this!" he silently told himself. "You have to stop this! You're not a murderer!"

The sound of Ravager fire was deafening: a mass slaughter of the innocent that was taking place globally. Ironically, it was a beautiful August day. Such unthinkable evil in such wondrous beauty. The final nails were steadily driven into mankind's coffin. There was no turning back.

***

Zonfer's master quarters were comparable to his awe-inspiring base of operations. The ceiling stretched twenty feet high. Bookcases lined the walls bursting with all sorts of literature on various topics. Subjects ranged from science and technology to historical fiction and everything in between. It was a wealth of knowledge of past, present, and prophecy.

He finally managed to find a night to rest. A massive 300-inch, wide-screen ratio viewing screen hung on Zonfer's wall, with the evening international news telecast in progress.

"If you are just joining us, the breaking news of the day is the systematic extermination of a large amount of the population around the world. This action was allegedly initiated by Z-Defense Industries. The worst fears of all governments involved with Z-D were realized today. It appears to be the ultimate power grab by the corporation's CEO, Wolfgang Zonfer."

The telecast now showed a picture of Zonfer from his latter AAF days.

"Let's now go to one of our national security correspondents, Ron Wise. Mr. Wise, with this unthinkable scenario playing out before our eyes, what should the international response be?"

"Well, Christina, unfortunately, it looks as if Zonfer has a very good chance at getting what he wants—global rule. I've been speaking to people on the inside of Z-D and they're telling me that in the countries where they are stationed, the governments have been totally eviscerated. Z-D is going to step in and take over everything. The company's forces are countless in number. Bringing Wolfgang Zonfer to justice will be nearly impossible. If we had understood the danger earlier, we could have stopped this. However, Zonfer has been allowed to dig himself into every government in the world. I don't see any turning back from this point."

The telecaster scratched her head and continued. "I think the obvious question would be, how could Z-D win an election after doing something like this?"

"That's a good point, Christina, but the fact is that Z-D is denying all involvement in the act. Their public relations department has been inundating the press with denials. The polls say it's working."

"A very ominous analysis. Thank you, Mr. Wise. We leave you tonight with footage from the afflicted areas of the world."

It was as if a reel of images had been ripped from Zonfer's visions and broadcast to the globe. Most of the images were from Africa. Once pristine beaches were now soiled with crimson pools of blood, bodies of small children, pregnant women—utterly unimaginable horror.

If he had been awake, Zonfer's psyche wouldn't have survived. The reality of what he had ordered would have surely broken the man. However, Zonfer had more important matters to address.

The muffled mutter of a late night program droned while Zonfer slept. Suddenly, he found himself somewhere else. A voice confronted him.

"Please walk forward, Mr. Zonfer."

Zonfer realized that he was no longer in his safe haven.

"What is going on here? Where am I?" He called out to the darkness. The echo seemed infinite.

"Come forward, Zonfer!"

Reluctantly, he slowly walked toward the darkness. The blackest of black washed over him, totally engulfing him. Suddenly, a tunnel of light surrounded him, growing to a blinding burst of white light. Then he found himself in a majestic hall lined with massive opal-colored, cylindrical pillars. The walls were covered with red and gold velvet banners. Zonfer looked about him in shock. Finally, a voice once again confronted him.

"Come forward, Zonfer. You have much to answer for."

As he gained his bearings, Zonfer approached the end of the hallway. Two enormous red doors appeared in front of him. They slowly opened, revealing his captors. An alien being sat upon a large throne. A deep red carpet was scrolled out on the floor leading to the throne.

"Hello, Wolfgang. My kind finds yours in a dire time. My race is known as the Seers. We dwell in a realm between the physical and spiritual, observing your journey through existence. We have never been granted the opportunity to physically interact with human beings. This unique time warranted it."

Zonfer looked at the being in astonishment.

"This isn't real. I'm dreaming," he said.

"Not true, Zonfer. Let me show you what you have ordered."

The entity closed its eyes and raised its hand. Suddenly, Zonfer found himself on the soil in Africa, the site of the largest slaughter. He could only watch as Directive 84 was initiated. He watched as countless Z-Defense soldiers stormed the area, killing every living thing in sight.

As soon as it had started, it was over. Zonfer once again found himself in the room with the Seer.

"Do you understand why I've called you?" the Seer asked.

"I don't answer to anyone, let alone some alien. I'll be leaving now."

Zonfer turned to leave. The Seer swiped its hand in a downward motion, and a burst of platinum light exploded in front of him. Zonfer screamed in pain and staggered forward.

"Zonfer, there are consequences to actions! The human race has strayed from its path, your personal actions being the final calamity. The punishment will be exile. You will choose your kind's fate. Stay and die or leave and survive, the choice is yours. You will find that you have captured what you sought. We hope you think it was worth it. Let the scar upon your face be a reminder of our meeting."

"What do you mean by 'exile'?" Zonfer asked, trembling.

The Seer seemed to dodge the question. "We shall meet again," it concluded.

A burst of blinding light knocked Zonfer to his knees. He awoke in the safety of his bed in a pool of sweat. A soft, blue glow from the still active viewing screen illuminated the room. He recalled every second of the encounter.

"Exile..." he thought to himself.

***

A new day dawned in the mountains of Austria. It was an especially overcast day, with thick black clouds surrounding the top of Zonfer's grand erection. Directive 84 had been successfully executed. All entities considered hostile had now been exterminated. Zonfer awaited his board of advisors for the post-directive briefing. He stared out the huge window in his main office, thinking about his encounter. He wasn't sold on its bearing in reality. Then, as he observed the rolling clouds in the reflection the window provided, he noticed the large scar that stretched from the top of his right brow and ended on his right cheek. The Seer's voice echoed in Zonfer's mind. "Let the scar upon your face be a reminder" and "your punishment will be exile" and all the other prophetic words spoken to him. He found a modicum of his usual strength and snapped out of it. "Hogwash," he thought. But before he had an opportunity to explore this newfound strength, Zonfer's security detail entered.

"Sir, the panel is here."

"Send them in."

The motorcade of advisors piled into Zonfer's office. The clap of their expensive footwear bounced off the walls of the huge room, creating an eerie resonance.

"Please take your seats, gentlemen," Zonfer ordered.

The panel was somber, not a smile among them. One of Zonfer's main advisors was noticeably absent.

"Where's Deshlocke?" Zonfer inquired.

"He hung himself late last night, soon after the international news telecast," Stinton informed him.

Zonfer's head dropped. "I see. Now I understand the air of dread about all of you. This is unfortunate but it will not stop us. Deshlocke had the idea that solidified Z-D's standing in the world. I am ready to lead this planet into the future."

The panel was quiet. The pure determination of Zonfer's attitude struck them. Finally, Stinton broke the uncomfortable silence.

"Deshlocke's plan was ingenious. He planned the Great Slaughter immediately before the International Election Day. Tomorrow, Z-Defense Industries is predicted to win in a landslide victory. The PR campaign has caused people to gain trust in the company. Deshlocke assured the press that Z-D had nothing to do with the killings. As far as the press and citizenry are concerned, the governments ordered Directive 84, not the company. It appears that the fear factor has worked, sir. This time tomorrow, you will be the ruler of our planet."

Zonfer once again turned to his wonderful view. He looked into the reflection of his eyes, the scar taunting and reminding him of his actions. He scowled in intense defiance as he thought about his supernatural visit from the Seer. His ambitions and father's expectations were about to be fulfilled.

The U.N.-mandated international election took place the next day. The outcome was as Stinton and the pundits expected. Zonfer now held absolute power over the planet. Zonfer's will was now the Earth's.

Chapter 13: The Beginning of the End – 3025 A.D.

The streets of Vienna were flooded with activity. Larger-than-life banners displaying the Z-Defense motto and crest scrolled across every street and public area. The Austrian people were proud of their native son, who now possessed global supremacy over all. The Austrian financial markets immediately reaped the benefits of Z-Defense's sudden rise to global power. Stocks skyrocketed. Z-D Inc. saw the largest single-day rise in worth ever recorded. With his incredible wealth and vast infrastructure of forces, the fifty-one-year-old Zonfer was seemingly invincible.

An older and bored Blaine Danken traversed the sidewalks of his homeland. He glared at the banners in disdain, trying his best to ignore them. He sported a close-cut beard and mid-length hair. Cast casually over his shoulder was a gym bag filled with the needed materials for a good workout. He still wore his old AAF outfit. He longed for the days of the War for Humanity. His bloodlust still existed but he now managed to keep it under control. He found that working out, particularly lifting weights, took the edge off of his cravings for murder. However, he didn't completely abstain from questionable activities.

Immediately after the Great Slaughter, Danken left Z-Defense. He gave no reason to Zonfer, just a vague message left in his inbox. It was all the same to Zonfer. He had always found Danken somewhat difficult to deal with. During the last few years, Danken had been secretly compiling a Resistance force against Zonfer's rule. The force had already attempted small-scale attacks at various outposts throughout Austria—nothing serious, just provocative actions.

Danken had always loved Vienna. The Parliament building was a frequent stop for him. Even a psychopath could appreciate the beauty of the structure. As he passed it, he couldn't help but think about destroying it. It would be a pleasure to destroy such a grand structure. The thought passed quickly. He continued on his way to his destination, "Planet Fit." It was the premiere fitness center in the country. Every famous bodybuilder had frequented it at some point.

As he entered, he observed another large Z-Defense banner splayed across the Planet Fit front windowpane. He shook his head in disgust. "Not here too," he thought to himself. The now-familiar scent of testosterone-laced sweat invaded his nostrils. In a passive-aggressive manner, Planet Fit's atmosphere fulfilled something inside Danken that nothing else but killing could. It calmed him.

He approached the dumbbell storing rack and picked up two fifty-pounders. He noticed that his regular spot was vacant. He took it and began his muscle tearing. In the reflection of the massive mirror, he noticed a stranger whom he hadn't seen at Planet Fit before. He was unbelievably enormous. He was spread out on one of the benches doing a nonstop set with a bar filled with what Danken calculated to be around five-hundred pounds. The man was a monster. After the hulk had completed his set, Danken observed him take a leisurely stroll to the vending machines. He watched him procure a bottle of water. "He would be perfect," Danken thought.

Danken sat his muscle-building apparatus upon the floor and started for the vending machines. The massive man sat at one of the stools next to the machines, gulping down his water. His height, at seven foot one, was as impressive as his bulk. Danken got his own beverage and stood near Hercules.

"So, how much were you benching over there?" Danken asked.

"Me?" the man asked, seeming surprised at the question.

"No one else here, bud," said Danken.

"I've been doing about five-fifty for the past year. Can't seem to break that ceiling."

Danken's right cheek raised and he laughed. "Break it? Goddamn—"

"This is something I take really seriously. I'm hoping that someday I could be a professional bodybuilder."

"Name?" Danken inquired.

"Huh? Oh—Fillmore Jayson. You?"

"Blaine Danken—just call me Danken."

"Right. What's your deal?" Jayson asked.

Danken's infamous crazy stare ensued. "Glad you asked, friend. Let me ask you something. How do you feel about—" Danken's voice trailed off as he motioned toward yet another Z-D banner.

"What?" said Jayson, tilting his head.

"About Z-D getting all the power?" Danken said softly.

Jayson shrugged. "It's fine—I guess. Better an Austrian company than an American."

Danken flinched. "So you're just fine with one man holding all the power in the world? And I assume you think Hitler was a great guy—right?" he said sarcastically.

Jayson was already feeling the pressure of Danken's influence. Danken possessed an ability to make a person feel dejected over his own beliefs if they didn't jive with Danken's. The monstrous man recoiled and bowed his head.

"No—no—not at all. I guess you're right. But what can we do about it?" Jayson said somewhat sheepishly.

"That's what I do, Jayson. I've been organizing a Resistance to Zonfer's power. His rule simply can't continue unopposed. I'm hoping—someday—that Zonfer will pay for his arrogance."

Jayson's attention was fixated on the psychopath. Danken's ability to manipulate and deceive were that of a true cult leader.

When he observed the look in the huge man's face, Danken knew he already had him.

"I'm in. Hell—I've been selling televisions for the past five years. You're the one I've been waiting for," Jayson said without a moment's hesitation.

Danken grinned and slapped the big man on the shoulder.

"I believe this is beginning of a beautiful friendship."

***

The Zonfer Era of human existence had officially begun. The bland, boring war-free environment made Blaine Danken restless. His ambitions for supremacy had caused him to leave Z-Defense and form an opposition group to Zonfer's rule. This ragtag group became known as the Resistance.

And so the human race atoned for its actions in the most extreme manner. The Plague came and the human race was exiled from their only universal safe haven. The planet Tento was now humans' only hope and home for the future.

Chapter 14: 20 Years after Arrival (A.A.)

With the chaotic civil conflict between Zonfer's forces and Danken's Resistance now only a distant memory, mankind's utopian existence on Tento had gradually taken shape. The Erectorbots worked day and night constructing the human race's new home. A fortified gateway marked the Capital of Humanity, Tento City. Its glistening, golden walls symbolically portrayed mankind's new reality. The walls provided ample protection from Tento's more dangerous natives such as the Tilothans. Zonfer's loyal defense forces patrolled the streets, creating a sense of security for the citizenry.

Slowly but surely, the human race was making the planet Tento its own. Zonfer's planetary development team projected that, within the next thirty years, expansion into the more remote regions of the planet would increase tenfold. Zonfer found himself intrigued by the Tentonian wilderness. The craters and fissures, the ebbing and flowing plains, the winding rivers, the brutal climate, the unorthodox cloud patterns—all of these qualities piqued Zonfer's interest. A small outpost in the harsh wastelands of the planet had been prepared for him to perform research on organisms and compile cartographical information.

Tento City embodied the essence of mankind's determination to survive. The streets hummed with constant activity. Businesses boomed and families flourished, with the population reaching previously unimaginable numbers. Crime and violence were negligible factors. There was the occasional rebellion by determined individuals hell-bent on overthrowing Zonfer, but they never got far. The citizens realized that Zonfer had earned the right to call himself the leader of mankind. Setting aside all of his transgressions, the man had single-handedly saved the human race from extinction.

Several memorials had been built to honor fallen heroes of the past. The most impressive was the Great Slaughter memorial. A massive, golden statue of a grieving mother collapsed on the ground and holding her murdered infant stood in front of Zonfer's headquarters in Tento City. The inscription beneath the statue read, "In eternal remembrance of the collective sacrifice of mankind. We shall never forget." —Wolfgang Zonfer.

The Great Slaughter victims were widely considered martyrs for mankind's survival by most people, including Zonfer. During one of his liaisons with the Seers, they had told him, "All things, tragic and otherwise, happen for a reason. You were allowed to carry out the actions you performed. You may never know why." Zonfer took this to heart. It aided in alleviating his weary conscience.

Zonfer had spent the better part of the last twenty-plus years attempting to make amends for the unthinkable atrocity. Through his own personal journey, he now understood that every action had a reaction, a consequence. The human race had taken many wrong turns during its time in existence. Zonfer's Great Slaughter proved to be the breaking point. Through the punishment of exile, he hoped that whatever greater power existed would forgive his crime and not condemn the entire human race. Zonfer's New Beginning appeared to be a successful venture.

The Renaissance still resided on the same spot where it had touched down. This site would also be ordained a memorial at some point in the future. For the time being, Zonfer decided that it should remain in working order in case of an unforeseen event requiring a safe haven for Tento's citizenry.

Much was still unknown about Tento's brutal nature. Zonfer's science department collected and studied the biological information of its new intergalactic residence. The randomness of the planet's weather and season cycle puzzled all minds involved with the research. Just when a definite cycle appeared to be taking shape, the planet decided to make a turn. In certain cases, unexplained phenomena such as electrical storms and massive storm fronts had wiped out entire communities. For this reason, Zonfer relied on the Renaissance as a backup plan. Earth's original conditions had been perfectly emulated inside the enormous craft, making it the ideal shelter.

Human beings had been permitted a second chance to live in harmony with their surroundings and with one another. The now psychologically healed and enlightened Wolfgang Zonfer vowed to preserve his race and be its salvation.

***

A past-retirement-age Dr. Hannibal Schiller stood inside a dank and grungy room filled with seemingly useless computer systems. "What the hell does he expect from me, a miracle?" Schiller muttered to himself in bewilderment.

The task in front of him was daunting. He found himself in one of the long-abandoned science labs recently discovered by Zonfer's planetary development team. It was the most remote of any other pre-Earth Exodus structures. Zonfer had ordered Schiller, now the head of his science department, to rehabilitate the outpost and attempt to recover any data from the old servers. It wouldn't be an easy feat. The systems had been dormant for a very long time and it was likely that they wouldn't reboot for anyone. Schiller decided to deal with what he knew best first. He squinted at one of the old, rusty desktops. He swept off the surface as best he could and set up his laptop. He activated his still experimental bioscanner software and hoped it would do what it was built to do.

"Well, this job isn't going to do itself," Schiller sighed with only himself to talk to. He found the main power board for the facility and crawled underneath the console. He inserted a flashlight into his mouth and took a deep breath. With teeth clenched, he examined the internal workings of the power console. He shook his head in disgust. "I'm not an electrical engineer. Why did Zonfer think I could do this alone?" he thought in frustration. He tweaked a few wires with his snub-nosed pliers, hoping for a miracle. Then he heard clicks and beeps emitting from somewhere.

"Couldn't be that easy," he muttered with the flashlight still between his teeth.

He scooted out from under the main console and looked at the old systems. They were all inactive. Realizing his tweaking had done nothing, he suddenly became aware that the clicks and beeps were coming from his laptop. The new build of the bioscanner software appeared to be processing at a furious rate. It was collecting and organizing the biological makeup of mankind's new home. As Schiller observed the data, the similarity to Earth astonished him. He smiled in amazement while he skimmed the readouts. "Fantastic," he thought happily. "Taber's programming alterations will surely make this program the wave of the future."

Suddenly, the servers boomed and then hummed with activity as they resurrected after lying dormant for hundreds of years. Old Hannibal Schiller was quite proud of himself. But he soon realized he had nothing to do with the sudden operational state of the servers. Schiller followed the laptop and the bioscanner's progress. Apparently, the program could sense the hibernating information and decided to awaken the servers from their slumber. It immediately began downloading all information from the ancient equipment.

"This program is only in beta!" Schiller shouted out loud in delight and amazement.

***

Zonfer's new headquarters made his old digs appear lackluster. He spent the majority of his spare time on the Renaissance during the construction period mapping out the plans for his new base of operations. He kept the basic layout of his Earth home as the framework for this new monstrosity. It was made up entirely of cloned Earthling materials. Through bioengineering techniques, Zonfer's science department had found a way to accurately recreate every mineral on Earth. Hence, in terms of materials, mankind didn't miss a beat. Because of this technological advancement, the Erectorbots had an unlimited amount of materials to work with and building could continue indefinitely.

Zonfer was eighty-one years old and weary. But not looking a day over forty, he was now certain that the benefits of his Tier One conditioning outweighed the tortures he had endured. Every member of Zonfer's defense force underwent a mandatory conditioning program. Hannibal Schiller had perfected the Tier Five conditioning techniques and their implementation was elementary.

It pleased him that it appeared that mankind had escaped damnation. He had enjoyed the past twenty years, leading his people, studying different forms of government, combining ideas from different systems and implementing them into the fold, studying the latest astronomical and astrological finds. Zonfer spent ninety percent of his time reading and governing. The other ten percent he dedicated to sleep. The time was fast approaching for Zonfer to step down from his post. He now spent most of his days assembling the way government would function after he was gone. The final preparations were being made for him to take his post in the Tentonian wilderness. This was where he fully intended on spending his last days.

Zonfer wondered why the Seers hadn't contacted him recently. He found himself thinking about these meetings more than ever. Why had they chosen him? Who were they? At times, he wondered if they were just a hallucination. Then, every time he looked into a mirror, the scar on his face reminded him of their reality. As he sat in his main quarters, he closed his eyes and attempted to will a meeting. But nothing happened.

He sighed and walked slowly to his desk. He pulled out a pad of paper and a pen and began writing. Realizing everyone would want to know his full life story, he was slowly compiling ideas for his memoirs. Suddenly, he wasn't able to control his hand. He stopped writing and shook his hand in frustration. He regained control and began to write again. Then, the loss of control returned. But this time his hand continued to write. Zonfer stared at the page as the Seers made contact through his handwriting.

"We are no hallucination," the page read.

***

Schiller found himself lost in the bioscanner readouts. He shifted his attention to the room he was working in. He gazed around like a child at a carnival. All at once it struck him that this mission should be considered a privilege and not a tedious task. In this very structure, hundreds of years ago, scientists just like Schiller were attempting to unravel the mysteries of this new planet. Planet Earth's indifference had terminated the research far too prematurely. With Schiller's bioscanner technology, hundreds of years' worth of research could be completed in hours. This was a truly exciting time for the seasoned veteran of science.

He continued to study the information that poured out of the program. In each specimen, he noticed a unique code structure. For the first time in human history, a scientist looked upon complex, extraterrestrial biological information. As the bioscanner continued its work, Schiller made an astonishing discovery. His eyes widened.

"Wait a minute—it can't be. I need to check that again," he whispered.

He accessed the recently downloaded information. He scanned the lines in search of the biocode anomaly he thought he had seen. He found it and confirmed the information. The old scientist activated his communication link with Zonfer's science department.

"Kilman, it's Hannibal. I need to speak with Zonfer immediately."

"Yes, sir. Please hold," the science department communications official said.

After a brief wait, a strong voice greeted the scientist.

"Dr. Schiller, how is the recovery mission going?"

"It was a rough start, sir, but things are going more smoothly now. The recovery mission isn't why I'm contacting you."

"I'm glad to hear that. Those old research documents will be very useful. Is there a problem?" Zonfer inquired.

"I wouldn't call it a problem—necessarily. But I thought it warranted your immediate attention."

"What is it, doctor?"

"The bioscanner picked up an anomaly in Tento's biocode. I checked it multiple times and it's definitely correct," Schiller said and paused.

"Well, doctor?"

"I'm sorry, sir. I'm searching for the right way to explain this. Sometime in the past, this planet was home to another race. The residuals of their biocode are present in some of the readouts."

"Are you saying that we might not be alone here?"

"Certainly not—this is why I was unsure about telling you this. First of all, the bioscanner is still very experimental and might be misreading something. Second, the readouts clearly show that these are only markings left behind by something. Now, the obvious question would be: Is it possible that these former residents might make a return? Unfortunately, I can't answer that question. But I wanted you to know the circumstances for your consumption," Schiller concluded.

"All right, doctor, I appreciate the report. Please report back to me when the research data is archived."

"Yes, sir, Schiller out."

As he sat in his majestic headquarters, Zonfer folded his hands and scowled. The New Beginning was in full swing and he didn't want negative press to dull the optimism. He decided to keep Schiller's discovery a secret. He continued writing after the brief interruption.

Silence pervaded Zonfer's office. His advisors had their marching orders to guide the human race past Zonfer's time. All the preparations for Zonfer's stepping down were in full swing. The Erectorbots now focused on building the New Senate Complex. This was where the new leadership for the human race would govern from. Planetary elections were slated for 30 A.A. As he penned the last letters of the Tentonian Constitution and the Bill of Will, he rested his writing implement upon his desk for the last time. He exited his office and met one of his security forces.

"Strauss, please deliver this to Advisor Stinton. This is the will of the future."

Zonfer handed a steel briefcase to the loyal member of the Defense Force.

"Yes, sir—sir, I would like to thank you."

"For what, son?"

"For saving us all."

For the first time in what seemed like decades, Wolfgang Zonfer smiled. As he walked the halls of his headquarters for the last time, Zonfer realized that his father's vision had been fully realized. Mankind had gotten its second chance. Whatever humans did with it would be up to the generations of the future. Zonfer approached the transport that would spirit him to his final destination. Before he boarded, he looked back at the shimmering façade of his headquarters. As the latest version of the Griffin Wing lifted off, another smile lit up Zonfer's face.

The End

Epilogue: A *Tentonian Chronicle* Series: *Exploring Human History*

"The Tyrannical Savior: An Intellectual Analysis of Wolfgang Zonfer"
January 01, 0025 A.A.
By: Hans Witheim - *The Tentonian Chronicle*

By all accounts, during his existence as an Earthling, Wolfgang Zonfer embodied a ruthless tyrant. Through no fault of his own, his psyche and ideologies were manipulated; he was a victim of experimental science that should have been banned before a single application attempt.

His more atrocious actions could be explained by his fear of loss. Given his relationship with his father, one could deduce that Zonfer constantly prepared for change. Over the years, he began to fear that change. Finally, in a position to nullify that change happening, Zonfer did so. Perhaps this small understanding could help Tentonians move past their feelings of disgust over some of Zonfer's revolting deeds. Most sane people cannot accept the idea of a decent member of society, let alone a cultural hero, extinguishing a large portion of our kind. Let there be no illusions. Mr. Zonfer's decision to systematically eliminate all of his political rivals was disgusting as well as criminal. However, one can find deeper understanding of this particular action given the man's tribulations and tortures.

Collectively, as members of the human race, we should all be able to agree that if it weren't for Mr. Zonfer's unshakable will and prophetic vision, mankind would be extinct. During the time of the enigmatic Plague, Zonfer experienced a rebirth of conscience. If he had been in that mindset—that social awareness—before the Great Slaughter, one wonders if it would have happened at all. The very logical argument could be made that Mr. Zonfer wounded the potential for great human advancement with this grievous action. With his indiscriminate bloodletting, Zonfer damaged our species, potential geniuses undoubtedly present in the millions slaughtered.

Perhaps it was a prophetic logistical decision, beyond his knowledge, some higher power guiding his hand in preparation for mankind's new predicament. After all, those extra members of the human race would have made the Exodus from Earth considerably more difficult. The answers will forever be elusive.

Fortunately for Tento, Zonfer is still alive. Perhaps, before his death, he will clarify for us his motives and motivations during that awful time in human history. Personally, I doubt the man would not care to discuss it nor perhaps even remember, but the possibility isn't entirely nonexistent.

In the final chapter of his life, Zonfer is still a servant to history. Currently, he resides in a small outpost in the farthest-reaching area of the Tentonian wilderness, supposedly mapping and researching all aspects of Tentonian life. The man's advanced years have afforded him a vast store of knowledge and understanding. One marvels at Zonfer's intelligence. Most who have met the man are changed forever. Apparently, according to many personal accounts, Zonfer has become gentle in his elderly years. Fishing in Tentonian streams for days on end, smiling and laughing at the sight of small creatures—difficult to imagine given the man's history and past transgressions.

The only viable explanation is that Mr. Zonfer did truly experience a transformation of personality. Perhaps his biological makeup recognized the toxic levels of brutality that he had accumulated, finally "rolling back" his psychosis.

Nevertheless, we should all look on high to whatever, if any, higher power exists and give thanks. If it weren't for Mr. Zonfer's moral awakening, we would all be nonentities.

"A Brief Tentonian History Lesson"
February 02, 0025 A.A.
By: Hans Witheim – *The Tentonian Chronicle*

Planet Tento's early relationship with mankind is a peculiar one. Scientists worldwide were baffled by the discovery of Tento. It was as if the planet had been birthed from nothing. Countless astronomers and space telescopes had thoroughly researched the area and found nothing in the way of inhabitable planets. Evan Tento, a passionate astronomer who lived to observe the cosmos, stumbled upon it during a night of intensive cataloging for the university he worked for at the time. He speculated that it might have been expelled from a white hole. While the collective scientific community didn't put any stock in this hypothesis, it was the closest thing to an answer anyone could muster.

Soon after its discovery, all U.N. participating nations on Earth met and discussed the possibility of an international space expedition to the planet, the first mission being a small team of astronomers including the discoverer himself. All parties involved agreed, and the U.N. Erectorbots were immediately launched toward Tento. Located in the nearest galaxy to the Milky Way, travel wasn't a problem. With modern space travel means, the trip could be made in a few years. Cryostasis technology had been used for centuries in deep space missions and had been perfected.

The only other scientists who had the privilege of researching Tento while on its soil either left or had been exiled hundreds of years prior. Any scientist worth his salt knew about the United Nations-organized mission to Tento in 2400 A.D. (Earth Timeline) and the conflicts that had taken place between the various nations' science departments.

For reasons lost to history, the various international science departments descended into all-out war on Tento. The U.N. received reports of rival factions planting bombs in one another's research facilities. Eventually, it culminated in a breaking point, with the U.N. sending peacekeeping forces to quell the violence. All hostile entities were imprisoned on the U.N. craft and prevented from ever returning to Tento on future missions.

This marked the only interesting era of Tento's history until Wolfgang Zonfer's reign. After research of the basics and preliminary tests of the conditions, people lost interest. Tento's future seemed to be doomed to obscurity. But fortunately for mankind, Tento had been discovered and was known to be habitable. No one, most of all Evan Tento, could have ever imagined the importance of his discovery.

PART III

ORIGINS OF ANNIHILATION

Prologue

Last Memoirs of the Great Conqueror Wolfgang Zonfer
Info Capsule #3010
Transcribed through: 5aMbot 19, model 1

"REPARATIONS & PREPARATIONS"

His enemies finally pooling at his feet (in more ways than one), Wolfgang Zonfer suddenly found a few moments of clarity. His empire had succeeded in bringing peace and—most importantly—saving humanity from itself and the by-products of its once-doomed existence. But he was unsure of how the Tentonians would fare in times to come.

The Plague had continued to rage and build to a catastrophic maelstrom of efficient destruction. Zonfer kept eyes constantly glued to its progress reports, his gleaming eyes lit by the backwash of flashing consoles within the darkened room. The Plague's strength had grown to a mighty fury, reducing nearly all it encountered to an unrecognizable graveyard. Earth was left a barren dump of ooze and dust, with swirling winds taking the surviving particles (whatever horrendous form they occupied) and tossing them irreverently to all corners of the wasteland.

It was widely believed by the citizens of Tento that Earth was now a fiery place. The sun was so blotted that its natural light was obscured, leaving only a few mercurial rays of disease and fever penetrating the cloud layer to shed scant light on whatever grotesque and mutant organisms could thrive in such filth.

Zonfer had other thoughts to occupy his mind: he was heir-less and unsure of how to hand over his empire. He suffered nightmares, seeing this exchange of power suffering the unfortunate fate of a child handling a glass sculpture of unmentionable delicacy. He balked at the idea of attempting to place such enormous power upon the shoulders of a raging, rabid Tilothan, its barely-formed motor skills failing as it shook with extreme nervousness. He could already imagine the abundance of instant ulcers the ill-prepared creature would form.

He often wondered how the old societies had managed to simply switch power from person to person, as though rewiring some tiresomely intricate jury-rigged motherboard. Zonfer was old, but he

still remembered the silly politics of the now-ancient
governments. Some had merit, he could admit now, though he had
not seen it then, and Zonfer found he wanted the best for his people.
They had accepted his burden of dictatorship for perhaps too long.
 Zonfer's days were a blur for him now, broken into shards of
fragmented memories, all swirling about his central preoccupation—
the question of who should be his successor.

Then on one unforgettable day (now celebrated as a statutory
holiday on Tento), while conducting research in the Library of Tento
in the History of the Tentonians, Era I section, Zonfer took the time
to pull his nose out of the outdated media—containing records of the
former ruling styles of Earth before him—to glance at the scrambled
notes he'd made. They looked foreign and much like the diary of a
madman, as the saying went.

Just then he looked over and saw his cabinet approach him—
a group of men of various ages, mostly old like Zonfer, but some
fresh as morning dew. Zonfer had found that he hated to waste
talent, regardless of the other characteristics of the individual in
which it was encased. (The people of Tento would never let Zonfer
forget this rather prominent feature of his personality, especially
considering what it had cost him and the Tentonians with Danken.)
 However, opinions remained generally high for Zonfer and his
administration. Some reports indicated that although life on Tento
was harsh, most citizens found this life more rewarding than the one
they had lived on Earth.

There, everything was wasted, spent, and gratification was
instant. On Tento, people worked for their living, and found a
cleansing ritual in the frugal though pleasant lives they lived.
At least that held true for the middle-class citizens. The wealthy felt
the change more painfully; they were far less patient and less tolerant
of such "down-grading." But of course, even on Tento the upper
class found ways to enjoy life more than perhaps they should have.
 Zonfer's attention snapped back to the moment at hand. His
thoughts had been disjointed and rambling of late, mostly due to the
overworked problem of political succession.

As he watched his advisors in an angry mob marching toward
his table, Zonfer saw the future unfold before him, as if witnessing an
expert of the near-lost art of origami, filmed and played in fast-
motion.

"Zonfer, you've missed most of your meetings for the week!"
said one of the herd harshly. "In fact, you've been avoidant and

distant for some time. We've practically been running Tento City for you!" another chimed in.

At this, the last element for the crystallization of an idea already birthed in Zonfer's mind fell into place. The idea teemed with life and possibility.

"Gentleman," he said, "the problem has been solved. I have been pondering the succession of power to take place after my demise. I wanted it to be a secret project so that no influences but my own interfered. Apparently, secret though it was, its tolls were not. I will be making a speech tonight, of importance unmatched since our original freedom from fear and war at the conclusion of the Civil War."

Zonfer's advisors were shocked at the gravity of the situation. It was a heavy load for heads already filled with worry; the only thing keeping the panic back was the devout faith his advisors had in him to solve problems. All they needed to do was look out the windows at the Tentonian landscape to see proof of this.

***

Throughout the day calls were made telling of the great news Zonfer was about to reveal. Nearly all lines of communication on Tento were in use. Excitement ran high; the citizens sensed the magnitude of the speech. Zonfer himself was no exception. With a smile on his face from the contentment of a decision well made, he made a few calls of his own, requiring of the recipients only an answer and a promise of secrecy, at least until after the speech.
 That night, Tentonians crowded around their holo-sets, or gathered elbow to curious elbow in the Central Square of Tento City, eagerly awaiting what important news was about to be divulged to them on the square's huge holo-screen.

Zonfer appeared. He began solemnly: "Greetings, my good citizens of Tento. Long have I ruled for you, and longer I wish I could, but I am old and tired. The Battle against the Resistance and the settling of Tento have been more than enough excitement for one Administration." Citizens exchanged befuddled looks. "I have decided to stand down from my position of duty and responsibility and to leave control of Tento to you, the more than capable citizens who have proven their worth and love of Tento over and over again." A cheer went up, but the citizens were still confused. "A special Senate has been appointed, hand-picked by me, to act as the senators of old, taking in requests of the people, and acting on them appropriately. All members of this Senate have been notified and are here with me tonight, having only learned of and accepted this responsibility today." With a gesture of respect and a tear in his eye, Zonfer indicated a curtain behind him. With all the majesty of the grand theaters of the world, the curtain whirled away, revealing the Senate in a breathtaking display. Each senator came forward one by one, with Zonfer shaking their hands, symbolizing the exchange of power. Each made a short speech, promising hard work and open ears.

At the close of the ceremonies, Zonfer announced, "You have been delivered, people of Tento!" More enthusiastic cheers went up, fists pumped in happiness, and everyone was swept into the energy of the moment. It was also announced that Zonfer wanted the Tentonians to approve of his appointments. A strange and awkward voting took place over the next few days. Some of the Tentonians had never voted, knowing only Zonfer's rule in their lifetimes. Perhaps as a result of this, or the lack of other running parties, or perhaps because the citizens of Tento were so well pleased with Zonfer's appointments, but at the end of the voting period, it was unanimous—Tento was officially under new management. It was decided before Zonfer completely disappeared from the governmental body that the current Senate members should rule out the rest of their days or until they felt unfit to govern. A majority could oust any member, but the citizens would be able to offer opinions as well. Many checks and balances were set up. Legislation was a lengthy process to complete, as an honest attempt to represent all views was made, and much voting and re-voting occurred. However, all steps were completed efficiently; it was simply the sheer number of steps that caused the delays. As work was always being done, the Tentonians didn't mind, and in fact gradually learned to enjoy living at this new, more measured pace.

As a final act of decision-making, Zonfer suggested to his new Senate that the people choose its constituent members in the future. Then, seeing all was in place as he and his people desired, Zonfer retired and quietly disappeared, his whereabouts known to none.

***

Zonfer spent the next few years of his life making amends for his former dictatorial actions; repenting and making reparations to the groups he had hurt or lost in the crossfire. He encouraged the construction of monuments, he observed holidays, did occasional interviews, and enjoyed being an ordinary citizen. No one knew where he lived, his former palace having been converted to Senate chambers that were more impressive than any history had seen.

 Too slowly to notice, Zonfer made his presence increasingly less frequent. With a wily grin on his face, he would close the door to the cottage where he'd lived for the past few months. Located on the as yet unexplored outskirts of Tento City, its occupant enjoyed a peaceful existence within its humble walls.

One night, taking a torch in one hand and his freedom in the other, Zonfer burned his cottage to the ground, disappearing into the smoke of his public funeral pyre. He was never seen again.

***

In fact, few knew about the fire. Its evidence was discovered many years later—a bizarre husk of a building, shrouded in mystery. The military had no answers; it was disregarded as just another old hideout of the Resistance, all of which had been mapped and turned into monuments. It figuratively shrugged its shoulders to historians and investigative agencies, and the question kept being passed until it reached the people themselves. Zonfer's home found its history obscured in years to come by folklore and word of mouth (not to mention several high-grossing holo-documentaries). It became the stuff of legend, told to tiny Tentonian children to maintain good behavior. They were warned that the "Ghost of the Wilderness" would get them if they didn't behave. Perhaps that is what Zonfer had wanted; perhaps he even ensured that certain parties would deliver results of any investigation in a certain way. Or perhaps not, and thus knowledge of it passed into eternity, and out of all minds, Zonfer's included.

For Zonfer was not dead, nor quite ready to die. He had set up one final secret before leaving office—an outpost station, to be used for the discovery and recording of the Tentonian habitat. A skeleton crew of scientists were the only ones to know of Zonfer's existence. He had decided to spend the remainder of his years exploring his lost passions of topography, geography, and geology. The scientists never revealed that Zonfer was still alive, for they had no desire to leave their outpost, content in study and scarcely aware

Zonfer had disappeared anyway. Zonfer had chosen them
specifically for their studious discretion. Besides, no one there had
even seen him; they just found mysterious packages of instructions
left at their workstations and knew only that they worked for a very
discreet pioneer.

More life and strength remained in Zonfer than he had
originally anticipated, though to everyone but himself he was little
more than a ghost and a memory. He would go on long outings,
develop his charts, fill in information, and be content just
discovering. He would signal the outpost when he felt he needed to
return for sustenance, or to drop off data packets, or just to see what
work was being done with his maps, photos, and observations. A
drop ship would appear for him and he would hop on back to the
lab.

Zonfer invented and designed survival gear, wrote numerous
manuals on the do's and don'ts of the Tentonian wilderness, and
even discovered alternate fuels. He invented several new industries,
all in secret, of course. All told, Zonfer discovered and traversed
nearly 58 percent of Tento's landscape, and left detailed instructions
and recommendations for completion. He hand-picked the new
pioneers of this frontier, feeling he knew best how the ancient
societies had felt when Earth was still separated into territories and
"New" and "Old" Worlds.

Spending his last days in a facility separated from but near the
lab, when his health finally did fail him, the great warrior, leader, and
explorer recorded his remaining memoirs. After his death they were
quietly entered into the records of the Library of Tento, to perhaps
be discovered by accident many years later by an aspiring young
academic.

With a device hooked to his brain to record his final thoughts
and a Transcriberbot waiting nearby to convert the information,
Zonfer lay upon his deathbed. With his last breaths hitching in his
throat, Zonfer gazed out his window at the Tentonian landscape and
the stars beyond the night sky, imagining he could make out the
shimmer of Earth. He contemplated the Plague, wondering vaguely if
he had caused it or could have prevented it.

By morning Zonfer had exhaled his last breath and was
pronounced dead by the Medibot at his bedside. His body was
disposed of in accordance with his wishes, which few knew of. Once
the operation was complete, all of Zonfer's robotic aides self-
destructed, leaving a neat little debris pile that caused the scientists of

the outpost to scratch their balding heads. But then, they were used to strange occurrences around the complex by now.

Recorded only in a file that might never be discovered were Zonfer's dying musings. The morning sun shone upon his face as he wondered...

"What is Earth like now?"

Chapter 1: The New World – 200 A.A. (after arrival)

The Tentonian landscape remained the same since its discovery. However, since the arrival of the Earthling refugees two hundred years prior, the production of new buildings and the discovery of important archeological sites never ceased. Tento City had a new name and face. Zonfer City, as it was now known, stood tall and proud. Boundless skyscrapers littered the landscape and skyline. Aerial transportation of various kinds could be heard in all the major cities on Tento; however, the majority of inhabitants decided to reside in Tento's super city—Zonfer City.

Hovercrafts were the main mode of transportation for the majority of the Tentonian citizens. The affluent could afford Transwarpers, miniature wormhole creators worn on the wrist like a watch. These were entirely experimental. Tests were conducted during the production of these devices and, overall, they were deemed safe by all major governmental agencies.

The Zonfer Era had long passed. After Wolfgang Zonfer's death, there was a major power struggle between his closest advisors and associates. In the end, none of them came to power. As much foresight and intelligence as Zonfer had, he never named a successor. This was a very deliberate action. Zonfer enacted an especially secret commission during the last years of his life. He organized a group called The New Senate. The group comprised close allies of Zonfer as well as former enemies. It was a kind of "who's who" of Zonfer's history. All of them had one thing in common: the knowledge that Zonfer was not a man to be crossed.

After the initial group of New Senate officials had died off, democracy took hold. As the old senators died, they were replaced by elections. The laws of the land were written and enforced by this body. History, as it seemed, was repeating itself.

Over the years, the subject of the Exodus from Earth became more palatable for Tentonians to discuss. It was a topic desperately in need of serious discussion.

What were its origins? Could there be a cure?

"What was Earth like now?"

***

Dr. Tobias Schiller stood at the exit from Zonfer City leading into the Tentonian wilderness. The exit gates creaked and moaned. They were massive, as one might imagine the gates of hell to appear. The gate attendant glared in Schiller's general direction.

"Papers please," the attendant requested.

Schiller slowly pulled out a small, badge-like object. He handed it to the attendant, who examined it thoroughly. He paused and looked up at Schiller with a humbled expression.

"I apologize, sir. If I had known your security status, I wouldn't have wasted your time."

"It's your job. No need for an apology. However, I should be getting on my way," Schiller replied.

"Yes, sir," the attendant politely responded.

Schiller was an impressive-looking man. He stood at six feet one inch tall, with long, cropped, jet black hair and the popular Tentonian choice for facial hair, the Fu Manchu. His mission would be a daunting one. The Tentonian Institute of Science (TIS) had assigned him the task of cataloging various Tentonian life forms. The former residents of Earth had been living on Tento for almost three centuries yet little to nothing was known about native Tentonian life forms. The motivation was always present to learn about this new world. However, TIS was only recently capable of putting any kind of study into action. The old studies were hundreds of years old. The new technologies and better understanding of reality would be a great tool in understanding the complex makeup of this planet's chemistry.

The old studies revealed little in terms of life forms. Basic chemical makeup and action/reaction thereof were explored and well documented. Surprising as it seemed, little to no research had been done on actual life forms. This was Dr. Schiller's task. TIS wanted a thorough and concise report on all Tentonian life forms.

Obviously, this mission would be long and tedious. Schiller was the only scientist at TIS who was willing to even consider this massive undertaking. Hence, his only company during this task would be his own thoughts.

Schiller was a deep thinker. He liked being alone with nothing but the distant sound of the strong Tentonian winds in the background. It wasn't uncommon for him to get lost in his own thoughts for hours at a time (months, in this case). He knew that he was the only one capable of fulfilling the obligations that TIS set forth for this mission.

Perhaps subconsciously he had always known that he would be accorded this task in the future. Years prior to the discussion of this mission, Schiller spent years researching the old studies that had been done during Zonfer's reign. Some of the data packets dated back to before the massive Exodus from Earth. This time period fascinated Schiller. His feeling was that this period marked the true end of human decency. Most history books painted Zonfer as a caring leader, a tyrant who learned to truly care about the people he ruled. Schiller found it impossible to accept that a man who could kill innocent women and children ever had a shred of decency in his body. The Zonfer reign had its share of outrageous events. One event, however, overshadowed the rest.

It was widely speculated among the religious that the Plague was punishment to the human race for Zonfer's drastic "cleansing" of the human race. They held the thought that actions so atrocious must have some sort of consequence. Debate on this matter would continue for many generations.

Fortunately, most of the research materials that had been compiled by the first group of scientists to work on the Tentonian landscape were cataloged, recorded, and preserved in the massive database of knowledge that was the Library of Tento. Many hours of research were clocked in on these reports. Most of the root understandings of Tento's biological makeup came from this research and the resulting reports.

In terms of life forms, research of the old studies on Tento revealed more questions than answers. It appeared that most, if not all, of the life forms discussed in the reports were extinct. To everybody's dismay, however, the Tilothans were still roaming. The monstrous creatures roamed the outskirts of Zonfer City regularly. They didn't bother the inhabitants. No one knew or really cared what the Tilothans ate. Perhaps this was something that Schiller would learn during his studies.

The sight of these creatures was truly astonishing. The first human encounter with a Tilothan, although indirect, was memorable. On the first mission to Tento, research scientists and prestigious professors from various universities were the only travelers. Evan Tento, the astronomer who discovered the planet, was the only other passenger.

***

Evan peered through the large, spherical window next to him. He observed the landscape of this new world that he had uncovered buried within the infinite vastness of the cosmos. He was dumbfounded by one topographical feature of the planet—how perfectly flat it was. A brief survey of what he had encountered so far indicated the presence of hilly or mountainous terrain was sparse. Fissures and dropping points into boundless blackness seemed far more prevalent. As the craft continued on its journey, Evan listened intently.

One of the scientists suddenly broke the near silence. "Does anyone hear that?"

Beneath the deep, pulsating, monotone hum of the craft's power core, another reverberation was heard. It was thunderous. However, they couldn't tell if the source of the sound was close or in the distance.

Then one of the scientists cried out, "Would you look at that!"

Evan peered towards the position of interest. What he saw left him almost speechless—a creature so massive that its visage enveloped the entire row of portholes on the craft. Its size was so grandiose that the passengers thought it was part of the Tentonian landscape. The sound was of it moving. It was like watching a living, wooly mountain. The team was awestruck.

"Good eye, Dr. Tilo. Looks like you have an organism to name," stated Evan.

"I'm never any good at that," replied the doctor.

The planetary scan that was done from Earth revealed that Tento was, at one time, uninhabitable. Apparently, at some point during its history, Tento was a gas giant. The planet had undergone a massive biological and chemical transformation at some period in time. Scientists could only hypothesize as to how something like this could occur. The scan revealed that massive amounts of radiation were still present in Tento's atmosphere. The amounts were so high that analysis of Tento's orbit exposed that the space around Tento was also tainted by the radiation. However, it was not present on land. This completely baffled scientists. Tento truly was a planet of mystery and intrigue.

The Earthling spacecraft had orbited Tento for several weeks before its actual landing. Scientists wanted to conduct scans and analyze the conditions near and around the planet before they attempted a landing. At the conclusion of their studies, all parties concurred that Tento was a safe habitat for human existence. The planetary scans that had been carried out on Earth were correct.

The spacecraft was now nearing the Tento Interplanetary Port. Soon after the discovery of the planet, the notion of studying it manifested immediately in the science community. Hence, multiple nations' science programs allied to gather the funds for Tento studies. After the completion of the planetary scan, the science communities' enthusiasm piqued. It would be possible to physically reside on the planet to study it.

Plans were immediately put into action for construction of necessary facilities on Tento. Erectorbots, U.N. funded nation-building tools, were instantly deployed and production began at that time. By the time the expedition took place, all the required amenities were in place for the team. The structures were unimpressive. Nonetheless, the fundamental requirements for a successful study were present.

Tension ran high among the members of the research team. Evan found the mood puzzling, almost toxic. Perhaps each party longed for the exclusive bragging rights that would come with being present at the first Tentonian expedition, and the more accompanying scientific talent, the less the focus on any one individual. In his mind, Evan understood this line of thinking. The planet, after all, had been named after him. He didn't enjoy the notion of having to share that honor with anyone.

It had been a long day. The team arrived at their destination with little more complication than a scare from the native bestial habitation. Evan lay in his quarters at the research outpost. He peered through a massive window that was positioned bedside. While the cold, relentless winds of Tento blew that night, Evan pondered. What would the future hold?

Chapter 2: The Discovery

Schiller sat on a Tentonian rock, lost in the midst of one of his literal brainstorms. He had been studying the habits of an amazingly interesting insect. He observed that it secreted a white, milky substance when it suffered an injury. Surely, tests would need to be performed on it.

When Tobias Schiller entered this state, nothing could bring him out of it. He could hear the sounds, taste the tastes, see the sights, and smell the scents of his mental gestations, as if he experienced them while in a conscious state. Perhaps Tobias had discovered a method of tapping into another level of consciousness. He didn't understand the spells himself. He could remember every detail perfectly, as if his mind had recorded the thoughts.

At times during these spells he wandered physically, somewhat akin to sleepwalking. As well, during these interludes, he often speed-read. In a matter of two hours, he had consumed most of the research reports that had been filed on the Earthly Plague. While studying at the Tentonian Institute of Science, he wrote his entire thesis while in this state. It outlined possible theories on the origins of the Plague. He won the Tentonian Award for Scientific Achievement for this work, an honor bestowed upon few in the field. Given the fact that he was only twenty-four years of age at the time, calling this an "amazing" feat would be a gross understatement. Indeed, a mind like this was useful for a scientist.

As Schiller sat, wandering throughout the winding maze of his subconscious, a psychological light switch flipped in his mind. The minute organism he had been studying might hold much more importance than he first thought possible. He began to emerge from his latest violent brainstorm. There was work to be done.

***

Schiller initiated the startup sequence of his mobile lab unit. His excitement to immediately begin this latest foray into understanding Tentonian life piqued. He did not understand why his mind told him to perform these tests. However, when these notions came, Schiller never ignored them. The spells, as inconvenient as they were, often birthed tangible results.

For the next four hours, Schiller calculated, observed, and recorded. These events are unexplainable to the common mind. Only Schiller understood what everything meant. Tiny eyedroppers containing various mixtures littered the console of his mobile lab. He measured intricately. The slightest error would mean failure.

As Schiller entered the final calculations into the mobile lab's keyboard, his eyes lit up like the display on the MLU. He had done it again.

Chapter 3: Return to Zonfer City

It seemed that only a day had passed to Schiller. In fact, it had been nearly a year. In this time, Schiller managed to catalog approximately 80 to 95 percent of all Tentonian life forms. TIS scientists, to say the least, were amazed at these results. Schiller proved that he was the only man for the job. He imagined this accomplishment would finally make him a senior official on the board at TIS. And TIS would undoubtedly not be the only pleased party.

The cataloging of life forms would pale in comparison to the findings that were recorded in his MLU for that fateful day on the rock. Today would prove to be a red-letter day.

***

Schiller stood at the entrance/exit gate to Zonfer City. A communication panel flickered in front of him.

He leaned toward the microphone. "Tobias Schiller, TIS."

It was the same attendant. "Ah, yes, Dr. Schiller, it's great to finally see you back. How did everything go out there?"

Schiller was somewhat aggravated. "Fine. You know, I've been out here for a long time. I'm looking forward to seeing Zonfer City again."

The attendant noticed the curt tone. "Yes sir, right away."

Schiller, in turn, noticed his rudeness. "I apologize, I've been traveling all day and I'm a little tired."

"Say no more. I completely understand," replied the attendant.

"I appreciate your understanding. It was nice seeing you," Schiller replied.

"You as well, sir."

"What's your name?" Schiller inquired.

"Siegfried Danken," replied the attendant.

The shock could be read on Schiller's face. Surely a person with the last name of *Danken* would choose to change it.

He wiped the expression from his face as soon as he caught himself staring. "Pleasure to meet you," he finally replied after an awkward pause. He exited the gateway swiftly.

***

Schiller's excitement piqued as he sat in the hover transport on its way to Zonfer City center. His confidence level was high. He knew his discovery would make him a senior member of the TIS board.

He exited the transport with a gleam in his eye and a smile on his face. He set his foot on the sidewalk outside TIS. Zonfer City bustled with activity. It mirrored the feelings that Schiller was experiencing in his heart. This was the most excited he had been in a long time, perhaps ever.

Schiller stood in the middle of the presentation floor of the TIS main office. He wished his presentation could present itself. He dreaded making speeches. They made him uncomfortable. In most cases, the material he reported on couldn't be explained in everyday terms.

The chairman of the TIS board stood at the head of a massive boardroom-like table.

"All right, Dr. Schiller, let's get started," the chairman said.

"Thank you, Mr. Zimmerman. Ladies and gentlemen, I come to you today with an exciting discovery. For the past year, I have been traveling the outskirts of Tento's mapped territories in pursuit of cataloging Tentonian life. Most of you are aware of this operation. I never would have guessed that this mission would yield such an astonishing revelation. I will ask that you keep open minds, gentlemen."

With that last statement, chatter began and sighs could be heard.

"Now, I understand that the Exodus from Earth is a—"

The chairman interrupted. "No, no, no. No discussions on that. We need to call a special session for discussions on the Exodus. Reports on the Exodus need to be recorded and filed with the government."

"Well, in that case, I call a special session," Schiller replied.

"All right, Dr. Schiller, but we need to do some preparatory work for a session such as this. There shall be a short recess and we can continue," the chairman stated.

Schiller sighed. He thought he could be done with this promptly. He was excited about discussing his discovery but not the speech. Nonetheless, his enthusiasm for the discovery he had made eventually overcame his feelings of dread.

***

The preparations had taken longer than anticipated. Schiller could feel a cold sweat forming on his brow. There were not many things that could make this man break a sweat. With his hands folded in his lap, Schiller sat closed-eyed. He took long, deep breaths. Only he and the almighty knew what thoughts were running through the valleys of his mind.

The chairman finally spoke. "Dr. Schiller, we are ready for your presentation. I apologize for the delay. We needed to contact certain government officials before we could begin. They proved to be more difficult to get hold of than I had anticipated. The board and I are eager to hear your findings."

"Thank you, Chairman Zimmerman, I would be more than glad to get started. Ladies and gentlemen of the board, as you know, I have been assigned the task of cataloging all of Tento's life forms. With the benefit of hindsight, I must confess, if it weren't for this discovery, I might have been tempted to turn this mission down. However, with that said, I come to you today with a profoundly exciting discovery."

Schiller paused, took a small sip of water, and gathered his thoughts. He was visibly nervous. He padded his brow with a handkerchief.

He cleared his throat and continued. "Our generation is almost the first to call Tento home. Certainly, we have all heard the tales of mankind's past—wars, dictators, prophets. Quite frankly, most of it sounds like a fairy tale. If it weren't for the accurate multimedia records in Tento's library, most of us wouldn't believe it. Thank science for sustainable databases that are self-decoding."

Schiller felt himself losing grip of the topic at hand. These were the moments he dreaded. He awkwardly paused and regained his footing.

"I spent a year in the Tentonian wilderness. Never, in a million centuries, did I think I would find what I eventually found.

"Let us go back to the year 3034 on the Earth timeline. As we are all aware, Wolfgang Zonfer was the leader of the entire human race. We also know that this was the final year that Earthlings would call Earth home. Enter the enigma that is 'the Plague.' Soon after its emergence, the human race found itself without many options.

"The ultimate decision, made by Zonfer, was to evacuate the planet. At the time, this was an unprecedented feat to achieve. Now, it seems like a commonsensical notion. It is common knowledge that Tento has had an evacuation plan since any of us could remember."

Chairman Zimmerman stated, "Dr. Schiller, we are on a schedule. Is this going to be considerably longer or—"

Schiller realized he had digressed and interjected. "My apologies. I'm not very good at these presentations. I shall get to the point."

"Quite all right. Please continue," Zimmerman replied.

Schiller nodded. "The greatest mystery of human existence is what the Plague really was. Virtually everything about it is shrouded in mystery and uncertainty. The only research that was done on it was at the time of the Exodus from Earth. Most of the conclusions and calculations were hasty, to say the least. One thing is for certain: the Plague is and was a mesmerizing destructive force. To this day, Earth is periodically monitored to observe the progression of this abomination. We can say, with a good amount of certainty, that Earth is dead. It is a mere husk of what it was. However, on the other hand, the Plague has met its match. Ladies and gentlemen, I present to you, on this day in the year 201 A.A., the cure!"

Schiller raised a small vial of white fluid. Gasps were heard. It wasn't easy to impress these people.

"The content of this vial is a secretion from the xenocite, one of the many organisms I cataloged. When I observed the biological makeup of this organism and its secretion, I noticed something astounding.

"As most of you know, before I was given the cataloging mission, I had been researching Wolfgang Zonfer. In the countless drives and data disks, I ran across a bioscan of the infamous Plague. I uploaded the information to my MLU for later study. During the routine cross-check of biological scans between the xenocite and known organisms, this amazing discovery was revealed. The xenocitian secretion is the 'anti-Plague.' How this could be is something beyond my knowledge."

Schiller used a remote to turn on the massive presentation screen.

"As you can see, the bio markers are unmistakable. Ladies and gentlemen of the board, I appreciate your time and attention," Schiller concluded.

The applause exploded. This was the greatest discovery since the theory of relativity had been proven. Schiller had made history. Now, what should be done with this knowledge?

Chapter 4: A Past Revisited

Wolfgang Zonfer sat in his office at the United Nations in New York City. His latest peacekeeping mission in Africa was not going as planned. The government of Nigeria had given him its word that the genocide would stop. The killing, however, was not subsiding. Zonfer thought it was time for action.

He grabbed the first flight to Nigeria and prepared for diplomatic combat. This might have seemed like a contradiction but it wasn't. Zonfer didn't need to lift a finger to intimidate. His blazing gaze could make a lion run for cover. Being a former Austrian general, he had plenty of combat training. If the situation permitted, he could defend himself quite efficiently.

In this day and age, peace was flourishing. All the nations of Earth were united and strong. From time to time, a leader may think he can oppress the people of his nation and get away with it. In this rare happening, Zonfer was the entity to intercede. To put it bluntly, leaders that opposed Zonfer usually ended up ousted or dead. He had his methods.

The Nigerian president sat at the end of a massive dinner table. Zonfer entered the room.

The president began, "Hello, Mr. Ambassador. What, may I ask, is the problem regarding my nation? I understand that you only show up when there is a problem."

Zonfer was in top form.

"Yes sir, that is correct," Zonfer replied.

"Well, what is it?"

"Sir, we have been getting reports of genocide taking place here in Nigeria. As you know, Africa, as a whole, has had problems with genocide and ethnic cleansing in the past. The U.N. wants confirmation of this rumor," Zonfer explained.

The president was shaken. He felt Zonfer's eyes glaring through to his soul.

He began, "I can assure you, Mr....Zonfer, is it?"

Zonfer glared. "That is correct."

The president coughed. "Right. I can assure you that there isn't any genocide or ethnic cleansing taking place in my nation. I am well aware of the past and I would never repeat it."

Zonfer knew he was lying. He could smell it. In one quick action, Zonfer pulled out a pistol-sized machine gun. He put a full clip into the president of Nigeria. He then opened the window to the dining room of the president's palace. The U.N. chopper was hovering nearby. Zonfer made a quick leap out the window, clinging to the landing gear of the chopper. A U.N. peacekeeping force member grabbed Zonfer's arm and hoisted him onto the chopper.

Zonfer proclaimed, "Let yet another revolution begin."

Chapter 5: The Way Forward

After Schiller's presentation at TIS, discussion immediately began within the Tentonian scientific community regarding a return to the former homeland of the Tentonians. Schiller assumed this would be the result of his report. He didn't necessarily agree with this idea. Certainly, there were many questions that needed to be answered about the final days on Earth. However, the theory of using the xenocite's biological chemistry found in its defensive secretion as immunity to the Plague's destructive powers might well be viable. The harvesting of xenocites had already begun—immediately after Schiller finished his report to TIS, it passed a new initiative to harvest and study the xenocite. The obvious focus of the study would be the organism's defense mechanism.

The way forward was not without obstacles. Schiller's findings definitively concluded that the xenocite secretion was the "anti-Plague." This much he was certain of. However, the effects on humans were unknown. The introduction of the xenocite's biological defense mechanism to the human immune system could be fatal. Many tests would need to be conducted in the near future to evaluate how the biological makeup of the xenocite's defense mechanism could be safely introduced to the human immune system. Billions of Tentonian tax credits would be spent on this project, dubbed "Project Heilmittel."

Schiller would spend the next months conducting projection tests in his TIS lab. Projection tests were a new technology that used advanced artificial intelligence. to create a 100 percent accurate "prediction." They could be thought of as a prophetical tool that had saved many lives. There was no longer any reason for test subjects to be put in danger of new vaccines or medicines. The projection test modules would automatically generate countless hypothetical human DNA structures and analyze the effects of the material being tested. Through this process, dangers to human life were uncovered.

Through its projection test trials, the xenocite secretion was not without its red flags. Fortunately, all of the inherent problems were negotiable. Every danger could be countered by another element being added to the code. This made for a complex and expensive serum. Hence, the production of the cure would be short and in a small quantity. Unfortunately, this would make multiple expeditions to Earth a nonstarter. It would be a one- or possibly two-time deal.

When the projection trials ended and a serum code had been compiled, production began. Physical serum production was limited to seven injections. However, the recent innovation and implementation of A.I.-based biosuits made it possible to mimic the effects of the serum code while in a biosuit. However, the physical effects on the human body past a few months were unknown. This outlined a relatively bright future for missions to foreign and hostile planets.

By the end of 201 A.A., the projection test trials and production of the serum code were complete. Project Heilmittel was a success. The expedition to Earth was that much closer.

Chapter 6: The Mission to Earth

It was now 202. The end of the xenocite projection test trials marked the first serious discussions in the Tentonian Senate about a mission to Earth. Only the Senate could authorize a mission to Earth. This would normally be TIS territory. However, the sensitivity and seriousness of the mere notion of a return to Earth would stimulate countless hours of discussion in the Tentonian Senate. It was time for these discussions to take place.

The floor of the Senate was now open. The chairman, Adolph Heinmeche, opened the session with the topic of a mission to Earth.

"Recently, as many of you are aware, a scientist from TIS, Doctor Tobias Schiller, discovered something extraordinary. While studying life in the Tentonian wilderness, he discovered the 'anti-Plague.' This word has been thrown around in the science community for almost a hundred years. However, there has never been iron-clad proof of the existence of such a notion. Dr. Schiller has concluded in his studies that he has indeed found the anti-Plague biocode. Obviously, this has started the discussion about an expedition to Earth. In my personal opinion, this mission is long overdue. Our kind knew Earth as home for almost four millennia. We only have basic knowledge of its original chemical makeup. If possible, a mission to Earth should be a no-brainer. I would like to start the session with this topic. All in favor vote 'yea.'"

The senate voting results came with a unanimous "ye."

Heinmeche continued, "Right. So the first order of business would be the funding for the project. Immediately after the successful completion of the xenocite projection test trials, I authorized TIS to put together provisional cost predictions. Funding should not be a problem. We have had a billion credit surplus for as long as I can remember."

"Mr. Chairman, what were the results of the xenocite projection test trials?"

Heinmeche squinted at his interlocutor. "Didn't you get the memo, Mr. Fellermen? The PTTs were a total success. I wouldn't have brought this to the floor if they weren't. As important as a mission to Earth is, I wouldn't risk one Tentonian life. Now, if that is all cleared up, I would like to bring a new vote to the floor. All in favor of funding a mission to Earth please vote 'yea.'"

Again, the touch screens in front of the senators blinked and pulsated. The final vote on the floor was a unanimous 100 percent in favor. It was official. There would be a Mission Earth.

***

Schiller stood in the TIS dry-docks. The building of the craft that would return to Earth had already begun. Schiller recognized one of his colleagues.

"Mark, when did this start?"

"Confirmation of the Senate funding came in early in the day. The team began assembling the parts immediately. Our science engineers have been chomping at the bit to start this project. If it was up to them, they would have been working on this immediately after your presentation to the TIS board. At any rate, word came down the channels pretty quickly," replied Mark Pinter, a science engineer.

"I see. This is encouraging. At this rate, we will be in Earth's orbit in short order. Have you named her yet?"

"She'll be known as the Phoenix. We thought that was fitting."

"Indeed," replied Schiller.

Pinter inquired, "Are you going to be on the expedition?"

Schiller was defiant in tone. "I damned well better be. They'll need me on that mission in case anything goes wrong with the xenocite code. As flawless as the PTTs are, anomalies can occur. A reworking of the code would need to be done and I'm the only mind in TIS that could do something like that on the fly. Bottom line is that I am going."

"Well, I guess that's a 'yes,'" said Pinter sardonically.

Construction of the Phoenix had been under way for most of the day. Luckily, word came in early about the Senate's decision on funding a mission to Earth. TIS contacts inside the Senate relayed the good news without delay.

A hypothetical design for a craft had been worked up in the past. Most designs of larger spacecraft still glorified the great mother ship, the Renaissance, that had been used to transport the residents of Earth to Tento. The original ship could still be visited just outside Zonfer City, a reminder of a past they might never fully understand.

The Engibots would have most of the Phoenix completed by the end of the week. After some human preparations, the launch could take place.

Chapter 7: Assembling the Team

With the Phoenix now ready for launch, the human factor was all that remained. The majority of the team would be biochemists with Schiller as the lead scientist. In the off chance that they might encounter some kind of hostile force, they would need protection.

The Tentonian Senate tapped an independent contractor for the job. His only known identity was Rayne. Great military leaders in Zonfer's time would use only one name. Perhaps he thought of this as a throwback to those times. Most people didn't take him seriously. Rayne knew this and didn't enjoy the notion in the slightest. It wasn't a very fair view to have of him. He had proved himself in keeping Tentonian citizens safe in times of crisis. However, his attitude was a bit of a parody of a military figure. He seemed to take himself somewhat too seriously.

Schiller, Rayne and three other biochemists would make up the field team. Two pilots would make up the remainder of the team. The Senate refused to clear more than seven members for the team. This was because the physical xenocite serum had not been mass produced. Only seven injections were made. The A.I. biosuits had not yet been field tested. Hence, the Senate insisted that the crew not comprise more than seven individuals. If the A.I. Biosuits proved to be as efficient as Schiller predicted, a larger team could be deployed on a future mission. For now, they would have to make the best of the current situation.

In terms of research equipment, the Phoenix would have it all. Every bioscanner and condition analyzer known to mankind would be present on the vessel. If there was a danger, the team would know far before their lives were at risk. With regard to physical dangers on Earth, the chemists weren't aware of any. Life on Earth, aside from the mysterious Plague, had ended.

The Plague had changed everything on Earth. From the basic composition of the atmosphere to the minerals found in the soil, Earth had been transformed into a chaotic maelstrom of unpredictability. However, with the xenocite code, the human race would be safe from this chaos. If a human so much as entered the Earth's atmosphere without protection, he or she would immediately be vaporized by the destructive force of the Plague. At this point, one might well rename the planet Plague. All of the properties found in the mysterious organism could be found in the basic chemical makeup of the planet. To this day, the greatest and best minds at TIS couldn't understand how something like this could happen. It defied every law in the books. Nonetheless, bioscans of Earth revealed all of this was taking place on a day-to-day basis. The Tentonian Institute of Science had been monitoring Earth since the organization's creation. The progression of what was occurring on Earth was astounding and nothing and no one could explain what was happening. For this reason, a mission to Earth would benefit scientific understanding on many fronts.

In order to understand the biological and chemical effects that the Plague possessed, analysis of Earth's new makeup would be a hands-on undertaking. The bioscanners at TIS could only do so much. Thus the Phoenix was equipped with a full function bioscanner for the crew to observe and record every biological happening on the planet in real time. The resulting log would be a virtual tour of the crew's stay on the planet. The accuracy and thoroughness of the bioscanners findings would be greatly increased by being located in the same area it was scanning. When the bioscanner was first invented on Tento, TIS did a dry run of the new technology. During this short dry run, TIS discovered more about Tento and its biological and chemical makeup than in years of study using conventional means. Bioscanners existed prior to the TIS invention but in a much more primitive form. Soon after its internal workings and procedures were streamlined, TIS altered its operating scope. At this point, a bioscanner could be pointed and aimed at any single point in the universe and begin gathering data about the given coordinates. Tentonian scientists began unlocking the mysteries of the universe with this amazing new technology. Now it was time to reveal the answers to the mysteries of the past with the technology of the future.

***

Schiller had begun the relatively long journey of returning home to the Tentonian countryside. Zonfer City was beautiful but he found the countryside to be much more to his liking. The bustle of the big city quickly became tedious and mind-numbing to him. He found great pleasure and relaxation in the howl of the Tentonian winds. Most days on Tento were cold and dark and Schiller loved it. He found comfort in the desolation of the planet he called home. For the people that were adversely affected by the lack of sun, there were "sun bars," as they had come to be known, located all over Tento. Here, patrons could enjoy the simulated rays for as long as they desired. The dangers of the real sun were absent. Occasionally, Schiller enjoyed a sun bar visit. For the most part, however, he loved the natural Tentonian state.

Schiller was contemplating purchasing a Transwarper. With his new senior position at TIS, his pay upgrade would permit him new perks. As a lackey TIS biochemist, he had made a comfortable living. Now, he and his family could enjoy much more than they had previously been accustomed to. At this point, however, he was still restricted to driving his old 190 Protek Cruiser, a very reliable hovercraft. At a steady 90 kilometers per hour, Tobias inched closer to his home. Soon, he was pulling up to the driveway. His humble abode looked identical to the day he left for the cataloging mission. The cylindrical design was something that he had fallen in love with from day one. At the time he had it built, it was trendy to have a house that looked so different. Now, cylindrical structures were the norm on Tento. Tobias had always insisted that he started the trend.

He exited his junker and started toward the door of his dwelling. He hesitated in opening the door. His wife, Emma, could sometimes be difficult after he returned from a long mission. Schiller's profession sometimes made it hard for the people in his life who loved him. His work demanded his time far too often. He held his breath and entered the house.

He hung his TIS jacket on the coat tree hanging from the wall in the entranceway.

He called out, "Em…Em."

He entered the living room. The holocube was on and flickering images of the day's news. Tento's last bit of sun for the day flooded in through the massive window in the living room. He entered the kitchen to find his wife.

"Emma, I'm home. I was calling for you. Didn't you hear me?"

She was a bit down but better than normal.

"Yes, I heard you. I wasn't expecting to see you until later tonight."

"We finished the debriefing sooner than I thought."

Emma smiled. "I'm happy to see you. I've missed you more than I can express. I thought I would get to see you before this. You returned from your mission days ago. When TIS sent someone to get the craft, I was beginning to worry. I didn't understand what was going on."

"Sorry, Em, there was too much to do before now for me to come home. Things started happening immediately after my address to the TIS board. By the way, I made senior member."

Emma's smile grew wider. "My god, that's amazing! You've wanted that forever. Congratulations, Toby. I'm so proud of you."

"Thanks, Em—that means a lot to me."

They embraced and kissed. Tobias leaned in again for another. They made their way to the bedroom and did what humans love to do. After their session, Tobias's cell rang.

He answered. "Schiller—yes—this has been confirmed? Thanks very much, Mark. I'll be in contact."

Emma felt what was to come.

"Who was that?"

Schiller solemnly answered, "Emma, I have to talk to you about something. I haven't had a chance to tell you about why I made senior member. I found something amazing on the cataloging mission. This is the biggest discovery since the proving of the theory of relativity."

Emma's eyes widened. "What is it, Toby?"

"It's the cure to the Plague."

Emma was stunned. She too was a biochemist and this was the Holy Grail of discoveries.

"You cannot be serious."

"As serious as cancer was before nanomeds," Tobias jokingly retorted.

"How could you have not told me about this sooner?"

Schiller rolled his eyes.

"Emma, you know protocol. No one knows about this yet. You needed a level one clearance at TIS to even know about my cataloging mission. Did you forget that the secrecy at TIS was the reason you left?"

Emma was immediately distant.

"Toby, hearing this, I think I know what's coming next. Am I right?"

She could read him like a book. He knew he couldn't fool her if he wanted to. Secrets didn't exist between the two of them for a very long time.

After a slight pause, Schiller responded.

"I could leave as soon as the end of the week."

Emma Schiller's eyes widened and swelled with tears.

"I didn't realize it would be that soon. Are they positive that an expedition to Earth will be safe?"

"You understand better than anyone that there are risks in all missions, Emma. Hell, anyone on Tento could be killed by the microscopic Tentonian ticks that carry diseases mankind has never known. We know they exist. It's only a matter of time before people start dropping like flies from unknown illnesses that are off all the medical books we have today. I'm not telling you anything you don't already know. I'm just trying to prove a point. All of us are risking our lives twenty-four hours a day on our own planet. On Earth, ironically, I'll be safer than I am here," Schiller concluded.

Emma knew he was dead on with everything he said but she still didn't feel good about it. Basically, she didn't want Tobias going on yet another expedition that would take him away from her for an extended period of time. She couldn't be blamed.

Before the cataloging mission, Schiller had spent most of the last three years from home, at TIS studying Wolfgang Zonfer's latter-year experiments and observations of Tentonian life. Schiller concluded that Zonfer had been a genius. He'd had primitive equipment to aid his studies but he managed to be almost 100 percent accurate in his findings. Even with current technology, that would be an admirable feat to achieve.

Emma gazed in disbelief. Yet she had known that Tobias would be one of the few biochemists qualified to head a mission to Earth. He had studied Earthololy more than any scientist at TIS.

Emma sighed. "I knew what I was getting myself into marrying you. The pros still outweigh the cons. You do what you have to do. You're going to anyway."

Tobias felt terrible. If he was going to be honest with himself, he would have to admit that he had been an absentee husband for the last few years. His work had taken over his life. However, if it weren't for his studies and findings, mankind's understanding of the planet they lived on would be far more vague. Emma knew this to be true. Part of the reason she had married him was because of his brilliance. She found that to be his most attractive attribute.

She had waited for a response long enough. Emma pulled her fingers through her long, wavy, bluish black hair.

"You don't need to say anything else. I understand."

Tobias was solemn. He felt bad but he knew that he had to go on this mission. He had been training his entire career for this one assignment. This mission would be the crowning achievement of his life's journey.

***

Schiller had begun his journey back to Zonfer City. He was glad he had taken the time to travel home and visit Emma. She had been a very understanding, supportive force in Tobias's life. He couldn't ask more of her. The least he could do was be present in her life as much as his time permitted. Emma was forced to tolerate a great deal.

During his journey back to TIS in Zonfer City, he contemplated seeing Earth for the first time. This would be the first time mankind had entered the vicinity of Earth's orbit since the Exodus over two hundred years ago. He imagined what the team would find on the Earth's new landscape.

Their landing zone would be the purported site of Zonfer's ruling headquarters. There were rumors that deep beneath the basement level of the headquarters lay a vast library of historical documents that the Earthlings had been unable to take with them on their journey. The information contained in these documents, if they even existed, could reveal information vital to understanding human history prior to Zonfer's reign. Tentonian historians were frustrated with the fact that there were so many gaps in human history. They had a good record of Zonfer's time but before that there was little information available. Schiller hoped the rumors were true.

Schiller arrived at the entry gates to Zonfer City. He had been coming to this gateway to enter Zonfer City for years. Even so, every time he saw it, his stomach lurched a little. It was massive. At the top of the gateway was a huge sculpture of a likeness of Wolfgang Zonfer standing with one arm raised with a closed fist. At the base, an inscription read "HERE IN THE YEAR 100 AFTER ARRIVAL, WE DECLARE WOLFGANG ZONFER OUR ONE LEADER FOR LIFE. EVEN THOUGH HE IS NO LONGER WITH US, HIS IDEOLOGY LIVES ON. —Benjamin Kodder – Chairman of the New Senate." At midday, the sun would be directly above the massive statue. The metal armor covering Zonfer's likeness would shimmer in the sunshine. The site was truly awe-inspiring.

Schiller entered TIS's parking facility for hovercraft. He saw a familiar face approaching the entrance to TIS.

"Davies, are you on today?"

"No, well, I wasn't supposed to be, but I got a call from Mark Pinter in engineering. He said that I was needed for something pertaining to Project Heilmittel," Davies responded.

"Welcome to the team," Schiller chimed.

Davies was confused. "You know something I don't—of course you do. You have level one clearance. That's a stupid question."

Schiller winked at Davies. "You'll find out soon enough. Come on, let's get going."

Schiller and Davies entered the craft parking facility entrance to TIS. They went through security and proceeded to the board meeting room. The entire crew was present at the meeting. Rayne was seated in the first chair on the right-hand side of the boardroom table. Next to him sat Dr. Thomas Hindler. Davies and Schiller took their seats next to Hindler. Dr. Stanley Dobbs rounded out the biochemist team.

Chairman Heinmeche of the New Senate was present to address the team. Additionally, the chairman of TIS, Randolph Zimmerman, was present to deliver the mission briefing details.

Zimmerman began, "All right, gentlemen, let's get started. I want to thank all of you for assembling so quickly. Also, I would like to personally thank Chairman Heinmeche of the New Senate for attending this meeting on such short notice. Gentleman, this mission to Earth has been a long time coming. Over the years, our people have been asking questions about our history that we have been unable to answer. What was the Plague? What are its origins? Finally, we possess the protection required for a manned mission to Earth."

Davies looked at Schiller in disbelief.

"This was your doing," Davies whispered.

Schiller nodded.

Zimmerman continued, "This is why you have been summoned here so hastily. The construction of the craft that will take you to Earth, the Phoenix, will be complete within days. When the construction is complete, you will be briefed in full on the equipment. You will find in front of you a data node that can be placed in your MLUs. Rayne, you will be briefed by Chairman Heinmeche. Contained in the nodes are all the details of the operation. Also, there are contingency procedures provided in case of emergency situations that may occur on the Phoenix."

Zimmerman cleared his throat and continued.

"Now, the main mission priority will be to land at Zonfer's headquarters and recover the historic documents."

Dobbs interjected, "We don't even know if these documents exist!"

Zimmerman raised his brow.

"Don't we? Now, after you secure the documents, Dr. Schiller's priority will be study of the Earthling soil. This is vital to understanding the new dynamic of Earth's form. In the unlikely event that you encounter hostiles, Mr. Rayne will be your main defense.

"Mister?" growled Rayne.

Zimmerman sighed. "I apologize—*Rayne* will be taking care of that. Now it's time to discuss protocol and positions on the Phoenix. Schiller, you are the lead biochemist on the team. You will be making all of the decisions on this mission. Second in command is Dr. Hindler. If something is to happen to Dr. Schiller, Hindler is to be the mission leader. Dr. Davies, your main function will be collecting physical samples for research. Dr. Dobbs, your main function will be decoding and earmarking bioscanner readouts. You are the leader in this field and this is why you have been tapped to go on this mission. Also, you will serve as a second hand to Schiller, Hindler, and Davies. Mr. —I mean, *Rayne*, your main objective is to keep the entire crew safe. Be prepared for any danger that you could aid in putting down. All right, gentlemen, this concludes the mission briefing. Chairman Heinmeche, would you like to make your closing statement?"

Chairman Heinmeche stood at a height of five foot ten. He was a stately-looking man. He had been presiding over the New Senate for over ten years. He was a seemingly honorable man. Fortunately for the population, his intentions were always geared toward the common good of the people. He was just as passionate about Earth as the TIS scientists.

"Gentlemen, I don't need to explain to you how important this mission is. The people of Tento deserve to know more about their history. Until now, it was impossible to explore the possibility of a mission to Earth. Now, this formerly impossible mission is going to happen. The success of this assignment will lie solely in your hands. Understand that you have the full support and backing power of the New Senate. Virtually all members of the New Senate voted for this mission. We, as the leaders of Tento, realize that understanding the past will play a large role in shaping our future. In closing, I would like to thank you for your commitment to science and advancing human understanding of our history. Know that this will be the most important mission of your lifetime and you are the sole crew members. Throughout this mission, I ask you to keep in mind the importance of your assignments. Realize that as you are shaping the picture of our past, you are also altering our future. Thank you."

Now that the briefing was over, preparations for the launch would begin. By the end of the night, the Phoenix would be near completion. A new era of human understanding was approaching.

Chapter 8: Launch Day

It was a typically cold and desolate day on Tento. The winds were consistently strong on the planet. The science program had grown accustomed to the brutal conditions on Tento. When they prepared for a launch, they assumed the conditions on the ground would be less than desirable.

The launch strip for the Phoenix was miles long. At TIS, launches took place at their landing strip. The site was nothing special, aside from the length of the strip. The length of the launch strip needed to be such for the Phoenix to warm up. The craft needed to have a certain amount of momentum built up in the engine to maintain the operational conditions for launch. Warm up procedures had already begun. The time had come for the crew to assemble and get ready for launch.

Schiller took the hoverbus from his loft in Zonfer City. He could hardly sleep the night prior. Heinmeche's address had left a lasting impression on him. This was the mission of the century and he was fully aware of that fact. When he arrived at the TIS landing strip, the team had already begun assembling at the Phoenix. Much could be said about prompt arrivals. Schiller was the team leader, yet his team was already assembled at the craft. This wasn't exactly a good way to build respect within the crew. If he was going to lead these men, they would need to respect him. They didn't have any training programs at TIS for leading a crew into a danger zone. This wasn't something they dealt with on a normal basis. However, this was far from a normal mission.

Hindler, Davies, Dobbs, and Rayne were finally all assembled at the area near the Phoenix. Tobias Schiller could feel the tension in the air.

"Good to see you all ready for launch," Schiller commented.

"Glad you decided to make it, Dr. Schiller," Hindler sarcastically snipped.

"I deserved that. I apologize for my delayed arrival. You know how public transportation is. Now, what's the status of the Phoenix?"

"Sir, the warm up started about twenty minutes ago. The itinerary is right on schedule," Dobbs informed him.

"Excellent. I must admit that I was shocked when I received the call from Zimmerman this morning that the Phoenix was being prepped for launch so quickly. I never thought we would be leaving today. The earliest projection I heard for the completion of the Phoenix was the end of the week. This is a pleasant surprise."

A voice suddenly boomed from the loudspeakers throughout the TIS landing area.

"Phoenix is now ready for launch. Repeat, we are go for launch. Dr. Schiller, please organize the crew and begin takeoff protocol."

"Copy, homestead. Okay, team, you heard him. Let's get going."

Schiller was the first to enter. The interior was unimpressive. However, the technology involved in the on-board computers was revolutionary. The bioscanner displays flashed with activity. They would be the main workhorses on this mission. Without them, the mission would be impossible. It would take years to analyze Earth's new constitution through conventional means.

Schiller took a deep breath. "Here we are, gentlemen. I hope you like your new workplace."

Hindler sarcastically commented, "Just like home."

Roberts, the pilot, entered.

"Lets get you guys strapped in. We're taking off soon."

Chapter 9: Journey to the Past

The crew of the Phoenix was restless. Perhaps they weren't used to being in zero gravity. Manned missions into the cosmos were a rarity. TIS rarely received authorization from the New Senate for interplanetary travel. Reasons for this were not known. Early in the New Senate's life, the then members of that governmental body created legislation that made future missions into the cosmos more difficult to get funded. Perhaps the Plague was still too fresh in the minds of the leaders at the time. In all likelihood, they didn't want to tempt fate into creating another nightmare scenario. This time, there would be no refuge from a horrific destructive force. Only missions that the New Senate dubbed worthy went through.

***

150 A.A.

When TIS bioscanners picked up possible life forms other than simple-celled organisms on Tento's moon, the New Senate immediately authorized a manned mission to Tento's moon to investigate. This was unprecedented at the time. There was a massive celebratory cast off for the crew of the mission, even though they were only going to be gone for a matter of days.

The crew of the mission had no idea what to expect. In the instant the bioscanners picked up initial signs of life other than the normal single-celled moon organisms, there was a fatal error in the system. All the data that the bioscanners had picked up was immediately erased. This had never happened before. TIS scientists were flabbergasted.

As the craft entered the orbit around Tento's moon, the crew immediately knew something strange was going on. As the dark side of the moon approached their window, they could see a massive black cloud near the moon's surface. Instantly, the crew thought of the stories they had heard about the Plague. Could this be a resurgence of the menace that had threatened the human race so many years ago on Earth? For people who studied the information that was known about the Plague, this would be a ridiculous notion. The cloud that surrounded the moon had an ominous aura, but it was far from the seemingly organic movements of the Plague.

Archival video of the destructive powers of the enigmatic Plague were popularized over the Internet 3.0 on Tento. One of the more popular videos was footage of the entire Earthling continent of Asia being devoured in a matter of minutes by the Plague. These videos were eventually outlawed by the New Senate for being "overly provocative." It was probably the right decision. People had heard of the destructive power of the Plague until it was now legend, and seeing it in full color video was too much to bear for some. The videos had been leaked onto the Internet by a member of the Tentonian Institute of Human History. The member was immediately discovered and prosecuted for the crime. This person caused the deaths of suicide victims who couldn't take what they witnessed in these videos.

The question still remained: what was this cloud? The crew remained clueless as to its source. At the time, mobile bioscanners had not been invented. They decided to land on the surface.

The craft landed at a safe distance from the cloud. The crew cautiously exited the craft. They peered into the cosmos above Tento's moon searching for the large cloud. They found it and moved toward its epicenter. goats they got closer to the source of the cloud, they could see that this source was a downed object. They decided to call in a bioscan from Tento. This was something that TIS liked to avoid at any price. The costs involved in a pinpoint bioscan could fund a million missions to Earth. However, this mission was important and they needed to know the origin of this smoke cloud.

TIS authorized the action and the area was deemed safe. As the crew approached the downed object, it was clear that the object emitting the smoke was small. Then the crew leader noticed a high-pitched hum coming from the device. He had a bad feeling about it. Suddenly, the high-pitched noise became louder. The crew leader feared the worst.

"Team, retreat from the site immediately! Get back to the craft!"

But it was too late. Almost as soon as they had landed, the team was annihilated. A massive explosion that originated at the smoke's origin erupted with fury, and the team was incinerated instantly.

***

The Phoenix had entered into the orbit around Tento. The Crater of the Unknown could be seen on the moon. Schiller looked in awe. This was the first time, and probably the last, that he would ever see the crater up close. This incident that had happened over fifty-one years ago still remained a mystery. The New Senate ordered many investigations into what had happened but the site was a loss. Any evidence of what had happened had been destroyed beyond any possibility of examination. Schiller didn't like empty spaces in history. He had often pondered the disaster to no avail.

But this was not the matter at hand. As Schiller gazed out the side window of the Phoenix, Hindler broke the silence.

"Schiller, where were you just now?"

"You know me—my mind's always running."

"Yes, I am aware of your condition. Do you take anything for that?"

Schiller was taken aback. "I don't know if that is any business of yours—but no. I'm not the medication type. Honestly, I don't regard it as a disorder. It's often a good tool. Concentration is a valuable research asset."

Hindler squinted. "What do you make of this mission?"

"Well, the human race deserves answers to questions about our history. We need to learn as much as possible about the new makeup of planet Earth. This will reap valuable information about

the Plague and possibly its origins. We need to know our history
to be able to manage our future."

Hindler's brow rose.

"With that statement, it is clear that Chairman Zimmerman
made the right decision. You are the right man to lead this mission,
the only man."

This was a rare moment of civility and recognition on
Hindler's part. "Thank you, Tom, that means a lot to me. I hope we
can carry this attitude throughout the entire mission. We need to
back each other up. It will be vital to the success of the mission. We
will accomplish nothing if we are working against each other."

"I understand, Tobias. I am as enthusiastic to find answers as
you are. This is the greatest mystery the human race has ever
encountered. Our ancestors called Earth home and we barely know
the first thing about it in its current state. My hopes are high for this
mission."

Schiller nodded, smiled, and continued to peer out the
window of the Phoenix.

Schiller and Hindler were not without a volatile history.
Schiller had passed over Hindler several times in terms of positional
promotions within TIS. This was not because Hindler wasn't as
bright as Schiller, quite the contrary. Mainly, it had to do with
bureaucracy and luck. Hindler had confronted Schiller on several
occasions regarding promotions that Schiller had been awarded. This
left a sour relationship between the two. Understandably, Hindler
wasn't happy to hear the Schiller would be the lead biochemist on the
mission. In reality, Schiller had never done anything to undermine
Hindler. Mostly, a very common human emotion could be blamed—
jealousy.

The TIS reward system that had been in effect since the
creation of the institution had much to do with Schiller's luck and
talent, and subsequent rise in rank and clout. It also helped that
Zimmerman and Schiller had been research partners in the past.
Zimmerman held great respect for Schiller. He felt that Tobias was
bright enough to lead TIS himself. In all likelihood, this would be the
case in the future. Rumors abounded that Zimmerman had already
named his successor in his final will and testament. Schiller was
candidate number one for this honor.

Schiller was lost in thought gazing out of the window of the
Phoenix when the co-pilot entered.

"Gentlemen, it is time for you to enter cryogenic stasis until we arrive in Earth's orbit."

Schiller nodded. "Right, thank you, James. All right, let's get to the chambers."

***

Schiller's foot touched the Earth's soil. He couldn't believe that his foot was on a planet that the human race hadn't traveled to for two hundred years. A feeling of dread filled his mind, but he couldn't put his finger on the reason. Something didn't feel right. Suddenly, he heard a noise in the distance that sounded as though it was getting closer—an animal creature, perhaps. He heard the muted voice of Hindler.

"Schiller—Schiller—wake up."

"God—how long have I been out of cryostasis?"

"James, the co-pilot, scheduled the chambers to open about an hour ago. I was the first to wake up. Dobbs, Davies, and Rayne are still out."

Schiller furrowed his brow and squinted at Hindler.

"And you let them sleep, huh? That's interesting."

"Come on, Toby, you are the mission leader. You need to get ready for descent."

"We're that close? I guess that's why I'm not a pilot."

Hindler nodded. "Roberts and James informed me that I needed to get you and the rest of the crew up and strapped in for descent. We will be entering Earth's orbit within the hour. Oh, you need to see Earth. It's unbelievable. We haven't been able to see the planet for so long—well, you need to see for yourself."

Schiller sensed a bad vibe in Hindler's tone. He exited his cryochamber and started for the Phoenix's cockpit. He inched closer to the windshield. What he saw took his breath away.

"My god—that cannot be the same planet."

Any defining aesthetic feature of Earth that Tentonian scientists understood Earth to possess was gone. Earth's beautiful white clouds and sea blue skies were no more. The new visage was absolutely frightening. The blue skies had been replaced by a terrifying shade of red. It was as though the planet had been cut and bled into the atmosphere. Most bodies of land no longer existed. The steaming sulfuric oceans spewed into the air with violent persistence.

It looked as if this mission would be shorter than anyone had anticipated. This place was hell. Then Roberts discovered something.

"Look," he pointed. "There is a massive landmass across that large pit."

Schiller peered at the landmass. "I don't believe it. Do you see those ruins in the distance? That's Zonfer's palace. Even in ruins I can recognize it."

Schiller was right. Amazingly, parts of the structure still stood. Their interest lay in the basement of the structure. Hopefully, the historical documents would be intact. No one knew if the documents, some of them paper, could have withstood the constant ravages of the Plague. Most likely, they would enter the basement to find nothing.

Roberts began, "All right, we've found our landing area. Time for descent."

By this time, Davies, Dobbs, and Rayne had joined the crew and were strapped in for descent. The human race had returned home.

Chapter 10: The Homecoming

The Phoenix's landing gear touched down on Earth's tattered soil. The landing was flawless; Roberts was the best pilot in the TIS academy. Not a bump could be felt upon landing. Roberts knew it was a flawless landing. He broke the silence.

"Well, how does it feel to be on Earth, gentlemen?"

Schiller was overwhelmed and speechless. Not surprisingly, so was everyone else. Roberts' adrenaline overtook him. "I think it's great," he enthused.

Schiller snapped out of his trance. "This is a historic day, gentlemen. I am happy to be sharing this moment with all of you. This is a day that will be going down in the history books as one of the most important days in human history post-arrival on Tento. Let's get to work."

Schiller had a way with words when he felt inspired. The crew unhooked their protective harnesses and made their way to the main door of the Phoenix. Schiller pressed the opening mechanism on the door, the airlock disengaged with a hiss, and the door lowered.

"I can't believe we are here," commented Davies.

The first out was Schiller. To the eye, it appeared that a film grain filter had been applied to the brain's programming. The air was thick. They could feel it in their lungs as they breathed. This could have been because of Earth's new biological makeup. As they stood, the on-board bioscanners on the Phoenix were compiling a profile of Earth's new makeup. Dobbs would be staying behind to monitor its progress.

Hindler, Davies, and Rayne followed close behind Schiller. All members of the TIS biochemist team had their mobile lab units in hand. The group trekked toward the ruins of Zonfer's palace. As they inched closer, they passed demolished architectural masterpieces. At this point, they were unrecognizable. One could infer from what remained that this had been a majestic palace at one time. Zonfer had been the leader of the human race. His palace would have had to be impressive. Schiller was the only crew member who was familiar with Earth's history, *Earthology*, as it had become known. He found the period of time that Zonfer dominated to be extraordinarily interesting from a historical standpoint. Most of pre-Zonfer history was not known. Schiller's hope was that this mission would shed light on the shadowed past of the human race as Earthlings.

The team now stood at the entrance to the palace. Nothing remained in the main hall. The building had been gutted. As they continued on through the once great palace, Dobbs chimed in on the team's comm links.

"Dr. Schiller, I have been watching the bioscanner readouts. We might have a serious problem."

Schiller immediately responded, "What exactly do you mean, Stan?"

"Well, I'm working on it now. At this point, nothing is certain. I'll keep you informed."

"Copy that," Schiller responded.

Suddenly, Rayne found something of interest. "Dr. Schiller, you need to take a look at this."

"That's amazing. This door looks like nothing has ever touched it," said a confused Schiller.

The large steel door appeared to be pristine. This seemed impossible compared with the rest of the surroundings. Zonfer's entire palace comprised steel and stone—nothing remained intact. It was almost as if the door was immune to the Plague's effects. How could this be possible?

Schiller started up his MLU. He attached the bioreader to the steel door. The MLU holoscreen lit up with activity. Schiller observed its readouts. After a few minutes of biocode pattern, Schiller's fears were confirmed.

"Well, gentlemen," he said, "it appears that our hero Zonfer wasn't a hero at all. This steel panel's biocode has been altered to be Plague resistant. That means that—"

"—Zonfer knew the properties to the anti-Plague," interjected Hindler.

Rayne's rage boiled out. "No—that's impossible! Zonfer was the savior to the human race! Without him, we would not be here now!"

Schiller inhaled deeply. "There are other possibilities. However, at this point, this appears to be the case."

"What do you mean 'other possibilities,' Schiller? It's obvious what happened. Zonfer wanted to dominate the human race. He created the Plague as a weapon to scare the human race into evacuating Earth," Hindler hypothesized.

"There are so many problems with that theory I don't know where to begin," argued Schiller. "I studied the Exodus from Earth extensively. Zonfer was dedicated to the New Beginning. I find it very hard to believe that he would have or could have created the Plague. Come on, Tom, we know how hard it would be to biologically engineer a weapon as powerful as the Plague. In my opinion, it would have been impossible in that time of history to create something like the Plague. Very little is known about it to this day," he concluded.

"You are the Earthology expert here, Toby. I'm not claiming to know the history. I am merely using common sense here. Clearly, Zonfer had the anti-Plague biocode," Hindler stated emphatically.

"He makes a good point, Schiller," added Davies.

"I know—bear with me here. What if other beings are present here on Earth?"

The reaction was silence. Finally, Hindler responded.

"Aliens, that's your retort? That is most entertaining, Toby. Out of the entire universe, aliens are going to choose to land on this rock? That's a revolutionary theory! Good work, Dr. Schiller. I see you are truly the man for this job," Hindler erupted sarcastically.

"That's mature, Tom. Why is that so ridiculous?"

"Because there is no life other than us, Schiller. It has always seemed statistically impossible, but that is what the research says," Davies responded.

"I know that!" said Schiller impatiently. "Think about this, though. What if the Plague wasn't a natural occurrence? What if the Plague was a weapon used by alien beings to destroy the human race?"

Hindler had had enough. "This is mindless speculation. Let's get this door open."

"Hey!" Schiller exploded in anger. "Who is the mission leader here, Tom? Huh? Am I incapacitated? I don't feel incapacitated! I'll tell you who! It's me! Don't you try and take over this mission, Tom! I'll send you back to the Phoenix quicker than you can say *aliens*."

Hindler shivered back in shock, realizing he had hit a nerve. Schiller wasn't known for his violent outbursts.

"Look, Toby, I—"

"No more of that *Toby* crap! Only my wife calls me that," Schiller interrupted.

"Listen, I stepped over the line. You are the mission leader. No one is questioning that."

"You're damn right I'm the mission leader—and I flew off at the cuff myself. Honestly, you were right. We were wasting time. Let's get that door opened."

Hindler nodded in agreement. "The door looks pretty solid. How we are going to crack it?" he asked.

Suddenly, Rayne exploded into action. He pulled out a plasma blade and sliced the steel door in two like a hot knife through butter.

"Well, wasn't that convenient? Thank you, Mr. Rayne," said Davies.

Rayne grunted in disapproval of Davies' ignorance.

Schiller entered the door. He wasn't sure what to expect. The team slowly made their way down the long corridor.

"Well, gentlemen, I think we can assume we have found the way to the basement," Schiller proclaimed.

It seemed as if the corridor led to the depths of the planet. Soon, they reached a massive room, similar to a mess hall. It was completely empty.

"No, I don't believe it. It's impossible! Maybe there is a false wall, or something of that nature."

"Schiller, the walls are solid steel," Hindler responded.

Schiller was determined.

"Dobbs, I need a full bioscan at our coordinates."

Chapter 11: A Defining Moment

Dobbs began the bioscan of the massive room.

"Whoa! The bioscanner is going nuts! Give me a minute, sir. It might be malfunctioning."

Schiller waited with bated breath. He was convinced there was more to this story. Chairman Zimmerman all but confirmed that TIS knew the historical documents were inside Zonfer's palace. This could be the only location the documents could be found.

"I don't understand this," said Dobbs. "I have never seen code like this. Dr. Schiller, do you have your MLU booted up?"

Schiller swiped his finger across the fingerprint reader on his MLU screen.

"I'm booted up, Dobbs."

"Great, I'll send the readouts to your MLU."

Schiller examined the bioscanner readout. His eyes widened with amazement. Once again, his studies were about to pay off.

"Unbelievable…"

Hindler was as excited as Schiller. "What is it, Schiller?"

"You aren't going to believe this. The bioscanner is putting out God code."

Hindler furrowed his brow and put on a sardonic grin.

"Yeah, right, that's a good one."

Schiller gazed at Hindler with fury. "Do you think I would joke about something like this? I studied God code for years. The theory went that if we could manage to find the right coordinates, we might be able to prove the presence of God. Bioscanner technology has improved so quickly that its power is mind-boggling now. Predictably, TIS didn't put much stock in the idea. However, I worked on it in my spare time. It was and is a very viable theory. Now, as I stand here—I can scarcely believe it."

Hindler knew that Schiller was not a crackpot. If he said a theory was viable, it probably was.

"So, what are you saying? God has been here?"

Schiller inhaled and pinched the bridge of his nose. "I can't begin to contemplate why the bioscanner is picking up God code here. I can only tell you that it is here. It is definitely here, no question. However, it's clear that it is only present in this room. The rest of Zonfer's palace and the surrounding areas are devoid of any presence of the God code."

Davies interjected, "Regardless, this is extraordinary. This proves that there is a God!"

"Not exactly," Schiller clarified.

Davies was confused.

"God code doesn't necessarily prove that God exists," Schiller explained. "The God code is merely a massive compilation of thousands of different biocodes that have been collected by Tento's main bioscanner at TIS. Part of the theory of God code is that, if you can find one point in the universe that contains all of those codes; it must be the presence of God. That is what the bioscanner is picking up now."

"Fine, but that doesn't mean, without a shadow of a doubt, that 'God has been here.'" Hindler remarked dryly.

"Obviously, Hindler, that's why it's a scientific theory and not a scientific fact. You understand the difference between a theory and a fact, don't you, Tom?"

Hindler was steaming. He knew he had been served.

"Dobbs, is the bioscanner recording all of this?"

"Yes, sir, at first, I didn't think it was going to record properly because of the volume of data it is trying to process. At this point, everything looks copasetic."

Schiller was pleased.

"Copy, we're about done here. We have to let the bioscanner run for as long as it needs. I'm going to drop some nanobots. Perhaps their analysis can shed some more light on what exactly is going on in here."

Schiller grabbed into his side bag and pulled out a small capsule. He cracked it and turned it upside down. The microscopic machines dissolved into the ground. Under a high-power microscope, they appeared insect-like. They would be absorbed into the soil underneath the steel floor in the room and would transmit information back to Schiller's MLU that would be recorded for later study.

Chapter 12: The Encounter

A feeling of shock and confusion rippled through the team. The main question was: what exactly had they discovered? The discovery of the God code alone would make this expedition historically priceless. Schiller relished the idea of reporting this discovery to Zimmerman. As chairman of TIS, he had been responsible for cutting the funding for God code research. This would certainly make him rethink that decision.

This had been an eventful day. However, the mission was far from over. The next mission objective would be for Schiller to do a full analysis of the Earthling soil. This would be the most time-consuming part of the mission. The bioscanners on board the Phoenix could only do so much. Schiller would have to do a "hands-on" analysis to reap the full benefits of the research. Samples would be taken and his MLU would record the biocode of every sample. This would be vital in understanding Earth's new composition. It would be much more helpful if they could bring back samples on the Phoenix but the risk of alien viruses was real. An alien infection would devastate Tento.

The team needed to find an area on Earth that most represented the entire planet. The new volatile behavior of the planet made this a risky task. All the bodies of water on the planet were boiling. The soil was an ashen red color. Plant life was all but extinct. It was obvious that the new makeup of planet Earth was drastically different.

The team appeared to be a wandering tribe, and at this point, that wouldn't be far from the truth. Back at the Phoenix, Dobbs was analyzing maps as the team traveled. The bioscanners, at close range, had the ability to map large areas and display them in a 3D map. It had completed mapping over fifty percent of the Earth's surface.

The old maps of Earth's surface that Tentonians had grown up learning about didn't even come close to what was now a reality. Entire continents had been reduced to islands. The beautiful blue oceans of Earth now were dark, brooding death pits. The appearance of the ocean was now that of a gigantic moving black bed sheet. It was terrifying to witness. To say the least, the human race had returned to a profoundly different planet.

Schiller and the team slowly and cautiously traversed the coastline near Zonfer's palace. Schiller wanted to get a sample from the body of water. He once again grabbed into his bag and pulled out a large scoop like tool. He dipped it into the black, rippling liquid. It steamed and hissed as he pulled it back out. The odor the amalgamation emitted was putrid. Needless to say, this was not drinking water. The consistency of the water was different, almost soupy. This was a clear indication that the fundamental makeup of the Earth's oceans had been totally transformed. Schiller stared at the liquid in the scoop-tool.

"I can't wait to see the analytical data from this stuff," he said excitedly. "I'll bet we'll find a plethora of anomalies—I can't wait."

Hindler smiled and nodded in agreement. "I don't want to be pushy but could we get moving? Being out here makes me—uncomfortable."

Schiller smirked. "Absolutely, just let me get this into a vial."

Schiller filled his sample vial and the team continued on its way. As they came closer to the coastline, something strange came to their attention.

"Schiller, do you see that?"

"Yes, Tom, I do."

In the distance, it almost seemed as though the Earth had ended. A massive black, writhing cloud obscured the path ahead. Davies was profoundly frightened by what he saw.

"I don't know about you, gentlemen, but I don't want to walk into that."

"No, I don't think that would be wise. Dobbs, I need a full bioscan of the area directly in front of us. You have our coordinates. Please do that now," Schiller concluded.

Dobbs arranged the scan quickly.

"It appears to be a Plague cloud but I thought they had all disappeared," Dobbs suggested.

"That was what we thought. We couldn't confirm it," Hindler clarified.

"I see. Schiller, I don't recommend you get near that cloud. The concentration of Plague code could alter your DNA. We know that's a bad thing," said Dobbs.

Schiller sighed. "Well, it looks like we have reached the end of this path."

The team members made an about face and started in the direction they had come from. As they continued on their way, one thing was for certain. The current state of planet Earth was depressing and unfortunate. A once vibrant and alive planet appeared to be dying from the inside out. Perhaps the ravages of the Plague had proved too devastating even for planet Earth to adapt to.

As the team got farther away from Zonfer's once great palace, Schiller turned his thoughts back and recalled the images of when Zonfer's palace was a great architectural masterpiece. It now represented the current state of Earth, a fallen angel of sorts.

Suddenly, Rayne equipped his pulse rifle that he had holstered on his shoulder for the entire mission. Schiller noticed this.

"Rayne, why did you ready your weapon? Is everything all right?"

"I'm picking something up in my motion HUD. There's movement somewhere near us. It might be smart to pick up the pace."

Schiller flinched. "Keep me informed."

The beeping of Rayne's motion detector resonated inside the team's ears. Each tone was like a hammer pounding them into submission.

Rayne said anxiously, "Sir, the objects are closing. We might have hostiles. We should get into defensive posture."

The team members powered on the force field protection on their biosuits. This function was used for hazardous environments. They were hoping they wouldn't have to use the function on this particular mission.

"Rayne, what is the status of the hostile?"

"Still closing, sir, I don't understand it. We should be able to see something by now. Where the hell are these bastards?"

Without warning, a creature shrouded in darkness propelled itself in the way of the team. Its shape appeared to be almost lion like but it was enveloped in a cloak of black. All that was visible were its pale, red eyes that became bright red at the sight of the team.

Rayne sprung into action.

"Everyone get behind me!"

Rayne fired at the creature, a few well-placed rounds of plasma hurling into the beast's face. The creature never had a chance. The plasma rounds hit their target with great precision. Rayne surveyed the territory for more targets. His motion detector stopped beeping.

Schiller took a deep breath. "Gentlemen, I think we just met our first Earthling. I guess not much has changed around here. They'll kill you as soon as they look at you."

Chapter 13: The Site

The team was shaken up by their encounter with one of Earth's new residents. Rayne now knew that he had a definite purpose on the mission. The likelihood that the team would encounter more of these hostile Earthling creatures was high and they appeared to be formidable.

They had been traveling for hours. The landmass where they touched down was enormous. It was almost as if several continents merged into one. At the center of this landmass was a huge craterlike indentation. Schiller spotted this and decided it would be the team's objective point. He thought this area would best represent Earth as a whole. This was because it appeared that this area once had water in it. To understand what had happened to Earth during the transition to its current state, research would need to be done in an area that encompassed all of Earth's new attributes.

The team now found itself at the edge of the massive crater. Davies was dumbfounded.

"My word, look at this. What could have created this?"

"Well, it doesn't look like an impact crater. The edge would be much more chaotic if that were the case," Schiller answered.

"What are you suggesting, Schiller?" asked Hindler skeptically. "It's a landing spot?"

Schiller sighed again and brushed off the comment. "All right, let's see what we can see," he proclaimed.

The crater was shallow enough for them to climb down to its bottom. When they reached the bottom, they saw that the soil was scorched. Hindler felt ridiculous.

"Well, I called it," he said. "It's a landing crater."

Schiller glared at him in distain.

"Not necessarily, but you know that. We need to set up shop in here. Dobbs—are you there?"

"Yes, sir, what do you need?"

"Send out the rover with the research equipment. I've found the area that I'm going to use to conduct the research. I'll send you the coordinates."

"Yes, sir, I'll get on that right away. Sir—"

"What is it, Dobbs?"

"I need to talk to you about something—in person. I have you on a private channel. Don't tell the rest of the crew that you are going to meet with me. Come back on the rover."

Schiller was concerned.

"What is this about, Stan?"

"I don't want to talk about it in this way. I need to see you."

"All right, I'll comm you when I'm near. I have to admit, you're scaring me."

Dobbs didn't respond.

Chapter 14: Beginning Research

The research equipment was on its way. Schiller couldn't wait to get to work. However, Dobbs' seemingly urgent request to discuss something with Schiller was interfering with the good vibe. He could think of little else.

In the distance, Schiller could see the rover approaching the research site. It looked like a hovercraft in the shape of a buggy racing vehicle. Towing behind it on a hover flatbed was the equipment that the team would need to complete their research. Schiller, Rayne, and Davies unloaded the equipment as Hindler set everything up for use. A mobile nuclear power supply was used to power all of the equipment. When all the preparations were complete, Schiller wanted to get going.

"All right, gentlemen, I'm going to personally drive the rover back to the Phoenix. I'll be right back."

Hindler was puzzled. "But, the rover can autopilot back itself. We need you here, Schiller."

"TIS will not be happy if something happens to that rover. I want to make sure it gets back safely. We have a teleport point set up. I'll use that to get back."

Hindler wasn't letting up that easy. "Look, we need you right now. Some of this equipment I don't even know how to use. You think I can just learn on the fly? I want to get back to the Phoenix as soon as possible, too. If you take the time to drive that thing back to the Phoenix, it's going to put us way behind."

Schiller didn't appreciate the tone.

"No—you listen. I am the mission leader. I really don't want to go down this road with you again, Tom. To tell you the truth, I need to talk to Dobbs in person. He's got something he needs to discuss with me."

Hindler knew that Dobbs wouldn't request a meeting if it wasn't something urgent. Also, he didn't hear anything over his comm link so that meant they must have been on a private channel.

"I'm sorry. I had no idea," Hindler said apologetically.

"Yes, that was the point. We need to get this mission over with as soon as possible. We didn't come here on a vacation. This mission is costing the government billions an hour. We're on borrowed time here," Schiller said.

Hindler recoiled in shame.

Schiller continued, "The longer I stand here arguing with you, the longer no work gets done. Most of the equipment that you haven't used yet isn't hard to operate. Trust me, just read the quick tutorial within the operation program. I know you will catch on quickly. Now, I have to go—right now."

"Okay, Schiller, I'll do the best I can, but I'm not making any guarantees."

"Listen, in the off chance that you can't operate something properly, I'll get us caught up."

Schiller turned and ran toward the rover. He opened the cockpit door and hit the accelerator hastily. Hindler didn't appreciate the treatment he was receiving from Schiller. As far as he was concerned, he was just as intelligent and capable as Schiller. The seeds of contempt had been planted long ago. They were beginning to sprout.

Chapter 15: Devastating News / An Amazing Discovery

The rover approached the Phoenix. Schiller could feel a lump in his throat. Dobbs' tone was especially dire. What could be so important? He exited the rover swiftly and entered the Phoenix quickly.

"Dobbs, I came as quickly as I could. What's the problem?"

"Sir, I have been looking at the readouts from the bioscanner. There seems to be an unforeseen circumstance to us being on Earth in its current state for a prolonged period of time. The bioscanner is projecting that there is a 50 percent chance that upon returning to Tento, we could die."

Schiller was flabbergasted.

"Have you run the facts on this?"

"I have been pursuing every angle of this since the bioscanner put out the information. All indications are that the projections are correct. When I was fairly certain this wasn't an error, I decided to request a personal meeting with you. I didn't want to broadcast something like this to the entire team."

Schiller didn't know what to say. Fifty percent was better than one hundred. He was a "glass half-full" type.

"Well, this is unfortunate, but we are here now and there is nothing we can do about this. I appreciate your candor and I want you to keep me updated on the status of your studies. Your initial instincts were correct about not telling the rest of the team about this. I would like you to keep it that way. The last thing we need is this bearing down on us as we are conducting the research—Dobbs, you haven't been out with us. Maybe you're safe. The Phoenix has its own oxygen system."

"Schiller, I was there when the airlock was opened. I'm just as at risk as you are. It's okay. I'm proud to be a part of this mission."

Schiller nodded and placed his hand on Stanley Dobbs' shoulder.

"This mission is going to benefit the science community more than even we can understand. We are making a difference in our field for years to come. You have been a vital part of the team, Stan—understand this. As your mission leader, I thank you for your work thus far. Keep up the good work."

"Thank you, Schiller. One more thing. The 3D mapping of the Earth is almost complete. It appears there is a gigantic structure a few hundred miles from where the team is now. It looks like a massively large, one floor structure. It looks to be intact."

Schiller couldn't believe that Dobbs didn't see the importance of what he had just told him.

"Stanley—are you sure?"

"Yes, look for yourself. I assumed it was just more ruins from when the Plague destroyed Earth."

"The only ruins that TIS knows about is Zonfer's palace. If you are telling me that there is another structure, this is a huge discovery."

"Well, I don't know how they could have missed this. It's enormous."

"Stan, they didn't miss it. It means that it was built after the Exodus," Schiller enlightened him.

"What?"

"That's right."

Chapter 16: A New Mission

Schiller returned to the research site with amazing news as well as devastating news. The research equipment was all set up and the team had begun testing samples and recording biological data. The information bank on Earth's biological composition had increased exponentially in the last hour. Schiller approached Hindler.

"How are things going, Tom?"

"*Hindler* will do, Schiller. It was a bit touch and go at first but I got the basics of it."

"Good. Davies, how is the gathering of samples going?"

"Going great. I've managed to gather enough samples to compile a preliminary outline of Earth's biocode."

"That's impressive, Davies. I don't think I would have been able to do that so quickly. Rayne, how is the security end of the mission going?"

"There is nothing to report, sir. My motion HUD has been silent ever since the encounter with whatever that was. The quietness is a bit unsettling, sir. If there is anything to report, I will see it. I have set up a lookout point at the edge of the crater. I will be sure to report any activity."

"Thank you, Rayne. It looks like it's time for me to get to work."

Schiller began to read the research information that had been compiled thus far. Immediately he saw something that caught his eye.

"Gentlemen, we have a new mission. According to the information acquired thus far, I think there is a good possibility that there is something beneath us. We need to dig."

Hindler snickered. "How do you intend on digging? We didn't bring any excavating equipment?"

Schiller looked defiantly at Hindler.

"They're just going to have to send it."

Hindler's eyes widened in disbelief. "What? you've got to be kidding! That will take a month to get here! I am not staying on this planet any longer than I have to!"

"If you don't like it, tough. That is what's happening."

"Schiller, I've had it! You've been leading this mission with an iron fist. You won't even consider alternatives," Hindler retorted.

Schiller was sick of Hindler's defiance and he knew where his attitude originated. It was time to call him on it.

"Hindler, we both know why you're being so difficult. We have some issues. We need to put them aside for the sake of this mission. I wouldn't suggest something that needs to be done simply to anger you. I need to focus on the mission. We have a very small team here and your attitude isn't helping. Now, we need to stop wasting time and continue our work."

It was done. What needed to be said had been said. How Hindler would take it would be his business. Schiller had more important matters to be concerned with.

Schiller knew what the next step would be. He needed to get authorization from TIS to send the excavation equipment.

"Dobbs, I need you to get in contact with Chairman Zimmerman at TIS and request a conference call with the TIS board."

"I'll contact him immediately. What is going on, sir?"

"I have very good reason to believe that there is something underneath us in this crater. I've been studying the sonar and bio samples of the area and there is something under here. I'm sure of it."

"All right, sir, when I have him on the line, I'll contact you."

"Copy that."

Schiller continued studying the research data. It wasn't surprising that Earth's new makeup was drastically different. The research data proved what Schiller had suspected. Gradually, over time, Earth had taken on the biological code of the Plague. How or why this happened could be a mystery forever. They would need far more information and time to gather it in order to understand that. The fact that a structure had been built post Exodus unveiled terrifying new questions. The main question in Schiller's mind was: Was the Plague a weapon used to drive the human race from planet Earth? Were they sharing Earth with a hostile race as Schiller sat studying the research data? Both these questions were constantly running through Schiller's mind. Those answers he could find, however, formed a confusing equation. He focused on what he could answer.

Chapter 17: The Conference Call

Schiller had been sifting tirelessly through the new research data. He finally paused to have a bite to eat. The TIS ready-to-eat meals were actually quite appetizing. As he began to take his first bite, Dobbs chimed in on his comm link.

"Sir, I have Chairman Zimmerman on the line."

Schiller couldn't believe the timing.

"Copy that. Patch him through."

Zimmerman's voice crackled through. "Dr. Schiller, I hope this call doesn't find you in a perilous state," he said.

"No, sir, I requested a conference call of the board because I need excavation tools on Earth. I have reason to believe that something of interest is underneath our research site. Sonar and bio data say that this is the case. I feel that if I were to ignore this, a potentially significant discovery could be overlooked."

Zimmerman and the board didn't appreciate this. The funding for the mission had been difficult to get from the New Senate in the first place. Now, with this considerable added expense, they would need to get approval from the appropriate authorities.

"Listen, Schiller," said Zimmerman, "this mission has come at a huge expense to TIS and the Tentonian people. This new request

is going to double the cost of the mission. I don't know if the
New Senate will even consider funding this request."

"Then don't ask them for approval. Mr. Chairman, if we
don't do this, the entire mission might turn out to be a failure. The
government wants us to succeed above all. I know we have an
unlimited bank account, sir. We need to do this."

"You're right—all right, let's take the vote. All in favor say
'yea.'"

The vote passed unanimously.

"Now, Schiller, you do realize that you are going to have to
stay on that planet for a considerably longer duration. We don't know
if the Plague serum will last for an extended period of time."

"Don't worry about that, sir," Schiller shot back.

"What are you talking about, Tobias? We are not going to risk
your life and the lives of your crew for this mission. No mission is
worth that," Zimmerman said with conviction.

"Sir…I can't explain the details but…you don't have to worry
about us. Just get the excavation equipment here as soon as possible.
The bioscanner on the Phoenix and our research equipment are
constantly sending information back to the main bioscanner at TIS.
This mission will be a success, no matter what happens to us."

Zimmerman understood the gravity of the situation.

"All right, Tobias. I don't know what else to say."

"One more thing, sir. I know that wormholing hasn't been
perfected, but can we try it to get the excavation equipment here as
quickly as possible? To be honest, the team is getting a little crazy
down here and no matter what happens to us, we can't complete our
studies if we aren't thinking clearly. Getting that equipment here
within the hour would do wonders for everyone's state of mind."

Zimmerman didn't want to say yes but he couldn't see a way
around it. "You are making my job very hard today, Tobias. We'll try
it. Expect to see the wormhole within the hour. I will get the
coordinates from Dobbs."

"Thank you, sir. I guarantee you won't regret your decisions."

"I'd better not, because you will have someone else to answer
to, someone not as forgiving as myself. Out."

The meeting could have been more cordial but it would do.
Schiller knew without a doubt that there was something beneath the
crater.

Chapter 18: Continuing Progress

The research was going swimmingly. Davies had collected enough samples to put together a full profile of Earth's biocode. Schiller and Hindler compiled the biological information into the research equipment that generated the code structure. Earth's new image was becoming clearer. The excavation was all that remained. Dobbs chimed in on the comm link.

"Sir, TIS has begun the creation of the wormhole. You will probably begin to see it develop within the next five minutes."

Schiller was pleased. "Copy that, Dobbs."

Schiller saw a tiny spiral forming in the sky directly above the site of the crater. In a matter of minutes, the wormhole covered the entire span of the sky above the massive indentation on the Earthling landscape. A hover flat containing the excavation equipment slowly descended onto the research site. Hindler looked on in hostility. He wanted to be off this vile planet. He longed for the overcast, dreary surroundings of Tento. The evil, brooding visage of Earth was disheartening to say the least. One couldn't blame him without being hypocritical.

The landing zone for the equipment was predetermined by Schiller and marked with a homing beacon. The flat slowly set down the massive autodigger. These were tools that were used by developers to burrow into areas that needed to be cleared out for building new superstructures. TIS had been developing them for years. The prospect of wormholing one of these, however, would be an expensive one, hence the reluctance of Zimmerman and TIS. But Schiller now had what he needed and he was elated.

As the equipment was unloaded, Schiller ordered the team to fold up the research equipment so the excavation equipment could do its job. As the hover flat reentered the wormhole, the team paused to watch this amazing sight. Wormholing was a new technology that hadn't been used in the field. This was the first time any Tentonian scientist had seen this new technology in action. The team was awestruck. As the hover flat entered the wormhole, the wormhole began to close. Then, almost as soon as it had appeared, the flat was gone.

Schiller broke the silence. "Well, that was an amazing sight. Now, Hindler, help me out with programming the autodigger."

Hindler didn't respond. He simply followed Schiller to the landing site of the equipment. The tension between the two was palpable.

Schiller added the autodigger to his MLU equipment profile and prepared to start the excavation. He prepped the autodigger software on his MLU.

"All right, team, is everyone clear of the dig site?"

Davies, Rayne, and Hindler all gave the green light.

Schiller confirmed, "Action commencing." He plugged the depth information into the autodigger programming and began the excavation. The enormous drill descended from the autodigger and immediately began to burrow into the Earthling soil. The team waited with bated breath to see what results the new mission would uncover.

Chapter 19: Lost and Found

The autodigger relentlessly dredged the soil. A cloud of dust and debris obstructed the view of the team. It was a mesmerizing sight to watch this piece of equipment work. It had millions of intricately engineered alloy blades that contoured around the object that was contained in the soil it was dredging. The synergy of its programming of various operating systems was a technological wonder. Hindler, even with his obvious feelings of disapproval with Schiller's decision, couldn't hide his excitement.

"Schiller, what do you think might be under there?"

Schiller was annoyed but felt vindicated by Hindler's enthusiasm.

"I don't know, Tom. Why do you think I ordered excavation equipment here? It wasn't for my health."

Hindler went on the offensive. "Nothing's been found yet, Tobias. Don't call the game before it's over."

Schiller looked down at his MLU monitoring the progress of the dig and didn't respond. He gazed at it longingly in search of validation of his instinctual feeling. Suddenly, the sonar began buzzing.

"The autodigger has started to slow the excavating process. It appears that its internal sonar system has picked something up—and it's close."

Schiller smugly gazed at Hindler. Vindication was a wonderful feeling.

Hindler skimmed over any awkward moment with an enthusiastic inquiry.

"What are the dimensions?"

"It's big, real big. It looks as if it might be a building that has been buried beneath the soil. The sonar mapping's preliminary model is producing an image that looks similar to late Earthling architecture," Schiller informed.

"How the hell do you know so much about Earth's past? I thought a main part of this mission was finding out about our past," Hindler asked.

"One has the ability to acquire a multitude of information if one is so inclined. I find it sad that so many people choose to ignore the information that is already available on Earth's past. It is true that there are many missing holes in the accounts. However, we are far from clueless in the realm of Earthology," Schiller retorted in an almost arrogant tone.

"You and that quackery," said Hindler sourly.

Schiller input the new coordinates into his MLU telling the autodigger where to move. As the autodigger moved to its new destination, the team observed what they had uncovered.

"It looks like a massive safety deposit box with a door," Davies commented.

Hindler rolled his eyes.

"Great, more structures that shouldn't be here."

Schiller rolled out an auto bridge for the team to descend into the pit. The team eagerly approached the vessel. Schiller examined the door. "It looks as if this requires a pass code to open it," he said.

Davies interjected, "I can take care of that." He powered on his MLU and attached the research module to the keypad. In a matter of seconds, the door was open. Schiller looked at Davies in amazement.

"You find out new things to do with our Mobile Lab Units every day, don't you?"

"I have my methods, you have yours," Davies responded modestly.

The door hissed, retracted, and revealed the inside of the vessel. Inside lay what the crew had thought to be lost forever. From wall to wall, metal file cabinets, ancient computer towers, and compact disk media covered the interior of the history-preserving container. The team was thrilled.

"Here is our priority one, gentlemen. How or why it got here I have no idea. Nonetheless, without this information, the entire mission would have been a failure," Schiller proclaimed victoriously.

The team entered the vessel. Davies made an observation. "Dr. Schiller, there are some stone tables over here. I'll run these through the Rosetta Stone program in my MLU."

Schiller was surprised. "You have the Rosetta program on your MLU?"

"It's the best TIS-certified program for decoding ancient languages. It's the only one, really."

Schiller felt quite accomplished at that moment. "I wrote that program," he said. Davies' astonishment couldn't be hidden.

"Schiller, I had no idea! That's amazing!"

"Well, many sleepless nights were spent on that monstrosity. Did you know that it almost didn't receive TIS certification? Zimmerman and the board insisted I verify my sources before they 'put stock' in their contents. Finally, they understood that I had done the best I could and they certified the program for use within the TIS community."

Davies was disgusted by Schiller's tale.

"Unbelievable. They tell you to assemble a program and you compile this comprehensive research tool. Then they have the ignorance to deny certification in expectation of an impossible task, just to prove sources that are impossible to contact."

Schiller nodded.

"I wasn't happy myself, Davies. Today, to my great pleasure, those sources may be proven."

"I'll scan these tables into my MLU and start running the Rosetta program immediately," Davies replied.

All the while, Hindler was examining and starting up the old computer towers. As far as Hindler was concerned, everything that Schiller and Davies were discussing amounted to nothing. Hindler believed only in what could be seen and even then, he needed some convincing. He scoured the computer files quickly. He found it painful to admit that he didn't understand what he was looking at. Earthology was the last sector of science he ever thought he would have to work with. As he so eloquently stated, it was nothing more than "quackery" —or so he thought.

Chapter 20: Unforeseen Events

The team was mentally exhausted. They had been compiling and calculating data for longer than they cared to think about. However, the fruits of their labors were paying off as the hours passed into history. The flickers of the biochemists' holoscreens illuminated the darkened time capsule they had uncovered. Rayne, standing outside the structure on the extended walkway that led back to the Earthling topography, constantly monitored the security situation. The team feared another encounter with an Earthling.

As the team members continued their studies, one question was prominent in their list of hypothetical questions. Namely, "who had buried this vessel and how?"

The story of the Exodus from Earth was well known. The Plague had quickly and viciously appeared and decimated Earth. Zonfer had to hastily organize and implement an escape plan. It was impossible that he had been the one who constructed this structure in the hopes of an eventual return of the human race to Earth. From his perspective, this would never be possible. So, the question would remain. Who had visited Earth and found it necessary to bury this information?

Without warning, the door they had entered slammed shut and locked. There was no keypad on the inside. Schiller immediately contacted Rayne on his comm link.

"Rayne, did you pick up anything on your motion sensor?"

"No sir, nothing to report," Rayne calmly responded.

"Could you please reopen the door, Rayne? I don't understand—"

Rayne interrupted, "Sir, we've got company."

Rayne could feel the tip of some kind of object pressed to the back of his head. Then he heard clicks and guttural noises that he couldn't begin to understand.

"Schiller, the hostile is trying to communicate with me but—"

"Obviously, you can't understand," said Schiller in frustration. "Gentlemen, I think we've just been captured. Apparently, we've walked right into an alien trap. Ironically, we're the aliens."

Hindler frowned in confusion. "Captured by whom, Schiller?"

"I think you already know the answer to that, Tom."

Rayne updated the situation. "Sir, this thing is coming in."

The airlock reopened and as the steam from it faded, the team got their first look at a race that until now was not known to mankind. The being that stood in front of them was frightening and repulsive. Its skin was an ashen red color, similar to the color of the sky and soil. It was long and tall in stature and exceptionally thin. If the light hit its bald cranium correctly, one could very well be knocked back by the intensity of the beam of light. Its eyes were pitch black orbs. Its mouth was similar to a human being's aside from the teeth, reminiscent of shark teeth. Its clothing was armor like in appearance. However, one could distinguish that it was a fabric of some sort. Massive shoulder pads made of fur, perhaps a spoil of war, completed the terrifying figure. The team shuddered collectively at what would happen next.

After the creature entered the trap, it immediately tried communicating with the team. It made the same clicking and guttural noises that Rayne had heard. There was nothing random about these sounds. It was obviously the creature's language. When it was apparent to the creature that communicating in its own language wasn't working, it used a more familiar communication system— threats of violence. The alien pointed its weapon in the air and shot a single round into the ceiling of the structure. Then it motioned with its weapon toward the exit of the human mouse trap.

Schiller led the way as Hindler, Davies, and Rayne followed close behind. The alien could be heard faintly as the team walked back to the ledge of the crater. When they reached the ledge, a cylindrical, pod like vehicle lay in wait to transport the captives to their unknown destination. The alien transport emitted a droning, monotone humming noise. The alien made a quick motion with its arm and the pod morphed into a larger version of itself. The team momentarily forgot they had been captured, awestruck by the technology they were witnessing. After all, they were scientists. This was the kind of thing that a TIS engineer only dreamed about. Davies observed the material that the craft consisted of. It appeared to be a liquid form of metal. White light shimmered off the craft in brilliant waves. Davies could only hypothesize as to what the physical material was. He longed to attach his MLU sample reader to the craft. At this point, however, that might be a death sentence.

For that matter, it was unlikely that any of their research would be safe. The alien beings would probably destroy all of their research data. Schiller hoped that the servers jacked into the bioscanners back at TIS would have successfully recorded all of the research data they had compiled by the time the creatures realized what the research equipment contained. And there was the possibility that this was the only being on the planet other than them, a lone alien being. However, Schiller thought this to be extremely unlikely. Given the fact that there was a structure built on Earth post-Exodus meant that Earth had new residents and they didn't want visitors. One could deduce from the current set of facts that were known that Earth was being terraformed or manipulated to serve the living conditions of this race. A good hypothetical guess would be that the Plague was a weapon used by this race to drive the human race from the planet so that they could easily slip into their new home.

Schiller found it hard to believe that TIS wouldn't have noticed craft entering into Earth's space. According to the board, TIS was almost constantly monitoring Earth. One would assume this would include possible incoming craft. However, this wasn't necessarily the case. In terms of visual monitoring, TIS rarely took the time to update its archival images of Earth. This was the reason for the utter shock of the team when they observed the current aesthetic of the planet. It resembled Mars more than the original Earth in its current state. It was apparent that this transition had been centuries in the making. However, the final transition to its current state was almost instant. The slowly assembling Earthling biocode revealed this fact.

The alien being prodded the team toward the mesmerizing craft. Unexpectedly, out of the dimly lit expanse, a new kind of creature appeared in the form of a pride of the silent Earthling killers, showing only their deep red eyes and pristine, flowing black bodies. The alien being immediately reacted with fire from its weapon. Apparently, these creatures weren't even friendly with the locals. There were a considerable number of the Earthling killers. Yet the alien's accuracy was astonishing—each shot equaled a kill. In the end, a line of corpses lay steaming on the Earthling soil. This incident was enough of a distraction for Rayne to act.

He suddenly made one quick movement and blew a hole in the creature's throat with a hidden pulse pistol that was embedded in his bio suit.

"Hostile down, sir," Rayne announced with confidence.

Schiller could barely speak. He was a scientist. He wasn't used to all this action.

"That was—anyway, I think our next course of action is obvious, gentlemen. I received some information from Dobbs concerning a post-Exodus structure here on Earth. I didn't inform you about this because I thought it would interfere with your current objectives—"

Hindler exploded in a torrent of anger. "You have information like this and you fail to inform us? This is a new low, Schiller! We need to know about these things! If you informed us about a post-Exodus structure, we could have prepared for a possible attack! Rayne would have been prepared for something. Damn it! You're going to get us all killed!"

Schiller gazed at Hindler without any expression.

"Rayne, could you have done anything different if you had known about a possible threat?"

"No, sir, I had my motion sensors activated and nothing came up. This is my first and last line of preventive defense."

Schiller looked back at Hindler once again, expressionless. Hindler felt the pressure of being so blatantly shown up. After a very awkward silence, Hindler childishly responded.

"Whatever! This mission is insane and your leadership is going to get us all killed, Schiller! You'll be up on charges if anyone gets killed. You can mark my words on that one."

Schiller didn't respond. Hindler's empty threats and constant bad attitude were getting tiresome but Schiller knew he needed him. Davies and he alone would never be able to do all the cataloging and research that needed to be done. Hindler would have to cool down on his own time. Schiller's best response was no response at all.

***

Zonfer City was bustling with activity. The mission to Earth wasn't known to the general public but the Tentonian Free Press was digging and rumors were circulating.

The New Senate convened in an emergency session, the subject being the mission to Earth. Chairman Heinmeche had been monitoring the progress of the mission, and he was seriously concerned about the effect that the new knowledge this mission was uncovering would have on the Tentonian citizens. He began his address.

"Gentlemen of the New Senate, I thank you for gathering so swiftly to discuss this highly important topic; that is, protecting the Tentonian citizenry from destructive knowledge. I think I can assume that no one thought about this when we green-lighted the mission to planet Earth. I have had the time to contemplate the possible effects of knowledge that could arise from this mission that would do nothing but negatively impact the psyche of Tentonian people. The primary talking point, in my opinion, would be any knowledge that would question the ultimate authority of the New Senate in Tentonian affairs. The authority of our body has been given by our people. With this mission to Earth, we are dealing with potentially intangible, vague information. Subjects like alien life and 'other realms' are not subjects that the Tentonian people need to be concerned with.

"So, in light of my contemplation, I suggest we take an immediate vote on a new resolution. The Information and Knowledge Protection Act would, at all costs, protect the ultimate authority of the New Senate in Tentonian affairs. This resolution shall state that the psyche of the Tentonian people should be protected no matter the consequence. Finally, the ultimate decision of action will come directly from the New Senate chairman. All in favor say 'yea.'"

This concluded the New Senate session. How the governing body of Tento voted would determine the ultimate fate of the human race. However, as important a matter as this vote was, the vote was taken in closed session. We will never know if the resolution passed. In this moment, Tentonian government had done what past governing bodies ended up eventually regretting: overstepping its legal bounds and hiding behind walls of secrecy. Regardless of the actual vote, Tento had decided to go down a very dangerous and destructive path, the path to total annihilation.

Chapter 21: Rayne's Mission

Schiller, Hindler, and Davies had briefly returned to the structure that contained their research materials. They returned to find that all was well. Fortunately, the TIS bioscanner servers had downloaded and backed up all the research materials that the biochemists had recorded on their research equipment. Rayne remained at the edge of the crater keeping a watchful eye on the surroundings. To the team's comfort, Rayne's motion sensor remained silent. He kept his weapon close as he surveyed the territory.

Rayne observed the pod that would have served as a transport for the captives. As he studied its appearance, he imagined whether he could pilot the craft. He peered into the cockpit and gazed at the operating controls. The being that had taken the team captive had the device that controlled the pod on its arm. Rayne cautiously removed the operating device from the being's forearm and placed it on his own. He could feel it cling to his arm almost as though it were a living organism. At this point, the pod was in its larger state to accommodate the prisoners. Rayne made a pinching motion with his index finger and thumb with the hand of the arm that had the pod-controlling device on it. Immediately, the pod morphed into a smaller shape. Rayne decided to experiment and spread his fingers out again. The craft returned to its larger form. For fun, he spread and pinched his fingers quickly, and the pod adjusted accordingly. Rayne wished he could buy one. He was a confirmed transport enthusiast. His profession allowed him to pursue such an expensive hobby and this particular transport intrigued him more than any of the crafts he possessed back on Tento.

Schiller and the rest of the team had finished their tasks at the structure inside the crater and made their way back to Rayne's position. Schiller noticed Rayne admiring the pod.

"Pretty neat, isn't it?"

"That it is, sir. I wouldn't mind having one," Rayne responded.

"We might be able to arrange that. It would come at a cost though. Hindler, Davies, and I have been discussing the post-Exodus structure found in the northern region of the planet. After our encounter with this being, it is clear that Earth is inhabited by another race. We have concluded that the structure is probably an outpost for this race. A large library of information would be available at this structure for us to take and digest. As the mission leader, I have decided that this is priority one on our agenda. However, these beings are obviously hostile and combat isn't what we do—"

"Say no more, sir. I'll infiltrate the structure covertly and find out whatever I can. I'll take photographs and, if possible, download any information that I can to a mobile drive," Rayne interjected.

Schiller nodded and turned to converse with Hindler and Davies.

"Sir—"

Schiller turned back in Rayne's direction.

"I should take the pod. If there are other hostiles, any other foreign craft would raise suspicion."

"That's a good idea, but be careful. I'll input the coordinates into your HUD," said Schiller before he resumed his conversation with Hindler and Davies.

Rayne jumped into the pod's cockpit and quickly accelerated away. This was going to be amusing.

Chapter 22: The Citadel

The droning buzz of the engine inside the pod resonated throughout the expanse of the Earthling terrain. Rayne had quickly grown accustomed to the behavior of the craft. It handled better than anything he had ever driven. If he had been the type to do so, he would have yelled in excitement. Immediately upon traveling toward the structure, he noticed that a pathway had been blown by prior traffic. According to the coordinates, the path was leading right for the structure's position. Rayne prepared mentally for a possibly hostile encounter.

The craft inched closer to the coordinates that Schiller had programmed into the HUD unit contained in Rayne's helmet. Soon, he could see the structure in the distance. Upon first sight, Rayne knew that this was a fortress of some sort. Large cannon like weaponry protruded into the Earthling sky. Beacons glistened atop the massive structure. As light kissed and glided off of the structure's surface, it was apparent that this fortress was made of the same material as the pod. It was also apparent that there was a lack of activity at this citadel. The apparatus that would have provided lighting was dormant. Rayne was relieved. He was used to combat but didn't necessarily enjoy it. He would lead people to believe otherwise but this was in fact the case.

Rayne powered down the pod and exited at a safe distance from the alien citadel. He didn't want to push his luck. It appeared that the structure was vacant but nothing was certain. When all seemed clear, he decided it would be an opportune time to take some snapshots of this alien wonder. He readied the internal terra-pixel camera contained in his helmet. This device could take crystal clear photographs hundreds of miles away from the point of interest. Rayne was well in range for an excellent photo opportunity. As he completed the photo shoot, Schiller chimed in on his comm link.

"Rayne, what is your current status?"

"Currently, I am a few miles from the structure. I just shot some photos of the alien structure. It definitely seems to be an alien fortress of some sort. The front of the structure has a large identification sign in the same language as the pod console controls. Fortunately, it looks like no one's home. Apparently, our recently departed friend who wanted to take us captive was a caretaker for this place. Hopefully, he was the only one here. But sir, just in case he wasn't alone, I think it would be wise for me to go dark. The last thing we need is this alien race monitoring our conversations and being a step ahead of us."

Schiller understood and agreed. "Absolutely, Rayne, I couldn't agree more. This will be the last contact me or the team will make with you until you are clear of the alien structure. Good luck and god speed."

"Affirmative, sir. I will power down your communication channel but I will leave the line open so you can listen in on the activity. Rayne out," he finished.

Rayne was puzzled. What was with the sudden "God talk"? He chalked it up to the God code moment in Zonfer's headquarters. He probably wasn't far from being dead on. Schiller wasn't a confirmed atheist like most of his chemist colleagues. Faithful Tentonians were in the minority. However, through the years, for mostly financial reasons, some Tentonians found God. The pioneers of Tentonian faith groups sifted through the available texts in the Library of Tento. This inevitably led to the founding of different churches and religious groups on Tento. Until this point, most of the ancient Earthling faiths had gone dormant with the death of the last remaining native Earthlings. Now, Christian, Islamic, and Jewish holocasts could be viewed regularly on Tentonian holovision. Immediately following the resurrection of the ancient Earthling faiths, Tentonian scientists began reaffirming their atheist roots, citing the countless years of human effort in finding God amounting to nothing as proof that God did not exist. Also, there was the fact that the human race had been relocated. This didn't exactly make sense in any of the old Earthling religions. However, as it was two hundred years ago, it was a matter of faith. To the Tentonian faithful, nothing could disprove their beliefs. History truly did repeat itself.

Rayne proceeded by powering off his comm link. Now, communication would not be possible with the crew but they could monitor the situation remotely. In the howling Earthling winds, Rayne prepared for a sprint toward the alien outpost. After a few deep breaths, he began to contemplate the importance of his mission. He realized the importance of the discovery of an alien race. Knowledge was the prize-winning fish, human ingenuity the fishing rod.

Chapter 23: Silently Effective

The only sound for miles was the clop of Rayne's boots against the Earthling soil. His objective inching closer, he paced his breathing pattern, repeating to himself, "You're almost home. Keep it up."

As he continued on his jaunt toward the citadel, he began organizing his plan of infiltration. In this case, silence would be his best friend. Rayne might be a large man, standing about six foot five inches and weighting in at around two-forty, but he could be quite stealthy if need be. The last thing he needed was a hidden platoon of hostiles gaining knowledge of his presence and ambushing him. Rayne was a tactical genius. His book smarts were average at best but he thrived in the tactics of combat. He studied all the material he could on ancient and current strategic war strategies and tactics. His favorite tactic was flanking the enemy. He used it whenever the circumstances provided the opportunity. This happened to be one of those occasions.

Finally he approached the back of the facility. He pressed his back against the wall and listened for activity. The wall reacted with a high-pitched screech. Shocked, Rayne immediately backed away from the wall. Apparently, the alien material responded to touch. Rayne waited breathlessly in hopes he hadn't tripped any alarms within the alien fortress. He couldn't believe that he hadn't been more cautious. Perhaps his excitement was getting the best of him. Seeing that the rear wall to the citadel was nothing but a solid piece of the alien matter, Rayne took a deep breath and proceeded to the front entrance of the complex.

The mechanical scan of the area that would alert Rayne to any presence of surveillance equipment came back negative. However, he was well aware of the fact that the scan would probably not be of any use considering this was alien technology. It was very unlikely that the scan would pick up otherworldly devices. To Rayne's dismay, this was a situation that he could have never anticipated and trained for. He would need to adapt and adjust on the fly.

Rayne thrived in this uncertain environment. His senses were crisp and in tune. He could almost hear the next step he would make. Earth's moon shone overhead, cascading over all surfaces, including Rayne's bald, ample head. Before he allowed himself to make an erroneous step, he found himself at the front of the mesmerizing structure. He gazed up in amazement at its grandeur, all the while vigilantly searching for suspicious or potentially dangerous mechanical equipment. After all, how different could a surveillance camera appear? Then he thought about the alien matter the building consisted of and he wasn't as confident. For all he knew, an entire army of hostile alien forces might lie just feet from his current position, waiting for him to enter—and then pounce on him.

As he spied the point of interest—the entrance—Rayne noticed that nothing is conventional about this structure. Even the doors comprise unimaginable matter. The entranceway appeared to be covered by an alternate version of the shimmering alien material. This mass, however, literally shimmered and shook. It was visibly mobile. This forced Rayne to second guess his current plan of action. If he couldn't successfully enter the facility, nothing would be gained.

***

Schiller, Hindler, and Davies remained at the structure that had almost caused their capture. The structure had been a trap but the bait wasn't a fraud. Presumably, these alien beings had been studying human history and, more importantly, human weaknesses. The best consensual hypothesis of the group was that the Tentonians had much to fear for the future. All indications were that this race, if hell bent on interplanetary supremacy, could easily dominate the human race with the plethora of information contained in the historical documents left by Zonfer. Unfortunately, it seemed Zonfer's best-laid plans for the human race might end in human slavery or extinction. However, this was taking a "hypothesis" entirely too far. This unthinkable scenario was nothing more than a guess.

On the bright side, Dobbs informed Schiller that the percentage of survival for the team was steadily increasing. Apparently, the xenocite serum was more effective than the bioscanners had first projected. This was an enormous weight off Schiller's shoulders. He had been finding it increasingly difficult to keep this information from the rest of the team. These men were all dedicated to each of their respective positions on the mission. However, none of them had agreed to a one-way ticket to the grave.

Night had blanketed the Earthling landscape. The moon's light shone over the devastated expanse of the planet that humans had once inhabited and loved. Now, the Earth was a mere shadow of its former self, and one could feel the hairs on the back of one's neck stand on end when peering into the Earthling heavens. The moonlight gave the atmosphere a blood red color, another consequence of Earth's mutation into this vile landscape of incomprehensible horror. As Schiller peered into the Earthling skies, he imagined, *evil resides here.*

***

The pursuit of a safe entry plan was complete. Rayne used his internal camera as binoculars to zoom in on the door and study its functional apparatus. It appeared that the entryway material functioned similarly to the pod matter. His theory was that the pod controller that resided on his arm would make the door material respond in the same manner as the pod matter. Hopefully, this guess would pan out. Otherwise, he would have to prepare for plan B, demolition. This was not a desirable tactic in the current situation. If hostiles were present, this would guarantee a treacherous battle.

Rayne, while an effective warrior, couldn't take on an entire army alone. However, if necessary, he would valiantly attempt it.

He quietly sprinted toward the entranceway to the citadel. With deliberation, he squeezed his thumb and index fingers together, mimicking the motion that resized the pod, with the arm equipped with the alien technology. Immediately, the material that served as a secure door compacted together, acting identical to the pod. It appeared that Rayne possessed a figurative skeleton key to this alien outpost.

Rayne gazed in awe at the expansive interior of the alien structure. The center of the enormous complex contained various alien craft, primarily the pods. Holoscreens were abundant, and alien text scrolled across the monitors in brilliant form. Foreign noises were plentiful. It was clear that any hope of ripping information to an external drive would be impossible. To the team's disappointment, alien hardware wasn't compatible with human peripherals. Rayne could only relentlessly photograph everything he observed.

It was apparent that the structure was vacant. Fortunately, Rayne had been correct in thinking their prospective kidnapper was the "off-season" caretaker for the facility.

Then, without warning, tones that were very obviously alarms began to sound. Rayne raised his pulse cannon to prepare for battle. However, his anticipation was met with inactivity. Soon, he observed activity on the holoscreens. He saw numeric code counting down on all the monitors. The countdown appeared to be a long one. It wasn't a self-destruct sequence; that was clear. He continued to contemplate the potential ramifications of the alarm. Finally, his questions were answered. One of the holoscreens revealed a huge army of the beings assembling and readying for battle, but they were clearly not on planet Earth. Rayne then put two and two together. The countdown was a timer for invasion. The hostile alien race was well aware of the human presence on their prized planet and they didn't like it.

Rayne immediately flipped on his comm link and contacted Schiller.

"Sir, this is Rayne. Do you copy?"

"Yes, Rayne. What is the current situation?"

"Sir, the citadel is vacant. However, I have good reason to believe that there are a massive number of hostiles on their way as we speak. I have no idea how long it will take them to reach us, but according to this alien timer we should seriously consider abandoning the mission."

Schiller was devastated. The Earthling biocode was nearly complete. However, it needed more ample physical samples to complete the structure of the code.

"Rayne, do you believe that we have hours or minutes?"

"Judging by the number of characters on the time, I would guess hours, sir. Honestly, I can't be sure."

"Then I don't have much time," said a frustrated Schiller.

Chapter 26: Schiller's Determination

Rayne had just returned from the raid on the alien citadel. Exhaustion was setting in. The team had been through much during the course of this vital mission. However, the final biocode structure of Earth was still not fully constructed. The capacity of the on-board bioscanners of the Phoenix was limited. More hands-on research would be needed to fill in the gaps. Schiller was determined to complete the Earthling biocode structure. Without this, the mission would be considered a failure. Schiller, Davies, and Rayne were gathered at the makeshift checkpoint outside the alien trap, discussing their current situation. Rayne was briefing Schiller on the events of the raid. Davies was engrossed in the research data as Schiller and Rayne discussed his findings. Hindler was nearby.

"...and the walls were entrancing," Rayne informed the others. "The material was similar to the pod. You didn't need to open a door. I used this alien device to open the shimmering doorways. It was similar to the material that the pod was constructed of. This alien technology served as a key to the citadel. I photographed and archived everything I saw in this place. See, these markings must be the language of this alien race,"

Schiller was enthralled. "Rayne, TIS, the team, and I owe you a great debt of gratitude. You didn't have to put your life on the line like that. You have proven yourself to be a vital part of this mission's success. There were some sketchy moments during the infiltration," he admitted.

"Thank you, sir, but I would be lying if I said I was doing it for you or TIS. I am an independent contractor who is paid based upon performance. Financially speaking, infiltrating that citadel was the only option for me. All of my actions are self-serving, sir. That's how I make money. Ultimately, that is why I am here with you," Rayne confessed.

Schiller grinned.

"Your candor is refreshing, Rayne. Nonetheless, you have been a great asset on this mission and you will be compensated accordingly."

Rayne nodded.

"That's what I expect and it will be greatly appreciated."

Schiller prepared to make his new case to the team. He swallowed hard and began.

"Gentlemen, I realize the exhaustion factor is setting in. However, at this current juncture of the mission, if we quit, the mission will be generally considered a failure. Dobbs has informed me that the Earthling biocode structure framework is stuck at ninety five percent in completion. Apparently, the bioscanner is waiting for further physical samples to complete the framework. I have decided that I will assume this task alone. I want all of you to return to the Phoenix immediately. You can monitor my progress on-board the Phoenix along with Dobbs. He'll be happy to have some company. Your Transwarpers are set up and the access point at the Phoenix is operational. This would be the time to utilize all that expensive equipment."

Hindler gazed at the Earthling dirt in shame. He realized how difficult he had been during the entire mission. Schiller had proved that he was the only man to lead the mission. As brilliant as Hindler was, his knowledge of Earth was limited at best. Schiller had prepared for something like this his entire career. Without him, the mission would not have been possible. Hindler decided it was time for a *mea culpa*.

"Schiller, I know that I've been a thorn in your side this entire mission. To be perfectly honest with you, I've finally recognized that my difficult attitude arose from my fear of this place. My whole career, I have disregarded Earthology. Now that I am confronted with the realities of this planet, I have had to question my own common sense. Perhaps I fear what I don't fully understand. I can now admit that I have ignored a serious part of human and scientific history. I want to sincerely apologize to you for my attitude during the mission. I realize that I've been a major obstacle at certain points during this operation and I appreciate your tolerance. If I were you, I would have thrown me off this mission long ago. I'm sorry, Tobias."

Thomas Hindler extended his hand to Tobias Schiller. Schiller took it with pleasure and placed his other hand over their handshake.

"Tom, don't think I'm not scared too. I don't know everything. I'm just as lost as you on most of what we've been uncovering here. I'm not God. I don't know everything there is to know. Honestly, I feel like we have gotten closer to Him on this mission. If He's up there…"

Hindler cringed. "All right, enough of the God talk. I'm transporting back to the Phoenix. Good luck, Tobias. I'll be in contact."

Hindler started the sequence and disappeared as the Transwarper beam showered over him and sent him to the access point at the Phoenix. Davies gestured to Schiller and did the same as Hindler. Rayne was last. He was concerned about Schiller.

"Sir, you shouldn't be alone—"

"Rayne, say no more. I will contact you immediately on your comm link if I need assistance. I'm going to find a safe location to perform the remainder of the research. Dobbs has been earmarking various locations on the 3D mapping of Earth that appear to be uninhabited. Coincidentally, this checkpoint happens to be near one of those areas. This planet is still in the transitional stages of its development in terms of wildlife. The bottom line is that I'm going to be safe. Thank you for your concern."

Rayne lowered his head.

"All right, sir. I just wanted to be sure this is what you want. You don't get extra points for being a hero in your profession. On the other hand, I do."

Schiller laughed.

"Move out! I need to get going. Thanks again, Rayne."

Rayne followed the rest of the team and activated his Transwarper. Schiller then embarked on his final task.

Chapter 25: The New Revelation

A weary and tired Dr. Tobias Schiller activated his Mobile Lab Unit once again. He gazed into the holoscreen of his MLU at the

3D mapping of the new planet Earth. He searched for Dobbs' nearest archived earmark that would provide him a safe haven in which to complete the final stages of research to bring the mission to a successful conclusion. The time of the invasion came closer by the second and this didn't help his state of mind at all.

Schiller had learned to put on a brave face in this intimidating landscape and in the face of potentially deadly circumstances. However, being alone in this environment played on his nerves. He could feel himself periodically checking his rear. As he beat the Earthling soil with his protective foot gear, his eyes jumped from wonder to wonder. Despite his nerves, being alone gave Schiller the opportunity to truly observe and relish the alien surroundings. Schiller was a confirmed nature lover. He chose to live in the Tentonian countryside for this reason. In the spare time he did have, he was known to disappear into the Tentonian wilderness for extended periods of time. It was a passion he would never outlive. But never had he imagined that one day he would trek the uncharted lands of a long-abandoned planet that the human race once called home.

Schiller arrived at an Earthling cave. He began taking samples and recording his observations on his MLU, and continued doing so for hours. Unfaltering, he tirelessly sifted through the research data to construct the final biocode of Earth, concluding the long and treacherous journey. The mission to Earth had turned out to be even more productive than he had first thought. The rest of his team remained on the Phoenix, observing and earmarking various observations of the bioscanners aboard the Phoenix. For the most part, the scanners were self-operating. However, it was good to have human involvement to mark any points of interest.

At the bioscanners sat Dr. Hindler and Dobbs. At length, Hindler inquired over the comm link, "Dr. Schiller, how are your studies progressing? Are the bioscanners aiding you in your observations?"

Schiller squinted intently into the holoscreen on his MLU. "Everything is progressing as I would think it would, Dr. Hindler—slowly. I have taken various samples of Earthling soil and uploaded the biocode to my MLU. Right now, it's building the final code. All the research at the crater has led up to the creation of this final code. I will contact you when its construction is complete."

"Thank you for the update, Tobias. We will inform you of any progress or complications here as well. There is no update on the alien time frame. Rayne can't project any accurate timetable. I would encourage you to hasten your studies. The sooner we can leave this rock the better,"

"Copy that, Schiller out."

As time passed, Schiller began to see the new biological code that Earth possessed. It was startling. He knew that the Plague had fundamentally changed the Earth's composition, but not to this extent. Literally every element that made up Earth's basic chemical structure had been altered. Schiller could have guessed this. The radically different appearance of the planet was itself a clear indication that everything had changed. However, seeing it play out on his holoscreen in real time made it a tangible fact.

Suddenly, the holoscreen flashed and blinked, seemingly an error of some sort. Schiller felt himself slipping into one of his spells. This was different. This was unnatural. Suddenly, he observed a conference instant message request on his MLU. The origin field of the message was marked "unknown." Schiller felt trapped in his own body. If he wasn't in one of his states, he would never have agreed to accept a conversation of unknown origin. He felt compelled, almost forced, to click *accept*. Schiller could hear his team trying to contact him on his comm link. However, he couldn't respond. The communication from an unknown origin began.

"Dr. Schiller, I don't have long to communicate. You will see this message as if it were communicated on your MLU screen. This is not the case. We have tapped into your subconscious. You certainly notice that you are in one of your spells right now. This is no coincidence. In fact, these spells that you have had your entire life have been a tool of my kind to communicate with your kind. You would know these people as psychics or prophets, individuals with ESP. My kind has chosen you to communicate a message to your kind. Do you understand, Dr. Schiller?"

Schiller understood. "Yes, I do. Who are you? Do you have something to do with the alien beings?"

"I have as much to do with the other race as I have to do with you. In your language, my kind would be known as the Seers. We are a race between the realm of physical existence and spiritual. We are everywhere and nowhere at all times. Through the authority of the Creator, we have guided you through your journey. For millennia, my kind has watched over your kind and warned certain individuals of dangers through your brainwaves. Thousands of years ago, on Earth, when the Creator created himself on your planet, we provided the script to preserve the word of history. When the human race strayed too far from its path, we provided the opportunity for a new beginning. Now the time has come for you to accomplish the task that you were destined to perform. This message will be recorded in your MLU. It will spark a flame in your kind's consciences that will put you back on the right path. Your fate isn't so bright. If we could change your fate, we would. After this communication, you will not exit your state. You will forever be trapped in the maze of your subconscious. However, be content in knowing that you have accomplished your duty. Know that, on this day, your kind will be protected from extinction. Finally, I must implore you and your kind, attempt no more travels or missions to the planet Earth. You have had your time here and there is a greater purpose for this place. We understand that this is much to take in but we know we chose the right person in you, Dr. Schiller. Do you understand?"

This was happening. Schiller couldn't reason it or begin to understand how it was happening. However, he knew it was real.

"I understand. I only worry about one thing. My wife, Emma—"

"She knows you love her, Dr. Schiller."

"Thank you for your message, Seer. My race will be eternally grateful for your help over our journey."

This was where the communication ended. The message window on Schiller's MLU remained on the screen. The team on the Phoenix had been trying to contact Schiller the entire time he was in contact with the Seer. At this point, they were concerned and on their way to Schiller's position to see what was going on. When they arrived at his position, they found Schiller sitting in front of his MLU, eyes open, unblinking, and in a catatonic state. Hindler ordered Dr. Davies to gather Schiller and his MLU and to return to the Phoenix immediately. Hindler was now number one in command. With Dr. Schiller incapacitated, Hindler decided that it would be best to end the mission. After all, they had obtained what they came for. Mankind's understanding of Earth, as it stood now, had increased tenfold.

Chapter 26: The Liftoff

Hindler contemplated the fact that the arrival of the alien race on planet Earth was fast approaching. Davies, with Schiller in tow, followed Hindler and Rayne back to the rover that lay outside the Earthling cave Schiller had utilized to complete his research. All of the research materials had been loaded onto the Phoenix to return to their rightful owners, the human race. The group piled into the rover and it hastily accelerated away from the cave toward the position of the Phoenix, where Dobbs, James, and Roberts prepared for an immediate exit from the planet. As the team awaited their arrival at the Phoenix, Hindler was in panic mode.

"Rayne, do you have access to the countdown at the citadel?"

"Sir, you know as well as everyone in here that I couldn't download any information from that place. The alien data was not retrievable, sir,"

Hindler continued to panic.

"Damn it, how do you even know if that was an alien countdown to invasion? It could have been anything!"

"All due respect, sir, fuck you. I did everything in my power at that place. I put my life on the line for something I can't begin to understand. You need to take a step back. I have two eyes and I saw an army preparing for engagement. You should be happy it wasn't here on Earth," Rayne sternly concluded.

"Right, so Schiller was the only one who could demand respect around here! Well, that isn't the way it's going to be! I am now the mission leader and I'm demanding proof," Hindler shot back arrogantly.

Rayne had had enough. "You want proof? There's your proof." He threw a print from an image of the holoscreen that showed the alien army preparing for disengagement.

Hindler was irate.

"You had these photographs the entire time and you didn't report them! I should—"

"Schiller knew about them, sir!" Rayne interrupted. "I informed him that I would be photographing the alien structure for archival purposes. Now, could we please cool down…sir,"

Hindler shut up. Obviously, Schiller was not telling everyone everything there was to know. Rayne was not to blame. The inflammatory atmosphere calmed when the team arrived at the Phoenix. The rover pulled into the bay of the Phoenix and the team immediately exited to start launch procedures. Roberts, James, and Dobbs had already begun the pre-launch procedures. By the time the team had arrived at the Phoenix, the engine was nearly ready to initiate.

As the team prepared for launch, Roberts helped strap in the incapacitated Dr. Schiller. Schiller stared blankly into the eyes of the pilot without responding. Roberts was alarmed and frightened at the same time. It was as if Schiller was completely comatose. After Roberts had strapped in Schiller, the final countdown to launch began.

Then, in a blaze of triumphant fury, the engines of the Phoenix resurrected. The lift off was clean. Then, in the distant sky, a foreign craft could be seen. As seconds passed, more and more appeared. Like passing ships in the intergalactic sea, the human research vessel, the Phoenix, barely escaped the alien invasion. Once again, the human race defied the odds.

Chapter 27: The Trip Home

No one quite understood what had happened to Schiller. Most of them were aware of his spells. However, this didn't seem like one of those. Even while in one of his deepest episodes, he could be snapped out of it in order to communicate with others. This was different. They all knew it.

Hindler informed the pilots of the situation and that he was now in command of the team and mission. Hindler inquired about the alien craft and if they appeared to be giving chase. Luckily for the team, the invaders didn't seem to be interested in them. The pilots had already started organizing the auto flight plan for the trip home. All that was left to do was input the coordinates. Then the team would enter cryogenic sleep for the duration of the trip.

Davies examined Schiller's MLU and noticed the communication window.

"Dr. Hindler, sir, I noticed this communication window on Schiller's Mobile Lab Unit. It seems that Schiller was in communication with an entity of unknown origin while we were trying to contact him on his comm link."

Hindler's eyes widened. "You know what this means."

"This is definitive proof of different realms of existence. As you are well aware, Universal Positioning technology makes a signal of 'unknown origin' impossible," said Davies.

"That is correct, Dr. Davies. This expedition has turned out to be far more fruitful than any of us could have imagined. The question is: what will we do with this information?"

"Also, sir, the question of authenticity of this communication is in question. Schiller's MLU reveals nothing in this area. The question I am asking is if this could be the alien beings misleading us. They obviously consider Earth their territory."

"That is something we need to consider. However, we can deduce from the contents of this message that these Seer beings have been present throughout our existence. This being knew about history far prior to Zonfer's reign. This is not information that would be readily available to some foreign being. Also, science has shown us that the existence of realms other than the one that we occupy very well could be fact. The 'unknown origin' status is what convinces me. If it were the alien race, Schiller's MLU would have immediately acquired the coordinates of its origin," Hindler reasoned.

"Well, I guess time and research will tell, sir. This is truly groundbreaking information."

Hindler paused and contemplated. "Absolutely. And we need to treat this information as such. I shall contact TIS and the New Senate and inform them of our findings."

Davies had one last thought. "I can't help but think that we'll be seeing those alien craft again. The human race, for the first time, will be aware of the fact that we are not alone. One wonders how the masses will take to this knowledge."

Hindler stared ahead, his arms crossed in contemplation.

"We can only hope for the best."

The mission had come to an end. The questions of the past had been answered. Now, however, the future seemed more uncertain than ever.

Chapter 28: The Unthinkable

The crew was exhausted. They longed for the moment they would enter their cryochambers for the trip home. But first, they would need to enter their final reports into their Mobile Lab Units. For the most part, it was tying up loose ends to the best of their abilities. Many questions had arisen from Schiller's current catatonic state. Hindler and Davies hoped that Schiller would somehow come out of the state. However, preliminary medical tests showed that this was unlikely. There were so many unanswered questions to what exactly had happened in the latter parts of the research mission. The questions were likely to remain unanswered if Schiller didn't recover from his current condition. Upon their return to Tento, transcriberbots would be used on Schiller to record any thoughts that might pass through his mind. Ironically, their fact-finding mission had created more unanswered questions than it answered.

As Hindler, Dobbs, and Davies finished up their final MLU entries, a disturbance arose. The blaring alarm tones of the Phoenix could be heard from the cockpit. Hindler immediately reacted.

"James...Roberts, what's going on?"

"Sir, it appears that we have a ballistic missile approaching! The warning systems have engaged and the Phoenix is currently entering evasive positioning," Roberts responded with urgency.

Hindler was frantic. "Do we know where the missile originated from? Is it from an alien craft?"

"I wish it was. This is the disturbing part, sir. The on-board weapons analysis system tells us that this is a Tentonian Intergalactic Defense Missile. I can't begin to understand this, sir," Roberts concluded.

Hindler understood all too well. The New Senate had been monitoring the progress of the mission since it had begun. TIS was also providing the governing body with periodic reports on the latest developments. After the wormholing of the excavation equipment fiasco had played out, the New Senate demanded that regular reports be filed. The existence of an alien race and other "realms" of existence didn't exactly solidify the case of human supremacy. Heinmeche had apparently grown accustomed to the absolute authority the New Senate possessed. Hindler grasped all of this and it made him sick. He and the rest of the crew could only listen in horror as the pilots went through evasive procedures. Panic filled the air. The crew of the Phoenix listened as their last moments ticked by. Hindler could only think, "Tento will never know..."

Then, the unthinkable…

The End

Epilogue: 3033 A.D. (Earth timeline)

Zonfer stood in a massive, majestic hall. He was conversing with a non-human being.

"We discussed this, Mr. Zonfer. The outcome is inevitable. You need to make a decision. I have been allowed to give you this information ahead of time. What you do with it is a matter that you must contemplate. You must not discuss this meeting or our race. The consequences of this would be dire. Breaking our agreement is not in the interests of you or your kind. The fate of planet Earth has been determined. There is no alternate pathway. The human race can either survive elsewhere or perish and fade into obscurity. It is your decision."

Zonfer was complacent. He knew this was the truth. He had no reason to not believe it. Sometime in the future, he knew that the human race would have to deal with an enemy it couldn't defeat. What could he do? How could he protect the human race? He prepared himself mentally for a dark future.

PART IV

THE CULMINATION

Chapter 1: Corruption

Nothing but the whisper of the howling winds uttered a sound in Zonfer City. Ordinarily, the bustle of constant activity could be heard resonating in the streets and back alleys. Absent was the monotonous hum of hovercraft on the ground and aerial transportation overhead that usually saturated the air. Today, however, marked a somber day and explained the chilling silence. The governing body of Tento, the New Senate, had announced to the Tentonian people that the mission to Earth had met a tragic and unexpected end. Chairman Heinmeche appeared on all the major Tentonian networks, informing the citizens of the unfortunate events and declaring a national day of mourning. The government took the hard line that the Phoenix had met with catastrophe when its engines overheated, causing the core to explode, resulting in the deaths of the entire crew. Confirming the fears of all parties involved, Heinmeche clarified that all research data had been lost. Only the Tentonian Institute of Science and government insiders knew the truth. However, all participating members of the government and their relatives had signed confidentiality agreements with the New Senate. The breaking of that agreement would result in immediate prosecution and conviction in the Tentonian Judicial Tribunal— "the Teege," as it had become infamously known as among its occupants.

The mission to Earth had been nothing more than a rumor until Heinmeche's address to the Tentonian population. He knew that brewing rumors of secretive missions would only help his critics' case for regime change. Thus he decided to disclose the information. He would have preferred that it not be necessary, but somewhere along the line information had been leaked. An investigation into the matter had already been opened.

Tento's current state of stability seemed invincible. The current government had ruled for two centuries without checks and balances, and it didn't come without a cost. In certain circles, mostly comprising paranoid conspiracy theorists, the scenario went that the Tentonian government consistently withheld any and all negative press pertaining to the New Senate. In any free society, some members of the population will invariably disapprove of their leadership. And given the fact that New Senate members served life terms, the feelings of disapproval of these minority groups were given ample time to fester and build a case against the governing body. With human beings sometimes living past one hundred and twenty years old, new elections took place rarely. Needless to say, any government will make mistakes over an extended period of time. In this case, the appearance of foul play in certain incidents during the New Senate's reign made a rebel movement inevitable. Slowly, with deliberate intent, this movement began to gain the support of more mainstream members of society. This movement, over the years, began to take shape and its member list was about to explode.

Heinmeche's address made the rounds on the various holocasts on Tentonian holovision. Its message reverberated in the cultural mainstream. Fair or not, the rebel movement began to surface in Tentonian media. Holocasters would appear on news holocasts declaring Heinmeche a criminal, citing various questionable tactics and rulings taking place in the New Senate.

The Tentonian constitution, its origin being the ancient Earthling governmental structure known as a Jeffersonian democracy, protected the government from any media reprisals. The New Senate, as controversial as some of its tactics seemed, never overstepped the boundaries of the constitution. This cardinal rule had remained unbroken for two centuries and Heinmeche vowed to keep it that way. He studied old forms of government frequently and realized the consequences of the people feeling thwarted or oppressed by the bodies that governed them. Feelings of oppression had inescapably led to rebellion and, in some cases, civil war, in the past governing systems. The human race had seen plenty of racial infighting during its time in the universe. Civil conflict was one issue the New Senate had always worked hard to prevent for the sake of governmental security and the greater good. "Peace at all costs" was the tag line of the New Senate. A giant placard hung atop the New Senate's main entrance inscribed with this motto.

Within the walls of the New Senate complex, the delegation sat in session. Debates and discussions were the only tools of a governing body in a state of absolute panic. New Senate members raised issues and howled in furious debate, the orderly conduct of past gatherings blatantly absent. Divisive topics often caused such an atmosphere and this particular topic more so than most; that is, dealing with the growing public dissatisfaction with their leadership. Over time, the feelings of discontent began to spread—the beginnings of resistance movements assembling and preparing to launch into action. The appointed leader of the governing body,

Chairman Heinmeche, stood in defiance of the chaos, jockeying for position.

"Gentlemen, gentlemen, you are all out of order!" Heinmeche yelled as the frenzied assembly continued its bickering.

"Gentlemen, I demand order!" Heinmeche roared in a commanding voice. The relentless banter finally abated.

"The current state of this discussion is unacceptable—this isn't even a discussion. We need to determine the best options and immediately implement them," he demanded.

"May I yield?" one senator requested.

"I yield to Senator Flemming," Heinmeche confirmed.

"Mr. Chairman, the gravity of the situation demands that we immediately take retaliatory action against any rebel movements. Our doctrine is to uphold peace at all costs. We would be doing our fundamental rule a disservice if we ignore the coming storm," the senator stated with conviction.

"May I yield?" another from the delegation requested.

"You may," Flemming said.

"This course of action will inevitably lead to greater opposition. The current atmosphere can be contained and minimized by means of public relations adjustments. We need to justify our actions to the people," the senator thoughtfully concluded.

"Chairman yields, I am leaning toward Senator Flemming's recommendation. The threat of a growing opposition force and civil war is far too serious for a simple PR adjustment. The Tentonian citizenry will understand that parties opposed to the New Senate Delegation don't hold their best interests at heart. Therefore—"

"May I yield?" the holder of the opposing viewpoint interjected.

"I yield to Senator Linden. Senator, can you please lower your tone. I want to keep this meeting in working order," Heinmeche sternly requested.

"Yes, chairman, I apologize. I think this topic deserves more thoughtful discussion before you make a vote call. I sincerely fear the consequences of military or legal action against citizens purely based on their views of the New Senate leadership. The first amendment to our constitution is freedom of—"

"Chairman yields, and I don't require a lesson on our constitution, Mr. Linden. The fact of the matter is that our governing power is at stake. We must not lose sight of this fact. The possibility

of a rebel force overthrowing this body is real and possibly an
eminent threat. Therefore, I believe a new vote is in order—"

"May I yield?" Linden loudly interrupted.

"No, sir, you may not!" Heinmeche exploded.

"The Tentonian Citizenry Protection Act states that any and
all entities opposing the New Senate ideology shall be subject to full
prosecution under the Tentonian Judicial Tribunal guidelines. Due
process shall be rescinded in applicable cases. New Senate Defense
Force deployment shall be permitted upon chair request and a vote.
Minimal dissemination of information regarding this act shall remain
paramount in our operation. All in favor, please vote 'yea.'"

The electronic voting panels were initiated for use. The once
inexhaustible crowd now sat in silence. Heinmeche stood dominantly
atop the chairman's podium, the massive holoscreen displaying the
vote tally for the act's support. He waited patiently as the final vote
count was calculated. Then the final straw was drawn for the
leadership.

"The 'yeas' have it. The act is ratified. This concludes our
current session. Thank you for your patience and vigilance in
pursuing this vital legislation. Know that because of your wise votes,
the New Senate's power shall remain uncompromised," Heinmeche
declared. His totalitarian attitude was unmistakable.

Heinmeche motioned to a New Senate Complex security
agent. The burly man dressed in militaristic garb ascended the
podium and consulted with the chairman.

"Jeffers, could you please escort Senator Linden out of the
building? He will no longer be a customary member of the New
Senate Delegation for personal reasons."

"Yes, sir," the NSC security agent responded.

Heinmeche looked on in satisfaction as his ideological rival
was strong-armed away from the debate room, his holographic file
viewer confiscated for obvious reasons. Heinmeche's ultimate power
grab had been successfully initiated.

***

A translucent mug sat in front of Emma Schiller as she
caressed the lip of the drinking apparatus. She felt as if only hours
had passed since Zimmerman had contacted her about her husband's
demise. Life for the once vital woman had come to a virtual
standstill. She had always attempted to prepare herself mentally when

Tobias would begin a new assignment. Being a former Tentonian Institute of Science biochemist, she understood the dangers involved. Unfortunately, no amount of preparation would be sufficient for what she was now enduring.

She stared blankly into the mug, the remnants of her beverage clinging to the bottom. Suddenly, her holoset lit up with life, the programming guide recognizing a broadcast of interest. A TNN live holocast from the TIS headquarters was underway. One of TIS's chair members, Zimmerman, stood at the podium addressing the media.

Without moving her head, Emma gazed up at the holoset. Her weary eyes blinked slowly as she listened.

"As all of you know, we have been conducting a thorough internal investigation pertaining to the Phoenix's tragic end. We had hopes that, with black box data reconstruction, we could get an ironclad answer as to what caused this unthinkable tragedy. I'm sorry to report that, with the research data, the black box recordings were also lost. With this final piece of the puzzle missing, it's virtually impossible to draw an accurate picture of the final moments of the crew's mission."

"What about the mission to Earth? Rumor has it that communication from an unknown origin was transmitted to the mission leader," one of the members of the press yelled.

"That is completely false. Dr. Schiller, while an honorable member of our institution, had a history of mental instability. Any communications that took place were between either TIS or the crew of the Phoenix. Dr. Schiller would sometimes engage in conversations with himself on his Mobile Lab Unit. Any reports of communications of unknown origin are fictitious.

"In terms of the mission to Earth, as the chairman reported, all bioscanner data and maps were destroyed. However, we continue to monitor Earth's transformation…"

Emma abruptly turned off the holoset. She had heard enough lies. She knew that it was impossible for information to be "lost." It was common knowledge to TIS members that any activity recorded by a TIS bioscanner was sent directly back to the TIS mainframe. It would take a catastrophic meltdown of the entire TIS server structure to lose anything.

Her anger had been accumulating within her mind and body for a long while, and she furrowed her brow in disgust. As she gazed at the brim of the cup, her frustration hit its peak. In one fluid motion, she picked up the drinking vessel and threw it at the wall in front of her. It shattered, the broken pieces of glass exploding then cascading through the air. She laid her face in her hands and wept.

While in the depths of her angst, Emma Schiller experienced a moment of clarity. She took a deep breath and wondered, "What could they be hiding?"

Chapter 2: The Face of Rebellion

A chilly draft blew across the flat Tentonian expanse in a relatively underdeveloped area. Only modest structures owned and rented by middle-class citizens littered the landscape.

Within this small community lay the beating heart of the rebel force, a movement concerned solely with the destruction of the New Senate. Simply, they fought for anarchy, believing the current system to be obsolete and laden with corruption. They lived a tribal existence, hoping for the dawn of a planetary revolt against its leadership and an abundance of chaos.

In the community square, the ragtag group discussed revolution. The apparent leader of the gathering preached their cause.

"...and know that the day will come when the New Senate will beg for mercy while lying at our feet. Though it seems hopeless now, I am confident the public will begin to awaken. The seeds of discontent are growing. Recruitment for our organization is progressing at an amazing rate, far quicker than I could have ever imagined. Heinmeche's day of reckoning is fast approaching!"

The congregation erupted in a fury of excitement. As the celebration continued, a lone hovercraft approached their position. The crew members lifted their primitive weaponry as the luxurious vehicle inched closer.

"I know this one, guys. Nothing to worry about," the rebel leader informed his team. He acknowledged the occupant with a wave while hoisting his machine gun over his shoulder.

The door to the transport flung open and a well-dressed man exited. He approached the rebel leader with a smile on his face.

"What's up, my man? I have amazing news. You know that New Senate Act I was telling you about that would make the citizens shit a brick? Well, it just went through a few hours ago," the man said enthusiastically.

The rebel leader smirked. "Recruitment has been going good…real good. This will only help."

"Yeah, besides the obvious…" the man responded.

"What you getting at?"

"Well, I'm sure New Senate Defense Forces are onto your location. You're gonna need to go underground. You're actions are the whole reason this act got passed. The delegation has been railing the NSDF for not finding you. You've probably cost a lot of people their jobs!" the man joked, laughing uncontrollably.

"This shit isn't funny, Donovan. I've been lucky thus far. If the Teege prosecutors happen to realize which holorecord I stole from the archives, I'm screwed! They can trace it right to my position. I've been writing out all of the incriminating information from the records because the drives on the unit can't be ripped, the encryption is—well, alien. Seriously, I have no idea what they encrypted their records with. It looks like some kind of different language. Anyway, everything has gone great thus far. All the material I've leaked to the press has been covered extensively and it's starting to take root in the people's minds," the rebel leader concluded.

Donovan Sterling motioned to the rebel leader to move closer to him. "Listen, Tento, I've always wondered…you related to the guy that found this planet?"

"Tell you the truth, I have no idea. My family tree is something I've never known nor cared about. They ask me that all the time," Tento motioned to the crowd of rebels. "They would like to think it—'The triumphant toppling of the corrupt government led by the great-great-great-grandson of our home planet's discoverer!'" he stated with a sarcastic tone and a sigh. "That's the crap legendary sound bites are made of."

"You got that right." Sterling responded. "Listen, the guys back at the New Senate send their best wishes. We miss you back there. Things are getting bad, Donald—real bad. I think Heinmeche is losing it. This protection act is nuts! Anyone who's caught talking against the government is going to be subject to prosecution!" he said, exasperated.

"Why do you think I started this thing? I'd been witnessing corruption near the top for years prior to my expulsion. Heinmeche losing it is something new, though. He was always a decent man. It further proves that absolute power corrupts absolutely." Donald Tento finished.

Sterling nodded in agreement. "Definitely. Listen, I should get going. I wanted to give you the good news in person. I'll be in contact."

Tento shook Sterling's hand. "Give the guys my best."

"Sure, Don, watch your back out here!" Sterling shouted as he ran to his vehicle.

Donald Tento, the leader of the Tentonian Liberation Organization (TLO), stared into the darkening Tentonian skyline. Zonfer City bustled with activity in the distance as he wondered, "What comes next?"

Chapter 3: The New Senate Defense Force

The barracks for the NSDF lay dormant, most of the lights off and little activity taking place. Private Raymond Abbot and Private Neil Strauss sat outside indulging in cigarettes.

"You know we'll be in deep shit if they catch us smoking," Strauss said.

Abbot blew a plume from his mouth. "What are they gonna do? Kick us out of the DF? At this point, if I weren't stuck in it, I'd leave myself."

"Yeah, city border patrol is getting boring. When's the last time we saw any action?" Strauss asked, more or less rhetorically.

"Since the New Senate elections—in other words, it's been a hell of a long time." Abbot confirmed.

Strauss flicked his cigarette. "You heard about the new act? We might be getting some action sooner rather than—"

"Nothing's gonna happen," said Abbot. "As soon as word of that act gets out, it'll crush any will for a revolt."

"I wouldn't be so sure, Abbot. Have you seen the news holocasts lately? People are getting sick and tired of the New Senate. Maybe we should be careful about what we ask for. I've never been in any big war. I'd be scared shi—"

"No, you wouldn't, Strauss. We've trained for combat. We'll be ready for anything," Abbot said with conviction. "Don't worry about it. Nothing is going to happen. The New Senate has been in power a couple of centuries. You don't actually think we'd be lucky enough to be the generation that sees a revolt, do you? Ha! That would be something."

Private Abbot dropped his cigarette and stepped on it, killing the flame in little, sparkling ashes beneath his black boot. He turned and entered the door that led back into the barracks. Private Strauss followed him. They walked through the halls, greeting their comrades. One of the soldiers yelled in passing.

"Hey, Abbot, Strauss, you guys been sucking dick again?"

"Go to hell, Owens!" Abbot retorted.

"I can smell the smoke! I'll report it if you guys keep that up!" he shot back.

They continued on their way and entered the mess hall. The resonance of soldiers in discussion ricocheted off the mess hall walls, with laughter and yelling prominent. A large holoset in the middle of the room displayed the evening news holocast. Privates Abbot and Strauss retrieved their dinner and found a seat. They searched for a table with familiar faces.

"So, anything interesting going on in the world?" Abbot inquired.

"See for yourself," one of the soldiers responded, pointing to the holoset.

A report aired on the massive display. The news commentator began the report.

"This is the TNN Nightly News for February 22, 202. Thank you for joining us. Shortly after Chairman Heinmeche addressed the nation today, a small protest took place outside of the New Senate. It was short-lived, however, when NSDF forces were deployed and thwarted any large-scale problem. This is the latest happening in a growing rebellion against the actions of the New Senate…one minute please…This is breaking news. The New Senate has just passed a new initiative that is effective immediately. The New Senate statement on the act is as follows.

"'The Tentonian Citizenry Protection Act will protect the people of Tento by protecting their leadership. Any and all entities that oppose the New Senate ideology shall be vulnerable to Tentonian Judicial Tribunal prosecution. NSDF deployment to troubled areas shall be permitted if warranted. This act is further proof that the New Senate is determined to keep the citizens of Tento safe.'

"Well, ladies and gentlemen, this is the new law of the land. The implications of this new act are obvious. We'll be right back after these messages."

Silence gripped the mess hall.

Finally, one of the group said, "Holy shit, that's pretty extreme. I mean, it was only a small protest. Why the hell would they pass such a crazy act?"

"Don't be stupid, Cal. This has been in the works for a long time. The citizens have been ball-less during Heinmeche's reign. Personally, I think this delegation has overstepped its bounds on a lot of issues," Abbot stated emphatically.

"Careful, Abbot. With this new act, they'll probably be monitoring every word we say," said Strauss.

"They already do, you dumb shit! That's my point. In the past, do you remember having to 'meet with a government associate' when someone you know said something against the delegation? No! I'm not saying I'm against the New Senate. They pay my bills, but I don't know—" Abbot confessed.

"I'm just saying I like you as a partner. I'd like to keep you," Strauss said.

"Yeah, well, you'd better. You're stuck with me," Abbot responded, playfully punching Private Strauss on the shoulder.

A tone sounded in the mess hall and a voice followed it.

"The dinner hour is concluded. Please report to your obligations."

Abbot sighed in disgust.

"Son of a bitch, back to the grind, Strauss. I really don't feel like watching those stupid Tilothans today," Abbot fretted.

"By the looks of things, we might be having more exciting times in the near future. The rebels are going to go ape shit after hearing the news," said Strauss.

"We'll see. I'll bet the rebels back off. I'll bet you, ten to one odds—come on!" Abbot joked.

"You're on!" Strauss yelled with vigor.

Chapter 4: The Insider and the Outsider

Donovan Sterling's hovercraft buzzed across a Tentonian highway, dodging and weaving through traffic as he sped toward his destination. As he concentrated on the roadway, his cell rang.

"Sterling," he answered.

"Have you met with the rebel leader?" the voice on the other end inquired.

"Yes, sir. I'm on my way to your residence. He's prepared for the next phase of the operation," Sterling said.

"Excellent. Weapons production is ahead of schedule. Delivery of the goods will be happening soon. You should inform Tento."

"Yes, sir. I'll be arriving soon." Sterling closed the cell and pushed the accelerator to its limit.

***

Senator Flemming sat in his mansion and examined various reports and paperwork. Pleased with Heinmeche's new initiative, he observed video of Senator Linden's extraction with pleasure. The intercom on his desk droned and he answered.

"Yes, what is it?"

"Sir, Mr. Sterling from treasury is here to see you," the assistant informed him.

"Thank you, please send him in."

After a short delay, the regal door creaked open and Donovan Sterling entered.

"Sterling, great," enthused Flemming. "Let's get down to business. Is Tento aware of the accelerated weapons production?"

"Yes, sir. I phoned him immediately after our conversation. He'll be expecting them."

"Perfect. Things are going just the way I planned. Tento's constant leaking of legislative information to the press has driven Heinmeche up a wall—that reminds me. Has Tento destroyed the holorecords yet?"

"No, sir. He wants to archive all the information before he destroys it. He was unable to duplicate the information through conventional means due to encryption issues."

"Right. We switched over to alternate means of encryption before the mission to Earth." Flemming paused, deep in thought. "So, he's writing down all the information by hand?"

"That's correct, sir. There was no alternative."

"That'll take forever! We need to keep our asses covered, Sterling. You tell Tento to kill that holorecord as soon as possible. The Teege prosecutors are looking for that record and they won't stop until they have their hands on it. That thing can be traced right back to me. I won't have that!" Flemming's voice trembled.

"He's working constantly on it, sir. It will be destroyed immediately after the last word is recorded."

Flemming nodded reluctantly and folded his arms.

"Yes—things are flowing in the direction we want them to, Sterling. Soon, talks of impeachment will surface and I'll be there to pick up the pieces—perfect."

***

As Donald Tento stood at the entrance to his rebel compound, the Tentonian winds swirled in his head. He took a minute to enjoy a cigarette, having recently finished archiving the holorecord data and destroying the unit.

As he inhaled, he spied an incoming vehicle. He dug in his tattered, military-issue jacket in search of a pair of binoculars. He peered into the device, adjusting the zoom with his finger. He identified the prominent crest of the New Senate, two hands embracing the planet Tento.

"Just like Sterling said," Tento muttered to himself. He raised a communication device to his mouth and began to speak. "Listen up. There is a New Senate marked transport approaching. They are not hostiles. Hold your fire and allow them safe passage into the compound."

The message boomed throughout the rebel fortress, and word traveled that an approaching vehicle was on its way. Rebel forces scurried in all directions, positioning for a potential ambush.

The massive transport entered the gate to the TLO hideout, and the engine turned off with a thud. Rebel forces slowly emerged from their defensive positions with arms drawn. The driver exited the vehicle.

"Tento, call off the dogs, would ya? Sterling sent me," the driver yelled.

"Hey, he's fine!" Tento obligingly told the rebel forces. "I told you this transport isn't hostile." The rebels reluctantly lowered their weapons.

"That's better. I got the goods in the back. The Tentonian taxpayers fronted the bill for these, so put them to good use," the driver said with a smirk.

Tento motioned to the rebel army and they hastily unloaded the advanced weaponry. He stood silent as the driver rambled on.

"So, you're gonna start a war with this stuff, huh? That's interesting. I've read a lot about the big civil war that erupted when Zonfer decided to get out of dodge. I guess you're like Danken, huh?"

Tento, with the speed of a feline, grabbed the driver by his coat collar. "Listen, why don't we just help the guys unload this stuff. It'll make time pass quicker—and save you a bloody nose. What'd you say?" Tento whispered harshly while glaring into the suddenly terrified trucker's eyes.

"Yes, sir. I g…guess I hit a nerve, huh?"

"Let's just say that I read history too and I didn't appreciate the analogy. Blaine Danken was a goddamn madman."

"Fair enough," the driver said with a sigh of relief.

As Donald Tento, the rebel force, and the driver all worked feverishly to unload the advanced weaponry, Tento realized that the driver's statement wasn't far from the truth. Tento's motives differed greatly from Danken's malicious intentions during the now legendary civil war, but the human toll remained the same.

Finally, Tento unloaded the final crate of munitions into the TLO armory. He removed the top of the container and examined at its contents. To his dismay, his conscience began to speak to him. He pictured images of rebel fighters armed with the formidable weaponry, relentlessly murdering soldiers whose only guilt lay in their loyalty. He caught himself feeling reluctant and shook his head in search of reprieve. He promised himself that this would mark the last occasion he'd remorsefully think about the enemy.

Chapter 5: Protocol Interrupted

The personnel rover traversed the Zonfer City border. Abbot peered out the window, pulse cannon in hand, as the rover prepared for their deployment. The rover continued on its course, passing

NSDF checkpoints and dropping off soldiers at their respective outposts.

"Hey, Abbot, where were you just then?" Strauss inquired, wondering about Abbot's silence.

"It's nothing. I have a weird feeling about today, can't put my finger on it."

"What're you thinking?"

"Never mind. I'm sure we'll just be watching roaming Tilothans just like any other day."

The rover pulled up to the last checkpoint on the journey and the privates disembarked. Being grunts, they got the less-than-desirable tasks. They walked through the checkpoint and checked in for duty.

"What's up, guys? Ready for another interesting and exciting day in the world of Tilothan watching?" the checkpoint manager commented sarcastically.

"Just stamp the card, man," Abbot said with disgust.

"Yeah, yeah, all right, I'm just trying to lighten up the mood."

"Don't bother."

Strauss followed close behind and approached the checkpoint manager. "Don't think anything of that. He's not himself—well, maybe he's more like himself today—I don't know. Things are tense back at base. It seems like they're in crisis mode. They're readying more combat groups than ever."

"It's fine. If I were patrolling the border all day every day, I'm sure I would have the same attitude. Any word of a promotion for you guys?" the attendant inquired. "You've been doing this for a long time, longer than any other crew I can remember."

"Nah, they think we need to pay our dues."

"Hey, Strauss, you coming or do I have to report you to our CO?" Abbot yelled in frustration.

"Coming, honey!" Strauss called out sweetly. He turned back to the attendant. "I'd better get going. Take care."

Strauss ran to catch up to Abbot and smacked him on the back of the helmet. "Hey! What the hell is the matter with you, man? Ron didn't do anything to you."

"I don't need to take that guy's bullshit. He isn't the one roaming this stupid border and completely wasting his time."

"Still, you don't have to be such an asshole! Everybody's just doing their job here. The last thing we need is bad feelings between us—just keep that in mind."

Abbot gritted his teeth in hopes of curbing his anger, but to little avail. "You want to know the last thing I need? My partner stabbing me in the back! If you can't understand why that pissed me off, you're dumber than him! Now could we just patrol—without talking, please?"

The privates silently strolled along the Zonfer City border. The distant sound of Tilothan footsteps bounced in the pair's ears. Suddenly, the consistent rhythm of the thunderous reverberation was interrupted.

"What the hell—you hear that?" Strauss asked in confusion.

"Last time I checked, those things can't tap dance."

Abbot's communication device sounded, demanding his attention. He fingered the button located on the side of his helmet near his ear.

"Abbot here. Copy that base. We're on our way back to the checkpoint. Out." A look of nervous excitement draped Abbot's face. "All hell has broken loose in Zonfer City! Those thuds we heard must have been explosions! Come on, Strauss, the rover is making the rounds to pick up reinforcements! Goddamn, I think I owe you some credits!"

Like two children playing tag, Abbot and Strauss scurried back to the remote checkpoint. As they arrived at the gateway, the rover roared up the hill toward them. The attendant, Private Ron Livingston, exited the doorway of the checkpoint gateway. Livingston, Abbot, and Strauss met as the rover pulled up to retrieve them for deployment.

Abbot's cynicism had all but disappeared. "Did they call you up for deployment?" he inquired with the enthusiasm of a twenty-year-old on the eve of his twenty-first birthday.

"Hell yeah!" Private Livingston responded with just as much vigor.

Abbot locked and loaded his pulse cannon. "Game on, boys." The trio jumped into the rover and prepared for battle.

***

Brilliant flashes and enormous booms filled the streets of Zonfer City. The New Senate Delegation sat in an emergency session as the chaos erupted around them. The chaos, however, wasn't limited to the outside environment.

Senators stood, screaming and pumping fists, as Chairman Heinmeche observed NSDF forces engaging the enemy. A rebel fighter laid fire on an NSDF soldier, taking cover behind a demolished hovercraft. The New Senate combatant pulled the pin on a combustion grenade and hurled it. With amazing accuracy, the explosive landed perfectly in the rebel soldier's vicinity. The rebel fighter hastily grabbed the ticking time bomb and attempted to chuck it back but he was too late. The ensuing explosion dismembered him. Another rebel, acting on pure instinct, flanked the soldier and made the kill, advancing further on the goal of reaching the New Senate Complex entry.

Heinmeche stood in disbelief while the horrendous battle raged on around him, his greatest fear realized. Suddenly, while he was mesmerized with the activity and ignorant of the danger, a sniper shot crashed into the window he was peering through. He fell to the ground in a helpless heap. Jeffers immediately ran to his aid to find Heinmeche was not wounded. But panic ensued as the delegation realized the severity of the situation, and senators' voices overlapped and combined in an unrecognizable bellow.

As combat continued to rage outside, plasma fire and frantic shouts of friendly and hostile forces alike resonated through the New Senate Complex, the walls seemingly closing in on the besieged organization.

Heinmeche saw the situation rapidly deteriorating and acted quickly. "Jeffers, would you kindly help me get to the podium?" he asked with pain piercing through his right leg.

"Yes, sir. But do you not require medical attention?"

"No, I believe it's only a sprain."

Arm in arm with Jeffers, he stumbled to a touch screen control panel behind the chair's podium and activated the NSC security "panic" system. The bedlam continued as the delegation debate room entered lockdown mode. Large titanium shutters cloaked the windows and doorways, and the final remnants of the auditory assault faded.

Jeffers took a deep breath and queried the chairman.

"Sir?"

"Yes, Jeffers, what is it?" Heinmeche responded, exhausted.

"We're not going home tonight, are we?"

"No, Jeffers, we're not."

Chapter 6: Combat Ready

Strauss and Abbot closely examined their plasma cannons as the combat rover barreled toward the conflict zone. While they checked their ammunition clip charges and adjusted their targeting systems, the commanding officer of Zonfer Company, Corporal Aiden Brewer, addressed his soldiers.

"All right, listen up, Zonfer Company. This is Brewer. The TLO has begun its offensive on Zonfer City. NSDF surveillance picked up cell communication confirming that the main strike would take place at the New Senate Complex. I have confirmation from Galant Company that the NSC has entered lockdown. All combat rovers that are not already in the combat zone are to report to the Zonfer City gateway. Further orders will be available at that time. Brewer out."

Abbot felt his eye twitch. "This is the real deal, guys. How are things looking out there, Livingston?"

Private Livingston's targeting system ticked and buzzed while he manned the heavy pulse cannon mounted atop the combat rover. "All clear—the rebel forces must be concentrated in Zonfer City."

The traveling rover clanked as it accelerated at top speed. Its hardy titanium treads hugged Tento's soil firmly. Then, as the rover passed an overturned hovercraft, an explosion rippled beneath it, throwing the rover on its side.

Abbot shook his head and regained his bearings. "Everybody all right? Strauss... Livingston?"

"Yeah, I'm fine, Abbot. Just banged my head a bit," Strauss said wearily.

"Livingston!" Abbot called with concern.

No answer. A swirl of wind entered the cab of the combat rover where Private Livingston had been perched.

"Look, Abbot!" Strauss pointed out of the open hatch. "He's gone. When the rover toppled, he must have fallen head-first," his voice cracked.

"Goddamn it! What the hell happened?" Abbot yelled, his anger mingled with fear.

"It felt like the explosion came from underneath—"

Abbot raised his index finger to his lips. "You hear that? I think we got company," he whispered.

The men lay motionless in the combat rover, waiting for the first sound of movement. The wind was now reduced to a breeze blowing ever so lightly. Suddenly, a crunching sound of footsteps could be heard through the rover's open hatch. The two held their breath in anticipation of rebel forces.

"Anyone in there?" a voice said from outside. "I'm NSDF, Williams Company! Looks like you hit a pulse mine!"

Abbot and Strauss looked each other in the eye. "What do you think?" Strauss whispered.

Without warning, Abbot jumped from the combat rover with pulse cannon drawn. A soldier dressed in NSDF garb stood in front of him.

"Whoa! What the hell? Calm down, Tiger! Private Landry, Williams Company," said the startled soldier. He held his hands in the air while pointing at his identification patch. "My CO got a call from yours and he sent me to check out the scene. My transport is about a half mile back. We should be getting back. Our company needs all the help it can get."

Abbot lowered his weapon. "All right, chief. Sorry. We were on our way to the Zonfer City gateway. I guess those orders are different?"

"Yeah, that's what my CO told me. Zonfer Company was deployed to the New Senate Complex to aid in combat operations. We have a more exciting mission."

Abbot noticed Livingston's body and approached it. He took the dead man's identification tags and placed them in his vest pocket. He then hoisted the fallen soldier's body over his shoulder.

"What'd you think you're doing, Tiger? There're lots of soldiers dying out there. We can't worry about that," Landry said solemnly.

Abbot glared at the private with disdain. "I'm taking him."

"Fine—but don't ask me for any help. You know, when we get to the rover, you'll have to leave the body behind anyway."

Abbot sighed and dropped the body with disgust. He regained his composure and the three began their journey to the rover.

"What do you mean by 'a more exciting mission'?" Abbot inquired.

"Williams Company has been assigned the mission of invading the rebel hideout. That's where we're going."

"No shit! I thought the hideout's location was unknown," said Strauss, surprised.

"Up until today, it was. I don't have the details—I just work here," Landry jokingly responded.

"I hear ya," said Strauss.

The soldiers picked up their pace, accelerating to a fast jog.

"Hey, there's the transport. Let's get going."

They ran toward the combat rover and leaped in. Three more combat troops sat in the rover awaiting the arrival of the three.

"You girls ready for some action?" one of the crew yelled.

Neither Abbot nor Strauss responded. An awkward silence followed.

"Well, all right then—I'll take that as a 'yes'!"

The combat rover roared to life as the treads tore into the Tentonian soil.

Chapter 7: Absence

The New Senate remained in lockdown as explosions and plasma fire raged outside. Chairman Heinmeche sat in a seat behind his podium, favoring his left leg. He made a successful effort to stand and addressed the members of the delegation.

"All right, gentlemen, I believe it would be wise to conduct a roll call. Given the current situation, it would be helpful to know who is among us."

The chairman activated the touch panel display on the podium and began the roll call.

"Senator Adelman...Senator Bainor...Senator Collins...Senator Flemming..." The chairman paused and awaited Flemming's response.

"Senator Flemming..."

Heinmeche peered about the debate room in search of the missing senator.

"It appears that Senator Flemming is absent. Was he scheduled to be elsewhere today?" Heinmeche asked Flemming's aide.

"No sir. As far as I know, he had no prior engagements."

"Interesting…" Heinmeche said under his breath. "Did you see him here today? I would hate to think he could have been in the complex at the time of the invasion."

"No, sir, I haven't seen him all session. In fact, I was about to leave at the time the invasion happened," the aide responded.

"I would like to request you try and contact the senator. If you are able to get in contact with him, please request a video conference. A serious debate that will require his input will be beginning soon," said Heinmeche.

"Yes, sir. I will try to contact him now."

Heinmeche inhaled deeply, puffing out his chest, feeling more powerful than ever. With his political rivals all but extinct, the pathway to total annihilation was laid clear.

***

Donovan Sterling paced in a grand hallway, the likes of which Wolfgang Zonfer would have approved. He talked urgently on his cell, clearly in a perilous state.

"…and if you think this isn't serious, you're seriously mistaken! You need to find those holorecords on the funding and make them disappear!"

"I'm doing all I can, sir. There are millions of drives in the database. It could take months to sort all the appropriations data," said the voice on the other end of the line.

"I'm well aware of that! Purge the entire system if you have to! I want that data gone!"

Sterling shut his cell violently. Suddenly, Senator Flemming appeared in the walkway. "Sterling!" he said. "How are things?"

"Going swimmingly, sir. Ev—everything's going as planned," Sterling said, fumbling over his words.

"You don't sound so confident. I'd hate to think my number one associate might be unsure of his duties."

"There's nothing to worry about, sir. The stress may be getting to me a bit, though. Anyhow, I just received a call from your aide at NSC. He requested an immediate video conference with the delegation. Apparently, Chairman Heinmeche has an ace up his sleeve," Sterling said sourly.

"Don't have that attitude, Sterling. This is exactly what I planned on happening. Tento's rebellion force has taken the first step. Heinmeche is taking the exact path I predicted. This civil war is going to rip the New Senate apart. Being the next in line to Heinmeche, I will be appointed chairman after his removal," Flemming said, laying out his plan.

"I understand all of that, sir. It's just that it seemed like…" Sterling paused to ponder his choice of words and rubbed his temples. "My conversation with your aide was…unusual."

"How so?" the senator inquired, his interest piqued.

"Well, his tone was ominous."

"Sterling, this is all purely speculation. We could fret over it all night. I'm going to find out more immediately."

The senator exited the hallway and proceeded to his home office. Sterling stared back at him and pondered the consequences of his own and Flemming's actions.

Sterling was well aware of the ramifications of the plan the senator had been carrying out. The Tentonian Judicial Tribunal would tear them apart given the opportunity. Checks and balances had been stifled by the New Senate and the TJT sought retribution for the senate's insolence.

Flemming entered his office and closed the door behind him. He approached his mini-bar and poured himself a shot of bourbon. He slowly walked to his desk, took a seat, and quickly consumed the beverage. Taking a deep breath, he activated his holo-conferencing system. The holoscreen glowed, displaying the "awaiting response" message. After a brief wait, Chairman Heinmeche appeared on the holoscreen, and audio of chatter could be heard in the background.

"Order!" Chairman Heinmeche asserted. The chatter quickly faded.

The enormous holoscreen affixed to the debate room wall displayed Flemming's video connection. The senators' attention immediately turned to the larger-than-life screen.

Heinmeche sat behind the podium, ready to begin the new session.

"Senator Flemming, thank you for your prompt response. It is greatly appreciated," Heinmeche said.

"I am glad to oblige your request, Mr. Chairman. I understand an important discussion is imminent."

"That is correct, senator. In light of the invasion of the New Senate Complex and our lockdown status, new NSDF orders will be needed. Would you agree, Senator Flemming?"

"Absolutely, sir. We have to take all measures against this new threat to our power."

"I hold the same conviction, senator. Currently, the NSDF forces are running operations all over Tento in hopes of defeating the rebel force quickly. However, early indications are that this battle will be a long one. The Tentonian Liberation Organization has recruited far more members than we could have anticipated. Most recently, I've received reports of common Tentonian citizens picking up arms and joining the rebel cause. This clear expansion of the opposition has made a new act necessary. Therefore, a new vote call shall be opened."

Heinmeche's power remained unopposed. Like a lamb to slaughter, he continued.

"The Leadership Preservation Act shall state that any and all entities that show allegiance to the TLO or other rebellion organizations are immediately subject to NSDF action. The citizenship of said entities shall be nullified, consequently eliminating constitutional rights."

Heinmeche paused and identified the expressions of shock on the senators' faces.

"Gentlemen, I understand this act is extreme. However, the current situation is…extreme! The New Senate's authority and our very lives are at risk! I encourage you to vote 'yea.'"

"May I yield?" one senator requested.

"I yield to Senator Wilkes."

"Mr. Chairman," said the first senator, "I think an expansion of the Tentonian Citizenry Protection Act is an unwise decision at this juncture. In my opinion, this is sanctioning genocide."

"Senator Flemming, you will get the last word," said Heinmeche.

"Mr. Chairman," said Flemming, "I am in agreement with you. Our leadership is in more danger than before. We need to eliminate all opposition—"

"Senator Flemming, you are in contempt!" Senator Wilkes yelled in anger. "*You* are the reason we are in such peril! In fact, your initial absence from this delegation is suspect. I want to suggest the opening of an investigation into your actions leading to this day!"

The delegation erupted in chaotic debate, senators rising and shouting in rage.

"Enough!" Heinmeche exploded. "I refuse to operate in this manner! I am passing the act citing the former act as authority!"

"That, sir, is in direct violation of the Tentonian constitution! As an active member of this delegation, I am calling for immediate removal of the chairman!" Wilkes fired back furiously.

"This is not the time for talk of this manner. I declare the act to be passed and active immediately. This ends the session," Heinmeche concluded.

Arguments reverberated off the walls of the New Senate debate room as the possibility of internal revolt mounted. But full dissent did not occur because the NSC security forces were ultimately dedicated to the chairman's safety. Heinmeche stood to dominate with an iron fist. History had once again repeated itself, elimination of populous in search of power.

Chapter 8: The Price of Extremes

The TLO hideout was relatively quiet. Considering that the rebellion was in full swing, this was understandable. Donald Tento stood outside the hideout awaiting the arrival of reinforcements. His cell phone rang.

"Tento here."

"Hey, buddy, it's Sterling. Listen, I was just talking to Flemming. He told me that Heinmeche has gone off the deep end. He's ordered that any and all enemy combatants be killed, no arrest or prosecution, mind you. Basically, it's all-out war now. You and your forces should prepare for a huge battle."

"I've been prepared, Sterling. This has been my life's mission since my eyes were opened to the New Senate's corruption."

"Well, Flemming told me to call you and inform you of the new act. Expect NSDF forces any minute. I'd better get off the line. They might be monitoring my conversations even now."

"I'm expecting reinforcements soon. This rebellion isn't going to die. I'm curious, Sterling—why is Flemming helping the cause?"

"He has his reasons. Let's just say that if I discussed them, he'd have me shot. I have to go," Sterling said, promptly ending the conversation.

Tento slapped the cell shut, impatiently awaiting his fighting force's arrival. Then, in the distance, he saw the heavily armored deployment vehicle approaching, and he smiled.

***

The combat rover containing the members of Williams Company continued on its journey toward battle. As the soldiers prepared for battle, the CO of Williams Company, Corporal Gerald Luther, addressed the NSDF forces.

"Men, this is Luther. The New Senate has just passed the latest act pertaining to the war. We have full authority to engage any and all hostiles, including citizens who appear to be loyal to the resistance movement. I understand that detention was the old method. Your new orders are to eliminate all combatants. I stress this order. It's vital to the success of our operation. Luther out."

The men looked at each other in shock.

"Goddamn, this keeps getting crazier and crazier," said Strauss. "First, we get orders to arrest anyone who looks as though they might be sympathizers of the TLO. Now, we're ordered to kill them at first sight? This is getting out of control."

"Listen, if you have a problem with the new marching orders, I recommend you quit your post now, son. The last thing we need is a hesitant pair of boots in our ranks," an older, seasoned member of the crew commented.

"Nah, I'm loyal to the DF. I'm just saying—"

"What! That you sympathize with the enemy?" another of the force interrupted.

"Hey, give him a break, Dillon. We're all feeling the pressure of today's happenings. This is the first action any of us have seen in a hell of a long time," the seasoned veteran interceded, defending his younger comrade.

Strauss nodded his head at the battle-hardened warrior in appreciation of his fatherly defense. The older man smiled at the nervous warrior and spoke.

"Captain Snell is the name, son. Glad to have you and your partner in the company," Snell said, shaking the hand of the private firmly.

Abbot remained silent through the exchange, staring out the rover's porthole. He made a point of noting their location.

"Looks like we're coming up on the hideout, guys," Abbot said with excitement.

Almost simultaneously, Corporal Luther chimed in on their communication links.

"All right, grunts, the rover is approaching the enemy hideout. What's the situation there?"

"Looks dead, sir. Not a light is on in the place," Snell responded promptly.

"In that case, gentlemen," said Luther, "I recommend you take the kamikaze approach on this one."

"Ah shit—" Abbot muttered under his breath.

"You got a problem, son?" Snell asked with a note of impatience in his voice.

"No, but I've only done this in training and I hated it," Abbot said shamefully.

"It's no sweat, son. You'll enjoy it in the field. It's invigorating," Snell responded with a smile.

The rover barreled at top speed. The six soldiers gathered at the rear hatch of the combat rover, poised for disengagement.

Snell stood at the front. "On my mark!" he commanded.

Abbot knocked on Strauss's helmet, searching for a reaction. Strauss raised a thumb in acknowledgement.

"Mark!" Snell yelled.

Snell jammed the hatch control switch with violent force. The hatch flung open, the members of Williams Company filed out. The rover continued on its collision course toward the rebel sanctuary. The soldiers gained their footing on enemy territory and watched as the rover flung toward its target. Finally, the rover approached its victim and with a massive resonance, slammed into the TLO hideout. The squad silently waited as they listened for activity. Soon, they heard shouting in the distance. Snell caught the small bursts of audio and motioned to his platoon to "go prone."

"Listen up, men," Snell ordered. "We're gonna camp here until we know we're clear. If we run straight in now, we'll be toast. We need to stick here and let our little ambush do its job." Then he pushed his communication device on the side of his helmet. "Base, this is Snell. My squad is going dark. I repeat...no communications to my squad. Snell, out," he whispered.

"Copy that, Snell," the base communications commander responded.

Like a pit of pythons poised to strike, the troop waited for their cue. Then, while the group covertly surveyed the territory, they heard a rustle in the bushes.

"It's at our twelve o'clock," Snell whispered as the soldiers readied their weapons.

As the phantom crackle approached, the fighters' targeting systems began to click and beep.

"Shit!" Snell said in frustration.

The NSDF combatants rose in unison, taking aim at their target. One lone rebel fighter stood before them. He raised his hands, unarmed, knees trembling. Dillon fired his weapon, penetrating the rebel's skull, killing him instantly.

"Dillon, that was totally unnecessary! That guy didn't even have a rock to throw!" Strauss yelled.

"Remember the orders, Strauss? Now, shut up!" Dillon retorted.

"He's right, son. We need to do our job. Just take it easy and stay frosty," Snell said in a low voice, consoling the inexperienced youngster.

Suddenly, pulse cannon fire broke the relative calm, originating from multiple locations.

"Move out! Keep your eyes on your HUDs!" Snell commanded while firing at hostile positions.

The members of Williams Company rushed toward the rebel hideout and their objective, Donald Tento. For the first time, battle raged outside Zonfer City. Heinmeche's new act of paranoia had been officially ratified.

Chapter 9: Contact and Conflict

Heinmeche wrung his hands nervously. He had been receiving regular updates on combat operations that had been taking place and progress was slow. NSDF forces continued to advance on enemy positions but their tactics proved formidable.

The atmosphere among the senators remained toxic; with conflicting views, they shouted in debate. Heinmeche contemplated ejecting all parties to cool off. At this rate, the leadership would fall apart and they wouldn't stand a chance of surviving the conflict.

"Gentlemen, we need to compose ourselves! I understand that you are under a tremendous amount of stress. We're all feeling it. Everyone needs to take a deep breath and relax," the chairman insisted.

The arguments and debates gradually subsided.

"Thank you. Now, I think it would be an opportune time to update the delegation on combat operations. General Pullman informed—"

Suddenly, a loud thud resounded throughout the debate room. The lights clicked and flickered out, leaving only the emergency lighting active.

"Jeffers, give me an update here. What's going on?" Heinmeche inquired.

"I'm assuming it's a power surge, sir. We have been running the debate room longer than ever before."

The debate room holoscreen suddenly began to flicker and hiss, with white noise prominent. The senators began to rustle in their chairs. Some of them jumped out of their seats and consulted their colleagues. Suddenly a communication was displayed on the enormous screen. The origin of the message was marked "unknown."

"What's going on? How is a transmission coming through? We don't have any power!" said Heinmeche, confused.

Jeffers shrugged, not knowing what to say to the chairman. The transmission began.

"Leadership of the human race, I represent a race known as the Seers. We have been watching over your kind for your entire existence. I need not explain my place any further. You should be well aware of us from my communication with Dr. Tobias Schiller.

"I informed Dr. Schiller that the human race would have one more chance for redemption. Your leadership has brought your kind to the breaking point. You decided to monitor planet Earth even after the warning you received from Dr. Schiller's communication. Now, you must pay the ultimate price for your ignorance. You have proven that your kind cannot live in unity with nature nor with yourselves. The ultimate decision to oppress and wage war with your own kind has, once again, damned you to destruction. Nonetheless, the Creator still holds you in favor. Therefore, you shall see a comfortable end. This marks the final communication my kind will provide. Our role has been completed. We wished for better. Alas, your fate was chosen far before we could have known."

The transmission ended, the lights flickered back on, and the holoscreen went blank. Heinmeche gazed at the screen in disbelief. Not a sound traveled in the debate room—the senators were just as shocked as the chairman. Suddenly, all hell broke loose.

"Mr. Chairman, we have to immediately confirm the origin of that communication!" one senator shouted.

"Yes, we know that there is an alien race present on Earth. This could be a threat of invasion!" said another in dread.

"I agree, gentlemen. I'm going to get Chairman Zimmerman of TIS on the line immediately. We need to calm ourselves! Panicking will get us nowhere," Heinmeche declared.

Heinmeche activated the communication program on the unit located on the chairman's podium. He typed Zimmerman's communication address in the unit. The debate room holoscreen initiated, and the senators' attention focused on the meeting about to take place.

"Chairman Heinmeche, I'm glad to hear from you. How can I be of service?" Zimmerman asked, curious about Heinmeche's call.

"Yes, Dr. Zimmerman, I am calling to inquire about the signal monitoring on planet Earth. I am curious to know if there have been any incoming transmissions from Earth. Our delegation received a mysterious message of unknown origin."

"No, sir. If we pick up any transmissions from planet Earth, we are mandated to immediately report them to the NSC—you know this," Zimmerman said.

"Yes, doctor. I assumed that given the circumstances, the regular protocol might have been interrupted. All right, Dr. Zimmerman, thank you for your time," the chairman said, leaning toward the console to end the communication.

"Sir!" Zimmerman said with urgency.

"Yes, doctor?" said Heinmeche.

"There is something I think I should mention regarding planetary stability."

"What is it, doctor?"

"Well, a few minutes ago, the main bioscanner here at TIS picked up a large culmination of energy forming just outside our orbit. It appears that it's slowly accumulating to form a ball of light. A preliminary bioscan on the energy put out God code. Now—"

"No, no, doctor, I don't want to talk about the God code. I told you I didn't want to hear another word of that after the failed mission to Earth. Keep me updated on the situation as you see fit. One last thing before I conclude the conference. What is the status of the Pacifier?" the chairman inquired while the rest of the delegation argued in confusion.

"It has been delivered to your appointed location, sir. As I told you in our private conference, I would err on the side of caution in using this device. It still hasn't—"

"Yes, yes, I understand all of that, doctor. I appreciate your time," Chairman Heinmeche concluded, promptly ending the communication.

One senator erupted. "Mr. Chairman, do you think that was very wise? I think this mass of energy Zimmerman talked about deserves further discussion! Also, what is this...Pacifier?"

"We all decided talk of the God code is a nonstarter. We need to deal with what we can make an impact on. This...situation...outside our orbit is being monitored. We can't do anything about it. We need to be focused on eliminating the rebellion. As for the Pacifier...that is a matter for my consideration only. It's better that you know nothing of that matter."

The senators slouched in their seats, feeling hopeless. Their normal method of debate had been mutilated. Heinmeche took the reins of every decision without input. The pathway to the future would be paved in uncertainty.

***

Abbot and Strauss shot furiously at the enemy positions. Snell aided the other squad members push the rebellion members deeper into the rebel compound.

"Strauss, get over here! I need some back up!" Abbot shouted as he fired on the TLO hideout.

Strauss quickly sprinted to Abbot's position.

"Listen, I need to get inside the gateway. I can't do that without cover. You provide suppressive fire and I'll rush the position. On my mark—"

Abbot checked his plasma charge and took a deep breath. "Mark!"

While conflict raged around him, Abbot raised himself from his prone position, rushing the enemy stronghold. His targeting system beeped with activity, acquiring new targets with each passing second. Abbot and Strauss dispelled the rebel opposition accordingly. Finally, Abbot reached the entrance to the TLO hideout. He activated his communication channel to address the growing NSDF presence in the area.

"All available units, listen up, this is Private Abbot! I've got the entrance to the stronghold clear! Move up immediately!"

The first to meet him was his loyal partner. Strauss approached Abbot, seeking his opinion on the next step for operations. "What comes next, bro?"

"Shit, man, I don't know. I saw an opening and I took it. It's up to the CO to determine the next step," Abbot said uncertainly.

"How did I know you'd say that?"

"'Cause you're an ass," Abbot joked, smacking Strauss's helmet in a friendly gesture.

Sergeant Snell approached the two, noticing their antics.

"You girls having fun?"

"Yes, sir. This is the first combat we've seen in a long time. I'm sure you understand…sir," Abbot responded with an undertone of sarcasm.

"Listen, boy, I'm still your superior. Don't think that mushy shit with Strauss means I'm soft. Good job on taking the gateway. Now, the real mission starts. We need to find Tento—quick."

Snell pushed his communication link.

"Dillon, you and Needler meet up with Strauss, Abbot, and me. We need to regroup and find Tento immediately. This is our priority one."

"Yes, sir. We'll be there in minutes," Dillon promptly responded.

Snell turned his pulse cannon to check his charge status.

"All right, boys, stock, lock, and cock. The real fight starts now!"

***

Donald Tento stood in the TLO operations room, the New Senate Defense Forces advancing deeper into the compound. He carefully contemplated his next move. His closest confidants surrounded him, offering what they could.

"Sir," one man said, "our forces are combating the NSDF forces the best they can, but I don't know how much more we can take. We weren't prepared for this type of combat. Our intention was to take this fight everywhere and thin out the New Senate Forces. As it is now, the fight is concentrated in our compound, the full might of the forces breathing down our necks."

"I fully understand the situation. We're going to have to regroup and flee the compound soon. If we stay here, defeat will be expedited. Send out a message on the encrypted communication channel to regroup at the garage."

"Yes, sir," the loyal attendant responded.

The entourage exited the operations room with pulse cannons equipped, en route to the TLO garage. They ran through the corridors of the makeshift headquarters, eradicating any hostile elements as they progressed. As they approached the garage, they noted that the task of escaping would be more difficult than they first imagined. The garage entrance had been blown open by a massive pulse charge, and NSDF forces were awaiting the enemy. Tento sensed the hostile presence and motioned to his support to stop.

"I have a good vantage point inside the garage. I can see that the entrance has been compromised. Send some of the forces outside in a flanking position. I'll give the call for engagement," Tento whispered to his top commander.

"Gillard, bring your squad in flanking position at the TLO garage entrance. Hostiles are inside, I repeat…"

Tento and the small rebel regiment waited as the new marching orders were issued.

"We are in position," Gillard informed the rebel leader.

Tento took a deep breath and mustered the required courage to take the next step.

"Engage, Gillard!"

Tento chucked a delirium grenade into the TLO garage. The NSDF soldiers reacted in the desired manner, screaming, covering their ears, and shutting their eyes.

Pulse cannon fire immediately exploded from the garage, the thunderous thuds echoing off the thick walls. The lead commander of the NSDF forces regained his composure and responded to the hostile fire with prompt action.

"They're at our six o'clock! Take defensive posture immediately!" the commander barked in panic.

The New Senate Forces turned to the rebel position as they piled into their once-silent sanctuary. At this moment, Tento ordered his troops to enter the conflict.

"That's our cue. Watch your backs!"

With that signal, Tento's crew piled into the garage, eyeing their targets and silencing them swiftly. Tento maneuvered to the massive combat rover provided by his inside connections. He entered it and prepared for disengagement. He quickly completed the final preparatory work and called a new order.

"All units, this is Tento. The combat rover is prepped for evacuation from the compound. Make your way to the TLO garage for immediate transport."

The NSDF attempt at defensive strategy was futile. The overwhelming number of rebel forces quickly dispelled the New Senate combatants. The rebel numbers quickly grew to an unmanageable amount as they piled into the combat rover for evacuation. The combat rover revved, ready for the next phase of the rebellion.

***

Snell's platoon of grunts slowly patrolled the inside of the TLO citadel. The calm atmosphere confounded the troops.

"This doesn't make sense. This is supposed to be the main sanctuary for the enemy? There's no one inside this place!" Abbot said, confused and frustrated.

"Stay frosty, son. You never know when a hostile might pop up. If you get too comfortable, you could find yourself staring at the sky—dead," Snell wisely informed the cocky youth.

"Yeah, yeah," Abbot carelessly replied.

Without the warning of his targeting system, a rebel combatant hiding around a corner blind-fired on Abbot's position. Snell accurately fired on the rebel, concluding his attack. Abbot took refuge behind a storage crate.

"Shit! Where the hell did he come from?" Abbot whispered to himself.

"You can come out now, private! The bogeyman is gone," Snell shouted contemptuously.

Abbot slowly rose from his pose of safety.

"What did I tell you, son? I guess this needed to happen to show you! I'm glad you aren't dead. Next time, you might not be so lucky," Snell said, reprimanding the private.

"Yes, sir…"

Snell's communication channel opened. He pushed the earpiece deeper into his ear canal in hopes of hearing better.

"Could you repeat that, Zonfer Company?" He listened as the instructions were repeated. "Copy that, we're on our way!"

"What's up, sarge?" Strauss inquired.

"We have to move out now! Tento's making his move. If we let him go, this whole mission's a bust!"

The crew sprinted toward the TLO garage. They quickly approached the enemy-controlled area.

"Strauss, watch my ass! We've got hostiles all around!" Dillon yelled in frustration.

"I've got it! I've got it!" Strauss responded, running backward and firing on the relentless enemy.

They finally reached the garage, which was thick with combat. As they approached, the massive combat rover began to pull out. Rebel combatants continued to fire as the rover entrance ramp closed.

"Son of a bitch, we've lost them!" Snell roared in aggravation.

"How the hell did they get one of the heavy combat rovers?" asked Dillon.

"That's a damn good question. I'm starting to think this whole rebellion is fueled by someone high up. I was wondering how they got their hands on NSDF-certified pulse cannons and weaponry. That's the only way to explain this," Snell said as he thought out loud.

"What's next, sir?" Abbot asked.

"Well, son, first of all, you and Strauss have been promoted. Congrats. What's next, you ask? We track that heavy rover," Snell said with conviction.

Chapter 10: Insanity Revealed

The war had peaked to a tumultuous crescendo of violence. NSDF forces spared no expense in carrying out Heinmeche's final act of absolute power: traversing the remote locations of Tento's countryside where the rebellion resided and laying waste to the opposition. They had brought out the "big guns," and throughout the streets and alleyways of Tento lay wounded and dead soldiers. Blast craters permanently scarred the conflict areas.

The New Senate Complex was quiet, the gloomy hallways empty. NSDF forces successfully pacified the enemy and pushed them back into Zonfer City. For the most part, the rebel forces retreated to areas outside the city. Combat operations in Zonfer City had decreased exponentially.

Heinmeche sat in his throne of tyranny, while the darkened debate room was now devoid of all activity. Heinmeche had successfully silenced every voice of reason that remained. The only sound that the demented chairman heard was the insanity of his thoughts.

"Mr. Chairman, I would like to address the delegation," one of the senators said wearily.

"No. I need time to think," Heinmeche said with aggravation.

"Heinmeche, your leadership during this crisis has been lackluster, at best. Your unwillingness to listen to opposing viewpoints has put this entire planet in danger—"

"That's it!" said Heinmeche angrily. "Jeffers, get your squad and clear out the debate room! I can't think with this banter!"

"But sir, where do I house them?"

"Transfer them to the NSDF prison block—anywhere! Just get them out of my presence."

The remaining senators screamed in protest. Heinmeche deactivated the security system's "panic" mode, and the titanium shutters lifted in unison. The NSC security guards piled in with stun sticks in hand. The guards, while threateningly beating their weaponry in their palms, lined up the embattled senators and guided them out of the debate room.

The security force paced in front of the new prisoners. They awaited the transport vehicle to take them to the prison block.

One of the senators panicked. "Jeffers, you have to listen to us! Heinmeche is insane! You can't allow him to rule without consequence. The planet will be doomed to destruction!"

"I understand, sir, and the security force is taking the necessary action to keep this delegation safe. You and your colleagues have nothing to worry about. We have control of the situation," Jeffers said in response to the senator's concerns.

Jeffers peered out of the main NSC entrance in search of the transport. He spied a heavy combat rover approaching the New

Senate Complex. He attempted communication with the NSDF transport.

"Approaching heavy rover, this is NSC Security General Jeffers. You are aware of the current situation. Please approach the NSC cautiously. We need to get the senators into the transport quickly. Do you copy?"

There was a brief pause and static. Jeffers squinted in confusion.

"Do you copy, heavy rover?"

"Yes, sir," a voice on the other end stated. "We have been patrolling the city and rebel forces are not present. It would be safe for the senators to line up outside. We can expedite their transfer if we get them all on board at once."

"Copy that. Some members of the security force will be accompanying the delegation members to the prison block," Jeffers concluded and turned to address the senators.

"All right, gentlemen, your ride is here. We need to move you outside to hurry your transportation."

"That's insane! It's a war zone out there!" a senator complained.

"That rover has been patrolling the city. The coast is clear for transport. All right, everybody line up, single file, at the main entrance."

The senators complied while bickering among themselves. The massive lock to the entrance disengaged and the senators began to file out of the New Senate Complex.

With the entry hatch in front, the heavy rover approached their position. The rover engine remained active, growling at the group of terrified leaders. The entry hatch lowered, slowly revealing the rover's interior. To their great shock, poised in front of the senators stood the rebel force with pulse cannons drawn. Jeffers was more surprised than anyone.

"We'll be taking these tyrants. I don't think you'll be attempting to fight us with those stun sticks. That wouldn't be wise," Donald Tento said with pride.

"Get back in the NSC, men. We've lost this one," Jeffers said in acknowledgement of his failure.

"That's the wise decision," said the rebel leader arrogantly.

The helpless senators piled into the rebel transport, now at the mercy of the enemy. Donald Tento's cell rang and he answered.

"Do you have the cargo?" the voice on the line inquired.

"I do indeed—I really can't believe how far you're taking this. I never thought you would put the entire delegation—"

"I told you. I have to see this operation through. The future of the planet depends on it," the voice interrupted.

"How far is Flemming willing to go, Donovan?"

"As far as it takes, Donald. He's expressed his intentions very clearly. He wants Heinmeche gone. That's why I'm contacting you. The next phase of this operation needs to happen now."

"What's that, friend?"

"I want you to…eliminate every senator."

"Are you nuts?" Tento responded in shock. "That will send the planet into chaos!"

Donovan Sterling's end of the conversation went silent. He covertly transferred the conversation to a monitored communication channel. Tento heard rustling in the background and a new voice spoke.

"Private, don't question, just act," a strange-sounding voice said.

"This action is insane! This is crazier than anything Heinmeche has ever done! You need to think of something different."

"Private! Just whom do you think you are talking to now?"

"I damned well know who I'm talking to! And why are you calling me 'private'? This is—"

"Let me clarify. This is Chairman Heinmeche. I am insisting you carry out your orders. NSDF forces don't disobey orders given by superiors, let alone the chairman. Do you understand what I am saying to you?" Flemming's disguised voice said.

Tento froze. He thought about what Flemming was doing. It was brilliant.

"Yes, sir. I'm sorry about disobeying the order. Our signal was weak and I missed it. I understand and will carry out the action immediately," Tento responded.

"Very good, private. Unfortunately, this difficult action is the last reasonable option that remains."

Tento approached the senators.

"What do you want?" cried one senator frantically. "You can have every credit that's in my name! Please don't kill us!"

"Heinmeche killed you," Tento said enigmatically.

"What! What are you saying?"

Tento loaded and locked his pulse charge.

"It doesn't matter. I suggest you close your eyes, gentlemen."

Without warning, Tento turned to the group of defenseless men, unloading his weapon on them furiously. Chucks of flesh flew against the heavy rover's inside wall as the rebel leader relentlessly fired upon the group.

After the brutal action had been carried out, Tento stared at his hands, then at the wall covered in blood. He thought about the promise he had made to himself at the TLO hideout. Suddenly, he realized he had just broken that promise.

***

General Pullman, grand commander of the NSDF, sat in Central Command inundated with various matters. His office phone rang and he answered.

"Pullman here."

"General, I have a vital new initiative that needs to be carried out immediately."

"Yes, Mr. Chairman, what is the action?"

"The last bastions of this rebel force will soon be eliminated. However, there will be remnants of the rebellion's ideological advancements. I believe it would be wise to eradicate this threat before it ever has a chance of reorganizing in the fashion we have witnessed. This day has taught me a very important lesson, General."

"What is that, sir?"

"That mankind needs suppression. Absolute peace is impossible. There will always be opposition to leadership. However, the beauty of technology holds the answer. I would like you to initiate the device TIS delivered to the detention facility," Heinmeche hissed.

"Yes, I was curious about that. What exactly is—"

"Stop right there, General. You always operate on a need-to-know basis. I don't think I need to say anything more," Heinmeche interrupted.

Confused, Pullman hung up the phone. He walked slowly to the prison that held the alleged enemy combatants, most of whom were unlawfully detained. A TIS scientist sat in the area where the device had been deployed.

"I got the thumbs up from the chairman," Pullman informed the scientist.

"I was hoping this wouldn't happen," the scientist replied.

"Why is that?" Pullman inquired.

"Do you know what this does, sir?"

"No, the chairman wouldn't tell me its purpose."

"Yeah, I could have guessed that."

Pullman's interest piqued.

"What does it do?"

"The scientists at TIS call it the Pacifier. It emits a pulse that destroys the part of the human brain that contains feelings of discontent. This might seem like a good thing but trust me, it's not. This thing hasn't passed one Preliminary Test Trial. Damage to other parts of the brain is a serious possibility. This device could effectively make every inhabitant of the planet go brain dead," the scientist informed Pullman in a matter-of-fact tone.

"That's crazy," said Pullman. He paused, thought about Heinmeche's recent actions, and reached a conclusion.

"You know," he said, "I've been more than concerned about the chairman's state of mind lately. This confirms my fears." He flicked his cell open, accessed the directory and selected a number.

"This is Pullman. Plan B's a go." He clapped the cell shut promptly and turned to exit.

"General, do I activate the device?" the scientist asked.

"Don't even touch it!" Pullman yelled, exiting the prison block.

Chapter 11: In Pursuit

Snell's unit sat in the familiar combat rover awaiting updated details on the status of the heavy rover. They had left the TLO hideout in pursuit of the rebel force. Abbot's heart pounded. He suddenly realized that he had grown accustomed to the humdrum days of Tilothan watching. He thought about the intense combat he had just experienced, and his hand trembled slightly.

"All right, Williams Company, this is your CO, Corporal Gerald Luther. I've received word that Tento's crew is headed toward Zonter City's gateway. We recently picked up their tracking signal. It took us a while to find the serial number of the particular heavy rover

Tento got his hands on. Apparently, Tento's crew had been wreaking havoc in the city. Your number one objective remains Donald Tento. Without him, the rebel cause will fall apart. Our planet's future depends on you, men. Luther out."

"You heard him, guys. Gear up," Snell said.

The members of the combat force rose from their seats and retrieved ammunition for their weapons as they prepped for combat. The combat rover traversed a rugged Tentonian trail in an area not fully developed by the inhabitants.

The rover relentlessly barreled toward the Zonfer City gateway. As the rover approached its destination, the godlike statue of Zonfer, the legendary leader, became visible, the late Tentonian daylight gleaming off its surface. The combat rover slowed as it approached the area of interest.

"Any sign of the heavy rover?" Snell asked, pushing the communication device deeper into his ear.

"That's a negative, Captain," the operations commander responded.

"Let's lay low for now. We'll see what happens. Cloak up," Snell said, the rover fading immediately into obscurity.

"I don't want a single channel open. All communications are to end right now. Let's see what we can see, boys," Snell concluded.

The team waited patiently for the first sight of the rebel transport. Abbot looked out the porthole of the rover, reluctantly anticipating the hum of an engine. Suddenly, the sound of a rover on the move filtered into the NSDF combat rover.

"You hear that, boys?" Snell whispered to his troop.

Then the sound abruptly ceased. The fighting force froze, clutching their weapons in anticipation. Finally, they heard an explosion close to their position.

"I think we might have a bogey, guys! We need to move out!" Snell yelled urgently.

The sound of an approaching missile hissed closer. The members of Williams Company filed out of the rover, ready for combat. A projectile struck the cloaked rover, and the enemy rover's position was suddenly apparent. The explosion knocked Strauss on his back. Abbot grabbed his partner's NSDF-issue jacket, pulling him to safety.

"I got you, buddy," Abbot whispered, gripping his partner's shoulder.

"Thanks, man, I owe you one."

"You're damn right you do," Abbot said, grinning.

"Would you two lovebirds shut the hell up?" Dillon spouted in frustration.

The squad stood silently as they waited for another attack on their position. They heard shouts of rebel combatants coordinating an attack on foot. Another projectile shot from the heavy rover. It slammed into the massive statue of Zonfer. The effigy rocked in instability, its formerly flawless appearance scarred.

"Those sons of bitches," Snell said in disgust of the rebels' actions.

Snell peered cautiously around their protective position behind the rover and addressed his troops.

"Listen up. Strauss, Abbot, and Dillon flank them from the eastern wall of the gateway entrance. Needler and I will advance up the middle. Let's move out!"

Abbot, Strauss, and Dillon ran with their heads down and pulse cannons readied. They ducked behind the gateway wall, monitoring their tracking systems for new rebel positions. Their targeting systems beeped and clicked, revealing the enemy. Dillon rose, putting suppressive fire on the rebel positions. The rebel fighters returned fire, temporarily distracted from Snell and Needler's new action.

Snell and Needler rushed up the center, screaming and shooting at the rebel combatants, killing most acquired targets. Pulse cannon fire and explosions burst from every inch of the battlefield. Multiple rebel combat rovers pulled up to join the battle.

"Abbot, Strauss, Dillon, enemy reinforcements have arrived! You're gonna need to double time it to flanking position!" Snell roared.

"Yes, sir, we see them. You heard him, guys," Dillon said to his partners. "We can't take this one safe. Let's move!"

Dillon led the group, with Strauss and Abbot following close behind and providing cover for their comrade. The three sprinted to meet their squad leader, who was in desperate need of support.

"Dillon, these guys are pushing hard. We need to take cover to regroup!" Abbot yelled.

"No can do, trooper! There's no time! Just keep on my ass!"

Perched atop a well-positioned hill, Donald Tento surveyed the conflict zone. His top commander stood next to him. He peered through the binoculars, carefully studying the NSDF tactics.

"Let's see what we can do," he whispered to himself.

He loaded the rail cannon and searched for a target. Tento controlled his breathing, brushing his finger on the trigger. Three NSDF soldiers bobbed slowly in the holographic targeting screen. Tento's nerves were as steady as steel. The aiming guide turned red and a tone beeped, confirming a lock on. Tento lightly squeezed the trigger. The rail cannon fired, kicking slightly.

Dillon, Strauss, and Abbot picked up their pace, while the rebel numbers grew all around.

"Come on! We're almost home free!" Dillon yelled, eliminating another enemy combatant.

Then, with the swiftness of a Tentonian insect, a precise shot annihilated Private Dillon's head. Abbot continued to run, tripping over the fallen soldier's body. Strauss and Abbot quickly took cover behind a titanium median divider.

"Shit! Strauss—you good?" Abbot asked frantically.

"I'm fine! But I can't believe—"

Abbot activated his communication channel. "All units, listen up. This is Abbot! We've got a sniper in the vicinity! Take cover immediately!"

"Abbot, Strauss, this is Snell. Make your way to the enemy heavy rover, and be careful! Needler and I have secured the parameters of the vehicle. We need to regroup," Snell's voice crackled over the communication channel.

"Copy that, sir, we're moving! Come on, you heard him!" Abbot said to Strauss.

Abbot and Strauss ran back to back, covering all enemy positions. Periodically, they stopped and ducked behind massive median dividers. With the finesse of hardened combat experts, the two soldiers moved with flawless intricacy.

Snell observed their dance of survival. "You see that, Needler?" he said with respect. "Those are two soldiers both of us can learn a lot from. They're true brothers in arms."

The dance continued as the soldiers made their way closer to the captain's position. Abbot and Strauss finally met their fatherly commander. The expressions on their faces told the whole story.

"Don't worry about Dillon. He could be overzealous at times. What happened was inevitable," Snell said in acceptance of the private's tragic end.

Abbot and Strauss nodded in unison. Needler peered carefully around the protection of the combat rover, accessing the situation as best he could.

"Sir, the NSDF forces have all taken cover. The sniper fire has ended since. My targeting system is no longer detecting an enemy position on the hilltop. This could be the opportunity we've been waiting for," Needler told his companions.

"Copy that, private," said Snell urgently. "It's time for this heavy rover to return to its rightful owner. Let's saddle up, boys!"

Snell jammed the entry hatch switch. The airlock hissed, and the massive covering gradually opened. As the last remaining light of the Tentonian sun gleamed off the heavy rover, a hideous sight was revealed. At first glance, Needler turned away, stumbling and throwing up whatever sustenance he had taken in.

Snell, too, was in a state of shock. "My god! What have these barbarians done?"

"It's the entire delegation!" said Abbot, covering his nose. "These maniacs have eliminated the entire governing body!"

The troops paced the inside of the rover, evaluating the mutilated corpses. They gathered all of the identification cards and credentials from the senators' wallets.

"This is cleaner than it appears, boys. These men were killed with a pulse cannon. I can tell by the wounds," Snell informed the group.

The shocked soldiers continued their assessment of the situation. They performed a full body count, identifying each dead individual as a member of the New Senate Delegation.

"Well, boys, by my count, we're missing two senators—Chairman Heinmeche and Senator Flemming," Snell declared.

"Yeah, it's a big shock that the chairman preferred to avoid this ending, right? That's mighty suspicious if you ask me," Abbot sarcastically commented.

"I didn't ask you, son. Although even I have to admit it's very odd. The rebel force has somehow gotten hold of NSDF-certified weapons. Now the entire New Senate Delegation turns up dead, minus the chairman and one of the few senators who supported Heinmeche blindly—I just don't know," Snell summarized the situation, slinging his pulse cannon over his shoulder.

"I do, sir. The chairman has gone off the deep end. We need to—"

"Stop right there, Strauss. Believe me, the NSDF has a contingency plan if that turns out to be the case. Checks and balances are important when dealing with a powerful body such as the New Senate. We are one of the things that keep the New Senate

Delegation humble. If something needs to be done, we'll be the first to know," Snell said, his wisdom shining.

Needler had managed to compose himself. He felt compelled to contribute to the discussion.

"I think Strauss is right, sir. I think it's safe to assume Heinmeche is behind this. How else could the rebels get their hands on the NSDF weaponry? As far as I'm concerned, it's obvious."

"We're not in possession of all the facts, private. We shouldn't be jumping to conclusions. We are assigned the task of defending the leaders of our planet. Heinmeche is one of those leaders," Snell wearily stated. "Still, I've got a bad feeling about this, too."

The sounds of combat had ended. It appeared that the rebels had retreated to a safe region. Tento's rail gun antics had proved effective. The four companies of the NSDF regrouped and began planning a pursuit operation. It was far from over.

Chapter 12: Fruition

Donovan Sterling's hovercraft buzzed down a Tentonian highway. Flemming sat in the passenger's seat. The opportunity had arisen to leave Flemming's estate and travel to the New Senate Complex. Flemming's plan was progressing as he had imagined. As the two sat silent, Sterling's cell rang.

"Sterling here. Yeah…perfect. Thank you for the update. I'll be in contact." He clicked the phone off.

"What's going on, Donovan?" Flemming asked.

"Good news. That was Pullman. He gave us the green light."

"That was fast. Well, it looks like you're looking at the new chairman of the New Senate," Flemming said arrogantly.

"Mr. Chairman—" Sterling said, bowing his head jokingly.

"This is no joke, Sterling. We've been working toward this moment for longer than I can remember. Now I can't wait to see Heinmeche in a cell. That man is going to rue the day he crossed me. Soon, he'll find himself at the Teege gallows awaiting execution!" Flemming said, his voice trembling with anger.

"You're a true hero for Tento, sir. Heinmeche has been a thorn in the side of free-thinking Tentonians for far too long,"

Flemming went silent, staring intently at the road ahead. The hovercraft continued on its course, the highway cleared of all traffic. The roar of combat rovers and jets boomed across the planet as the war continued. Sterling drove at a furious speed to expedite their arrival at the New Senate Complex.

***

The only sound that could be heard was the occasional clop of New Senate Security Forces patrolling the hallways. Heinmeche stared open-mouthed and unblinking. The realization of what he had done was too much to bear. The NSDF report containing details of the assassination of the delegation rested on the floor next to him. He had sealed his own fate. Throughout the darkened hallways of the New Senate Complex, the buzz of Sterling's luxurious hovercraft became louder and louder. Heinmeche noticed it and peered out the same window the sniper had taken a shot at.

Sterling sat in the hovercraft awaiting New Senate security support. Jeffers ran to the craft with pulse cannon in hand, cautiously looking out for hostile activity. He activated his communication link.

"The coast is clear, sir. You and Senator Flemming can make a safe passage to the complex."

"Thank you, Jeffers,"

The hovercraft door lifted. The two moles quickly entered the complex. Flemming looked around, observing the devastation. "It looks like I've missed a lot, Jeffers."

"Yes, sir, it's been quite a day," Jeffers wearily responded.

"I'll be giving you your leave soon, but there's one more bit of business I need you for," Flemming said.

"What would that be, sir?"

"Would you escort me to the debate room?"

"Absolutely. Follow me, sir."

"Listen, Jeffers, I suspect the chairman might have had something to do with the kidnapping and murder of the delegation. We need to handle the chairman very carefully. His psyche may be quite fragile," Flemming whispered.

"I'm on the same page, sir. Steps have already been initiated in this matter. General Pullman has initiated Plan B."

"I am more than pleased to hear that. This has been quite a day, Jeffers."

"That it has, sir."

Donovan Sterling, Security General Jeffers, and Senator Flemming slowly walked to the debate room. NSC Security forces paced the hallways with pulse cannons armed. They had successfully expelled the rebel forces that had infiltrated the New Senate Complex. To protect their territory, the security forces remained at their posts. Eerie creaks and cracks occasionally sounded, causing Flemming and Sterling to hold their breaths in anticipation of conflict.

Finally, they arrived at the New Senate debate room. Upon arrival, they realized the room's door was sealed. Jeffers pushed the intercom button to address Chairman Heinmeche.

"Sir, this is Jeffers. Senator Flemming has arrived with Donovan Sterling. They thought it necessary to come here based on the latest turn of events."

After a brief pause, the channel opened with Heinmeche's voice.

"Why did you come here, Flemming? You were safer at your estate—away from all of this."

"I don't have personal security at my estate, Mr. Chairman. I thought it was the wisest decision to come to here for my protection. I think it's a serious possibility that the rebels will try to assassinate me. You and I are the last remaining members of the New Senate. We should be together at all times," Flemming concluded.

"I beg to differ," argued Heinmeche. "For that very reason, we should be apart. Nevertheless, you are here. I'll cycle the door."

Heinmeche pushed the door lock button on his console. Three high-tone beeps rang and the door coiled back. The three entered the debate room. Heinmeche was slouched in his seat, covering his face with his hands. He rubbed his temples in an attempt to sooth the ache in his skull. The only light that flickered in the debate room was the console in front of the chairman. Slowly, the chairman lowered his hands and gazed at the three men in front of him. Flemming searched for words.

"Mr. Chairman, I offer my condolences. The New Senate has been devastated by these rebels. We need to regroup and prepare for a new era," Flemming said in an attempt to quell the ominous atmosphere.

Heinmeche simply sat in his seat, motionless, staring at his audience. The pressure of the war had obviously taken its toll on the chairman.

"A new era—you call this situation a new era? This is the end, Flemming. The rebellion has successfully infiltrated and extinguished every active member of the New Senate Delegation. Even if we kill every member of the rebel forces, we still cannot claim victory. If this is the start of a new era, it's an era of anarchy and chaos."

Flemming sighed and took a deep breath. He turned and glanced at Sterling, then he closed his eyes and nodded at his colleague. Sterling understood and said, "Sir, can I speak to you for a minute?"

"Of course, Mr. Sterling," said Flemming.

The two walked to a private position and consulted. This was merely a charade, for they already had everything planned. After the short interlude, the conspirators rejoined Chairman Heinmeche and Jeffers.

"Mr. Chairman, Sterling has been in constant contact with the Tentonian Bureau of Surveillance. They intercepted a recording that greatly disturbed me. Sterling…"

Flemming signaled to Donovan Sterling and crossed his arms. Sterling flipped his cell open and held it up. Flemming's manipulated conversation with Donald Tento began to play. At the conclusion of the recording, Jeffers stood flabbergasted. Heinmeche sprung out of his seat in a rage.

"This is preposterous! I've never spoken to the rebel leader!"

"Mr. Chairman, this is why I am giving you the opportunity to explain this communication. It is obviously you on the other end of this conversation."

Heinmeche's brow arched as his blood began to boil with rage.

"I'm telling you, Flemming, I've never had any kind of communication with Donald Tento, let alone conspired with him!"

"Well, sir, I have provided this information for the record. I believe it is your responsibility to disprove it. Until then, I think the only appropriate action is for you to step down from the chairmanship position."

Heinmeche stood motionless behind the chairman's podium. If looks could kill, Flemming would have breathed his last breath.

"I see exactly what's happening here—you're setting me up! This is outrageous! Jeffers, take Flemming and Sterling into custody!"

With disbelief, Jeffers looked at the chairman. He shook his head in confusion. He glanced at Senator Flemming in search of guidance.

"Now you know why I needed you, Jeffers. I am enacting the Leadership Corruption clause of the Tentonian constitution. Chairman Heinmeche, I formally charge you with treason against the NSD. Jeffers, please take Heinmeche to a holding cell."

Jeffers looked as if he had been punched in the gut. He approached Heinmeche.

"Sir, could you please put your hands behind your back?"

Heinmeche balked. "Jeffers, you know I didn't do this! You know me better than this!"

"Sir, this is already a difficult thing for me to do. Could you please not talk and put your hands behind your back?"

Heinmeche stared at Jeffers with a defeated look.

"How did it come to this? What have we done to deserve this future?"

Heinmeche turned with his hands crossed behind his back. Jeffers clipped on the restraints and began to usher the deposed leader out of the debate room. As Heinmeche approached Flemming, he stopped abruptly.

"I don't know what you did to make this happen but mark my words—this is not the end!"

Flemming stood expressionless. As the debate room door cycled and Heinmeche exited for his cell, Flemming smiled a grin so sinister the devil himself might have cringed.

"It is complete. So—this is what Wolfgang Zonfer felt like."

Sterling, too, smiled in satisfaction.

"Congratulations, sir."

"Thank you, Sterling. My first order of business will be tying up loose ends."

"What do you mean, sir?"

"This."

In one swift, fluid motion, Flemming pulled out a plasma pistol and fired a single, precise shot at Donovan Sterling's head, destroying the misguided man's skull. The lifeless body dropped to the floor. Flemming ran quickly to Sterling's corpse and placed the sidearm in his victim's hand. With impeccable timing, the New Senate Security Forces piled in through the debate room door.

"Sir, are you all right?!"

"I'm fine, soldier, thank you. Mr. Sterling shot himself. I don't understand—this has been one hell of a day."

For the first time since Wolfgang Zonfer's reign, one man held absolute power over the human race. Fate must have a morbid sense of humor.

Chapter 13: A History Repeated

Security General Jeffers walked with former Chairman Heinmeche by his side. The two strolled at a snail's pace, as if time had slowed to a trickle. Numbly, Heinmeche watched the cracks in the NSC floors pass underneath his feet as he inched closer to his holding cell. Jeffers stared ahead with his attention focused solely on his destination. As they turned the corner for the detainment wing, Jeffers spoke.

"Sir—Mr. Heinmeche, I feel that I have gotten to know you over the years of my service at this institution. I happen to believe that you were framed for this action."

The deposed leader raised his brow in hope and astonishment.

"Jeffers, I assure you, your instincts are correct. I should have seen this coming. Ever since he came into office, Senator Flemming has had his eye on absolute power."

"Yes, sir, I agree. However, he hasn't been your only cause for concern. Unfortunately, there are many entities within the governmental structure that have been craving absolute power. Let's face it, sir. Flemming needed plenty of help to carry out this plan," Jeffers said.

As he completed his thought, they arrived at the chairman's holding cell. Heinmeche humbly bowed his head and sat on his cell cot in the pristine cell. Jeffers cycled the cell door shut and said, "Well, it isn't Zonfer City Hotel but it will have to do. Sir, I want you to know that you still have a friend in me. As far as I am concerned, this isn't over."

Heinmeche smiled in relief that all hope was not lost. He searched for words and spoke. "You know, Jeffers, I haven't been a perfect leader. I'm the first to admit that. However, I have always prided myself on the fact that I lead by my conscience. I tried my best to focus on the greater good of the people of this planet and ruled accordingly. Perhaps I lost sight of what were acceptable actions. The clear warning that was laid out by the seer to Dr. Schiller should not have been ignored. We continued surveillance of Earth despite that counsel—I truly believe that was the final misstep."

Heinmeche rubbed his facial hair in contemplation of the future. Jeffers' voice cracked his concentration.

"I guess I'll start the countdown to the end of our existence," he said with a slight grin.

"We'll find out soon enough, friend."

Jeffers turned to exit the holding cell when Heinmeche bobbed his head upward.

"Jeffers—"

"Yes, sir?"

"Thank you."

Jeffers nodded and cycled the detention wing door shut. Heinmeche swallowed hard and breathed calmly. He felt relieved. He couldn't understand the sudden feeling of contentment. He thought to himself, "a countdown to the end." He laid himself down on the hard, uncomfortable cot in search of mental solace. He closed his eyes in anticipation of rest. In the stark blue glare of the holding cell, Heinmeche had a moment of peace within the chaos of reality.

***

A new day dawned on Tento. As the light of the nearest star began to cascade over the planet, a sudden and astonishing change was apparent in the Tentonian skies. The cloud cover that had embraced Tento's skies for so long miraculously disappeared. It was both exciting and disconcerting.

Zonfer Company had set up camp for the night. The warmth of the intense light that Tento had never experienced before hit Sergeant Strauss's pale and dirtied face. Experiencing the light for the first time, he squinted in its intensity.

"Abbot—Abbot, get up!"

"Just a few minutes more," Abbot grumbled drowsily.

"Abbot, you have to see this—actual light! The sky is beautiful!"

Abbot tossed and turned and finally gave in to Strauss's calls.

"Man, Strauss, this better be—"

Suddenly, the wondrous light hit Neil Strauss's face. He immediately ceased complaining.

"What the hell? When did this happen?"

"It must have been overnight. Have you ever seen anything so amazing?"

"Even I have to admit, Strauss—it's pretty awesome. It's so odd! There isn't a cloud in the sky."

Captain Snell emerged from his makeshift dwelling looking as if he had been awake for hours, full of vitality and well rested.

"All right, boys, we need to make good time. The pursuit operation is fully planned. Reinforcements will be making their way here any minute and we'll begin the mission."

"Sir, may I suggest you take a look at the sky?"

"Very funny, Abbot. I've already noticed. The science people think it's a natural cycle of the planet. We have more important things to worry about. We've received word that Tento is planning on invading the Renaissance memorial site."

"What the hell would he want to do that for?" said Abbot, perplexed. "That thing is practically falling apart."

"You would be surprised, Sergeant. They don't make things like they used to. I'm not supposed to say this to anyone, but it's important to the mission now. When I was a New Senate security guard, I was part of the crew that would fire up the Renaissance."

Abbot and Strauss looked at each other in confusion.

"Are you serious? I thought it was just an artifact from our past," Strauss said.

"Most people do. We never fired the engines, just went through the startup procedure. Trust me, everything on it works."

"Man, that's incredible," said an astonished Abbot.

"Now you understand why it's vital for us to stop Tento from capturing the Renaissance," said Snell. "Who know what crazy ideas that bastard might have."

"No doubt about that one, sir," Strauss responded.

"I'm gonna roust the rest of the maggots. The other companies are gonna be arriving soon."

"Which other companies will be joining this mission?"

"All of them, son."

Snell walked away as Abbot and Strauss looked at each other and smiled.

***

It was a frightening sight. Chairman Flemming sat perched upon his throne of totalitarian authority, his sinister plan finally realized. The plan for his hostile takeover had been in the making for some time. Soon after Heinmeche's imprisonment, Flemming called his closest advisors for a meeting of the minds. Heinmeche's traitors gathered together in the NSC debate room, poised in their new positions as council to the chairman. Zonfer's dying will of a just government led by the people's will was now a distant memory. The first order of business was eliminating the TLO for good. The corrupt leader began his statement to his group of cronies and yes-men. The address was also holocasted live on Tentonian holovision.

"With the tragic and unforeseen assassination of the New Senate Delegation—brought on by a malicious order from the former chairman—it has become apparent that a new, more aggressive military campaign must be waged to eliminate the threat to our planet. This new operation, which I have dubbed Operation Foothold, has already begun, with all companies of the NSDF assembling to engage the enemy at their last known location, the Renaissance memorial site. My friends, this appears to be the final stand for the disgusting abomination that is the Tentonian Liberation Organization. My fellow Tentonians, we need to stand strong in the face of these murderers. I strongly urge all citizens to report any and all suspicious activities to the surveillance department of the Tentonian government. Preemptive action is what will provide us safe haven from future terrorist organizations metastasizing. Thank you for your attention on this tragic day. Ladies and gentlemen, look out your windows. This is the dawn of a new era in our existence."

With the address complete, the new dictator could begin his reign.

"That was exactly what the citizenry needed to hear, sir," one of the advisors commented.

"Nothing but lip service. My only concern is eliminating Tento and the rest of the TLO," Flemming said with a maniacal facial contortion.

Suddenly, the debate room lights began to flicker. Hues of light bounced from wall to wall. Jeffers stood at the debate room entrance.

"It's probably just a power surge, sir. There's no need for any concern," Jeffers said.

Flemming looked around in fear. He hadn't been exposed to this unorthodox activity. His absence from the New Senate during the infiltration had its perks but also its drawbacks. As the giant holoscreen in the debate room displayed an incoming communication, Flemming recoiled in terror. The origin field once again was marked "unknown." The message began.

"With each passing second, you further prove your kind's inability to reconcile. We have seen this exact scenario play out thousands of times in your past. Unfortunately, we now know that your kind cannot live without boundaries. We see your future. In your ignorance and greed, you will attempt to destroy the new culture that is developing on Earth. This is unacceptable to the Creator. Hence, your new existence will be hastened.

"If you have looked into your skies on this day, you will have noticed a drastic change, a sign. We recommend you enjoy this gift until the time. This marks the last communication our kind will engage in with yours. It is disappointing that this is necessary. The Creator was anticipating interaction."

Flemming was manic. His newly acquired power appeared to be useless.

"What is this? Someone explain this! I want an immediate trace on that communication!"

"I'm beginning to think the TLO is trying to use scare tactics, sir," said one of Flemming's advisors. "We received a similar communication during the infiltration. This is nothing more than the enemy attempting to sway our intentions. I'm sure Tento was listening to the address. He knows we are coming for him,"

"I'm not so sure, sir," said Jeffers, attempting to promote another perspective. "I have been security general here for a long time. I've witnessed these communications as well. The consensus of the delegation was that these Seer beings are real. With our modern tracking systems, a communication origin 'unknown' is unheard of."

"Regardless, the final operation of this war is at hand. I am not going to listen to a communication of unknown origin when it comes to the future of the planet," Flemming stated with conviction.

"Sir, you read the same message I did. It said that we can't reconcile. All due respect to you and the former Senate delegation, I would wholeheartedly agree with the Seer's assessment," said Jeffers, holding his ground.

Flemming furrowed his brow, appearing almost rat like.

"Listen, General, I can have you incarcerated as an enemy combatant quicker than you can think about pulling your sidearm. I want talk of these Seers stopped immediately."

Jeffers knew Flemming was right. He was in no position to be saying anything, let alone dictating policy.

"I apologize, sir—it won't happen again."

Jeffers gazed at Flemming with barely hidden contempt. He knew the coward had set up Heinmeche for the ultimate fall. Heinmeche would have listened to the communication and considered its validity. Flemming's ignorance was blazing brightly.

With the Tentonian citizens now aware of their new circumstances, fear and panic would be inevitable. This sudden occurrence was bound to make the population question how Flemming came to absolute power. After all, Flemming didn't mention anything about future elections. However, the mere notion of future hostile organizations would lull the masses into submission. Alas, the final chapter would soon be written.

Chapter 14: The Greatest Battle

The rumble of hundreds of combat rovers could be heard from every inch of Tento. Zonfer, Williams, Vankman, and Galant companies assembled in their war machines to bring the rebellion to an end. Their destination clear in their hearts and minds, the warriors prepared for the final conflict. Abbot, Strauss, Snell, and Needler remained together. Having proven their effectiveness, they thought it wise not to split.

"All right, boys," announced Snell, "we're coming up on Renaissance Lane. The rest of the force is converging from different positions. We have the tough job. I'm going manual pilot. You can put your bottom credit down on the rebels littering this road with pulse mines."

"I wouldn't mind never coming across one of them ever again," Strauss said.

Snell climbed into the small pod like piloting chamber of the combat rover. Not many NSDF soldiers knew how to successfully pilot a rover. It was rare that the craft's automatic on-board navigation didn't calculate the best path.

"It's been a while, baby. Don't worry; I'll treat you right," Snell said, comforting the machine.

He grasped the wheel and took a deep breath. The auto-navigation feature clicked off and the heads-up display appeared, casting a glow over Snell's face. The radar showed what he had feared—hundreds of red hazard blips indicating the presence of mines.

"Boys, we're going to have a bit of a bumpy ride. I need to take the unofficial shortcut to the Renaissance."

Snell made a huge cutting turn off the main road into the dusty, undeveloped terrain. The combat rover launched over the protective median, crashing ungracefully onto the rugged topography. The sound of small rocks and pebbles ricocheting off the combat rover's body resounded within the craft. Abbot, Strauss, and Needler sat silent, patiently awaiting the time for battle.

Snell struggled with the small margin of error he had. The landscape was awash in hazard blips. The TLO had done a comprehensive job of securing the parameters of their new base of operations.

"Shit! I'm going to hit this one, boys! Hang on!"

The combat rover swerved toward the pulse mine, triggering the arming mechanism immediately. The loud screech of the warning tone penetrated the protective cabin of the rover. The rumble of the explosion under the soil gripped the warriors' steely hearts. The topography of the affected area rippled, catching the back of the combat rover. It lifted the massive machine easily and awkwardly sent it airborne.

"Hold on, boys! This might be a rough landing!" Snell said, gripping the wheel tightly.

As the front end of the rover met the soil, it first spewed dirt and rocks into the air. Then, in an almost poetic motion, the back end greeted the land with similar enthusiasm. As it gained its bearings, the rover's engine roared as if in delight.

"Man! That was some serious skill, Cap!" Abbot shouted over the engine's roar.

"You don't drive these things for fun for nothing!" Snell shot back.

Snell continued to dodge and weave the pulse mine positions.

"We're almost home free! Get combat ready back there!" Snell yelled.

The rover approached the final resting place of the legendary Renaissance. It rested upon a massive pedestal, appearing almost like a trophy. Snell slowed the rover and contemplated a suitable parking area. He decided on positioning the rover near the base built around the Renaissance, a structure intended to keep it hidden from rebel eyes.

Snell crawled out of the piloting pod. He paused and raised his index finger to the air.

"You hear that? The rest of the girls will be here soon. Everyone geared up?"

"Yes, sir!" the three others said in unison.

"Well, all right then! Let's move!"

Snell cycled the rover door open. Like a theater curtain, it slowly rose. The NSDF had never seen a more effective fighting force. They stood poised and ready, awaiting the rest of the NSDF. Soon, the infiltration would begin.

***

Donald Tento peered out of a porthole in the Renaissance engine room. His fellow TLO members scurried about the ancient craft in an attempt to revitalize the operating systems. Over two centuries of nothing but a yearly startup had taken its toll on the remarkable craft. But Snell had been correct. Amazingly, all electrical and mechanical apparatus were fully functional.

A TLO engineer entered the engine room and approached the rebel leader.

"Sir, I've completed a full test of the craft's operating systems. Everything is fully operational. However, the engine hasn't been fired since the craft landed. So I don't know if we could fly this thing."

As he gazed through the porthole, Tento rolled his eyes at the man's ignorance.

"Why do you think I'm in here? I already knew all the electrical systems were fully functional. I worked for the New Senate—remember?"

Feeling quite foolish, the engineer bowed his head in shame. Tento sighed and realized his harshness.

"Listen, I'm sorry, Slater. I want to get this thing fired up as soon as possible. Would you examine the engine's internal works and report back?"

"Yes, sir, and thank you for the apology."

Tento returned to observing the outside landscape. Suddenly, his mobile personal computing device began chiming. It was the tracking devices picking up movement on the parameters of the Renaissance. As he examined the radar blips, his eyes widened in shock.

"Holy—"

He accessed the communication channels on the device. Then he hacked into the NSDF secure channel and listened.

"All companies are currently en route to the site of the rebel stronghold. All company commanders should meet at the agreed upon rallying point."

Tento closed the NSDF channel, opened the TLO channel and addressed his forces.

"Listen up! I need all members at the Central Living Quarters common area! We're going to have a lot of company—very soon!"

The final stand of the Tentonian Liberation Organization would soon take place. Tento ran to the meeting area with excitement coursing through his veins. He knew the significance of this action. Launching into the cosmos with the two-century-old craft would make a powerful statement. His plans past getting off Tento weren't yet fleshed out. However, this action alone would serve the rebellion by showing the citizens of Tento the freedom that came with serving the TLO, thus creating more members for their eventual return.

***

Abbot, Strauss, Needler, and Snell ran quickly with their heads low. The NSDF rallying point had been set at the Renaissance Memorial gate. The entire NSDF fighting force was converging on the new TLO stronghold.

"Move, move, move! We need to get to the rallying point before the rest!" Snell said emphatically.

As the four approached the main gate, the presence of approaching enemy forces became apparent. With the sound of marching boots getting closer, they took cover at the rallying point.

"You hear that? That's quite a rumble. Can we get a visual on how many we're dealing with?" Abbot inquired.

Snell gazed into his helmet's heads-up display and examined the territory ahead.

"Well, boys, it looks as if they aren't as close as we think. The echo through the memorial gateway is playing games with us—"

Abbot, Strauss, and Needler waited impatiently for the captain's assessment of the situation.

"Yep, this is gonna to be the big one."

While the four had been discussing the battlefield, the collective forces of the NSDF had arrived. The roar of the combat rovers had become deafening. The generals of Williams, Galant, Vankman, and Zonfer companies ran to meet Snell and the others.

"What's the situation, captain?" Corporal Brewer inquired of Snell.

"Well, sir, it appears as if the TLO is amassing in the Renaissance's Central Living Quarters. It's located at the very front of the craft."

"Do we have any indication that Tento has successfully fired the engines?" asked Luther.

"Not so far, corporal," said Snell. "If they do get them to fire, I don't think there's a chance in hell that they could get it off the ground."

"Well, we can't take any chances," said Brewer. "We need to engage them immediately. If they manage to get off the planet, the implications would be dire."

"I understand, corporal. We'll do our best."

Brewer touched the communication link on his ear and addressed the NSDF.

"All units, this is Brewer. Move out, storm the front!"

Suddenly, the sound of countless combat rover doors cycling blared across the territory. In a frighteningly orderly fashion, a perfect line of NSDF warriors filed into the memorial gateway. Then, the deafening roar of the Renaissance's ancient entry hatch opening sounded.

"This is it! All units stand ready!" Brewer shouted.

Snell stood near the front with his three compatriots. Gripping his pulse cannon tightly, he spoke from his heart.

"Boys, you're the best three men I've ever served with. Whatever happens, it's been an honor."

Nothing else needed to be said. The time for talk was over.

Chapter 15: Salvation or Damnation?

Emma Schiller sat in the house that she and her husband had shared. She observed the evening holocast of the news.

"…The highly secretive mission to Earth was led by Tentonian Institute of Science board member Tobias Schiller. The biochemist was a leading voice on Earthology. Unfortunately, Chairman Heinmeche revealed today that all data had been lost in the tragic explosion that destroyed the craft and its crew. As we sign off tonight, we salute Dr. Tobias Schiller, and thank him profoundly for his service to our planet, present and future."

A picture of Emma Schiller's husband was displayed with "Dr. Tobias Schiller: 167 – 202 A.A." tagged on the bottom. The image slowly faded from the holoset. Her eyes welled with tears, and grief gripped her soul. She had been in constant mourning since Zimmerman had phoned her. She walked to the bathroom with a heavy heart. She approached the sink and turned the hot valve. The warm water ran into her hands, soothing her frigid spirit. She splashed water over her face in hopes of relieving her angst. She sighed and wept into her hands, her attempt at relief a failure.

Suddenly, she heard a low monotone hum outside. She looked out her bathroom window, searching for its source. Immediately she saw a bright, piercing light covering the landscape. She blinked and angled her head, attempting to gain some perspective. Failing at that, she ran through the bathroom doorway and left the house.

Upon exiting the house, she was knocked backward by the glorious radiance that confronted her. In wonder, she stared into the brilliant, clear Tentonian sky. A shimmering, spherical mass slowly descended from the heavens.

***

"Get down, get down!" Abbot screamed as plasma fire shot past the squadron.

The battle at the Renaissance memorial blazed on. Zonfer, Williams, Galant, and Vankman Companies engaged the relentless enemy from the entrance, attempting to push their way inside. The final remnants of the TLO remained holed up in the ancient craft that had saved the human race from extinction.

Within the legendary craft, in the engine room, Donald Tento screamed orders at his forces.

"Keep them back! We need more time!" he barked at the operations commander.

"Sir, we can only do so much! The NSDF forces are advancing fast!"

"I know that! Just do your best. We don't need much longer."

Donald Tento walked toward a man working furiously at the engine and spoke.

"How are things looking?" he inquired.

"I think we'll be up within the hour," said the man.

"I'm not sure we have that long. I want this thing up and running ASAP!" Tento demanded in frustration.

Sergeant Abbot threw a grenade at the enemy's position near the entrance. The subsequent explosion killed the majority of the combatants.

"That was for Snell, you bastards!"

He ran headlong in the direction of the conflict zone, leaving his protective position behind the combat rover. Strauss called out as Abbot began his rush.

"What the hell are you doing?"

Suddenly, while Abbot advanced, an explosion of light erupted overhead, knocking most parties to the ground.

"Ah! What the hell was that?" Abbot screamed in confusion, covering his face.

The conflict gradually subsided, and a lull overtook the combatants as rebels and NSDF forces alike gazed in amazement at the sight. Abbot, his eyes as large as saucers, stood catatonic. Without warning, a shot burst out, hitting him in the chest.

"Abbot!" Strauss shouted from behind the combat rover.

At this tragic event, the battle started anew, with both sides attempting to regain their bearings.

In distress, Sergeant Neil Strauss dashed to his partner. As he ran, he fired precise shots at the enemy who had downed his friend, silencing them forever.

Strauss fingered his communication device. "Move up! The entrance is clear!"

The NSDF forces ran toward the enemy-occupied craft, pushing the battle to inside the Renaissance. Strauss panted in exhaustion and approached his comrade, kneeling and embracing Abbot fervently.

"Abbot, let me take a look! You're gonna be fine!"

"Strauss, look at the light," said a delirious Abbot. "It's so beautiful—it's coming down from the sky to meet us—" He collapsed backward.

"Don't worry about that—we're gonna get you fixed up. Can I get a medic over here?" Strauss demanded.

A combat medic immediately joined them and evaluated Abbot's condition. Strauss remained by his side, attempting to keep him conscious.

"Goddamn it, Abbot, you stay with me!" Strauss cried, refusing to accept his beloved partner's fate.

Abbot roused himself. "Hey, Strauss. I guess I owe you some credits. This thing turned out to be the big one. You know where I keep my money," he croaked.

"We're gonna use your credits together, buddy. We'll go to our favorite sun bar and live it up after all this is over."

"Ha, we might not need those sun bars anymore if the cloud cover is gone for good," Abbot coughed.

As he breathed his last breath, his eyes remained fixated on the brilliant glow as it continued to descend toward the land.

"It's so beautiful…"

Strauss gripped his partner's hand tightly, fearing the next event. The light mass made contact with the planet Tento, flowing over all its entities. A warm embrace hugged rebel and NSDF soldier alike, the scourge of conflict no longer a factor. A single tear trickled down Sergeant Neil Strauss's face as he experienced what his dying partner had sensed. He squeezed Abbot's hand tighter as the final seconds of his physical existence faded.

***

The New Senate Complex remained dormant; the debate room was darkened and vacant. Smoldering impact craters dotted the landscape surrounding the NSC. Heinmeche sat in his temporary cell awaiting transfer to the NSDF detention block. With his head in his hands, he contemplated his future. As he sighed in sorrow at all he had lost, a blinding light suddenly burst through his cell window. He gazed in awe through the glowing plasma bars that covered the windowpane. Suddenly, someone entered.

"Mr. Chairman, do you see that? What could it be?"

"I don't know, Jeffers," said the chairman wearily.

Jeffers exited as quickly as he entered. Heinmeche looked on in continued wonder as the massive, shimmering orb descended to the Tentonian landscape. As he watched, the sound of distant explosions filled his head. Then there was silence. He thought about the contact with the Seer. Had his leadership caused this? Could this be "the end" that the being had predicted? In truth, Heinmeche didn't care. He knew his future lay in a Tentonian prison. His totalitarian power had bloated to an unacceptable culmination of corruption, resulting in the deaths of his fellow senate members.

The feeling of wonder dissipated and despondence set in. Heinmeche took a seat in his cell, the beginnings of a massive headache accumulating at the base of his skull. Cradling his chin in the palms of his hands, he watched the glistening sphere make contact with the planet, the glow streaming into his cell. Then, in a brilliant peak, a massive explosion of light engulfed the planet Tento. As he sat, peering out his cell window, Heinmeche remained motionless. He was prepared for anything.

***

In panic, Emma Schiller entered her home, not understanding what she witnessed descending from the Tentonian sky. Furiously, she dialed a number on her video phone. It rang five times before an old woman answered.

"Mom, do you see something in the sky?"

"Yes, Emma, I've been watching the news on TNN. They have been covering the ongoing war and this—this event—for a while now. If you don't have it on, put it on now."

"All right, I'll do that now. I was washing my face in the bathroom and I saw this big explosion of light. I went outside and I saw this huge ball of light coming down from the sky."

Emma grabbed the remote control of her holoset and turned it on. A field reporter stood in a crowded street; behind him, citizens stood motionless, staring into the sky.

"We're live at TIS Way, just outside center Zonfer City, where the war rages," said the reporter. "We are witnessing a large ball of energy descend from the sky— people here are awestruck by the sight."

The holocast continued. Emma Schiller sat on her couch with her mother still on the line.

"Yes, yes," her mother continued, "on my street, people haven't been going outside because of fears of the war coming here. We've been lucky. We've only heard explosions in the distance. People have been streaming out of their houses gazing into the sky. It's funny. I haven't heard many explosions since."

"Mom, I have to go. I want to watch this. That ball of light is almost on the ground."

"All right, honey. Call me if you want to talk some more. I saw the tribute to Toby. I love you," Emma's mother said.

"I love you too, Mom. I'll talk to you later."

Emma hung up the video phone and watched the holocast with wide eyes. Far from the reporter's position, the radiant ball of light touched down on the Tentonian landscape.

"The light just touched down!" said the reporter. "It's so..." His words trailed off. He could find no words to describe what he was just witnessing.

In a rolling pulse, the radiance cascaded across the planet. The reporter dropped his microphone, turning to view the happening. As the light approached people in its path, their skin began to glow. Citizens looked at their arms in shock, not understanding what was happening. However, not a whimper could be heard. In a strange way, the light was calming, a warmth similar to an Earthling spring afternoon.

In a final supernatural happening, the citizens affected by the light were slowly raised into the air and limply floated in space. In the blink of an eye, they were delivered to the epicenter of the radiance's touchdown point. Suddenly, the live signal from TIS Way went dead.

Emma Schiller looked longingly at a picture of Tobias and herself. She picked up the holographic photograph and embraced it, weeping. Gradually, the light grew more intense, pouring through the windows of her home. While gripping the photo of her eternal love, the warm light engulfed her being. Her body rose slowly from where she sat and gradually disappeared.

The Culminating Chapter: The Reunion

Weightless, floating in the void, the human race rested in the protection of a presence. The physical—the past. The spiritual—the now. The names of the past and present joined together, migrating to their soul mates and loved ones. In the distance, bathed in the intense light, the horizon of their new reality could be seen. Like newborn babies, their eyes tried to focus. It was a rebirth.

* * *

"Wolfgang? Are you there? It's so bright."
"Alexia…I've missed you so."

* * *

"Em? Emma? I know that's you"
"Toby…finally…I love you, my darling."

* * *

"I told you the light was beautiful, Strauss. You see it now?"
"Yeah, buddy. *I see the light…*"

* * * *

The four soul mates finally reunited. The two brothers in arms remained united. It was complete.

* * * *

The breeze on Tento blew as it always had; the cold and desolate atmosphere had been unchanged since its discovery. However, a new quality hung in the air. After mankind's deliverance, the orb of light quickly ascended into a clear Tentonian sky, clinging to Tento's orbit like a newborn sun. A giant halo remained where the mysterious force had touched down. The planet had served a far greater purpose than anyone could ever have imagined. The final era of human existence had been determined centuries before, and the ensuing events were merely a pathway to salvation.

Now, Tento would be folded into the new intergalactic union of the alien race that resided on Earth. Soon after the final human being was delivered, the alien race approached the planet Tento, ready to initiate Tento's next phase of existence. Plague clouds engulfed every landmass and crevasse, and the initial phase of the alien terraforming began.

The culmination of events had been completed, ending mankind's journey. Ultimately, humans acquired a peace they would have never known in a physical existence. Their tribal unity would last an eternity and create a peace impossible during mere physical existence.

And the Creator smiled, for his ultimate will had been fulfilled.

The End

Epilogue: A New Universe

The new stewards of Earth and now Tento had colonized many of the far-reaching parts of the universe. The new era of our universe was now in full swing. An intergalactic war for supremacy would be a possibility. The Creator's purpose for hitting the proverbial reset button was to begin an era of intergalactic unity. There was a lesson to be learned from mankind's tenure. The Creator hoped the new residents of his creation understood. New races and alliances were being formed every day. The human race had barely touched the new frontier. Their end marked this new beginning. Perhaps the Creator wished to spare mankind this new struggle.

With a new era comes a clean slate. With hope, the new residents of the universe would choose more carefully than mankind had chosen.

Man may abandon God but God shall never abandon man.

Author's Note

In a time where the existence of God is a matter of faith, the secular mindset is prominent. I understand the difficulty of "believing without seeing." At one point in my life, I had a similar mindset. Through a personal journey and certain experiences, I've come to my faith. Through this narrative, I am hoping you are encouraged to do the same.

My purpose with this work is not to "convert" or make a case for anything. It is my hope that, in the end, this work will simply challenge you to ponder the notion of a God—not a particular religion or ideology, just the idea of a Creator. After you read the last page, I would be delighted if you would Google "theology" and just browse. Have a look at the many faces of belief.

As a Christian, I believe it is my mission to witness for Jesus Christ. I hope, perhaps in some abstract way, that this narrative will stir the readers' consciousness. I believe this is what I was born to write.

"Into thy hands…"

—Jason W. Egroff

Dedications

*I dedicate this work to my **mother**: You have been the continuous light in my life and without you, I would be nothing. I will forever appreciate your belief in my abilities to achieve my dreams. I will love you past time itself.*

*I dedicate this work to my **father**: When I was seven, you were taken from me. However, in those seven years, you showed me what it meant to be a father. I look forward to us meeting again... sometime.*

*I dedicate this work to my **grandmother**: Thank you for taking the time to read this novel. Your encouragement was priceless.*

*I dedicate this work to **God**: Hopefully, the true purpose of this work will be realized and I can help your case. I can only attempt to show a door. Perhaps you could help them receive this and walk through it. Without You, this story wouldn't have been possible.*

*I would like to dedicate this work to my network of friends (**The Quids**): To Balt, Bill, Mario, Mike, David, Caleb, Izzy, Sam, Chuck, et al, you have enriched my life and stimulated my senses. Our times together are always priceless and I wouldn't trade a second for any amount of personal gain or money.*

*To my cousin **Brent**: It's impossible to express in words the amount of fun we had in the past.*

*A good teacher is worth their weight in gold. To **Mr. Richard Alluni**, **Mr. Micheal Kushmerick**, **Mr. Thomas Krempasky** and **Mr. Jan Mroz,** you are masters in your profession. You made the educational process enjoyable. Know that you have touched this student in the best possible manner.*

*Finally, to my editor, **Arlene Prunkl**, I felt this section wouldn't be complete without a "thank you" to you. You have made me a better author. I hope you enjoyed our working relationship as much as I did.*